A Different Turf

JON CLEARY

A Different Turf

HarperCollins*Publishers*

This novel is entirely a work of fiction. The names,
characters and incidents portrayed in it are the work of
the author's imagination. Any resemblance to actual
persons, living or dead, events or localities is
entirely coincidental.

HarperCollins*Publishers*
77–85 Fulham Palace Road,
Hammersmith, London w6 8jb

Published by HarperCollins*Publishers* 1997
1   3   5   7   9   8   6   4   2

Copyright © Jon Cleary 1997

The Author asserts the moral right to
be identified as the author of this work

A catalogue record for this book
is available from the British Library

ISBN 0 00 225597 9

Set in Times Roman by
Rowland Phototypesetting Limited
Bury St Edmunds, Suffolk

Printed and bound in Great Britain by
Caledonian International Book Manufacturing Ltd, Glasgow

A Different Turf

Chapter One

'A typical woman,' said Clements, but with affection. 'You ask her a question in the dark and all she does is nod her head.'

'If she doesn't have a headache,' said Lisa, 'that's all you need.'

'Don't be crude,' said Malone. 'Not in front of the b-a-b-y.'

It was hospital bedside chat, just another coverlet to keep the patient warm. Romy Clements, breast-feeding her day-old daughter, smiled at the three of them. She was a goodlooking, square-jawed woman, dark-haired and looking still a little peaked from what had been a difficult birth. She had insisted on a natural birth and had given the doctor the edge of her tongue when he had suggested a caesarean. She had wanted to tell him she knew all about pain, both mental and physical, but she did not have that kind of conceit. She had wondered, but not discussed it with the doctor or any of the midwives, if her aversion to the knife on her own body had something to do with the fact that, as Deputy-Director of the Institute of Forensic Medicine, she assisted in the use of the knife on bodies in the city morgue almost every day in the week.

'Russ' parents are coming up from Cootamundra tomorrow. Their first granddaughter.'

Clements explained: 'My two sisters have five boys between them. Mum will be out of her mind with this one. It's a pity –' Then he abruptly shut up, tripping over his tongue.

Romy put out a hand to him. 'It's all right. As you say, it's a pity my mother couldn't have seen her. But . . .' Her mother had been dead twelve years. No mention was made of her father, who had suicided after committing three murders. Malone, looking at the infant Clements, wondered how she would be protected against her heritage.

Clements was a big man, over six feet tall and weighing more than a hundred kilos. His *forte* was untidiness, though since his marriage to Romy two years ago there had been some improvement in his outward appearance. His mind, however, was a stuffed garbage bag; he could fossick in it and come up with a fact that nailed a piece of evidence to any number of courtroom walls. He was a senior-sergeant, the field supervisor in Homicide, Major Crime Squad, South Region, and some day he might make chief inspector. But he would go no further, he had left his run too late, and by then the Young Turks, with their tertiary education degrees and untainted by the old police culture, would be running the Service.

'Have you decided on a name?' asked Lisa Malone, who liked life to be neatly catalogued. She was Dutch, though she had spent very little of her life in Holland, and there was a Dutch neatness to her that Malone and their children gently derided, though they would not have wanted her any other way.

'Russ wanted to call her Marlene. He has some idea that all German girls are called Marlene or Romy or Brunhilde. She's going to be Amanda.'

'She'll be called Mandy,' said Malone, who liked Amanda but not the diminutive.

'No, she won't,' said the new mother and Malone knew Amanda Clements would never be called Mandy. Not if the child had her mother's willpower.

'The girls and Tom will be in to see you,' said Lisa. 'They are already looking on her as their cousin.'

Malone looked again at the new baby, tiny face pressed against its mother's breast. He tried to remember his first sight of his own three, but couldn't and felt a certain shame. A man should remember something like that; after all, he was partly responsible for their entry into this life. He did remember that at the time he had had no worries about them, not even for Tom, the youngest, now almost fifteen; when they had come into the world the future had still looked reasonably bright. Sure, Australia had been on the verge of a recession when Tom arrived, but the country had weathered earlier recessions and two Great Depressions, in the eighteen nineties and the nineteen thirties; the national anthem had always been *She'll Be Right, Mate* and somehow things had always come right, mate. But now the new century was just round the corner of the calendar and the future was

2

a mess of lines on a computer screen. Old certainties had been shattered and Malone had begun to worry now for Claire, Maureen and Tom. And, because of his love for Russ Clements and Romy, he would worry for Amanda.

'Time we were going.' He stood up. 'Can I kiss your wife while she's got her breast bared?'

'I dunno,' said Clements. 'Ask *your* wife.'

As the Malones walked down the corridor of the hospital Lisa said, 'I'm glad for Romy. Today she starts a new life.'

'In more ways than one.'

'That's what I meant. She can forget her father now.'

'I hope so. If she doesn't, then her old life isn't over.'

Lisa looked at him with love, put her hand in his. 'There are things about you that still touch me. Don't ever change.'

They were a handsome couple, though they never thought of themselves as such. He was tall and broad-shouldered and still reasonably presentable round the waist; he had the sort of face that, because it did not run to fat, would look handsomer as he grew older. Lisa was of medium height tending towards tallness, which was accentuated by her upright carriage. She was better than merely goodlooking, but she had no vanity about it. She had kept her figure with diet and once-a-week aerobics; she ran a tight house and kept her husband and her children from ever being slobs. Appearance counted with her, but not for appearances' sake. She just had, as Malone did, standards.

'This way.'

Malone opened a door that led to a flight of stairs. Romy was in the private wing of St Sebastian's, but Malone, ignoring the hospital's underground garage, had parked the car in the doctors' section outside the main general wing. Anything to save a dollar or two, Lisa had said, but had gone along with his parsimony. She had lived with it so long she had palpitations on the rare occasion when he splurged money.

The stairs ended at a door that opened into the reception area of the Emergency ward. It was Saturday night – Butchers' Picnic Night, as Malone had heard one ambulance medic describe it – and the casualties had already begun arriving. A young boy with a broken arm; a motorcyclist who, helmetless, had gone through the windscreen of a car; a woman who had cut her wrists and was screaming she wanted to die: they stood, sat, lay in the waiting area like wreckage from Bosnia. Then, stretched out on an ambulance gurney, Malone saw a man he recognized, though his face was a bloody mess beneath the pads taped to it.

'Just a minute,' he told Lisa and stepped across to the Triage desk. He had once looked up the word *triage*: the act of assorting according to quality. He could only assume that its use was designed not to hurt the feelings of those who thought they deserved first attention, that no one was more damaged than they. An ambulance medic was giving details to the duty nurse.

He finished, turned round and pulled up when he saw Malone. 'Scobie! How're things?'

'All right with me, Billy.' He looked around at the casualties, then at the man on the gurney. 'But you look as if you're already having a busy night.'

'And it's only eight-thirty.' Billy Logan was a wiry middle-aged man with close-cropped sandy hair and a lined face that could have been a mask; he had once told Malone that it was the only face he could wear on duty. 'It's starting to wear me down, this job. It's about time I applied for promotion and got into administration.'

'The feller over there, what happened to him?'

'You know him?'

'His name's Bob Anders, he helped me on a case once. He's with – or he was, maybe still – the Securities Commission. He's one of their investigators.'

'A-N-D-E-R-S?' The medic turned back to the nurse, gave her the name; then he turned back to Malone. 'He was bashed in Oxford Street about half an hour ago. A bit early in the night, they usually don't go around bashing 'em till later.'

'They?'

'He's gay, isn't he? This time they rolled him as well, took his wallet. That's why we had no identification. Poor bugger.' He looked across at Anders, then back at Malone. 'But there's gunna be a job for you, I'd say. The kid leading the bashers, he was shot.'

'Dead?'

'The third in two months. Looks like you've got a serial killer. Or a gay vigilante. Depends which way you look at it.'

4

Sunday morning Malone went to Mass with Lisa and the children. Lisa appeared to pay attention to the sermon, but Malone and the children all had the blank expressions of minds that were elsewhere. The sermon was based on a letter of St Paul to the Ephesians; Paul, whom Malone considered one of the Great Know-Alls, was not one of the family's favourites. Malone often idly wondered if anyone from Ephesus ever wrote back. Did an Ephesian ever come in from his mailbox and grumble to his wife, 'More bloody junk mail'? Such thoughts enabled him to get through a dull sermon.

Coming out of Mass his pager beeped. 'Oh, God,' said Maureen; and Lisa, Claire and Tom all rolled their eyes. There were disadvantages to being the family of an inspector, the Co-ordinator in charge of Homicide. There were, of course, advantages: seventy thousand plus dollars a year, good superannuation, the occasional chance that one might be a hero, a surviving one, that is. Yet, for all their complaints, Malone knew that none of them would want him to be anything else but a Homicide detective. Not so long as it was his own sole desire, which it was. Even though he could never fully explain to himself why.

In the church car park he unlocked the car and they all got in. It was a new car – his first in ten years – a Fairlane this time instead of the Holden Commodore he had driven for so long. It had hurt him to go out and buy the new car; he was not a car man, a petrolhead, and any vehicle that continued to go without falling apart was good enough for him. But the family, pleading social disgrace, had finally prevailed. And now they had the new car, complete with car-phone.

Detective Senior-Constable John Kagal was at Strawberry Hills. 'I was beeped to come in, sir. Surry Hills wants us to come in with their task force on the guy who's killing the gay-bashers.'

'Did you know your friend Bob Anders was bashed last night?'

'Yes.'

'Righto, I'll be in.' He hung up, cutting short any further discussion. He always tried to keep police business, especially murder, as remote from the family as possible. 'Sorry. I'll be as quick as I can. I'll meet you for lunch – where are we going?'

'Doyles at Watson's Bay,' said Lisa. 'If you're not there, I'll charge it to the Commissioner.'

'I love you four. I read about a family like you. The Borgias.'

'They'd have finished you off right quick.' Claire was twenty, as goodlooking as her mother and as serene.

'Can I come with you?' Tom was going on fifteen, almost six feet tall and broad with it; Malone hoped that his son might be a better fast bowler than he himself had once been. He saw more to laugh at in the world than either of his sisters, but he was not careless of its traps. 'I won't get in your way.'

'You can come with me the day you join the Service.'

'Oh, God.' Maureen was seventeen, more vivacious than the rest of them, a happy cynic who was beginning to trouble her father. 'Two of them in the family! Big Cop and Little Cop.'

Malone left the car with them and caught a taxi into Strawberry Hills. The glass-fronted building had once been a mail-sorting exchange, notorious for its union troubles, but now it housed an administration section of Australia Post and several Police Service units, including Homicide. The ghosts of union organizers still wandered the building, depressed by all the peace.

John Kagal was waiting for him, as immaculate and handsome as ever. He was dressed this morning in a blue cotton skivvy, well-cut navy blazer, grey slacks and black loafers. Lately he had adopted the fashionable haircut of Hugh Grant, but his eyes were too shrewd for the floppy, little-boy look. He was masquerading, but Malone felt that was his natural pose. He did his best to like the younger man, but something always intruded on his good intentions. Perhaps it was Kagal's slightly superior air, the knowledge that he had two university degrees and nobody else in Homicide had even one; perhaps it was that he had been to one of the more expensive private schools, that somewhere in his background was a family with money. Though he rarely, if ever, spoke of them. He was intensely private and that did not mesh with the police culture.

'Garry Peeples at Surry Hills asked us to come in.' It was typical of Kagal that he named rank only for chief inspectors and above; his own rank, or lack of it, seemed to trouble him. Peeples, Malone remembered, was a senior-sergeant in charge of detectives at Surry Hills. 'He seemed to think that the killings are getting out of hand.'

6

'Righto, let's get over there. Anyone else in here today?' Homicide did not run a duty officer at night and weekends, but there were always three detectives on call should local command detectives need them.

'Kate is coming in, just in case we need her.'

Kate Arletti was one of two women members of Homicide, a girl who held her own against the chauvinism, repressed but still occasionally visible, in the seventeen-men-plus-two-women unit. She and Kagal got on well together, often working as partners, and Malone had begun to suspect there might be something more than police work going on between them. So long as they didn't start holding hands in the office, he didn't mind. That was one of his standards.

On the way over to Surry Hills in an unmarked police car, Malone said, 'I saw Bob Anders last night at St Sebastian's. I was there saying hello to Russ's new daughter.'

'They both well, the baby and Dr Clements?' Malone had noticed in the past that Kagal always gave Romy her rank.

'Thriving. Your friend wasn't. He looked badly bashed up.'

Kagal nodded. 'I saw him first thing this morning. The bastards did a job on him. But he got one of them.'

'Who? Bob Anders? He did the shooting?'

'No, no. The killer. Or killers. There have been three in the past two months and there was one last year when we were working on the Huxwood case.'

'Why weren't we called in before this?' But he knew why. There was nothing so sacred as a patrol commander's turf; it was the civilized version of the animal kingdom's territorial imperative. 'No, don't tell me. Let's try and look like guests.'

Surry Hills police station was part of the complex known as Police Centre, a fortress-like building presumably designed to let the voters know that the police had a fortress-like mentality. A recent royal commission into police corruption, however, had shown that cracks were appearing in the mental fortress.

The patrol commander, a tall thin chief inspector named Neil Kovax, greeted Malone as an old friend and just nodded at Kagal.

'I'll get Garry Peeples in here.' He made the call on his phone, then sat back. He was bald on top but had full grey hair along the

7

sides; he had a thick military-style moustache which, over the years Malone had known Kovax, he had seen turn from black to grey to now almost-white. He was an old-style cop who, Malone guessed, had taken some time to come to terms with his current turf, a major part of which was the homosexual community's territory. 'This is a puzzling one, Scobie. I think we might be dealing with vigilantes.'

'An ambulance feller said that to me last night.'

Then Senior-Sergeant Peeples came in. He was tall, taller by a couple of inches than Malone, with broad shoulders and muscular arms that seemed to bulge out of his shirt. Malone, abruptly aware of the territory they were now in, could see Peeples being asked to strip for a photo in the gay press. He wondered how Peeples would react to such a request.

'Inspector –' He nodded at Malone and Kagal. 'Has the boss filled you in? No? Well, we're not sure where we're heading on these murders. Last night's was committed by a woman, the three previous ones by three different men. The connection on the three earlier ones was that the bullets came from the same gun – we think a Browning Thirty-two. There hasn't been an autopsy on last night's victim, so we're still waiting on the bullet. But we picked up a shell that's the casing for a Thirty-two.'

'The killings, they were all connected to a gay-bashing?' said Malone.

'The four we're concerned with. There've been other bashings, some gays, some straights, but they were usually just people being rolled for whatever they had on 'em.'

'And all four homicides were done by different persons?' said Kagal. 'Using the same gun? Assuming last night's gun *was* the same one.'

'That's the puzzle,' said Peeples. 'What've we got here? A group of gay vigilantes?'

'Was last night's killer a lesbian, maybe?' said Malone. 'Or a transvestite?'

'Could've been. The kids we interviewed all had different versions. You know what it's like.'

Malone indeed knew what it was like. No gaze was so fractured as that of a crowd. He had once interrogated ten witnesses to a murder in broad daylight and come up with ten descriptions of the murderer.

Who, when he was finally arrested, proved to look like none of the descriptions.

'Who was shot last night?'

'Kid named Justin Langtry, seventeen. Lives – lived – in Erskineville with his mother and three other kids, she's a single parent. I sent one of our girls out to see her last night. I thought I'd go out this morning. Unless you'd like to?' he said hopefully.

Malone knew when the buck was being passed; he'd lost count of the number of times he had knocked on doors to talk to bereaved wives and mothers. 'Okay, I'll do it. But first John and I'll go up and talk to last night's victim, Bob Anders.'

'You know him?' said Kovax.

'He's a friend of John's,' said Malone, and Kovax and Peeples looked at Kagal with wary interest. 'Then we'll go out and see – what's her name? Mrs Langtry? – in Erskineville. What's the address?'

'Billyard Street, it's off –'

'I know it,' said Malone. 'I was born in the next street.'

Driving the half a dozen blocks up to St Sebastian's, Malone looked out at Oxford Street, the main artery that led from the city out to the beach suburbs. Twenty, thirty years ago this had been a working class shopping area: small shops that even then had been wondering what their future would be. Now it was gay territory, from Whitlam Square, named after an ex-Prime Minister of liberal persuasion, up across Taylor Square where drunks had once congregated like seals on the small island in its centre, to the slope past Victoria Barracks, where the vestiges of an army command still lingered like faint memories of wars that everyone else had forgotten. The first few blocks up from Whitlam Square had a mixture of shops, small restaurants and pubs that catered for the gay community; there were also baths and the offices of a gay newspaper. Beyond Taylor Square were more gay hotels and in a side street The Wall, the high stone wall of an old jail where male hookers now paraded. It was all territory which Malone, carrying the baggage of another generation's moral sense, had always avoided, glad that he had never been posted to Surry Hills or Kings Cross, the other turf on to which the gay community spilled over.

St Sebastian's was one of the older hospitals that had survived, aided by additions and face-lifts. Anders was in one of the general wards, his battered face half-hidden by dressings. He smiled wanly at Malone and Kagal as they approached his bed and put out a hand to Kagal, who took it and pressed it.

'Hi, Inspector,' he said through bruised and swollen lips. 'I'm a sight for sore eyes, the nurses tell me.'

Malone remembered him as a tall, goodlooking man who had worn an earring; his right ear was now a torn mess painted with yellow medication. The dark moustache above the swollen lips had none of the bristly defiance Malone remembered; it looked limp and drab, like the shadow of a glum mouth. He was still holding Kagal's hand, clutching it with – love? Malone wondered.

'Bob, we have to ask you a few questions. Do you know the woman who came to your rescue last night?'

Anders moved his head slowly on the pillow. 'I hardly saw her. I was on the ground, the young shits were kicking me –'

'Where was this?'

'Up by the barracks. I was walking down from Paddington town hall, I was heading for the Albury –'

Malone knew of it: a pub mainly for drag queens. Something must have shown in his face because Anders said, 'I'm not into drag, Inspector. I had to meet someone there, a guy who's a nurse. I have a sick friend –'

All at once he closed his eyes, looked ready to weep and Kagal squeezed his hand. 'It's all right, Bob. But we have to ask questions, we have to find out who's doing these murders.'

Anders opened his eyes; there was a shine of tears at the corners. 'Why?'

Kagal looked at Malone. There was a sudden silence in the ward; the other three patients lay in their beds looking at Malone as if waiting on his answer. 'We are cops, not judges,' he said and even in his own ears he sounded limp and priggish.

One of the patients got out of bed, pulled on a faded dressing-gown and went unsteadily out into the corridor. The other two men turned away, one to a book, the other to stare out the window.

'So you can tell us nothing about the killer?' said Malone.

'I'm sorry, Inspector – no. I was too busy trying to protect myself – the shits were trying to kill *me*, that was all I was thinking . . .'

10

His voice trailed off; then he recovered: 'What will you do about the kids who weren't shot? Who did this to me?'

'I presume they'll be charged. But that's not in mine and John's area, we're strictly homicides.'

'They'll be taken care of,' said Kagal and pressed Anders' hand. 'I'll see to it, Bob.'

They said goodbye to Anders and walked out into the corridor. There the man who had got out of bed was waiting for them. He was in his sixties, a small hard nugget of a man, crumbling at the edges but with a core of bitter prejudices. Malone recognized his own father in the man: the hatred of bosses, of police, of anything and anyone who tried to run his life. *Us and Them* would be his motto. And Them would include everyone outside the norm of his narrow outlook. Malone had seen it so many times in Con Malone.

'That poofter in there, has he got AIDS?' His voice was as rough as his looks. 'The nurses won't tell us.'

'No,' said Kagal and Malone marvelled at the younger man's control. 'He just has a bad case of assault and battery. Any more questions?'

Then he walked on and Malone was left with the bigot. 'No one deserves what that man has had done to him. Not even poofters.'

'Speak for yourself,' said the man and stomped back into the ward.

Outside, where the brightness of the November day mocked the misery and pain in the hospital, Kagal was standing by the police car parked in the section reserved for doctors. A hospital security guard was reading the letter of the law to him.

'You'll have to speak to the Inspector,' said Kagal. 'He's the senior officer.'

The security guard was a young man who took his duties seriously: 'You know you can't park here, sir –'

'No, I didn't know that,' said Malone. 'If you look up the Police Service Act, section seventy-seven – paragraph B, I think it is – you'll find that police on duty can park anywhere they like.'

He said no more, got into the car, waited for Kagal to get in behind the wheel, then they drove out of the small parking lot, leaving the security guard staring angrily after them.

'What does section seventy-seven say?' asked Kagal.

'I have no idea. But then neither does he. Let's go up to the crime scene.'

They swung into Oxford Street again, passed the Albury Hotel where Anders had been heading last night, and drove the quarter-mile up to the entrance of Victoria Barracks and turned in. A uniformed sentry barred their way.

Malone introduced himself. 'We're investigating the murder last night, the one just down the road there. Can we park in here for ten or fifteen minutes?'

'I guess so, sir. You don't intend to arrest the GOC, do you?'

'Not today. If he starts another war, we will. Were you on duty here last night around eight o'clock?'

'No, sir.' He was no more than twenty, fresh-faced under his digger's hat: too young for war. But then, Malone remembered, though he had never been a soldier, it was the young who fought wars. 'The guy who was, he's on leave today. But he was inter-viewed last night by the police. I understand he saw nothing, heard nothing.'

So much for the defence of the nation; but Malone didn't voice the thought. 'Righto, we'll be back in a few minutes.'

Fifty yards down, on the lawn that ran below the high stone wall of the barracks, the Crime Scene tapes still fluttered in the breeze. A police van was parked on the footpath and as the two detectives approached a uniformed cop stepped out of the van and began to take down the tapes.

'You're from Surry Hills?' said Malone, introducing himself and Kagal.

'No, sir.' He, too, was young, no more than twenty; but his face had none of the fresh-faced innocence of the soldier. He had already seen the dregs of the life the other was supposed to defend. 'We're from Paddington, up the road. We were called in to stake this out. The job's finished now – for us, I mean.'

'Lucky you. Has anyone come forward with any information?'

The young cop shook his head as he wound up the blue-and-white tape: the gift tape, as Malone thought of it, that wrapped up a death. 'Hear no evil, see no evil . . . You don't get much co-operation, not in this street.'

After a few more minutes with the young officer and his colleague, a senior-constable, Malone and Kagal walked back up and in through the gates of the barracks.

'We'll be a few minutes,' Malone told the sentry. 'We want to compare notes.'

He and Kagal got into the car and wound down the windows. Malone sat gazing out at the scene before him. He had played in a charity cricket match here on the parade lawn years ago; before the game, because he was history-minded, he had looked up the story of the barracks. It was built in the eighteen-forties by convict gangs and some of the first senior officers who came to occupy it had fought at Waterloo. Though it was named after the new Queen, the style was Regency; it was built in time to escape the heavy fashion of later years. He sat in the car and looked across the wide parade ground at the main building, the length of two football fields. This morning, a Sunday rest day, the barracks looked deserted. It was peaceful, no suggestion of what it was designed for, the training and accommodation of soldiers. The high stone walls even closed out the sound of traffic in busy Oxford Street. A boy had died and a man had been almost kicked to death not a hundred yards from where he and Kagal now sat; but this, built for the military, was an oasis of peace.

'What notes have we to compare?' said Kagal, breaking the silence. He had sat quiet, knowing Malone had something on his mind.

Malone turned to him. 'John, I've got to ask you this. You are a – a close friend of Bob Anders, right?'

'Yes.' Malone could almost see the young man close up, tighten. 'I have to ask you this, too. Are you homosexual?'

Kagal looked at him sideways. 'Does it matter?'

'On this case, yes, I think it does.'

Kagal didn't answer at once. He looked across the parade ground at some movement on the far side. A small detachment of soldiers was falling in; it was time for changing of the guard. A shout floated towards them, as unintelligible as all military commands, like an animal bark. The detachment began to march along the far side of the ground.

At last he turned back to Malone. 'I'm half-and-half. Bi-sexual – double-gaited, if you want to call it that. Fluid is the in-word.' He was silent a moment, then went on, 'Okay, so I guess you can

13

call me gay. I don't like to be called homosexual.'

'Why not?'

'I just don't, that's all.'

'I don't like to use the term "gay". You — you people took away a word that used to be one of the — well, one of the most evocative in the language. Nobody talks about Gay Paree any more or having a gay time, things like that. What bloke would sing a song like *A Bachelor Gay Am I* these days?'

Kagal gave a small smile, though he was not relaxed. 'I know quite a few guys who would.'

Malone didn't return the smile; he, too, was uptight. 'That's why straights don't use the word any more for fear of being mis-understood.'

'That's your — their problem, isn't it?'

'Have you ever researched the origin of gay as a slang word? I have. We're taught as detectives to do research, right? The original slang use of gay was coined in the sixteenth century in London — maybe earlier. It meant the cheapest sort of whore you could buy in the alleys off the Strand, the up-against-the-wall knee-tremblers. An English poet and playwright named Christopher Marlowe —'

'I've read Marlowe.'

Which was more than Malone had ever done; it had been enough while at school to plough through Shakespeare. 'He used to use the gays, the women hookers. Whores were called gays up till about the end of the last century.'

'You're sure Marlowe didn't use the word the way we do? The first speech in one of his plays, *Edward the Second*, is about as close as you can get to a male love song.'

Malone didn't answer; his education went only so far.

'You seem pretty interested, doing all that research.'

'It was just curiosity. I'm not a closet queer.'

'Is that the sort of word you'd prefer? Queer, fag, pansy? Maybe I can give *you* a lesson in etymology. You call yourself a heterosexual?'

Malone nodded.

'That word was coined in the eighteen-nineties — about the same time, I guess, that the word "gay" stopped meaning a whore. Hetero-sexuality was used to denote sexual perversion — "hetero" means "other" or "different". How does that strike you? It was meant to describe someone like me, a double-gaiter. It was not until the nineteen-fifties or sixties that the meaning was changed. And it was gays who gave it the meaning that's acceptable to you now.'

It was no longer a dialogue between a senior and a junior officer. The guard detachment was now closer, the sergeant in charge barking to the rhythm of the marching. Behind the police car the sentry had come to attention, then dropped stiffly into the at-ease stance.

'Righto, I don't like fag or queer, either. I just wish you had chosen another word but "gay". It's a cruel thought, but I've sometimes wondered if a man dying of AIDS still feels gay — in the original meaning.'

Kagal's face had stiffened, but he said nothing. The guard detachment was close now; it went by with a thump-thump of boots, came to a stamping halt. The two detectives sat in silence while the guard was changed; then the detachment moved on, the sergeant's bark dying away as it moved on down the long parade ground. The defence forces were currently debating whether personnel suffering from HIV-infection should be allowed to stay in the army.

'In your language —' Kagal was now distinctly, if coldly, hostile. 'In your language, are you homophobic?'

'No, I'm not. People's sexuality is their own business. Except for paedophiles and fellers who bugger sheep.'

'Like New Zealanders?'

'So you're racist, too? Or nationality-biassed, whatever they call it.'

'It's a joke, for Crissake!' Kagal was angry; then he struggled to relax. It suddenly occurred to Malone that this conversation was as awkward for the younger man as it was for himself. 'Look, the Kiwis say the same thing about us, only we have more sheep, more opportunity, they say. It was an Aussie joke originally, that you only got virgin wool from the sheep that could run faster than the shepherd.'

Malone laughed, not at the old joke but as a release. 'There's the one about the bachelor farmer counting his sheep as they go into the pen — sixty-seven, sixty-eight, sixty-nine — hullo, darling — seventy-one, seventy-two . . .'

The time-worn jokes seemed to oil the tension. They sat in silence

15

for a while, then Malone said, 'I'm anti some of the things you get up to –'

'You don't know what I get up to.' The tension crept back in.

'Right. Gays then, full gays.'

'The Mardi Gras – I know you're against that.'

'Yes. I think it's a grown-up version of the game that five-year-olds play – you show me yours and I'll show you mine. But my two daughters think it's just a load of fun.'

'And your boy – Tom?'

'He's like me.'

'Is he going to grow up to be a poofter-basher?'

'You think I might encourage him to?'

'Sorry, I shouldn't have said that.'

There was another long awkward silence; then Malone said, 'John, I'm dead against poofter-bashing, gay-bashing, whatever you want to call it.' He was walking on eggshells; or anyway on words that kept tripping him up. 'But cops my age, we carry a lot of baggage – prejudice, if you like. Though I hope I'd never be like that old bloke in the hospital corridor this morning.'

He paused and after a long moment Kagal said, 'Go on.'

Jesus, he thought, this is like confession used to be when I was at school. But all he said was, 'Righto, let's get back to Bob Anders. Are you and he –?'

Kagal smiled without amusement. 'Lovers? Is that the word you can't get out? No, we're just friends, the best of friends. He's had his own partner for ten years, he's never played the field. Unfortunately his partner did – he's dying of AIDS. That was why he was on his way to the Albury to see the nurse. He's been looking after his partner on his own.'

That, for the moment, left Malone without words. An officer, a major, appeared from somewhere, coming at them from the back of the car. He leaned in and looked at Malone on the passenger's side. 'Are you going to remain parked here for long? If so, we'd prefer you moved over there.' He waved a swagger stick towards the far side of the ground.

'Are we cluttering up the place?' The words slipped out; Malone was still caught in the tension with Kagal.

'Since you ask, yes.'

16

Just in time, Malone caught a retort; instead, he nodded at Kagal. The latter started up the engine, turned the car round and drove out through the gates. The sentry came to attention and saluted; Malone didn't know whether it was from habit or whether it was satirical. Though he belonged to a service that had its own discipline, its own play-by-the-rules culture, he didn't think he would ever have been happy in the army. For the next few weeks he was not even sure that he was going to be happy in the Police Service, not in the wash from this latest case.

They had driven a mile or more back towards Strawberry Hills before Kagal said, 'Am I still on the case, then?'

'Do you want to be?'

'Yes.'

'Then you are.' It struck him that he would need Kagal to lead him through the shoals of prejudice, on both sides, that lay ahead.

Kagal nodded; then said, 'Erskineville now?'

'No, I don't think so.' He looked at his watch. Time to be heading for lunch with the family; he had broken enough eggshells this morning. Normally he liked to keep at a case, not to let it cool; but: 'Let Mrs Langtry have another twenty-four hours to get over it. I'm not up to treading on someone's grief this morning.'

Gazing straight ahead he felt, rather than saw, Kagal glance curiously at him.

3

Kate Arletti offered to drive him out to Watson's Bay in time for lunch.

'In your what? Goggomobile? G-O-G-G-O —' He spelled it out as in a well-known Yellow Pages TV commercial.

'The very same. Unless, boss, you'd rather not.'

'No, I'm game. My kids will love to see it.'

As he struggled to fit himself into the tiny bubble-car he thought of an old joke — 'I've been in bigger women than this' — but didn't tell it to Kate. He was always decorous in dealing with women staff and not just because of the current wave of sexual harassment cases.

Driving out to the farthest of the eastern suburbs in the thick Sunday traffic, Malone felt as exposed as if he were on a Mardi Gras float. At traffic lights Mercedes and Volvos loomed up on either side of them like behemoths; the drivers and passengers looked down on them with superior amusement. At one traffic light a turbo Bentley pulled up beside them and Malone waited for the driver, a burly man with a fierce moustache, to lean down and pat them on the bubble.

'Enjoying yourself?' Kate Arletti was a small blonde Italian, neat in body but not in dress; she seemed to have great trouble keeping her shirt buttoned and her skirt seams straight. Today she was in slim dark blue slacks and a pink shirt that, as usual, had a button or two undone; her hair was hanging loose, not in its usual chignon, and she looked casual and pretty. Beside her, still carrying the weight of his discussion with John Kagal, Malone wondered if he looked as old as he felt. He found himself hoping that the people in other cars, staring at the two in the plastic bubble, took Kate for his daughter, not his date.

'It's my brother's car, he bought it and rebuilt it. It's a family joke. He's on holiday down in Victoria, I'm looking after it for him. You'd be surprised the number of thumbs have been raised for a lift when they see me in it.'

'They're interested in you, Kate, not the car.'

She glanced at him out of the corner of her eyes. 'Don't flatter me, boss.'

He felt suddenly protective of her. 'Have you taken John Kagal for a ride in this?'

She gave him the sidelong glance again. 'Why do you ask?'

'You go out with him occasionally, don't you?' Why had he not minded his own business?

'Occasionally.'

'Sorry,' he said, abruptly retreating. 'It's none of my business.'

She didn't answer, all at once appearing to find the thick traffic threatening. She concentrated on her driving, only relaxing for a moment to raise her middle finger as a carload of youths, surfboards on the roof of their battered Holden like warriors' shields, went by with a yell of derision. Then she glanced at Malone again. 'Sorry about that.'

'What?'

'The finger. I suppose in your day a girl would've poked out her tongue.'

In my day . . . 'Probably. Though I never went out with aggressive girls.'

'You think I'm aggressive? In *this*?'

The Goggomobile crawled up the Rose Bay hill like a translucent bug, the sun shining on its plastic bubble and Malone, inside, wishing he had taken off his jacket. The traffic whirled by them, but Kate seemed unperturbed, even when some of the cars, driven by jokey show-off drivers, came perilously close. She seems able to handle anything, Malone thought, but how will she handle it when she finds out John Kagal is double-gaited? Or does she already know?

When Kate dropped him at the parking lot outside the famous fish restaurant, Lisa and the children were just getting out of the Falcon. Then beyond them Malone saw Lisa's father and mother getting out of their green Jaguar. *Oh crumbs*! He had forgotten that Elisabeth and Jan Pretorius were coming to lunch with them. He opened the Goggomobile's bubble and stepped out.

'Thanks, Kate. Hold it a moment while the kids admire their dad's chariot.'

'Oh, my God, it's so *cool*!' yelped Maureen.

'It isn't, actually. It's bloody hot.'

'How did you get him into it, Kate?' said Claire.

'He just commandeered me and the car,' said Kate and flashed a smile at Malone. ''Bye, sir. Have a nice lunch.'

On the spur of the moment Malone said, and later he wouldn't know why, 'What are you doing for lunch? Have it with us.'

'Yes, do,' said Lisa behind him in that wife's voice that said she hadn't been consulted.

'Come on, Kate.' Tom was walking round and round the car, shaking his head in admiration. 'Dad'll buy you lunch and then you can drive me home in this.'

Kate got out of the tiny car, grinned at Lisa and the two girls. 'He knows how to woo a girl, doesn't he?'

Malone had gone across to greet Lisa's parents. Elisabeth was close to seventy, but she had inherited good bonework and married money and the two had kept her looking attractive. She had never aspired to High Society, if there was such a thing in Sydney; but she

19

swam on the edges of what passed for it and, as far as Malone could see, was happy in the shallows where she had made her life. Jan was in his seventies, goodlooking in a heavy way, with a thick thatch of iron-grey hair. He was a serious man who still dreamed, however sadly, of the Dutch colonial life into which he had been born and in which he had grown up. Emigrating to Australia after Indonesian independence, he had worked for Dunlop, then gone into his own business and made a fortune in rubber heels. He was conservative in every way and once, half-drunk on wine from his expensive cellar, had confided to Malone that he would be happy if the world ended before the new century began. Still, Malone conceded and was glad, he wore his disappointment and pessimism with dignity.

Malone kissed Elisabeth, smelling the expensive perfume she always wore. Earlier in the year, when there had been a minor boycott of French goods because of the bomb tests at Mururoa, she had stopped wearing the perfume; but it had been like giving up something for Lent, not really a protest at the French. 'You look frizzled, Scobie. Is it that tiny car?'

'Yes,' he said, because it was easier. Whenever he was on a job he always wore temporary scars from it, but this was the first time he had been *frizzled*.

'A pretty girl,' said Jan, who never let his conservatism blind his roving eye. 'She's a policewoman? I always thought they looked like Marie Dressler.'

'Who?'

Jan smiled. One of the few things he and Con Malone had in common was a memory for old-time film stars. 'Some time, over a bottle or two of wine, I'll tell you about the loves of my youth. Claudette Colbert, Kay Francis – so elegant, the rumour was she was a nymphomaniac –'

'Who was?' said Tom, suddenly at his grandfather's side.

Jan Pretorius gently punched his grandson's arm. 'I thought they only taught you computer sciences at school these days?'

They went into the big restaurant, packed as usual on a Sunday. Closest to the harbour view, with the city skyline in the distance like a row of ancient monuments, Stonehenge on the Harbour, were a large group of Japanese and an equally large group of Koreans; they were the ones who ordered crayfish or crab, the two most expensive items on the menu. The rest of the diners were a mixture of natives, all of them able to afford the prices, even if at the lower end. Waiters and waitresses whirled amongst the tables like tail-borne dolphins. It was noisy, but with no walls to hold in the sound it was bearable, unlike some other restaurants Malone had visited where noise, apparently, was designed as part of the menu. I'm getting old and cranky, he told himself, a sentiment seconded by his children.

Lunch went well until Jan, on his third glass of semillon and holding it well, said, 'What case are you on now, Scobie?'

Malone saw Lisa's look of disapproval, but her father missed it. Malone said, trying to sound casual, 'The murder of a boy last night in Oxford Street.'

'Oxford Street? A homosexual?' Jan Pretorius was another who rarely used the word *gay*.

'No. He was with a gang bashing up a − a homosexual.'

'Poofter-bashing?' said Tom. 'You're gunna be mixed up in that?'

'Where do they learn these expressions?' Elisabeth asked Lisa.

'That will be the − what? Third murder like that?' Jan, retired and waiting for the end of the world, read the *Herald* and *The Australian* right through every morning, beginning with the obituaries. Malone, · too, occasionally read the obituaries, but murder as the cause of death was virtually never mentioned in the notices.

'Four, actually,' said Malone. 'Could we change the subject, Jan? I'm just about to cut up a dead fish.'

Jan changed direction, if not the subject. 'Are you on the case, Miss Arletti?'

Kate looked at Malone. 'I don't know yet, Mr Pretorius −'

'Possibly,' said Malone, cutting into his barramundi.

'Dad's anti-gay,' said Maureen.

'So am I,' said Tom.

'How do you feel about them, Kate?' asked Claire.

Kate shrugged. 'I'm neither for them nor ag'in 'em. But I don't like the idea of them taking the law into their own hands, which is what seems to be happening in these cases.'

Has she been reading the running sheets? Malone wondered. Or talking them over with John Kagal? He wanted to get off the subject. He looked imploringly along the table at Lisa, but for once she didn't read his expression. Instead she seemed to want to enlarge the subject:

21

'Is there much bashing of lesbians?' she said.

'A little, so I understand,' said Kate. 'But dykes, it seems, are not so conspicuous. Or maybe the bashers don't recognize them so easily. Maybe the gangs just like to harass their own gender, their own form of sexual harassment, I guess you'd call it. I don't know, really.'

Elisabeth delicately turned over her John Dory, lifted a forkful to her mouth. 'However did we get on to this subject?'

'The world isn't full of *nice* subjects,' said her husband. 'When else do I get the opportunity to talk to Scobie about his work? I'm interested in other people's jobs. I was always willing to talk about my work.'

'Rubber heels?' said Lisa.

'Do you know any gay guys, Kate?' said Maureen.

Malone glanced at Kate; but she seemed to be avoiding his gaze. 'One or two.'

'I know a couple,' said Maureen. 'Guys I met at a disco. Nice guys, treated you with respect, no fooling around.'

'Urk,' said Tom.

'Grow up,' said his sister.

Claire glanced at her father. 'You're quiet, Dad.'

'I just don't like working seven days a week, that's why.'

Jan Pretorius took the hint: 'Sorry, Scobie. I should have thought of that.'

'Indeed,' said Elisabeth round a mouthful of fish.

'Will you like working amongst the gays, Kate?' Maureen persisted.

'We'll handle it, I'm sure,' said Kate and once again appeared to avoid Malone's eye.

He had the sudden feeling that the days, maybe the weeks ahead, were going to bind themselves tightly round him, that he could find himself floating on a stream that would run down to the place Lisa had once pointed out to him on an ancient map, the Sea of Doubt. It wouldn't be the first time, but always in the past the company had been straight, if criminal.

The Japanese had stood up and photographed the Koreans; the latter in turn stood up and photographed the Japanese. Then both groups turned their cameras on the natives, there were blinding flashes and the natives turned their smiles on the tourist dollar.

Chapter Two

1

The first phone call came at nine-thirty on Monday morning.

'Inspector Malone? I understand you are investigating the shooting in Oxford Street on Saturday night.'

'Who's this?'

'Let's say I'm the Twelfth Man. You played cricket, didn't you, once upon a time? There is always a twelfth man, isn't there, just in case?'

'Are you offering some information?'

'In a way, I suppose I am. But we're also offering help –'

'Mr – what's your name?'

'Don't hang up, Inspector.' The man's voice was soft and educated, almost precise yet not prissy; a man with respect for the weight and value of words. 'Why waste your time? The police have enough to do. We are contributing a public service –'

'We?'

'Oh, I thought you knew. We're a, shall we say, a consortium. Pest exterminators . . .'

Malone was signalling frantically to Clements in the outer office, but the big man was busy at a computer. Then Andy Graham, the unit's St Bernard, Airedale or any lolloping dog, came lolloping in: 'You want something, boss?'

'Get me –' Then the phone went dead in his ear. 'Hello? You there? Bugger!' He replaced the receiver. 'Get Russ for me, Andy. What are you on?'

'The Chiano job out at Maroubra. I'll get Russ.' He galloped away, hitting a swivel chair and sending it swivelling; his small world was chipped and scarred by his progress through it. But he was a good detective, his enthusiasm was not bumbling; he would never let go

23

of a case, his mind was a file of clues in unsolved cases. Malone, looking after him as he bumped into a desk, wondered how he would go if transferred to the Oxford Street murder.

Clements, looking happier than he had for the past few months, relaxed almost to the point of carelessness, came in and flopped down on the small couch beneath the window in Malone's office.

'Romy and the baby are great. I was in there before I came to work –'

Malone humoured him with a few remarks about mother and child. Then he said, 'I just had a call from some feller about Saturday night's murder.'

'We had three murders Saturday night –'

'So we did.' He had looked at the synopsis on his desk, checked it against the computer. 'Sorry. The one up in Oxford Street, the kid from the gang that bashing up – Did you know it was Bob Anders they bashed? John's mate.'

'I've read the running sheet.' Relaxed though he was, the big man's voice had an edge to it, as if to say, *You think I'm not keeping up with the job?*

'Sure.' What was the matter with him? It was as if he, the boss, had come on the job only half an hour ago. 'Okay, well, this feller rang, said he belonged to a consortium – yes, that was the word he used.' Clements had a big expressive face and when his eyebrows went up they showed large surprise. 'A consortium. He claimed they were the Twelfth Man – he knew I'd played cricket –'

'He must of looked you up. Who else remembers? No offence, mate. Nobody remembers yesterday's sportsmen . . . This – consortium – they offered to help?'

'He said they were contributing a public service.'

'Vigilantes? Christ, that's just what we need! Why don't these public-spirited bastards piss off? We get enough criticism without vigilantes claiming we can't do the job without them –'

'He hasn't claimed that yet . . . Have they done the autopsy on the kid?'

'Not yet, I checked. Forensic said Ballistics would have the bullet by lunchtime. You want to know if it's from the same gun as the three other poofter murders?'

He tried not to sound pious: 'Russ, no poofters were murdered.

And since we're now on the cases, maybe we'd better start calling the homosexuals something else.'

'Okay, gays. But what's on your mind?' They had worked together so long they read each other like husband-and-wife.

'I think I should stay at my desk.' As Co-ordinator, in theory that was what he was supposed to do. The nineteen detectives on staff, including Clements, were the field workers. But theory was always one of the first casualties of government service; it had the same fragility as charity and other high-minded ideas. 'Who have you got to spare?'

'Nobody, except Kate. I can spare John Kagal, but he's on call for three court appearances this week. Tomorrow, Wednesday and Friday. You mean you don't *want* to handle the Oxford Street murder and the other three? Why?'

Malone sat back, sighed; he could confide in Clements. 'I'm not comfortable with them —'

'Gays? You'd be a bloody sight more comfortable with them than I would. I try to be objective, but —' Malone shook his head. 'You can handle it. How d'you think you'd be if you were on a pedophile murder? You'd feel like committing murder yourself, wouldn't you?'

'I guess so —'

'You know so!' Clements was no longer lolling on the couch; he was sitting up. 'Take Kate with you, she's used to them.'

'How do you know?' Sharply.

'I mean, women are more comfortable with them, aren't they? Romy is always lecturing me on my prejudices —' He got to his feet, looking unhappier than when he had come into the room. He was not fat, though there was fat on him, but his bulk always made any room seem smaller. Malone had a sudden image of him with his daughter, the baby lost in the massive arms. 'You always say you're not gunna be chained to that desk. You're on the Oxford Street job, mate, this is your Unit Supervisor speaking. Wear an earring, you'll be comfortable.'

'Up yours.'

'I wouldn't use that expression in the company you're gunna be keeping.' He grinned, then spread a huge hand. 'There I go again with my prejudices.'

He went out to the big main room, but was back in five minutes.

25

'I've just run through the computers. There have been twenty-six gay murders in the last five years.'

'Murdered by bashing?'

'No, some by their partners. It looks now as if they're striking back. This consortium, I'll leave you to work on it.'

'Thanks. Send Kate in.'

She came into his office, smart and neat; but it was early in the day. 'You're on the Oxford Street murder with me, Kate. We're going out to Erskineville to talk to the boy's mother, then we'll see if we can talk to the kids who were with him when it happened.'

Kate drove, in an unmarked police car this time, not the Goggo-mobile, and, because she drove fast, Malone, always a bad passenger, sat with his toes clenched inside his shoes and his belly tense against his seat-belt. He gave her directions and it was just as well, for Erskineville was a maze of narrow streets and lanes that seemed to be looking for each other. But he had known this area in his boyhood and youth, it was as plain in his memory as a birthmark.

'You know your way,' said Kate as she pulled up the car.

'I was born in the next street. My parents still live there.'

Billyard was almost a dead ringer for the street where he had grown up. Narrow terrace houses stood shoulder to shoulder, as if for security. Narrow front verandahs, protected by spiked railings, were only one step up from the footpath. Some houses had been painted, their doors varnished or painted a bright colour, fancy brass knockers added; two or three had barred windows and security doors. On an opposite corner and running down a side street some new townhouses, the terraces of the future, were going up; somehow they looked like a new sore. Gentrification had crept in, like a hesitant make-up artist; but not all the way, not yet. Number twelve was rundown, the paint on the front door was peeling, exposing the timber; half the front window was boarded up like a half-shut eye. There was no knocker, though a patch of lighter paint showed where one had once been. Kate rapped firmly on the panels of the door.

It was opened by a teenage girl. 'Yeah?'

Malone introduced himself and Kate. 'We'd like to talk to your parents about – was it your brother?'

'Yeah, I'm his sister Jillian. Come on in. Mum!'

They followed her down a narrow hallway that, carpeted with a length of runner as threadbare as a beggar's shirt, led past closed doors to a small kitchen at the back of the house. Through an open door Malone could see a backyard, as familiar to him as his office at Homicide and not much larger. An equally familiar smell hung about the house, the odour of over a hundred years of cooking, of bodies, of living.

Though times had been tough in the Malone household, he had never seen his mother as worn and desperate as Mrs Langtry. She was small and thin and prematurely grey; her sorrows were etched in her face. She had a soft voice with a whine in it, for which he couldn't blame her; her life, if not this house, had collapsed in on her.

'I dunno what I can tell you. Justin just went out Sat'day night and —' She stopped.

And never came back. He had heard it before: some lives just ended like that. 'Have they taken you to identify his body?'

She nodded dumbly.

'Do you have a husband, Mrs Langtry?'

Again the dumb shake of the head. The kitchen was small, everything in it looked chipped and worn, but it was clean, it was not like some garbage dumps Malone had been in. A brightly coloured calendar hung on one wall, the only decoration; a flamenco dancer stamped her foot on the pages below; Malone wondered if Saturday's date was marked, but he wasn't close enough to check. A small boy, about five or six, stood in the back doorway, still as a statue. In one corner of the kitchen was a small wheelchair, with a large doll in it; then Malone realized with a shock that the doll was another child, a girl with a tiny head and a wizened face. He felt something tremble in his chest and he drew a deep breath.

'We'd like to talk to some of Justin's mates, maybe they can tell us something about what happened?'

'What happened was someone shot and killed my brother!' The girl Jillian was suddenly angry, as if she couldn't understand the stupidity of the police. 'Jesus Christ, what else d'you wanna know?'

Kate Arletti said gently, 'We want to know who killed him, that's all.'

'Does it fucking matter now? It ain't gunna bring him back!'

'Jilly —' Her mother went to her and put her arm round her; she

27

was shorter by two or three inches and twenty pounds lighter, but for the moment she looked the stronger. She faced the two detectives. 'Do I have to go and – collect his body from the morgue? I don't have any money for that –'

'I think we can arrange that, Mrs Langtry. Do you have any friends or relatives who can help you?'

'One or two, friends I mean. Our relatives don't wanna know us.' Then she looked embarrassed at such a confession. 'We'll manage, if you can just arrange for him to be – to be collected.'

'I'll see to it at once,' said Kate. It was obvious that she was finding the situation difficult; her held-back emotion was plain in her face. Malone knew that it had taken him years before he could hold his own face in a mask.

There was a sudden whimper from the child in the wheelchair; a withered hand was lifted to the tiny face. Mrs Langtry let go of Jillian and turned to the child to comfort it. 'There, Jasmine –'

Justin, Jillian, Jasmine: the names were like a mocking song in this falling-down house. Malone glanced at the small boy in the doorway, still unmoving, carved in pale wood; he wondered what the boy's name was, but dared not ask, afraid that he would laugh. But not with mirth.

'Jasmine has micro-ce-phaly –' The mother pronounced the disease with care. 'She's got scoliosis, too.'

Malone abruptly wanted to weep. Christ, what sort of bastard was God that He spilled such shit on this woman? With difficulty he said, 'I think we'd like to find Justin's mates.'

'I'll take you.' Jillian had swallowed her anger, looked calm and dependable. 'I won't be long, Mum.'

The two detectives said goodbye to Mrs Langtry, Malone ashamed that he was glad to escape. Outside the house Jillian turned left. 'It's not far from here. We can walk, if you like. They'll probably be playing basketball or skate-boarding in the park, over by the oval.'

'Do you go to school, Jillian? Or work?'

'I left school last year, we needed the money. I work at a computer place. The parts come in from Korea and we put 'em together and they go out as made in Australia. You cops oughta look into it.'

'We've got enough problems looking into Australian-made murders ... Did Justin work?' They were walking through familiar streets, but ones he had not trodden in twenty years or more; gentrification had rouged and painted them. Even the one street he did visit once a week had been tarted up, but Con and Brigid Malone had resisted: their house was light brown, their front door dark brown, the knocker black.

'Sometimes, off and on – he was a bit of a layabout.' She walked in silence for a few paces, as if she had said something treacherous about her brother. 'He'd help Mum occasionally. She does piece-work for a dress manufacturer. You know, out-work.'

Malone had heard the term. Women, sometimes whole families, who in the main were exploited, often earning no more than a dollar-fifty or two dollars a garment. 'I thought only migrants did that? Vietnamese, people like that.'

She grinned cynically. She was a plain girl, plain and overweight; but her eyes were bright blue and intelligent, her best feature. 'Mum's a natural to be exploited. She wasn't, once, but she is now.'

'Where's your dad?'

'Dead. He was a fettler on the railways, he was run over by a train three months before Jasmine was born. He was a dreamer, but they never last long, do they? He was probably dreaming the day the train ran over him.' She said it casually, without a smile or a tear, standing on the kerb, waiting for the traffic to pass before they crossed the main road. 'He wanted to call me Lillian. Lillian Langtry.'

The name had a faint echo in Malone's ear.

They crossed the road. 'There was a famous actress once, Lily Langtry. The Jersey Rose. Mum objected, said she didn't like the idea. So they compromised, called me Jillian. Just as well, I never grew into any sorta rose.'

'How old are you?'

'Sixteen.'

'There's still time.'

'Don't kid me. I'm gunna finish up like my mum, only fatter. But with no kids. Definitely no kids. There they are.'

They had come to a small park that had been spruced up since Malone's memory of it. In one corner was a children's playground; in another an asphalt court where a dozen or so youths were skate-boarding or throwing a basketball at each other. When the youths saw the two strangers approach with Jillian, they stopped throwing the ball and gathered together in a tribal huddle. The three who had been skate-boarding jerked to a stop with a screech and clatter, picked up their boards and joined the group.

'Les —' Jillian spoke to the tallest boy, evidently the leader. 'This is Inspector Malone and Constable Arletti.' Malone was surprised she had remembered their names. 'They'd like to talk to you about Justin.'

'Yeah?'

They were sullen, suspicious of cops. Malone looked them over and, mentally, shook his head. All of them wore Keppers or baggy basketball shorts; T-shirts with emblems that he didn't recognize; and all of them wore baseball caps, most of them turned back-to-front. They were the New American Colonials, marching backwards into the future. His old Aussie blood galloped through him. Then: *come on,* he told himself, *you're carrying enough baggage in this case.*

'You were with Justin when he was shot?'

'Yeah.' Les was about eighteen, a goodlooking boy spoiled by a perpetual sneer at the world in which he found himself. His cap was worn with the peak to the front, a New York Yankees cap. He wore a Mambo T-shirt, Keppers that came well below his knees and heavy black Air-Max shoes. Malone had the feeling he was in a foreign land. 'I was right beside him when he went down.'

'How far was the woman who shot him, how far away?'

'I dunno.' He looked about him. 'You guys?'

'She was right on top of him.' He was thin and sharp-chinned, the sort of kid who was probably called Foxy; he would run with the pack, but always on the edges, always trailing behind. He was dressed much the same as Les, as were most of the group. These kids might be unemployed or skipping school, but they didn't look poverty-stricken. Malone wondered how Justin had been dressed when he had died. 'I seen the gun first, it was long, like it had a silencer on it.'

'That was what it was,' said another youth, a fat boy who would never jump high enough to slam-dunk a basket. 'We hardly heard it when it went off. Just sorta *phut!*'

'What did the woman look like?'

'Shit, who knows?' said Les, the leader. 'She had long hair, dark.'

'Was she in a dress or slacks?' said Kate.

30

They all looked at her as if wondering how she had got into the act, a second-class citizen asking questions. Obviously they had less time for women cops than they had for men. Then Foxy said, 'Slacks, I think. She was there one minute, then she was gone. She could really run. I suppose dykes can run – fast, I mean. Lots of girls play sport, athletes, tennis players, they're dykes, ain't they?'

Malone and Kate didn't answer that. 'Was she wearing trainers, shoes like yours?'

'Jesus,' said Les, 'how would we know? She shoots down our mate right in front of us – have you ever had that happen to you?'

'Yes,' said Malone and for just a moment the group was silent in sullen respect.

'Have you been charged with bashing the man who's in hospital?'

There was no word for a moment, then Les said, 'Yeah, two of us. We're out on bail.'

'You haven't asked how he is.'

This time there was no answer at all; their indifference showed in their faces.

'Right, here's my card. If you remember anything else, anything at all, ring me. By the way, do any of you play cricket?'

The group looked at each other as if he had asked them if they played hopscotch. Then Les said, 'That's history, old man.'

Malone had meant to leave on a friendly note, but he couldn't resist it, his tongue slipping its leash once again: 'So is Justin. If you hadn't gone in for poofter-bashing, he'd still be here throwing baskets.'

He walked away, abruptly, and Kate and Jillian had to hurry to catch up with him. As soon as they did he said, 'I apologize, Jillian. I shouldn't have made that last crack.'

'No, you're right.' She walked in silence for a while. Then: 'You haven't asked why Justin would of been with them, poofter-bashing.'

All three paused. They were out of the park now, but still close to the small children's playground. Half a dozen very young children were clambering on bars, sliding down a slippery dip, rising and falling on a swing like discordant notes of music. Their mothers stood near them, tossing gossip as idly as the youths in the far corner were tossing the basketball. Some of the mothers had turned their heads to watch Jillian and the two strangers. Erskineville hadn't changed

31

in all the years: strangers were recognized at once.

'Tell us, Jill.'

Jillian looked around her, at nothing in particular; then she faced the two detectives. 'I told you my dad died. About six, seven years ago Mum brought home Bev. I dunno where she met him, he just was with her and moved in. Justin and I were too young to kick up much of a fuss, and Jasmine . . .' She paused, worked her wide mouth; then she went on, 'He was a truckie, he'd be gone every week, sometimes for a whole week. Kelly is his kid, my half-brother.'

Kelly: who had escaped the Justin, Jillian, Jasmine sequence.

They moved on, crossed the road, on their way back to the house that God had shat on. Malone could feel his faith beginning to tear like tissue paper. Jillian continued: 'Bev used to, you know, fuck around with Justin.'

'Sexually abuse him?'

She nodded; she found it difficult to discuss the subject.

'Did your mother know?'

'I dunno. Justin never said anything, he was about ten or eleven then. Maybe Mum did know and was afraid to say anything. Bev used to get drunk, he'd scare the shit outa all of us.'

'Where is he now?'

She shrugged. 'Who cares? He took off three months after Kelly was born. He said he couldn't handle four kids, especially one like Jasmine.'

'How long has she had —?' said Kate.

'Microcephaly?' She also said the word carefully, recited like a curse. 'She was born with it, she can't talk. Then she got the scoliosis —' Again recited carefully. 'That fucks up your spine and your joints, you get osteoarthritis.' She knew the diseases like the alphabet. 'I love her —'

Suddenly she stopped and began to weep. Malone put his arms round her and held her to him; sobs thudded through her like drumbeats. He looked at Kate over Jillian's head and saw that she had turned away, had her hand to her mouth. They were on the far side of the main road now, but the mothers in the playground were still watching them. Be grateful, he told them silently, your luck is better than this. It could not be worse.

Jillian recovered, withdrew from his arms and wiped her eyes.

32

'Thanks. Sometimes it gets to be too much, you know?'

Malone just nodded; he could not get out any words. Then Kate, turning back, said, 'Let's walk you home, Jill.'

They walked the rest of the way in silence. At the front door of Number twelve, Malone said, 'Do you own this house?'

'Are you kidding?' Again the cynical smile; maybe it was her best, her only, defence. 'We pay rent. A hundred and seventy bucks a week and the landlord says he's doing us a favour, he feels sorry for us. A fucking Greek.'

'Do you get any welfare help?'

She nodded. 'A bit. Mum gets a single parent's pension and something for Jasmine. But it doesn't go far, with all the drugs and special foods she needs, things like that.' She looked up and down the street, then back at them. 'Sometimes I wanna turn the gas on —'

'Don't, Jill —' But what hope could he offer? She might escape, but what of her mother and Jasmine and young Kelly?

She smiled again, less cynically this time. 'I won't. But it's a thought . . .'

They left her and walked along to the car. They got in and immediately Kate broke down. Malone reached across and patted her shoulder. 'I shouldn't have brought you —'

She shook her head, dried her eyes. 'I have to get used to it —'

'Not like that, Kate. You never get used to tragedy like that. Let's go back to the office.'

His mother and father would be at home in the house just round the corner, but he didn't want to see them now. They would ask what had brought him to Erskineville and the story would not bear repeating. Not the way he felt at the moment.

2

That afternoon Malone was at Surry Hills with Garry Peeples in the incident room that the task force had set up. Photos were pinned to the walls: of corpses, scenes of crime: a macabre gallery. Intelligence had supplied rough portraits of the suspects in the murders of the gay-bashers in the past seven months. 'Intelligence is still working on a description of Saturday night's suspect, a woman. So far she looks like a cross between Zsa Zsa Gabor and Whoopi Goldberg. I'm beginning to think all witnesses to a homicide are cross-eyed, astigmatic, or both.'

'Could she have been a transvestite?' Malone asked. 'Drag seems to be pretty popular these days.'

Peeples shrugged. 'Could've been.' He gestured at the portraits. 'There are three sketches for each suspect. The only common feature is the eyes, you notice? All dark, good-sized eyes, not squinty. Could be a woman's eyes.'

'You suggesting all four suspects could be the one person? That would do away with the vigilantes then. But the feller who rang me this morning said he belonged to a consortium. Unless they're a family. They could be the family of a gay who was beaten up, maybe killed, by a gang of bashers.' Then a thought struck him: 'How did he know so soon that I was on the case?'

'Search me. We haven't put out anything.'

'I got his call before I went out to Erskineville.' He looked carefully at Peeples. 'How many have you got on establishment here?'

'Ninety-odd. Ninety-four, I think. Come on, Scobie, you don't think it's someone from –?' He shook his head. He had thick wavy hair that he seemed to have difficulty in controlling; a curl fell down, an incongruous decoration to his broad aggressive-looking face. 'No, I won't pay that. We have a gay liaison guy here, a constable – he's on leave at the moment. But he's not the sorta guy goes around avenging gay-bashings. Besides, he wouldn't know you are on the case.'

'When he heard about the bashings and the murder, he'd have called up and checked what was happening. If he was a good cop.'

'He *is* a good cop.' Peeples still looked dubious. 'I'll check, but I think you're on the wrong track.'

'Garry, I'm not on any track at the moment.' He moved to a map taped to a wall, a map that covered the area within a radius of two kilometres from Surry Hills station. 'These pins, they're the locations? I mean, of our four homicides. I'm not interested in any others.'

'Yeah. The dates are there. Two in Oxford Street, one in Darlinghurst Road towards the Cross, one at The Wall. Whoever they are, this – this consortium keep close to home.'

'Assuming they all live around here.'

34

'What about Anders, the guy who was bashed?' Peeples said suddenly. 'He'd have told his mates you were on the case. Maybe he has a partner –'

'His partner's dying of AIDS, I don't think he'd have been in to see Anders. But yes, maybe he told someone else – G'day, Clarrie. Got something for us?'

Clarrie Binyan was a light-skinned Aborigine; he had been on the planet forty-five years but Malone was certain he was a million years old. Nothing ever fazed him; he took racial insults and service problems with equanimity. He was the sergeant in charge of Ballistics and it was his smiling boast that he could identify a tribal boomerang or nullah-nullah as easily as he could the bullet from a suspect gun. He had a child's smile and an old man's eyes. He and Malone were the best of friends, though only at work. It had only recently occurred to Malone that he had never invited Binyan home to Randwick nor had he ever been to the Binyan home in Dulwich Hill. He had tried to assuage his social conscience by telling himself he had never invited anyone home but Russ Clements. Nonetheless there was a feeling of guilt.

Binyan placed a plastic envelope on Peeples' desk. 'It's from the same gun. A Thirty-two, either a Browning or a Beretta, I'd say. There are other guns, ones you can fit with a silencer, that take Thirty-twos, but they're expensive and unusual – esoteric is the word I'm after, I think. But maybe this lot go in for them? What they do is esoteric by my standards.'

'Homosexuality or killing?' said Malone. 'We don't know that this lot, the vigilantes, are gays. A bloke called me this morning, told me what they were doing was a public service. If we find the gun, you could identify it enough for us to go to court?'

Binyan nodded. 'We found some nice individual characteristics – the distinguishing marks on the lands and grooves. You know it, every gun has its own fingerprint. This gun has it, in spades – "The child's grin". An old tribal saying.'

'Is he like this with you all the time?' Malone asked Peeples. 'Always mentioning the tribe? How his great-great-great-grandpa gave the finger to Captain Cook? Get on with it, Clarrie.'

Binyan was unoffended; he had made his way in this white man's world and felt secure. There was no one who knew more about ballistics than he. 'I think these people, whoever they are, may be in for a nasty shock one day. The gun's gunna backfire.'

'Let's hope it does it next time they try to shoot someone ... Well, if it's got such a distinctive fingerprint, at least we've got something to go on. Now all we have to do is find the bastards who are using it.'

'Console yourself that they're not using a Smith and Wesson. They're so bland they leave practically no individual characteristics.'

Peeples patted his hip holster. 'I must remember that next time I feel like shooting the Minister.'

All three grinned. The Police Minister was also the Premier, Hans Vanderberg, a Dutch immigrant who had come to Australia fifty years ago and seen the opportunities in State politics for a man with drive and a total lack of conscience. Good, honest men had come and gone and some were still around, but The Dutchman had been a permanent fixture, in and out of government, for so long that it had been suggested, in the current quest for a new flag, his image should replace the Union Jack on the upper left-hand corner. The prospect of Hans Vanderberg's evil grin fluttering from a flagpole had raised the possibility of a rush for emigration by monarchists and other conservatives.

When Binyan left the station Malone walked out with him. Ballistics was on the fifth floor of Police Centre; for all his easy-going affability, Binyan ran his unit like a tribal elder. The two men stood in the afternoon sun outside the main entrance. For some reason there was never much foot traffic into and out of the big building; it was almost as if the fortress was too forbidding.

'Clarrie, are there many Koori homos?'

'Some, I guess.' Binyan himself rarely used the politically correct terms for the indigenous; his people were either blacks or Aborigines or, occasionally but always with a dig at the whites he might be talking to, Abos. 'There are Chinese homos, probably Eskimos, too.'

'How are they treated?'

'From what I hear, not too well. There's a lot of homophobia amongst blacks – they think being gay or lesbian is a white man's disease.'

'Do they bash them up?'

'I haven't heard of much of that, but maybe they do. The com-

36

munity would keep it to itself, in any case. The other side to it is that I'm told being an Abo in the gay community isn't all beer and skittles, either. The homos have got their prejudices, just like the rest of us. Are you uncomfortable in this scene?'

'How'd you guess? But I feel sorry for the poor bastards, the ones who get bashed.'

'How d'you feel about the kids who are being shot?'

Malone wobbled his hand up and down. 'Ambivalent. I met a kid this morning, the one who led the gang that beat up the feller on Saturday night, Bob Anders. I don't think I'd shed any tears if he got the next bullet. But the kid who was shot Saturday night ... I met his family this morning, saw where he lived, heard about his mother's boyfriend sexually abusing him. I never knew the kid, but somehow I don't think he deserved a bullet.'

'You're gunna have some problems before this is over, mate. I'm just glad I'm upstairs, in Ballistics. All I deal with are instruments, all you ever have to be with them is objective. Guns, bullets, knives, you never have a moral problem with them.'

'What if some day we bring in a boomerang that's killed someone?'

Binyan grinned. 'My granddaddy killed a man once with a boomerang. Said it just slipped out of his hand. Look after yourself, mate. If you come out of the closet, let me know.'

Malone was afraid there would be a spate of jokes like that over the next few weeks. Homophobic humour had never been subtle nor did it have the sardonic dryness of normal Australian wit. He would have to take his own preventive care, put a condom on the jokes.

He had been back at Homicide half an hour when the second call came in. 'Inspector? Well, what do you think now you've met the poofter-bashers?'

'How do you know who I've seen? Have you been spying on me?'

'Let's not use the word spying, Inspector – that has a sneaky note to it. Surveillance, isn't that what the police call it? That leader, Les Coulson, he's real shit, isn't he?'

'You've talked to him?'

Malone was flicking through his memory. Who had been in the park besides the youths, the children and the mothers? At the far edge of his memory there was an indistinct figure – a man or a woman? – hovering there like a blurred passer-by in a photo focussed on the youths.

'I've listened. They make no secret of their feelings towards gays. You must have realized that, Inspector. We are doing a public service, you know. Why don't you recognize that?'

'I might, if I could meet you and talk it over –'

There was a soft laugh; then the line went dead. Malone put the phone back in its cradle, then signalled through the glass wall to Clements. The big man came into Malone's office, went to flop down on the couch, paused when Malone waved a hand.

'Stay on your feet. I've just had another call from the vigilante, the same feller. Get a warrant, I want a tap put on my phone. I've got a feeling he's going to call again. Tell the Phone Interception Unit you're getting the warrant. Try Judge Bristow, he's always on our side. Tell them I want them here this afternoon.' Then as Clements went to go out the door, he said, 'The bugger's been spying on us. He knows I went out to Erskineville this morning.'

Clements had stopped in the doorway. 'You think someone is tipping him off from inside?'

'I don't know. Maybe there's a network of homos in the Service, I just don't know. I've been looking up some figures – and I had a talk on the phone with the Gay and Lesbian Liaison Unit at Headquarters. There are eighty-one gay liaison officers throughout the Service – twenty-seven in the bush, fifty-four in the city. Not all of them are gay themselves – twenty-five per cent of them, they reckon. But whether there's a network . . .' He shrugged. 'If there is, maybe it'll be a help. Right now all we have to go on are a dozen garbled descriptions and a voice.'

'I'll get the warrant. I'm taking tomorrow morning off, okay? Romy and the baby are coming home.'

'So soon?'

'They don't waste any time these days. Next week she'll be back at work in the morgue.'

'You're macabre. The kid'll be helping her, I suppose?'

3

'Where are you going?'

'Out.'

'I guessed that. You wouldn't be dressed like that to have a shower. Where's Out?'

'Dad, I'm seventeen – don't you trust me?'

Maureen had always been the one who might be a rebel; now, it seemed, her time had arrived. She had grown from a tomboy into a pretty girl; no beauty, but attractive. Her dark hair was cut short and had a fringe; what Jan Pretorius, the old movie buff, called the Louise Brooks cut. Her figure was hoydenish, she did not have the curves of her sister or her mother; but clothes hung on it well and she wore them with a certain style. She was sitting for her Higher School Certificate and, if all went well, next year she would be going to university to do Communications. She wanted to be a public relations consultant, as Lisa had been after her stint on the diplomatic circuit in London where she had been the High Commissioner's private secretary; Malone could see Maureen being successful in the PR field, though, and he had never told his daughter this, he thought most public relations was bullshit. Maureen got on well with everyone; with everyone except himself, it seemed. The friction, which he didn't understand and which hurt, had been gradual over the past three or four months.

'Yes, I trust you.' They were alone in the living room. Lisa and Claire were out in the kitchen and Tom was in his room doing his homework. 'Have you done your homework?'

'Dad, I'm not like Tom, I'm not a fourteen-year-old. I know what I have to do and I've done it. Now I'm just going out for a coupla hours' fun, the disco down the Bay. Mum's okayed it. You really do treat me like a child. And that's one thing I'm not, not any more.'

'Righto, you win.'

She stared at him; he had the feeling their ages were reversed. 'Dad, it's not about winning. You've just forgotten what it was like to be young. You're humping as much baggage as Gran and Grandpa Malone, you're thinking *old*. It's a different world, Dad. I can take care of myself.'

Then she was gone, leaving him *feeling* old. She had spoken without heat, without cheek: almost with regret that he could not understand her. He looked across the room at the photo of his three children on the book shelves. It had been taken only nine months ago, in February; but the girl who had just gone out was a stranger to the laughing teenager in the photo. *Baggage*: she had used the word he had used to describe himself to John Kagal yesterday morning.

'What's up?' Lisa came into the room, settled on to the couch beside him. 'You and Maureen having words again?'

'Am I *old*?'

'Sometimes. Don't worry about her. She *talks* to me, I know what's going through her mind. She's not going to go wrong.'

'What if some bloke does her wrong?'

'She'd tell me. I don't think you have to worry. Neither of our girls is going to be done wrong, as you call it.'

'Are they on the Pill?'

She had a trick of looking at him out of the corner of her eyes. 'What will you do if I say yes? Their bodies are their own. We discussed it, both of them came to me – give them credit for that. I didn't ask them if they were sleeping with anyone, but I know they're not sleeping *around*.'

'I should bloody hope not! What about safe sex? Did you talk about that with them?'

'Don't get crotchety with *me*.' She was as equable as if she were discussing homework with Tom. 'Relax, darling. At least both our girls are straight.'

It was his turn to look sideways. 'Meaning?'

'Meaning I've noticed how edgy you've been since you moved on to this latest case. I don't think you could handle it if one of the girls came and told us she was a lesbian.'

'I might handle it better than you think.' But he knew he didn't sound convincing.

She kissed him, that condescending kiss that turns a wife into a mother; then she switched on the TV remote control. 'Time for *Sydney Beat*.'

Claire came in, flopped down in an easy chair. 'Oh God, not another cop show!'

'Your father likes to look at it to see how many technical errors they make. It's his version of *Wheel of Fortune*.'

'I don't believe it,' said Claire, picking up a book. 'You just want to get your menopausal flutters over —' She named the star of the show, a muscular actor who seemed to spend all his time off-duty with his shirt off. 'You'd better keep an eye on her, Dad.'

It was a one-hour series that had been running for three months, to critical acclaim and public indifference. It was shot with an in-your-face, up-your-nose camera technique that a lone dissenting critic had described as film school wankery. Malone had watched the previous week's episode, found no glaring technical errors, liked the script but grown tired of the close-ups of acne-riddled villains, of the flaring nostrils of the hero and the backs of the heads of minor actors whose only purpose seemed to be to block out half the screen while the camera focussed on a player in the near-background.

Tonight's episode was about a serial killer, someone who was killing off cops. The hero, shirt on or off, was the principal cop in danger. The actor was a big blond man in his mid-thirties; his sidekick was a younger, slim dark man. The script avoided the wise-cracking buddy-buddy set-up; there was a genuine relationship between the partners, much as there was between Malone and Clements. That, at least, was real.

He saw the last half-hour with only half an eye and heard it with only half an ear; he dozed through the climax, and was wakened by Lisa digging him in the ribs.

Ten minutes later he was in bed. Just before he dropped off a voice whispered on the edge of his consciousness, a soft echo, but before he could identify it he had fallen asleep.

41

Chapter Three

1

Clements picked up the snail from the carpet; it must have dropped off the single pot plant in Malone's office. He took a sheet of paper from Malone's desk, wrapped the snail in it, crushed it and tossed it into the wastebasket.

'Why did you do that?' said Kate Arletti. 'It's a living thing, just like you.'

'It took its chances. The bugger's been following me around all day.'

John Kagal laughed, but Kate just shook her head. The three of them were in Malone's office, ready for the morning briefing; all the other detectives were out, either on investigations or in court. Malone said, 'You're not in court this morning?'

Kagal shook his head. 'It's been stood over. The accused tried to hang himself last night in his cell.'

'Righto, let's get on with this. I don't know that I should stay on this case –'

'Why not?' said Kate.

Malone was aware that both Kagal and Clements were watching him. He was not going to admit that his prejudices, no matter how much he tried to stifle them, were confusing him. 'I think you and John can handle it on your own –'

'No,' said Kagal. 'With all due respect, boss, I think you should stay on it.'

It was a challenge: Malone recognized it. 'Why?'

'Without you, Kate and I are just going to be also-rans over at Surry Hills. We'll get the shitty jobs. You know what it's like, we're on their turf –'

'I agree,' said Clements, smiling widely; he had become boringly cheerful. 'As Jerry Seinfeld says –'

'Righto, Russ. Since you've become a father you're turning into a stand-up comic. I thought you were picking up Romy and Mandy.'

'Amanda. Ten-thirty.' He looked like a man who had got advance notice that he had won the lottery.

Kate went out of the office and came back with a small parcel. 'For the baby, from all of us.'

Clements beamed, but still looked embarrassed; he had a long way to go before seeing himself as a father. 'Gee, thanks from the three of us. I'll be in this afternoon,' he told Malone.

'Don't bother. You'll be bloody useless. Get to know Amanda.'

Kagal hummed a few bars of a song. 'Oh, Amanda . . .'

'Jesus, night club singers, too!' Malone could hear himself; why was he so testy? 'Okay, I'll stay on the case. But you'll have to go over to Surry Hills on your own this morning, Kate. John and I are going out to Erskineville again, see if we can talk to those kids out on bail.' Then he looked at his phone and its new attachment. 'I wonder if we'll get another call?'

'What am I supposed to do over at Surry Hills?' asked Kate.

'Their gay liaison man is due back from leave today. Talk to him, then go and talk to the lesbians. See if they've had any hassling. They seem to suffer much less bashing than the male gays do.'

'Maybe they don't,' said Kate. 'Maybe they just report it less. Women are always less complaining than men.'

'You're joking,' said the men.

As they drove out to Erskineville Malone said to Kagal, 'There's a playground we'll try first. If they're not there, I've looked up their home addresses on the computer.'

'Why did you want to go off this case?'

It was man to man again, no rank. He hedged: 'I thought you and Kate could handle it on your own. There's no need for three of us.'

Kagal did not reply at once, seeming to concentrate on his driving. It was a beautiful late spring day, summer's heat come as an early visitor. The sky had a glitter to it, like a distant ocean through which the red fin of a Qantas jet scythed like a bloodied shark. They passed a jacaranda, a purple burst of smoke in the tiny front garden of a scabbed and peeling house. The air, coming in through the open window of the car, miraculously was fresh and clean, as if pollution

43

had been turned off for the day. It was the sort of day that Malone dreamed of for his retirement.

'There is, you know,' Kagal said at last. 'Have you read this morning's papers?'

'Just the front page.' He usually read the morning papers over his salad sandwich lunch. Or, on the days when he went against Lisa's instructions, over his meat pie lunch.

'Daley Girvan is resigning.' Girvan was an Independent who held the seat of Bligh, the electorate in which most of the homosexual community lived. 'He has leukaemia. I've heard he has about three months to live.'

'I'm sorry to hear that. I only met him once, but he seemed a nice bloke.'

'Even though he's gay?'

'Even though. What are you getting at, John?'

'The Dutchman says he will make a run for the seat – he never wastes any time. Labor will put up a gay candidate – there are two or three in the party – it must put some of the old blue-collar unions guys on the verge of a stroke . . .' He broke off while he speeded up and took the car through an amber light, just beating the red. 'Anyhow, Vanderberg is going to beat the drum about helping the gays. There'll be no more gay-bashings, not if The Dutchman has to come out on to the streets and stop it. So he says.'

'How do you know all this?'

'One of his minders is gay, though Vanderberg doesn't know it. That's between you and me, okay?'

'You're everywhere, aren't you?' But Malone said it without rancour.

Kagal smiled. 'You'd rather we all lived in our own little pink precinct? That's what some of the activists want. I don't think that will get them anywhere. It would be reverse ostracism.'

'Then you're not in favour of the activists?'

'If they had their way, they'd bar half-and-halfs like me.'

'What about the activists who want to out all gays?'

Kagal shook his head. 'Like you said, everyone's sexual preferences are his own business.'

'You think it might be a consortium of activists who are killing these kids.'

44

'They're activists of some sort. This the place?'

They had drawn up outside the playground. The mothers were there with their small children; their faces turned like tiny satellite dishes as the two detectives walked through the playground and across to the far corner. There was no gang this morning, just Les the leader and Foxy.

'Where are the rest of your mates?' Malone asked.

'At school.' Les went on bouncing the basketball that he and Foxy had been tossing at each other.

Malone introduced Kagal, then said, 'This is Les Coulson, he's been charged with bashing Bob Anders.' Kagal showed no expression, just nodded. 'And this is – what's your name, son?'

'Steve Stefanopolous,' said Foxy. 'I ain't been charged, if that's what you're getting at.'

'Steve's father owns the house our mate Justin lived in,' said Coulson. He had stopped bouncing the ball, but held it as if he might hurl it at them. There was an arrogance to him that he must have acquired at an early age: it was case-hardened, a metal skin.

'You're Greek? Born here?'

'Yeah.'

'You work or still at school?'

'I work for my dad. He give me a coupla days off, to, you know, get over the shock. Justin being knocked off, I mean. You guys got the killer, that why you're back here?'

'Not yet,' said Malone. Coulson sneered. 'The reason we're back here, the killer was around this way yesterday morning –'

He stopped, got the effect he wanted. The two youths looked at each other, their aggression abruptly forgotten for the moment. Then Coulson said, 'Here? In this playground?'

'I dunno, maybe he was. But he knew I'd been to see you yesterday morning, so he must've been somewhere around here, watching us.'

Coulson laughed. 'Christ, that's a joke! A killer tailing the cops and they dunno anything about it!'

Malone held his temper, but felt Kagal stiffen beside him. 'He might've been around before we got here. Tailing you. You're the ones he's after, not us.'

The laughing stopped; Coulson bounced the ball, once. Stefanopolous blinked as if something had just flicked him across his sharp-featured face. On the other side of the playground a child screamed and there was a rush of mothers towards a see-saw where a child had fallen off.

'Did you notice any stranger around here yesterday?' Kagal spoke for the first time. Malone could feel the tension in him, as palpable as if he had his hand on the younger man's arm.

'There might of been.' Coulson was less arrogant now; there was tension in him, too. 'People come and go all the time through here. It's a short cut to the other side of the park. We'd of noticed him, though, if he was a poof.'

'Really? How does a poof look? Like this?' Kagal was baiting him; he put a hand on his hip in an exaggerated stance. Malone let him coast: Bob Anders' friend had a score to settle here.

'Some of 'em, yeah. But you can smell 'em, if you know who you're looking for.'

'And you go looking for them every Saturday night?' Kagal took his hand off his hip; Malone relaxed. For a moment he had feared that the situation was going to get out of hand.

'Friday nights, too. It's open season all week round.' Occasionally Coulson showed flashes of another personality, one who had had some education.

'Are you still at school or do you work?' asked Malone.

'He's just finished his first year at uni,' said Stefanopolous with some pride; but Coulson didn't look pleased at the disclosure.

'What are you taking?' said Kagal.

Coulson was off-handed, as if he preferred the subject had not been raised. 'Arts. History.'

'What happened to you?' said Malone. 'Turned you into a poofter-basher? Did something happen to you as a kid?'

He wondered if Justin Langtry had ever mentioned to the gang what his stepfather had done to him. He felt Kagal look at him, but he didn't return the glance. He felt certain Kagal would raise the question with him later.

'Jesus!' Coulson half-turned away in disgust. 'Why does anyone have to be molested to hate gays? It's just fucking natural, isn't it? I mean if you're natural. Normal?'

'Homosexuality has been around a long time,' said Kagal quietly.

'Sure it has. The Greeks invented it, didn't you, Steve? Socrates

and his boys, stuffing it up their bums and telling them to be philo-
sophical about it.'

Stefanopolous did not look happy at belonging to a nation that
supposedly had bred homosexuality. 'Ah shit, I dunno about that —'

'I think it was long before the Greeks,' said Kagal, still quietly.
'The Sumerians practised it. Didn't they, Inspector?'

Malone hadn't a clue who the Sumerians were. 'All the time.'

Coulson looked at Kagal with sudden interest. 'Hullo, a cop who
knows some history. Yeah, I guess the Sumerians might've had a go
at it. Who knows, even Abel might've put the hard word on Cain
before Cain slew him? Or shoved a jawbone up his ass.' He giggled
at the weak joke, but only Stefanopolous laughed, a forced laugh.
'The point is, it's fucking *un*-natural and nothing has had to happen
to you to hate the fucking idea of it!' He was abruptly angry.

Malone decided the discussion had gone far enough. 'Whoever
started it, the Sumerians or the Greeks or whoever, it's with us, it's
a fact of life. Stay away from Oxford Street and the Cross —'

'There are poofters up the road here in Newtown,' said Stefanopolous. 'And dykes, too. We gotta stay away from there?'

'You just don't go out looking to bash them up. Obviously the
killer — or the killers —'

'Killers?' said Coulson; he had been about to bounce the ball
again, but stopped. 'There's more than one of them?'

'We think so. Three men and a woman. The woman shot Justin,
but there have been three other kids shot, poofter-bashers. The killers
in those instances were men, three different men. Any one of them,
they call themselves a consortium, they could be looking for you to
be next. Now they know who you are.'

'Do we get police protection then?'

It was the cops' turn to laugh. 'You've got a hide. Write your
local MP, tell him you're an innocent victim. Maybe he'll ask the
Commissioner to do something about it, but I doubt it.'

Coulson turned slowly, right round, then he faced the two detectives again. The arrogance had gone, he looked uncertain, though not
afraid. 'If he comes after us, can we shoot him in self-defence?'

'Do you have a gun?'

'No.' Meaning not yet.

'Don't get one. You could finish up like Justin. Or he might even

47

go berserk and kill more than one of you. I mean it, Les – don't start playing cowboys and Indians. Leave it to us to catch these people.'

'You haven't done much so far, have you? In the meantime, we're just sitting ducks.' He looked around him again.

'You should've thought of that before you went out poofter-bashing.'

Malone looked around. In the park beyond the playground several people sat on park benches, reading newspapers, tossing crumbs to the pigeons, leaning back with their faces turned up to the sun: all innocent. Could he and Kagal go over and ask each one to identify himself or herself, ask them to empty their pockets or handbags? They could, but he could imagine the complaints within the half-hour to Police Headquarters. There were always voters who cried out for more law and order, but baulked when asked for their own contribution. He turned back to the two youths.

'Stick with your studies at university, Les. History will tell you amateurs should never take on professionals.'

'You think these killers are professionals?'

'Yes.' He wasn't sure what they were, but it was the best argument in the circumstances.

'Even the woman?'

'The female of the species . . .' said Kagal, chiming in. 'You must have read Kipling?'

It seemed that Coulson had not read Kipling, but he was not one to confess ignorance. 'Yeah, well . . . Okay, no gun. But if the bastards kill me, I'll come back to haunt you.' He grinned, but the grin had trouble staying on his lips. Beside him Stefanopolous had blinked again, flinching a little. 'One question, though. Are you guys on the gays' side?'

'Yes,' said Malone before Kagal could answer. 'We're on the side of anyone who's being bashed for no reason at all. Gays, women, kids. It's what cops are for.'

He and Kagal left the two youths and walked back to their car. The mothers watched them like Indian scouts: this was not cop territory. In the car Malone said, 'Did the Sumerians, whoever they are, practise homosexuality?'

'I don't know.' Kagal smiled. 'But neither did he.'

Malone looked at him approvingly. 'You've got the makings of a good devious cop.'

'My ambition. Where to now?'

'Out to Woollahra. We're going to interview the two gays who were bashed in the first killing.'

2

Woollahra lies between the self-conscious trendiness of Paddington and the sun-bleached brashness of Bondi and hints it would rather not know either. Its streets are tree-lined and its buildings vary from Victorian mansions to the occasional expensive but unattractive blocks of, not flats for God's sake, but apartments. Consulates occupy some of the side streets, foreign flags fluttering from masts like travel banners; some masts are bare, consulates of empires and countries no longer whole. The main street, Queen Street, is a collection of antique shops, small galleries, one or two restaurants and every-day-living shops where even the delicatessen aspires to be chic. Whether it is the consulates, the Goethe Institute on the main cross-street, Ocean Street, or the sense of privacy in the side streets, there is a suggestion that the small suburb could be European, a section of Paris or Vienna. The inhabitants are overcome with delight if one makes the suggestion.

Walter Needle lived in a three-storied Victorian house in a side street. A wide garden fronted it, a garden as manicured as a display centre. Needle was an architect, a boutique practitioner who had won several awards for his designs for houses and small buildings. Malone had no idea what sort of houses he designed, but this pale-rose Victorian mini-mansion hinted he might go in for heavy opulence. Malone, having learned that Needle worked at home, had phoned ahead before leaving Homicide.

Needle himself was in his early sixties, heavy if not opulent, grey-haired and florid-faced; he looked as if he might have played rugby or lacrosse in his youth, some blood sport. On the other hand his partner, Will Stratton, was pale and bloodless, someone who might have played croquet or crocheted; his handsomeness was almost too delicate. Needle introduced him as 'my partner' and Malone was at

49

first unsure whether he was his associate in business or marriage.

'Come in, come in!' Needle swept them into the house, led them through a wide hallway papered in red silk and into a large sitting room that looked out on a high-walled garden as equally manicured as the front plot. Huge ornamental pots held glowing flowers that appeared to have been ordered not to sprawl or festoon. At the far end of the garden three manicured small cypresses stood at attention; in one corner of the high walls a Japanese maple had been allowed to droop, but not obsequiously. Crumbs, thought Malone, I wonder if the wind is allowed to blow around here?

'Will keeps everything just so,' said Needle and Malone knew then what sort of partner Stratton was. 'So you're dragging up all that horrible business last February? God, we'd hoped it was all forgotten.'

Needle was too bulky and heavy, even a little old, to flutter, yet he gave that impression. He had motioned for Malone and Kagal to sit down, but he moved around the room like a restless bull. Stratton sat in a chair opposite the detectives, cool and poised. He was dressed in a black long-sleeved polo shirt, black slacks and showed six inches of yellow silk sock above black loafers as he crossed one leg over the other. He did not clash with the room, which had one black wall and two yellow walls and the huge window that looked out on to the garden. The colour scheme of the furniture, all of it elegant, almost too delicate to be sat on, certainly not to be *lounged* on (Malone was glad he had not brought Clements), was black and yellow.

Needle must have pressed a bell somewhere, because a Filipino houseboy appeared with a tray holding coffee and biscuits. Needle continued talking, 'We've done our best to put it all behind us. They almost killed Will, you know, what they did to him. He was beautiful —'

'Still am,' said Stratton. 'Inside.'

Malone had now had time to study the younger man. He was slim to the point of being almost girlish; and yes, he might have been beautiful once. His face now was a pale mask; if one looked closely, one could see the faint scars. He had not smiled either at meeting the detectives or since they had come into this room; his face, it seemed, was set in the one grave expression. His dark blue eyes and his sleek dark hair accentuated his paleness.

'The doctors had to re-build his face,' said Needle, still moving around the room. 'I could have killed – well, I shouldn't say that to you, should I?' He had a wide smile. 'But why come back now?'

Malone explained about the three murders since last February's. 'It's a consortium, they call themselves. We suspect they are gay –'

'What makes you say that?' said Stratton.

'Righto, maybe they're not. But for the time being we're focussing on the gay community – they may have talked to someone, let slip who they are and why they're committing these murders.'

'It's pretty obvious why they're committing them, isn't it?'

This pretty boy is going to be difficult. 'Yes, it is, Mr Stratton.'

'If we had heard anything of these – these murderers, don't you think we'd have been in touch with the police?' Stratton had not taken coffee or biscuits, just sat without moving, one leg still crossed over the other.

'Perhaps,' said Kagal. 'But perhaps you felt that justice had already been done. I mean, for what happened to you. Were you bashed too, Mr Needle?'

Needle sat down at last, a buffalo in a Regency chair. 'A little, nothing like Will was. I managed to hold them off for a few moments – I used to play rugby when I was young, thirty, forty years ago. It was like being in a ruck – you know, fists and boots. Then the – the killer appeared, fired his gun and it was like the referee blowing his whistle to stop the mayhem. Everything stopped for a moment, then the – the killer took off. One of the bashers made a grab at him and that was when he lost his wig. And –' He stopped. 'God, I'd forgotten all about them. Where's my cream linen jacket, Will?'

'In your closet –' Stratton looked at Kagal and suddenly smiled; or rather his face seemed to crack. 'It took Walter a long time to come out of it.'

'All right, all right,' said Needle. 'Look for it, will you? There should be some glasses in one of the pockets.'

Stratton rose leisurely, taking his time, and went out of the room. Needle looked after him. 'He hasn't been the same since – since the bashing. He's developed a real hatred of the world.'

'It's understandable,' said Malone. 'Certain sections of it, anyway. You have your offices upstairs?'

'No, I have a suite of offices in town – that's where my staff work.

But since what happened to Will, I've worked at home – to be with him. He is all I have,' he said and all at once looked old and sad.

Malone and Kagal remained silent. Malone glanced at the younger man, but Kagal's face showed nothing. Was he feeling pity for Needle, was he seeing himself like this years down the track? But, of course, Malone reminded himself, Kagal's loved one could be a woman.

Stratton came back into the room; he moved with the grace of a dancer and Malone wondered if that was what he had been. He handed a pair of horn-rimmed glasses to Needle, sank gracefully into his chair again and crossed his legs. There was an indifference to him, an attitude that he was outside the discussion, that he had built up a screen between himself and what had happened to him last February.

Needle passed the glasses to Malone. 'You see? I think they're fakes, stage glasses. That's clear glass, not prescription lenses.'

Malone squinted through the glasses. 'Did the police see these? Forensic?'

Needle shook his head, looked embarrassed. 'No. I picked them up, I don't know why, it was just a reflex action. Then I turned round and saw what had happened to Will –' He looked sympathetically at his partner. 'I must have put the glasses in my pocket without thinking – I forgot all about them. It must have been about a week later, when I sent my jacket off to be dry-cleaned, that I found them. By then I was so worried about Will – they had operated on him and said there would have to be more . . . I should have passed them on to the police, but frankly, by then I didn't care whether they caught the man with the gun. I still don't care.' He didn't say it belligerently, but there was no doubt he was adamant.

'You put the glasses back in the pocket of the jacket when it came back from the dry cleaners? Why?'

Needle shook his head again. 'I honestly don't know. I haven't worn the jacket since, I've even thought of giving it to the St Vincent de Paul. I guess I just, subconsciously, want to wipe that out. We both do,' he said and looked at Stratton, who showed no reaction.

'You saw the man who fired the shot?' said Kagal.

'Of course. Not clearly, everything was so mixed up, a brawl.

When six or eight hoodlums are bashing you, you don't exactly have your wits about you. But yes, I caught a glimpse of him. He wasn't big, medium-sized, I'd say. I couldn't tell you whether he was blond or dark, but he wore a dark wig – that was the one the police found. I do remember he was very spry – he took off like a rabbit after one of the gang tried to grab him.'

'Can you remember if he said anything when he first appeared? If he yelled at the gang to back off?'

'I don't think so. It was almost as if he was there to kill, not to save us.' He looked at Stratton, but the latter was still impassive. 'One minute there was just the bashers and us – the next, there he was. He came in from one side, held up his gun and fired it. I didn't hear the sound of it – I heard later he had probably used a silencer. One of the kids who was kicking Will just suddenly went down – the police told me he'd been shot in the head, but I didn't bother to look. I was concerned for Will –'

'What happened then?'

'Well, like I said, he just took off. I think one of the thugs tried to chase him, but gave up. The gang turned their backs on me and Will – I think they'd been shocked stupid by what had happened to one of their mates. Then other people started coming towards us – I remember yelling for someone to call an ambulance –' He stopped, his voice trembling.

'That's enough,' said Stratton, rose unhurriedly and went to him and put his arm round him. 'That's enough for you, too, Inspector. We want to forget it ever happened.'

Malone rose. 'I can understand that, Mr Stratton. But the fact remains there are killers still loose –'

Both men looked at him. 'Killers?'

'I told you they call themselves a consortium.' It occurred to him that they really hadn't been listening to him when he had explained about the other murders. 'Saturday night's killer was a woman. Or a transvestite, maybe even a transexual, we don't know. But we've had a couple of calls, they say they're a consortium –'

'Well, well.' Stratton for the first time seemed to relax; the mask cracked again. 'We have our own secret little army. You can't expect us to be unhappy about that, can you?'

'You don't expect me to answer that, Mr Stratton ... I'll take these glasses, Mr Needle. It's too late for Forensic to do anything about them, but they *are* evidence. Thank you for your co-operation this morning.'

'Don't flatter us, Inspector,' said Needle. 'We haven't co-operated, all we have been is polite. The bashings will go on, I suppose? And there will be further killings? It's rough justice, but that's better than none at all, isn't it?'

'Police are not supposed to engage in polemics,' said Kagal. 'That's left to lawyers.'

Stratton escorted them to the front door. As they stepped out on to the portico Malone said, 'I admire your garden.'

'So just-so, you mean? My life used to be the same,' said Stratton and shut the door in their faces.

Malone looked at Kagal. 'I meant it as a compliment.'

Kagal said nothing till they were outside the front gate, standing beneath a canopy of plane trees. The street was deserted, as quiet as the back street in a pleasant country town. Bashings and murder were something in another country.

'I'm not sure whether he remembers me, but we met at a couple of parties – that would've been before he came to live with Needle. He was beautiful, *too* beautiful. Women and guys fell over themselves to get to him.'

'You too?'

Kagal smiled. 'I've never fallen over myself to get to any man. Or woman.'

Malone could well believe it.

3

'We've gotta strike while the irony's hot,' said the Premier.

Where did he dig up that one? Ladbroke wondered; some bugger's trying to sophisticate him. He would have to tell the other minders to mind their own business.

'Send out a press release today, we're gunna protect the homosexual community by hooks and crooks.' That was more like The Dutchman, who would have made a fearsome trio with Mrs Malaprop and Dr Spooner. 'Nothing specific, you know, your usual airy-fairy stuff, something they can't pin down. Make me sound like Churchill or Roosevelt.'

'They're a bit dated, Hans. I don't think they ever had to deal with homosexuality.'

'You got another think coming, Roger son. What I read, Eleanor Roosevelt was a lesbian. Maybe it's just gossip. I hate gossip –' The way he hated breathing. 'Just gimme some nice airy-fairy rhetoric –'

Ladbroke, the Premier's press secretary and principal minder, made a pretence of making a note. Hans Vanderberg was too wise to believe that rhetoric was argument; but he never credited a voter as a man with any wisdom. Rhetoric they would get, airy-fairy stuff, Churchill let loose on the crime scene, law and order fought on the beaches, et cetera et cetera . . .

'Hans, aren't you a little premature? Daley Girvan hasn't resigned yet. The poor bugger's dying, don't chop him up before he's dead.'

'You think I have no sympathy for him?'

Yes, thought Ladbroke; but kept the thought to himself.

'I'd give him a State funeral, only the homos would wanna turn it into a Mardi Gras parade. But he resigns, we gotta have a by-election, right? We take Bligh, we get the homos on side, and we don't have to worry about the bloody Independents arguing with us about which way they'll vote in the Assembly. We can stuff it up the do-gooders and the Greenies and the wowsers in the Council, too.' He worked his mouth as if he were chewing up those who tried to thwart him. 'From today I'm the homosexuals' – what do they call 'em?'

'Partner.'

'That's it, the homosexuals' partner.' And a more unlikely partnership could not be imagined. Except maybe Lady Thatcher in bed with Arthur Scargill or Newt Gingrich hand-in-hand with Eddie Murphy.

The Premier and Roger Ladbroke had been partners, though never chums and certainly never lovers, for fifteen years, in and out of government. The Dutchman was a bantamweight septuagenarian who dressed as if he had just passed through a jumble sale; he had his own image and he had killed off as many image-makers as he had political opponents. He had a face like an evil parrot, one that mothers tried to prevent their babes from seeing when he was on the campaign trail; but when he actually got to leer at the infants they, seeing in his face their own potential perfidy, actually gurgled in glee. Ladbroke was a plump forty-five, an expensive dresser though somehow never immaculate, with a face as bland as pink custard; he could tell lies, which was his job, yet at the same time convince the State press gallery that The Dutchman had only the voters' welfare at heart, even though there was no evidence that Vanderberg had such an organ. They were a formidable pair.

'I'll talk to Leeds –' said The Dutchman. Leeds was the Commissioner of Police, an honest cop suffering at the moment from the revelations about bent cops and their corruption. 'Get him to ginger up the investigations of these killings, find out who's doing them. We can kill two birds with a brick, get on side with the homos and polish up the image of the police.'

'If they catch the killer and he turns out to be gay, how's that going to get the gay vote? I've heard from Bill Zanuch –' Zanuch was the Assistant Commissioner, Crime. 'He says there are probably three or four killers, maybe more. Some guy has been phoning Inspector Malone, saying they are a consortium –'

'Malone?' said the Premier. 'Is he on this?'

'He *is* in charge of Homicide, South Region. It's in his territory.'

'Well, I suppose better him than some of those bent bastards.'

There had recently been a Royal Commission into police corruption and dozens of police and criminals, once they realized the Commission had video evidence of their corruption, had been rolling over like sinners at a Eucharistic Congress. Evidence at times had been hilarious and honest cops, the majority of the service, had had a hard time proving they were not part of the joke.

'Is he gay?' asked Vanderberg.

'Who, Malone? I shouldn't think so. He's got a wife and three kids.'

'Doesn't prove anything. Did you know animals are homosexual? Cows, for instance?'

'I'd heard that. But I don't think there are any cows or heifers in this case.'

'Don't smarten your arse, son. I'm being serious here. We're the homosexuals' partner, as from this minute. Give 'em the works in your press release. In the field of human endeavour, never had so few had to rely on the many, et cetera et cetera . . .'

Ladbroke would sort out the rhetoric later. 'Will you be flying a Spitfire up Oxford Street or just catching a bus?'

Chapter Four

1

When Malone and Kagal got back to Strawberry Hills, Kate Arletti was waiting in Malone's office with a young uniformed policeman. 'This is Darren Beane. He is the gay liaison officer at Surry Hills.'

He was a slim young man with close-cropped dark hair, regular features and an air of balance and restraint. He was what he was, he accepted it, and, without being aggressive about it, you could take it or leave it. He had a pleasant smile and a firm handshake. 'Inspector. It'll be a pleasure to work with you. Hello, John.'

'You two know each other?' Malone looked at Kagal.

'We were at university together,' said Kagal with a smile that said, *What else were you thinking?*

He went out to his desk in the big room and Malone sat down behind his own desk, motioning to Kate and Beane to take a seat. 'How'd you get on with the lesbians, Kate?'

The question had a blunt rudeness to it that Malone hadn't intended; but he noticed that Beane didn't flinch. Kate said, 'Not much response, sir. One of them, a reporter on the lesbian paper, was bashed on Saturday night, but they didn't bother to report it to us. It'll be in Friday's issue of the paper.'

'Did they say why they didn't report it?'

'They were a bit snarly. They think the boys are getting all the publicity.'

'That's because of the killings,' said Beane. 'So far the killers don't seem to be riding herd on lesbians, only gay men.'

'Maybe that will change now there's a woman with them,' said Malone. 'With the killers, I mean. Do you go into the baths and pubs where the gay men congregate?'

'Yes, sir. You want me to show you around?'

'No, thanks.' Malone smiled in an effort to take the edge off his reply. 'No offence. It's just not my scene. I'm going to have to rely on you younger people there. Have you picked up any gossip in the baths or the pubs? Are they discussing the murders?'

'They weren't at first, but they are now. There's lots of guessing going on as to who the killers are, but that's all it is – guesses. The one thing they're all agreed on is that the killers must belong to the gay community.'

'Do you think they are?'

Both young officers looked puzzled. Kate said, 'Don't *you* think they are?'

'I have an open mind,' said Malone, leaning back in his chair. 'Which means I haven't a clue. What if these people just like to kill and have chosen to do a public service, as they call it? They could be killing gangs that attack old ladies or girls travelling alone at night on the trains.'

'I don't think so, sir,' said Beane. He had a certainty about him, a faith in his opinions. 'These people are avenging gays.'

Even Kate looked at him, at the assurance in his voice.

'You say that, Darren, as if you're on their side.'

For the first time Beane looked uncertain; he beat a retreat.

'No, I'm not. But doesn't the evidence suggest that's what they're doing? I think all we can do is go on the evidence we have so far.' Then he looked back at Malone and added, 'Sir.'

'Would you like to take a guess at who they might be?' Malone's voice and expression were bland.

Beane was just as expressionless. 'No, sir. I've never been any good at guesswork.'

This bugger has his suspicions, but he's not letting on.

'It was suggested to me this morning by one of the bash victims that he wasn't unhappy about the killers. The secret little army, he called it. *Our* secret little army was what he actually said. I don't believe he has a clue who they are, but he felt no qualms about what they were doing. Killing people.' He was still leaning back in his chair, but he was not at all relaxed. *I'm pinning you down, son.* 'I hope you don't feel like that?'

'Not at all, sir. But if the killings stop the bashings, then something has been achieved, don't you think?'

59

'Darren,' Malone said patiently, leaning forward, 'if all the wife-beaters were killed off and the wife-beating stopped, do you think we – we police, I mean – do you think we should be satisfied with that? I don't know what the attitude is over at Surry Hills, but here in Homicide we are paid to bring murderers to justice. That's what these people are – murderers. If we catch them, they can argue their own case in court. But I'm not playing advocate for them and neither is anyone who works for me. Understand?'

'Yes, sir.' Beane's expression still hadn't changed.

'So long as you do understand it, Darren, we'll be glad to have you working with us. Let me know if you hear anything, go around the baths and see what the gossip is.'

Beane stood up. 'I'll be in touch, sir. Will you be coming over to Surry Hills?'

'Later, probably. Kate and I are going out to Homebush to talk to one of the other bash victims. Surry Hills has a stack of evidence on the four killings, but it still doesn't add up to anything concrete. Maybe I'll stumble on something you missed.'

'Good luck, sir,' said Beane and it sounded as if there was just a faint note of sarcasm to his voice.

He left and Malone looked at Kate Arletti. 'I can see you think I was rough on him.'

'You're the boss, sir.'

'You sound like my wife, Kate. Or my daughters when they think they know better than I do. Young Darren looks like a bright young cop, but he has a lot to learn about a cop's conscience. We're not supposed to have any, Kate. Not when it comes to catching murderers.'

'He's our best contact with the gay community –'

'I know that. But he has to make up his mind what comes first – being gay or being a cop. Yes?'

'Nothing, sir.'

'Come on, Kate. I know that look – you have something you want to say.'

'Well, let's say the killer, or killers, let's say they were killing thugs who were bashing up cops . . .'

'I'd still be after them,' he said and hoped he sounded convincing.

Kate considered his answer; then she stood up. 'Do you want me to keep covering the lesbian scene?'

'Yes, for the time being.' Eventually he would have to talk to the lesbians; he might even have to go into the gay baths. For the moment, though, he was still shedding prejudices: he was treading a different turf. Objectivity, something he needed in these cases, was never iron-clad. He looked at his notes. 'In the meantime you can come with me out to Homebush. We're going to talk to the second feller who was bashed, back in July, see if he remembers anything about the killing.'

Kate took out her own notebook. 'Roy Morpurgo. What does he do?'

'I don't know. He's not in the phone book or he's got a silent number. Maybe after being bashed, he just wanted to drop out. We'll take our chances. You've got another button undone.'

Kate Arletti did up the two buttons on her shirt. 'They just seem to undo themselves. I was as untidy as this at school. It must be in the genes.'

He was about to ask, *Your mother or your father?* Then remembered her father had committed suicide by shooting himself, always an untidy act.

They drove out to Homebush, along the traffic-packed Parramatta Road, the main artery west. This was the road that would be carrying hundreds of thousands of visitors to the Olympic games in another five years; those who set out to see the opening ceremony on the first day might be lucky if they arrived to see the finish of the marathon on the last day. Malone was not a supporter of the Sydney Olympics, reasoning that the money could be better spent on hospitals, roads and, yes, the Police Service. But the majority of local voters loved circuses and seemed prepared to wait two or three years for a hospital bed for elective surgery if it meant that a local athlete or swimmer or cyclist or gymnast could win gold. Malone kept his opinions to himself, because anyone who spoke against sport, even a sportsman as he had been, was considered guilty of worse treason than betraying the Constitution.

Homebush is part of the larger municipality of Strathfield. The latter, originally known as Liberty Plains, was where the first free settlers in the colony established their farms in 1793. By and large, the free settlers were not the abstemious, upright, hard-working types they had claimed to be; they had believed they were coming to a land of milk and honey, but the milk had proved sour and the bees savage and the soil poor. However, some persevered and survived, moving to the more productive soil of nearby Homebush. Gradually the area established itself. In 1841 a racecourse was laid out; bookies moved in to take the place of the bushrangers in fleecing the locals. By the 1880s wealthy citizens had moved out of central Sydney and were setting up small estates in Strathfield and Homebush, trying to re-create the life-style that they, or their forebears, had known in England and Scotland. All that got up their noses was the smell of the stockyards in Homebush; then came the abattoirs on the site of the old racecourse. But by facing south and breathing shallowly, the gentlemen and their ladies managed to ignore the smells and yells and bellowing on the other side of Parramatta Road.

Strathfield now is a solid middle-class suburb, still with many of the old mansions, though most of them belong to educational institutions. The area was once a bastion of Protestantism, but now most of the estates are owned by the Catholic Church; occasional earth tremors are felt in the neighbourhood as Presbyterians spin in their graves. The population, once almost exclusively English, Scottish and a few Irish who had learned some manners, is now a mixture, with a surprising number of Sri Lankan professionals. There is not a single hotel or bar in the municipality: the dead Presbyterians still hold sway. The abattoirs are now the site of the 2000 Olympic Games.

Kate and Malone turned off the main road, drove down several side streets, came to the end of a street that looked across a park to the huge development that was to be the Games complex. This was a quiet dead-end lined with young jacarandas that bloomed thinly, purple sunshades with the ribs showing through. Roy Morpurgo lived in a bluestone bungalow standing behind a front garden that was neglected, the grass six inches high and its bushes and shrubs withered by the spring heat. A late-model Mazda, looking as if it had not been washed since it had been bought, stood in the side driveway.

'Someone's home,' said Kate. 'Mr Morpurgo must be deaf.'

Music was blaring from the house, a symphony. They hammered on the locked security door. The music stopped and a moment later the front door was opened and a man peered out at them through the security mesh. 'Yes?'

'Police,' said Malone.

'What's it about? Someone complaining about the music?'

'No.' Malone introduced himself and Kate Arletti. 'Mr Morpurgo?'

'No.' The man opened the security door, revealing himself. He was tall, all skin and bone, as gaunt as a Rolling Stone. 'Roy died two months ago. I'm Jim Gable. Won't you come in?'

He led them into a small living room at the front of the house. It was nothing like the living room at the Needle house in Woollahra; not exotic at all, just plain suburban, not even suburban chic. The furniture came from discount stores along Parramatta Road, the prints on the walls were of Australian landscapes, the drapes were drab: Will Stratton in here would have looked like a macaw in a coalyard. A television set stood in one corner, a video recorder on top of it; beside it was a tape deck and a turntable and a table stacked with tapes and records. Malone, close to the video before he sat down on the cheap leather couch, saw the stack of videos. The one on top showed two naked men making love, which was enough exotica for him.

'I thought you'd come about the music.' Gable gestured at the tape deck. 'There's an old biddy across the road who is always complaining, says she can't stand classical music. She'd be across here to burn the house down if she knew the composers I play. Gays like Copland, Britten, Schubert – it was my partner's collection of tapes and records. It brings him back, in a way.'

He seemed to be talking as if to keep them here in the house, to keep him company. He had what was almost a cavernous face: deep-set eyes, sunken cheeks, a jawline that curved round like the rim of a container. Malone had to stretch his memory to think of anyone he had seen looking so sad without weeping.

'Did Mr Morpurgo die as a result of the bashing he received?'

'No, he died of AIDS. I'm HIV-infected, too, if you want to know.' Gable was not antagonistic; he offered the information as if they might like to question him on it. 'Why are you coming to me at this late date? I really don't want that – that experience brought up again.'

'We can understand that, Mr Gable. But we are trying to find the killer who shot the kid who bashed up your friend. Did the gang bash you, too?'

Gable nodded. He seemed to search in the bucket of his face for an expression; then gave up and just sighed, a heavy sound. 'Roy got the worst of it. They were starting in on me when this guy appeared out of nowhere, shot the kid . . .' He stopped, seemed to have some difficulty in getting his breath; then he went on, 'Some of the gang tried to grab him, but he got away from them. But he left his wig behind.'

Malone looked at Kate, who said, 'There was no mention of a wig in the running sheet.'

'The police probably didn't know about it,' said Gable. 'Most of the kids pissed off as soon as the police arrived.' He paused, frowned; his face was a congestion of lines. 'I remember seeing one of the kids holding the wig, it was a dark one –'

'Do you remember what the killer looked like? With or without the wig?'

Gable shook his head. 'I was too concerned for Roy – the gang had made a real mess of him. But he was conscious – I was surprised when he told me later he'd recognized the killer. Or thought he had.'

Malone leaned forward. 'Someone he knew?'

'I don't know. I asked him several times – even when he was dying. But he would never tell me – Roy could be bloody stubborn at times. He said he owed the killer his life – for what it was worth. He had AIDS then, the beginning of it. Roy also had a twisted sense of humour at times. But I miss the bugger,' he said and the dark eyes seemed to turn black.

'What did Roy do? I mean, where did he work?'

'We both worked for –' Gable named a well-known insurance firm. 'We were senior clerks, nothing more. Not executives, nothing like that. We worked together for nearly twenty years before . . .' He gestured with a big hand in which the knuckles stood out like knots. 'We were both in the closet all that time. Roy had been married – he had a wife and a boy, they're somewhere down in Victoria. When he died I tried to find them, but I had no luck . . .' He stopped again, once more seemed to have trouble with his breathing. 'Then one day Roy and I discovered each other, what we were. We lived together for the past four years – people at the office guessed, I think – we never really came all the way *out*. It's not easy at our age . . . Not till the bashing and then there was no point in hiding it. Roy had left work – we told people he had cancer –' He shook his big head. 'Jesus, the way you try to hide the obvious!'

'Perhaps it wasn't obvious,' said Kate gently. 'Not everybody recognizes AIDS when they see it.'

'Do you still work there?' asked Malone.

'No. After Roy died . . . No, I'm on a pension, I've got a little money set aside. I – we owned this house. The car out there – Roy insisted we buy it, two months before he died. Stupidest bloody thing we ever did . . . But I suppose you do stupid bloody things when there's no future?' He looked at them for confirmation.

'Probably.' Malone was not uncomfortable with Gable's confession; experience had taught him that. 'I hate to ask this – Jim, is it? Jim, you said Roy recognized the killer. Did he have other partners? Where did he pick up the HIV infection?'

'Yes, he had been with other blokes.' Malone had been trying to guess Gable's age: forty-five, fifty? He was apparently old enough still to use *blokes* instead of *guys*. 'Before we lived together. After that we were – true to each other? Is that the way to phrase it? Roy had had HIV for some years before it was diagnosed – I got it from him . . .' Suddenly he looked angry: not at his lover but at them: 'It's none of your business, is it? Why the hell am I telling you all this?'

'I don't know, Jim. Maybe you've just wanted to tell *someone*. Have you any friends to talk to?'

'Only the two women on either side of here. The wives – their husbands don't even give me the time of day.' There was no self-pity in his voice. 'It doesn't worry me, I'd always been a bit of a loner till I met Roy . . . Look, if you can find the man who killed that kid, good luck to you. But I can't help, tell you who he might be. I haven't a clue whether he is someone Roy had gone to bed with or whether he was someone he'd seen in a pub – I just don't know. All I can remember is he was young and –' He stopped, but not this time to get his breath. 'Yes, he held the gun in his left hand. I don't think I've ever seen a left-handed gunman, not even in the movies –' Then he smiled, a grimace in the gaunt face. 'No, there was a movie with Paul Newman, *The Left Hand Gun* or something. But that's the only place I've seen gunmen. In an insurance office and gay pubs, guns aren't your everyday fashion item, are they?'

Malone rose to go and Kate followed suit. 'Do you still go into the Cross and Oxford Street, Jim? Keep up with the gay scene?'

'I haven't been since Roy died – it wouldn't be the same without him.' He had followed them out on to the small front verandah. A slight breeze had sprung up and out in the street purple blossom floated down like one-winged butterflies. He nodded across towards the Games site. 'I'd like to last long enough to see that, the Games.'

'You're interested in sport?'

'I was, once. I almost made the four-hundred metres relay squad for the 1968 Games. I never had enough ambition, though, never tried hard enough. Athletics, I decided, was a mug's game. You trained your guts out all week, just to go out on Saturday afternoon and try to spend as little time as possible on the track. It's called breaking records. The apes in the trees must wonder if evolution was worthwhile . . . Well, goodbye and good luck.'

As they walked out to the police car Kate said, 'He's just waiting to die.'

'It's worse than that,' said Malone. 'He *wants* to die.'

'I suppose men can love as deeply as that.' Kate slid in behind the wheel. 'And women, too.'

'I guess so,' said Malone and wondered what she and John Kagal talked about when they were out together.

2

Malone was at his desk, catching up on his paperwork. Crime creates its own paper trail; sometimes it leads nowhere or round to its own tail. The computer has simplified and speeded up a detective's task, but even it manufactures paper. Eleven homicides were on his desk, some ready for court, some as vague as an idiot's scrawl. There were three simple domestics, two drug killings, two apparently motiveless murders and the four victims of the gay vigilantes. The simplest aspect of homicide was the arithmetic.

Then the phone rang. It had rung half a dozen times this afternoon and each time Malone had reached for it he had been expecting the same soft voice that had spoken to him yesterday. This time he was not disappointed: 'Inspector? You won't let sleeping dogs lie, will you?'

Malone pressed down the button on the tape. 'What do you mean?'

'You've been out pestering that poor man who was bashed in July.'

'That poor man is dead. He died of AIDS. Didn't you know?'

There was silence for a long moment; then: 'I'm sorry to hear that.'

'I thought all you gays knew about every AIDS death?' *Keep him talking*. The tape was running silently. 'Lighted candles and quilts, all that?'

'Who said I was gay? Or any of us?'

Malone changed tack: 'Are we still under surveillance? How did you know I'd been out to Homebush?'

There was a low chuckle. 'Police are always so obvious, Inspector.'

'I was in an unmarked car. And we're not always so obvious. Ask any undercover cop how easily he has trapped drug dealers. Or ask the drug dealers.'

'We have nothing to do with drugs.' A little primly.

'I'm glad to hear it. But that's about the only thing I find in your favour so far.'

'Oh, there are a lot of things in our favour, Mr Malone. Ask the gays who have been threatened or bashed. Or have you already been told we're not the villains you think we are?'

'Why don't you come in and talk to us then?'

There was a chuckle again, then the phone went dead. Malone put it back in its cradle, took out the tape, then called the Interception Unit. 'I've got the feller I'm after on tape. Do you have a voice expert?'

'We use a professor of English out at Sydney University, Professor Hamence. His number is—'

Malone rang the number, got the professor, who said, 'I'm just packing up for the day—'

'I'll be there in ten minutes at the outside. This is urgent.'

'Everything is, outside campus.' The professor had a sense of humour. 'All right, I'll be here.'

Sydney University was just five minutes up the road from Homicide, an island that tried to be aloof from the drab surroundings whose

67

residents paid it no respect. Built in 1850, it was in the Gothic image of the European and British academies it tried to imitate; its buildings suggested a cooler climate, a devotion to tradition. Since then it had been infected with a certain local larrikinism, but it still had its quota of conservatism. It had recently had its pride dented when it found itself listed below two or three other universities in the education stakes. It was as if Oxford and Cambridge had found themselves below Reading or Sussex; or Yale and Harvard below Podunk U. Smelling salts had been passed around amongst the Senate, as port had once been.

Professor Hamence was a small neat man with grey hair parted in the middle, pixy ears and, an incongruous note in the otherwise neat features, a broken nose. His room was small and neat, with its own incongruous note, a blue plastic laundry bag with a brief black lace brassiere hanging out of the top. The professor seemed oblivious of it.

'How long is the tape?'

'A minute, maybe a little more.'

Hamence looked at him quizzically. 'You're asking a lot.'

'I've managed a conviction for murder against a man just on a drop of blood on the victim.'

Hamence smiled. 'Voices don't have quite the same DNA value as blood.' He put the tape on the deck on his small neat desk, started rolling it. 'I've spent *hours* analysing some voices.'

He sat back in his chair, seemed to Malone to be too casual in his attention to the two voices as they began their short conversation. When the tape ran out, Malone went to speak, but Hamence held up his hand, leaned forward, rolled back the tape and then re-ran it. He sat back again, his eyes closed this time, then opened them when the voices ceased. He snapped off the tape-deck.

'If you want a full analysis of that voice – and I can't guarantee I can give it to you – I'll need much more than is on that tape. This is not an exact science, most of it is guesswork based on experience.'

'Make a guess on that feller.'

'The best I can do at the moment is say that it's a trained voice. I don't mean an educated voice, a *trained* one. A singer or an actor, maybe a professional speaker – you know, on the lecture circuit. They're everywhere these days.' He spoke like one who wished that

68

he, too, were on the circuit. 'He gives value to syllables, weight to certain words. He doesn't say guv'mint, like our politicians and union leaders, or Ostraya –'

'He doesn't use any of those words.'

'Sorry, I'm on my hobby-horse. No, he doesn't. Listen . . .' He switched on the tape again. 'There. *Pestering* – every syllable. Same with *police*. *Po-lice*, not *p'lice*. He's not being pedantic, it's perfectly natural with him. And unlike most Australians, he opens his mouth when he speaks.'

'Can you tell where a voice comes from? Here? Queensland? South Australia?'

The professor shook his head. 'I can't pinpoint a location. There are some people who claim they can nominate a North Queensland accent over a Tasmanian one. I think that's stretching it – I doubt if Henry Higgins could do it. You're familiar with *Pygmalion*?'

'I'm married to Mrs Pygmalion.'

Hamence nodded sympathetically. 'So many of us are.'

There was five seconds' silence while they contemplated men's subjugation. Lisa, with an educated foreigner's precision in English, had over the years got Malone to open his mouth, unclench his teeth and blow some life into his vowels. He wondered what Mrs Hamence, if there was a Mrs Hamence, did to influence the professor.

'There are differences in accent, of course,' said Hamence. 'The Melbourne upper classes – if there is such a thing – and the Adelaide establishment, they have an accent they try to make different. Some women from Sydney private schools, the same – a fluting sound. Sydneians, particularly the men, tend to speak too quickly. There's a certain cricket captain and a rugby league coach, too – they always sound as if they're trying to outpace the shorthand writers. North Queenslanders have probably the slowest, flattest drawls, but I've heard farmers out in western New South Wales with the same flat tone. All I can tell you at the moment is that this man has a trained voice. As I said, a singer or an actor or a professional speaker. Maybe even a barrister, some of them aspire to being actors.'

Malone grinned, remembering a few actors he had met in court. 'I'll just have to keep this feller talking then. Do you think he's psychotic, a nut?'

'On that? How can I judge? My first reaction would be to say no,

69

he's not. But I'm no expert on the criminal mind. I think you'll have to build up your own profile on him. I'll help with the voice, but that's all I can do. Is he getting to you with these phone calls?'

Malone made the admission: 'Yes.'

'Then that might be to your advantage. He'll keep going with the calls if he knows you're upset by them. Sooner or later he'll give himself away.'

'The sooner, the better.'

Malone thanked the professor and left, stepping round the laundry bag, about which Hamence made no comment. Outside in the quadrangle Malone paused. He had graduated from high school with reasonable marks that might have got him into university, but there had been no money in the family in those days to allow him further study; he had just joined the police force, liking it, when university fees had been abolished. He had no regrets that he had had no tertiary education, but he sometimes wondered where he would be now if he had come here or to one of the other universities. With hindsight he knew he would have studied law; but would he have been a criminal lawyer or one specializing in civil cases? Or would he have been one of the failures, the ambulance-chasers, hanging around courts looking for a brief? Whatever, he would not have met Lisa if, as a police officer, he had not been sent to London all those years ago. She was his success.

He went home, driving through the peak-hour traffic, one eye on the rear-vision mirror to check if he was being tailed. He had been tailed before and he had not enjoyed the experience. The foxhunter was not supposed to be looking over his shoulder for the fox.

He pulled the car into the driveway, got out to open the garage door. Lisa was in the front garden, hosing the two gardenia bushes she was cultivating. She was the family gardener, green-thumbed and enthusiastic; even tulips flourished for her, as if they knew she was Dutch, springing out of the ground at her. She turned off the hose and offered her cheek to his kiss. Instead of which he pulled her to him and kissed her on the lips.

'What'll the neighbours think?' Not that she cared what the neighbours thought. 'What have I done to deserve that?'

'I've just been to Sydney University. I decided you were better than a law degree.'

70

He drove the car into the garage, closed the door, took a look up and down the quiet street. This was middle-class suburbia: no gangs roamed here and if there were any gays behind the solid, respectable front doors, they were in the closet. Then he followed Lisa into the Federation-style house, his keep against the threats of the world.

That night, though he had an unlisted phone number, he got another call: 'I thought you'd like early notice, Inspector. We shot another basher this evening. There will be more, so long as the bashings continue. Why don't you let us get on with our public service?'

3

'It was attempted murder last night,' said Senior-Sergeant Peeples. 'The victim has a gunshot wound to the head, he's a long way from out of danger, the hospital says. This time it was lesbians, not male gays. A coupla girls walking hand-in-hand in Riley Street – just up the road, for Chrissakes! He's getting cheeky.'

'He's been like that for the past week,' said Malone. 'He? It was a bloke this time?'

The task force – seven detectives, including Malone and Kate Arletti, and three uniformed men – was in the Incident Room, though apparently no one at Surry Hills called it that. An extra coloured pin had been added to the map on the wall. There was no photo of the wounded basher; one had to be dead to merit such recognition. Glancing around the room, Malone wondered how many of the task force had their hearts set on solving these cases. Perhaps only Constable Arletti and himself. These Surry Hills men had lived for some years with the local gay community and maybe they were not unsympathetic to what the killers were doing.

'It was a guy, yes,' said Peeples. 'He was lucky to get away this time. Two of the gang went for him.'

'The girls okay?'

Peeples looked at Darren Beane, who nodded. 'I saw them this morning. They're shook up, but evidently the killer got into the act before the gang could really bash them up.'

'Anyone talked to the kid who was shot?'

'No, he's still in intensive care. This gang was different from the

71

others we've interviewed – they were kids from –' He named one of the more exclusive private schools.

'What happened to you? The kids bash you, too?'

Peeples was nursing a badly bruised right cheek. 'I got it at cricket practice. We were having fielding practice and I dived and misjudged the ball.'

'What are you, bowler or batsman?'

'Bowler. A quickie, like you.'

So someone remembers who I once was. 'Don't you know fast bowlers aren't supposed to exert themselves in the field? We're only there to maim the batsmen. There's a fast bowlers' union, Garry – you'd better join it ... So what happened with the kid? Is he going to be charged?'

'That depends on whether the women prefer charges. It depends on his dad, too.'

'Oh, who's his dad?'

'Judge Bristow. The kid's his youngest son.'

There was a sort of wry gloom in the room. Judge Richard Bristow was a 'hanging judge': the severity of his sentences was notorious. Police, Malone included, were always pleased when Judge Bristow presided over cases they were involved in. Malone decided that, if possible, he would stay well away from the Bristow kid.

'I'd like to talk to the girls,' he said. 'Kate and I.'

'Darren will take you,' said Peeples. 'They live only a coupla blocks away.'

'We can walk,' said Beane as he and Malone and Kate came out of the station. 'Unless –?'

'No, we'll walk,' said Malone. 'Have you picked up any gossip since I talked to you last?'

'I haven't talked to anyone, sir. Not any gays.'

'Why not?'

'Was I supposed to?'

'Yes.'

They waited at a traffic light, the morning sun warm on their backs. On the opposite corner was a restaurant where, not so long ago, Malone had seen crims and politicians lunching together to discuss life and other matters. Long before his time Surry Hills had been one of the toughest areas in the city; there had been sly-grog shops, cheap brothels and gangs who bashed you up for your purse and not your sexual proclivities. There were no longer any sly-grog shops and only one brothel, not a cheap one but one which took American Express and Visa cards and, so the rumour went, was classified for Fringe Benefits Tax. The workmen's terrace houses were now boutique offices for architects and fashion designers, when they were not the gentrified residences of those who were now flocking to inner city living.

The light turned green. 'I'll start asking around today, sir.'

'Do that.'

Nothing more was said till they came to the block of apartments where last night's intended bash victims lived. It was a big block, built on the site of what had once been the State's premier women's hospital; politics had moved the beds and the staff to where the government's voters had been, the hospital had been knocked down and the apartment block had gone up. It was progress, of a sort, Malone grudgingly agreed. His three children had been born in the hospital and it was a sacred site for him.

The two women lived on the second floor. A tiny brass plate on the front door announced: Bromley. A voice behind the door asked who they were; then it was opened by a girl in slacks and a checkered shirt worn loose. 'Police? We've already been interviewed –'

'Miss Bromley?' said Malone.

'No, I'm Liz Embury. *Miz* Embury.'

'May we come in?'

She was not welcoming at all, just stood there; then a voice behind her said, 'Of course, come on in! Don't leave them out there, Liz – all the old busybodies will have a ball. Come on, come on in!'

Greta Bromley was older by a decade or more than her partner. She was a flower girl of the Sixties, but looked as if she had been through a bad drought: faded, wilted, in need of a rain of good luck. She led the three police officers into a small, comfortably furnished room; Miz Embury followed silently, her reception like a chill on their backs. Malone glanced quickly around, not really knowing what he expected to find. Pictures of nude women coupling? An arrangement of dildos on the upright piano against one wall?

'Coffee?' Greta Bromley had a slight American accent. She had

73

once been goodlooking, perhaps even beautiful, in a square-jawed way; she had large, heavy-lidded eyes and auburn hair that hung down in a long curly frame round her face. She wore a kaftan and enough beads and bangles to have started a bazaar. All that spoiled her was that everything about her seemed to have lost colour, she was a washed-out picture of what she had once been. 'Liz honey, the coffee's still hot.'

Liz Embury might have been pretty but for her sullenness; or at least her present sullenness. She obviously resented the police presence; or did she resent just Malone and Kate, the straights? Though Malone noticed there had been no acknowledgement towards Beane; she had just ignored him. She went out into the kitchen without a word.

'Liz has been pretty upset by what happened,' said Greta Bromley. 'The bastards would've really hurt her if I hadn't gone for them. Then this guy with the gun suddenly popped up – Christ knows where he came from –'

'He always just seems to pop up,' said Malone. 'You hadn't been aware of him before that?'

'We were watching the kids. They saw us and crossed the road towards us – we were scared, but I couldn't believe it when the sonsofbitches just rushed us – they came at us like tackles –'

'Tackles?' said Kate.

Greta Bromley had a nice smile. 'I'm American, honey. Football tackles. My brother was one, I know the play –'

'And you got in front of one of the tackles?' said Malone. 'You were pretty game.'

She slipped down the loose shoulder of her kaftan, showed the bruising on her breast and shoulder. 'If I'd had the gun, I'd have killed the bastards myself. All of them. So would Liz, wouldn't you, honey?'

Liz Embury came back into the room, set down a tray with cups and saucers and a coffee percolator. She sat down on the couch beside her partner, her knees together, her hands clasped; she reminded Malone of the way his girls had been taught to sit by the nuns at Holy Spirit. 'You cops are doing nothing to protect us.'

'We're trying to find the man with the gun,' said Kate.

'Why him? Why don't you have police out on the beat, locking

74

up these thugs? You must understand how we feel, Darren.' It was the first sign that she knew Darren Beane.

'Liz,' he said patiently, 'they'd be out there if we had the men to spare. There aren't enough cops, everyone knows that.'

She changed tack: 'If you catch this man with the gun, what happens? He goes to gaol and the bashers still roam free? That's shit, if you ask me.'

Greta Bromley poured coffee, handed cups around. 'Look, guys, we appreciate what you're doing, but look at it our way. This guy with the gun—'

'There's a woman, too,' said Kate.

The other two women looked at each other, then Liz Embury said, 'Let me get this straight. Are you saying there's a lesbian in these murders?'

'There have been four murders and this attempted one,' said Malone. 'Haven't you been following the earlier cases?'

'Should we have been?'

Crumbs, thought Malone, is the division between male gays and lesbians as wide as this? Where does that put us straights?

'I thought any murder in the gay community—'

'I've been following the cases.' Greta Bromley seemed a little hasty to cover her partner's apparent indifference. 'I'd forgotten a woman had been mentioned. But why do you think she's a lesbian?'

'We didn't say that. We don't even know if the men involved are gays.'

'Men?'

'The killers in each case all looked different. What did the feller last night look like?'

The two women looked at each other again, then Liz Embury said, 'Slim, blond—he had his hair in a ponytail. And he had a beard, one of those stupid things they have on the end of their chins, a goatee—'

'Misplaced pubic hair,' said Greta Bromley. 'And you talk about the vanity of women!'

'Not Darren and me,' said Malone, glad that he was clean-shaven. 'This feller was blond? They've all been dark-haired up till now, haven't they, Darren?'

Beane nodded. 'Even the woman.'

'Did any of the gang run after him, after he'd shot one of them?'

Liz Embury shrugged. 'I dunno. I just grabbed Greta's hand and we ran for our lives. The bastards didn't come after us —'

'Tell me,' said Malone carefully, 'can you remember which hand the bloke was holding the gun in?'

'Who remembers that sort of thing?' said Greta Bromley.

Liz Embury had closed her eyes, almost theatrically; then she opened them. 'I do! His left hand — he held the gun in his left hand. Why?'

Malone looked at Kate and Beane. 'There are a lot of left-handed killers around or it's one and the same bloke.'

'Jesus!' said Greta Bromley. 'Whatever happened to love and peace?'

'I think the Age of Aquarius,' said Malone, 'got waterlogged.'

She looked at him with new interest. 'You know the zodiac?'

He shook his head, smiling. 'No, I just spent my early days as a cop on the beat, battling Aquarians. They weren't all a peaceful lot — having a flower stalk shoved up my nose during a demo wasn't my idea of a peaceful gesture. Were you at Woodstock?'

'How'd you guess? Oh, I was there! I was eighteen and thought life would be like that for evermore.' She suddenly looked ecstatic; memory was champagne. 'Jimi and Janis — Oh God, they were wonderful! I've told Liz about it —'

Liz looked as if she had been unimpressed.

'There were — what?' said Malone. 'Three hundred, four hundred thousand there? You think none of them has committed a crime since then? Murdered someone, beat someone up?'

'You're a cynic,' she said and looked disappointed in him; the champagne had gone flat. 'But I guess you're right. None of our dreams last, do they?'

She looked at Liz Embury, who looked away. There was an uncomfortable silence for a moment; the three police officers were outside whatever it was these two women shared. Then Greta Bromley looked back at Malone: 'So who are you going to arrest? The left-handed killer or the kid who tried to beat up Liz and me?'

'That's up to you, about the kid. We'll lay charges, if you want us to.'

'You bet!' Liz Embury was emphatic. 'The whole lot of the shit, if you can pick them up.'

'And what about the feller with the gun?'

'He's no concern of ours.' She looked at Darren Beane. 'Don't you agree, Darren?'

Beane said no more than, 'Inspector Malone is in charge.'

Malone stood up. He had had time to take in the room; it was as ordinary as Walter Needle's had been exotic. Except for her clothes and her hair-style, Greta Bromley had apparently abandoned the trappings of her youth; there were no posters of Jimi Hendrix or Janis Joplin, no Indian rugs or shawls on the couch or chairs, no incense sticks in a vase. There were two photos on the piano: one of a young Greta, looking much like she did now but before the bloom had faded; the other of a smiling Liz Embury, a studio portrait in which she looked more than merely attractive. The room was neat and tidy, a nest of domesticity, and he wondered which of them played housewife. Or both? He was still learning.

Once he, Kate and Beane were out in the street again, he said, 'What do they do? For a living?'

'Greta does nothing,' said Beane. 'She has wealthy parents somewhere back in America, I guess they send her money. Liz is an actress.'

'Oh? What? Films, TV, the stage?'

'The stage, mostly. She also sings, around the pubs, her own songs. She'd like to be the local k.d. lang. Or Melissa Etheridge or Robyn Archer. Really come out and sock it to them, what she believes in.'

'You know them well?'

'A little. Since I've been the gay liaison officer, I've got to know a lot of people I didn't know before.'

'That's why I'm relying on you, Darren,' said Malone. 'You're the one who's going to come to me eventually and tell me who the killer is.'

Beane said nothing, just looked uncomfortable.

Back at Surry Hills Malone and Kate picked up their car and drove back to Homicide. At a traffic light Malone said, 'Something on your mind, Kate? You haven't said much.'

She hesitated, then said, 'You were a bit rough on Constable Beane, weren't you?'

'Yes. If he's going to work with us on this, he's got to show a bit more enthusiasm. He hasn't got his heart in this. The gay community are never going to open up to us the way they will with him. You and I are not going to go into the baths –'

She laughed as she started up the car again. 'I should hope not! Not me, I mean.'

'Nor me.' He hesitated, then said, 'I'm depending on Constable Beane for that. And John.'

She looked sideways at him. 'John Kagal?'

'Yes. They'll accept him more than they would a middle-aged straight like me.'

She looked straight ahead again, gave her attention to driving. 'I suppose so,' she said in a flat noncommittal voice.

Why am I testing her like this? He had said that everyone's sexual preferences were his own business, but he was testing her as if she were his own daughter. And that, of course, he told himself belatedly, was the problem. In her he saw Claire and Maureen.

Chapter Five

1

There was no second phone call after the previous night's botched murder attempt and still none by week's end. On the Thursday Justin Langtry was buried at Rookwood in the outer suburbs. Malone, feeling guilty, did not attend the funeral; he could not bear to see again the misery of the mother's life. Instead, he sent Phil Truach and Andy Graham as observers.

'The killer may or may not turn up, but just in case . . .'

'Who do we look for? A woman or a bloke in drag or what?'

Phil Truach was Malone's age, the third most senior man in Homicide. He would probably rise no higher, at least not in Homicide, but he had no ambition and therefore no complaint. Tall and lean, he smoked like a man testing the limits of lung cancer, was imperturbable and, because he had no ambition, had few enemies, not even amongst the crims.

'I dunno. Anyone who looks like an outsider, suspicious.'

'I hate funerals.' Andy Graham, big and awkward as a tank, was the unit's enthusiast, though Malone was never sure whether it was from ambition or just natural exuberance. He had all the prejudices of the very young and the very old, sympathized with ethnics who couldn't help not being Aussies but gave them no quarter for their bad luck.

'Don't we all?' said Malone and knew how much he would have hated this particular one.

Truach and Graham went out to Rookwood and came back with nothing to report. 'It was just plain bloody misery,' said Truach and Malone was glad he had not gone. 'Some of the dead kid's mates were there. They recognized us as cops and just gave us shitty looks. But the mother and—' He just shook his head. 'I think I need a smoke.'

There were four other murders that came on the books that week. They were all domestics and local detectives handled them without calling in Homicide to help. A Muslim immigrant stabbed his fifteen-year-old daughter because she wanted to live the life of an Australian teenager, an unforgivable sin in his eyes; when the police, called by a neighbour, burst into his house the man was bent low to his prayer-mat and his wife sat like a statue holding the hand of her dead daughter. A woman, brutally beaten by her drunken husband, a weekly event, waited till he fell asleep and then cut his throat, after which she phoned the police; when they arrived she was having a cup of tea and finishing the vegetables she had been preparing when her husband had come home. A young man shot his girlfriend and her secret lover, his own best friend, then turned the gun on himself but had no bullets left; so he, too, phoned the police and, when they found him, was crying over the photo of his lost friend. The fourth murder was a euthanasia killing: an elderly woman gave an overdose to her cancer-stricken husband, put on her best dress and waited for the police. It was an average week in a city that, with apprehension, was slowly growing aware of the fact that violence, like a terrible weed, was growing rapidly.

'It's a symptom of the mess the last government left us,' said the Premier, who would have scored points off St Francis of Assisi if the latter, instead of talking to the birds, had talked to the voters.

By Thursday lunchtime Malone had cleared all the paperwork on his desk; crime, he sometimes thought, created as much paper as welfare. He had lunch: corned beef and salad sandwiches and two pieces of fruit, forced on him by Lisa; he would have preferred a meat pie and a couple of cakes. He went out into the big room and across to the coffee-maker, poured himself a cup: black with no sugar. Not only Lisa but now the two girls were at work on him: *Watch your weight, Dad*. Families, he had decided, were the original gaolers.

Most of the detectives were out on cases or at lunch. Gail Lee sat at her desk reading a book; there was always a book on her desk, but Malone had been hesitant about asking her what she read. She was the newest recruit to Homicide, from Physical Evidence: half-Chinese, half-Australian, with all the cool reserve of a mandarin and, so far, no hint of what she had inherited from her Australian mother.

John Kagal and Kate Arletti were sharing a desk and sharing lunch:

they were actually pulling a sandwich apart, each taking a half. He paused by them.

'Was any FACE imaging done on the early bash killings?'

'No,' said Kagal. 'I checked. Evidently the witnesses just didn't want to co-operate.'

'I think Bob Anders will,' said Malone. 'Is he out of hospital yet?'

'Yes. He's still pretty shaken up.'

'Who wouldn't be? Ask him if he'll come in.'

'The two women will co-operate, I'm sure,' said Kate. 'Maybe not Miss Embury, but Greta Bromley will.'

'Righto, organize it for tomorrow morning. How long will it take?'

Gail Lee had marked a page, closed her book and put it down; she had been listening to the conversation. 'An hour and a half, maybe two hours, for each witness.'

Malone was aware of Kagal and Kate, the two senior detectives turning slowly to face her. He knew that both of them had had experience with FACE, the Facial Automated Composition and Editing system; he had addressed his question to them. But Gail Lee seemed unconscious of the fact that she was treading on someone else's turf. She had a trick of being Orientally inscrutable at times.

'When I was in Physical Evidence I was the OIC several times. It's a tedious business.'

'Especially for the OIC,' said Kagal, turning back to Malone. 'You aren't allowed to open your trap. It's Jeff Belpage's show and he runs it his way.'

'All right, book him for tomorrow morning. Bring in Walter Needle, Bob Anders and Miss Bromley, bring 'em in an hour and a half apart. We'll take Miss Bromley first. We'll concentrate on the male image – let's forget there might be a woman in the consortium. There isn't one, I'm sure of that. You can be the OIC, John, but I'll be there for the start.'

'Will you want me?' said Kate.

'I don't think so. Maybe you can come with us, Gail. I'm not going to hang around for five or six hours. You can relieve John, since you know the ropes.'

He saw Kate's look of disappointment, but he ignored it. He had no intention of using Gail Lee on the cases; she had been with Homicide only a month and he was breaking her in easily. In Physical

Evidence she would have come upon bloody scenes, but he still felt protective of her. He had felt the same way towards Kate Arletti and, before her, towards Peta Smith. Who had herself been the victim in a bloody scene.

'What are you reading, Gail?'

She held up the paperback. '*The Female Eunuch.*'

He hadn't read it, but Lisa, approvingly, had read out sections to him. His reaction at the time had been a wish to meet Germaine Greer in a demonstration, on opposite sides. Undue force might have been the charge against him. 'That's a bit out of date, isn't it?'

'Parts of it. But most of its arguments, no, I don't think so.'

An ethnic feminist: just what he needed right now. Gays, ethnics, feminists: he'd head for Tibooburra if he had to investigate a Greenie murder. 'Get on to Jeff Belpage, tell him we'll be in at nine tomorrow morning. Get the witnesses – Kate will give you their addresses.'

'Of course,' said Kate, though her smile suggested she had bitten on something sour in her sandwich.

Malone put on his hat, went out for a walk, doing his best to take the shackles off his mind. He stopped once to watch an Aboriginal woman and a small child, temporary escapees from Redfern, frolicking in Prince Alfred park; the child fell over and the woman tumbled over it, their laughter drifting towards him like a breeze against the ear. If someone coming out of the black streets of Redfern could laugh, there was still hope.

2

Friday morning he, John Kagal and Gail Lee drove across to Police Centre. Gail drove, coolly and efficiently, giving nothing away to the male drivers in the peak-hour traffic. 'Where did you learn to drive, Gail?'

'I did the course with the Highway Patrol, sir.'

I might have guessed it. In the back seat Kagal, another expert at practically everything, laughed appreciatively.

Greta Bromley was waiting for them at Police Centre, ignoring the curious looks of the two uniformed officers behind the enquiry counter. The beads and bangles were gone this morning; she wore a pink blouse and a long beige skirt and sandals. The only real hint of the Age of Aquarius was the decorated band round her head. She looked fresher this morning, as if she had thrown off the memory of the night of the bashing.

'Thank you for coming at such short notice, Miss Bromley. Miss Embury didn't feel like joining us?'

'No, Inspector. I'm afraid Liz has opted out of all this.'

'Has she told you why?'

'Oh yes. She just thinks the killer is doing a public service.'

Malone ignored the two men behind the counter who had sat up, friendly Airedales turning to pit bull terriers. 'That's her own opinion?' he said.

'Oh yes. You never make up Liz's mind for her.'

'What about you? Do you think he's doing a public service?'

The pit bulls waited. She looked at them, then at the three detectives. 'You're waiting for me to say yes, right? Then you'll jump on me.'

'Never done that to a lady in my life,' said Malone with a grin.

She grinned back at him; then shook her head. 'In a way, yes, I suppose I do. But where do we go from here if we let him get away with it? That would be anarchy and not even at Woodstock did I believe in that.'

'Glad to hear it. Righto, let's all go upstairs.' They were all issued with security badges and he led them across to the lifts. 'How did you feel about law and order back in the old days?'

'Ah.' She pushed back her curls, adjusted her head-band. She treasured her memories, mainly because her father, a Baptist Republican who had made his money in soybean futures, thought them valueless. 'I didn't know what a serial killer was in those days. Everybody loved everybody.' Except, occasionally, one's parents. Malone raised a dubious eyebrow and she smiled wryly. 'Or so we thought.'

They rode up to Level 5 where Senior-Constable Jeff Belpage was waiting for them. He was a tall gangling man with a shock of red curls and a dark brown face that didn't seem to belong to him. He was affable, but he left no doubt that he was the expert in his field and he wanted no outside interference.

'You've seen our set-up, sir?'

'No.' Malone had always left this aspect of a case to junior officers. The last time he had been involved he had been a sergeant and they were still using the Penry Photofit system which meant the manual piecing together of transparent overlays of line drawings. He was now in the computer world; or rather on the outskirts of it. Jeff Belpage was very much a citizen of that new world.

'This is the most advanced system in the world, developed down in Melbourne. We've sold it to the Canadians, some American state police forces, the Brits are interested – this is a world-beater.' He waved a long arm around the narrow room in which they stood, at the computers, the camera lay-out, the stacks of files. It was his treasure-house. 'But ask the politicians for more money to expand this, give me more room, more staff – forget it. They can pour money into the bloody Olympics, but this –' Again he waved his arm. 'Nah, there's no votes in this.'

Malone agreed with everything Belpage was saying, but junior officers were not supposed to vent service spleen in front of civilians. 'Can we get on with it?'

'Okay.' Belpage didn't sound rebuffed; this was his domain. He had the confidence of the inexpendable. 'Miss Bromley, we'll start out with a basic face shape. I can't give you leading questions, other than to ask whether the face is round or square or oval or what. If I lead you, some smart lawyer in court will question the identification. Are you going to stay, sir?'

'Just for a while,' said Malone. 'John Kagal will be the OIC.'

'Okay, you understand you can't offer any remarks?'

'I understand.' Experts were taking over the world.

Greta Bromley had been watching Belpage with veiled amusement; her opinion that men thought they ruled the world was being con- firmed. Men had invented the computer, but one day women would invent the virus that would take it over. She smiled at Belpage, undaunted by him and his toys. She had liked, even loved a man or two back in the Woodstock days, but they had grown tiresome. As had Liz, lately.

'Go ahead, Constable. The man's face was oval.'

Malone stayed with the interview for half an hour while Belpage, a skilful artist, built up a picture of the blond man who had been the killer in the Bromley-Embury attack. Belpage was painstaking, eager

84

to show his skill and the range of his system but equally careful to do a meticulous job. Malone, impressed, went out to the main room of Physical Evidence, where Gail Lee waited with Walter Needle, who had just arrived.

'I suppose all this is necessary, Inspector? After so long, my memory may play tricks.'

'You're an architect, Mr Needle. Try and remember it as a face you designed.'

Needle laughed heartily. 'You have a flattering idea of an architect's imagination. But we'll try, we'll try.'

He appeared much more relaxed without his partner. He was fastidiously dressed as usual; he might have been a Macquarie Street doctor, specializing in wealthy women patients. He would have been successful at that, too, thought Malone.

'Do you think you'll catch this killer?'

'Do you think you'll ever build the perfect city?'

'Wrong analogy, Inspector. No.'

Behind him Gail Lee nodded in agreement. *Don't tell me she's studied town planning, too.*

'Righto, wrong analogy. But yes, we'll catch him. The difference between police and criminals is we have more patience.'

'Do you *want* to catch him?'

'Yes.' Flatly.

'Well, I'll do what I can to help.'

'And Mr Stratton, if we need him?'

'I'm afraid not.'

'Why not?'

'Will feels justice has already been done. The thug who bashed him is dead.'

His face had closed up; something that might have been pain tightened his eyes. Behind him Gail Lee was inscrutable.

Malone said goodbye, went out to the front of Police Centre. He was standing there when Clarrie Binyan came up the steps, briefcase in hand. 'I've gotta go to court this morning. How's it with you and the serial killer?'

'Clarrie, do you ever get the feeling that life ain't a bowl of cherries?'

'I didn't know that it ever was.' He grinned. 'And I don't mean

85

because I'm black. I was over in Longueville the other day. A nice leafy suburb, people there with comfortable incomes, maybe two cars. There was some graffiti on a wall – I hadda laugh. ''The Angels Sing – Always Fucking Off-key''. I don't think we were ever meant to win all the time, none of us.'

'Thanks, Clarrie. You've really cheered me up.'

Binyan smiled, patted him on the back and went into the Centre.

Malone went back to Strawberry Hills, found more paperwork on his desk, waded through it, waited for the phone to ring. It did, several times; but never with The Voice on the other end. He was not surprised, just irritated, that he was *waiting* for the killer to call. It was not the first time he had found himself chained to a murderer; the link was always there between a cop and a criminal. But The Voice had insinuated himself, had become – what? Not a friend, for Christ's sake. An acquaintance? Well, maybe; but that didn't really describe him. An influence? He would have to watch out. In that twilight stream immediately before falling asleep at night, freed of ethics and conscience, there had been momentary thoughts that maybe, after all, the killer *was* doing a public service.

John Kagal and Gail Lee came back in mid-afternoon. Kate Arletti came into the office with them as the coloured images were laid on Malone's desk.

'All the descriptions check pretty closely,' said Kagal. 'Whether blond or dark – they have the same facial characteristics.'

Malone looked at the faces staring up at him. 'Is there anyone in the files resembling him?'

Kagal shook his head. 'Half a dozen, but there's nothing to connect any of them with these particular killings. All of them had different MOs, none of them had any connection with the gay community. This guy's a one-off, boss.'

Malone continued to stare at the images. 'He looks familiar.'

'Constable Belpage said that's always a trap,' said Gail Lee. 'Actually, sir, he looks a bit like you, only you're older.'

Malone looked across his desk at her. 'Explain yourself, Gail.'

For a moment she showed an uncharacteristic uncertainty; had she gone too far? Kagal rescued her: 'He does look a bit like you, boss – I mean as you might have looked, say, twenty-five, thirty years ago.'

'Watch yourself. This bloke's supposed to be around twenty-eight, thirty at the most. You've just put me close to retirement.' But he wasn't smiling.

Kagal was adept at slipping through doors that threatened to slam on him. 'I take it back. Twenty years ago?'

'Fifteen.'

Kagal smiled and something like a smile flickered on Gail's lips. 'Okay, fifteen. Jeff Belpage told us about cases where witnesses have been brought in to describe someone who's attacked them. Halfway through the imaging he's realized they're describing themselves. The crimes never happened.'

'There's a big pit being dug here — you two are about to fall into it.' He saw a twitch of a smile on Kate Arletti's face; she hadn't had a hand in digging the pit. 'Are you telling me I'm seeing this bloke as the image of myself?'

Kagal dodged the slamming door, stepped back from the pit. 'No, boss. What I'm saying, what Jeff Belpage told us, is that we all have a store of faces in our memory — they come back to us, we can't put a name to them, but they're there, maybe for an instant, maybe longer. I think *I've* seen this guy's face, but for the life of me I can't remember where or when. This guy is anonymous-looking, he's got the sort of goodlooking face that you can forget as easily as you can remember.'

Malone looked at the two women. 'Would you remember him if you saw him in a room, on a TV screen, anywhere at all?'

Kate studied the face. 'No, I guess not. Not unless he smiled at me, made a pass. Then I might.'

'Gail?'

'I could say you all look alike to me.' It was the first time she had shown any humour; she had a very attractive smile. 'My father once told me one of the advantages to being Chinese was that most Europeans couldn't tell one from another. He said he should have taken up a life of crime. Instead, he chose to be a doctor.'

Malone smiled at her, trying to be patient. 'Take a stab, Gail. Would you remember him if you had a chance meeting with him?'

'No-o. Not unless, like Kate said, he tried to make a pass at me.'

'And if he did?' Malone looked at both women.

Kate studied the face again. 'Yes, I might. It's a nice face.'

'Kate, he's a confessed killer.'

'I know. But it's still a nice face. There's no – no *evil* there.'

Malone looked around at all three of them. 'Righto, we're looking for a nice killer. I'll remind you of that when we bring him in. In the meantime keep running through that store of faces Jeff Belpage says we all have.'

3

Saturday Malone came back from his weekly game of tennis with Keith Cayburn, his next-door neighbour, and two other non-police friends. Before he had a shower he got himself a light beer and slumped down on the couch in the living room. This was a room that Lisa, alone, had furnished and, looking around it now, he remarked that it had more character than Greta Bromley's had. There was a window-height line of bookshelves along one wall, the books both hardback and paperback and their contents eclectic. History, biography, novels but no crime fiction: Malone had given up on that. He did read books on corporation crime; against the grain he could only admire the gall of the entrepreneurs of the Eighties. There were a Margaret Olley painting of cornflowers, a gift from Lisa's parents, and two Drysdale prints of outback towns above the shelves. He found the blue of the cornflowers restful. The dry Drysdale outback towns reminded him too much of what Tibooburra might be like.

On the opposite wall, above the television set and the V C R, was a large painting of a seascape that Lisa had bought at a charity art show. In one corner was a Sumatran wood carving, a reminder of where her parents had spent their young lives; in another was a wooden Celtic cross that she had picked up somewhere and was a compliment to him and his parents. The furniture was solid and comfortable, with high backs to the couch and the armchairs to accommodate his height. It was a room in which he always felt at *home*.

He looked at his three children, all of whom were engrossed in their own affairs. 'Well, Big Daddy is home. Does anyone care?'

They all gave him a glance and a nod.

'What are you doing tonight? Maureen?'

'I'm going to a dance club in William Street.' She was reading her mother's copy of *Vogue Living*.

'With a feller or on your own?'

'With Sharon.' A friend from school. 'Safety in numbers, isn't that what you're always saying?'

'Not two girls, not enough. Unless you can get a man to take you, we'll pick you up. Mum's dragging me to the opera – what is it, darl?'

Lisa had come into the room, sat down on the couch beside him. '*La Boheme*. The new version.'

'Righto, that's it, then. Mum and I'll have coffee somewhere, then we'll pick you up at twelve.'

'Oh Da-ad –'

'If you and Sharon come out with a coupla fellas, we'll drive off.'

'You won't be able to park in William Street on a Saturday night –'

'I'll double-park and put the blue light on the roof.'

'Oh God! Not only am I being called for by my parents at midnight – *midnight*, for God's sake! – but in a *police* car!'

Malone turned to Tom, who was reading the *Herald*'s sports pages. 'What are you doing tonight?'

'I'm having Cameron over. We're gunna run a video.'

'Which one?'

'*Sliver*, with Sharon Stone.'

He looked at Lisa. 'She never has her clothes on. Is that what you let him watch?'

'He's your responsibility. He's a male.'

'Thanks. Righto, mate, no Sharon Stone. Get *Pocahontas* or some other Disney film.'

'Dad, you've gotta be kidding! I'm not a child –'

'Another one, not a child. All of a sudden the house is full of grown-ups.'

'You'd better believe it,' said his unhelpful wife.

'Get a Sylvester Stallone, then.'

'He's always taking his shirt off so's you can admire his muscles. You want me to develop into a poofter?'

'We don't use that word around here from now on, okay? What about you?' He looked at Claire, who was buffing her nails. 'What are you doing?'

She gave him her cat's smile. 'After listening to the Inquisition, Mr Torquemada, I reserve the right to be silent.'

Crumbs, am I turning into a Muslim father? 'I give up. Some day you'll all come running to me for help and you won't be able to find me.'

'We'll just look for the car with the blue light on the roof,' said Maureen. 'God, who else has family transport like that?'

He finished his beer, patted Lisa's knee, winked and got up and went in to shower. Under the soothing water he wondered where the nights had gone when the three children would have been in bed by nine o'clock and he and Lisa would listen to his old LPs of Benny Goodman and Errol Garner and Dave Brubeck; or look at a movie on television where Sharon Stone would have been chopped off at the neck by the censors of the day. He looked down at his streaming body, looking for signs of fat or ageing. Was he getting old? But no: the ageing wasn't there in his flesh; well, not much. No, it was in his mind, in his attitude. He was inching his way into territory that he had always thought he would deny.

He and Lisa went to the opera and, despite his expectations and against his inclinations, he liked the modern version by Baz Luhrman; if a few riffs from Benny Goodman's clarinet could have been worked in, he would have liked it even more. He and Lisa went up to the Intercontinental hotel for coffee and cake, enjoyed the pleasure of each other's company, wished they were childless and could go home to bed and make wild love without being overheard. Then they drove up to William Street.

The wide street, leading up to the vividly-lit sleaze of Kings Cross, was busy with both foot and motor traffic. On the south side the hookers posed like mannequins that had fallen out of store windows; cars cruised like sharks along the kerb, but the real sharks were the pimps checking that their girls were on the job. There was a bill before Parliament to legalize pimping, an act that stuck in Malone's craw, for his sympathy was always with the girls. He drew up the car outside the Emu Club (why were so many nightclubs named after birds?) to find Maureen already waiting on the pavement.

As she clambered into the car she said, 'Thank God I got out here before you put up the blue light.'

'Where's Sharon?' said Lisa.

'She's staying, she met a guy.'

Malone felt a momentary resentment: wasn't my daughter good enough for some guy? 'A good night?'

'Awful. You never saw such a collection of creeps. If I hadn't been with Sharon, I'd have walked out and gone home. Did you enjoy the opera?'

'Your father stayed awake,' said Lisa. 'For a change.'

The talk between them was easy as they drove home. Halfway to Randwick Malone became aware that a small white car was following them. He said nothing to the women, but kept his eye on the rear-vision mirror. Each time he turned a corner the white car followed. He was two blocks from home when he turned a corner, went halfway down the block and abruptly pulled up. The white car came round the corner and slid into the kerb.

'What's –?' said Lisa.

'Stay here!'

He was out of the Fairlane and halfway back towards the white car before he remembered he didn't have his gun. There was nothing to do but keep going. He reached the other car, a Mazda, as the door opened and the driver went to get out. Malone slammed the door, pushing the man back into his seat.

'Jesus! Who the hell –?'

'Why are you following me?' Malone leaned down close to the man, close enough to grab him if he went for a gun.

'Following you?' He was a young man with a long thin face and a high voice that cracked now with fear. 'Jesus, mate, I live here –' He pointed to the block of flats outside which his car had come to a halt. 'What's fucking got into you? Why would I be following you?'

Malone flashed his badge. 'Show me your driver's licence.'

The man fumbled in a hip pocket, with Malone ready to hit him if he produced more than a wallet. But that was all that came out of his pocket. 'There, that's me. There's my address –'

The address checked with the flats; Malone handed back the licence. 'Sorry. We've had some complaints about cars being followed –'

It was a lame excuse and he wasn't sure the man believed him. But all he wanted now was to get back to his own car; he had made a fool of himself. He straightened up and looked up and down the dark street, but there was no one in sight. An aluminium moon grinned derisively at him; somewhere a dog sounded like a laughing hyena. 'Sorry,' he said again and went back up to the Fairlane.

'What was all that about?' said Lisa.

'I thought we were being followed.' He started up the car.

'Why would anyone be following us?' asked Maureen.

'I don't know,' he said evasively. 'That car just looked suspicious, that was all. It was nothing, so let's forget it.'

'The guy in the car wouldn't have thought it was nothing,' said Maureen. 'A hulking big cop bearing down on him.'

Stop questioning me, he said angrily but silently. He might be a hulking big cop, but he was also a father and a husband and all he had been trying to do was protect them. But from what and from whom? He had felt foolish when he had identified the man in the car and he felt foolish now. But somewhere out there in the dark was the owner of the voice on the phone and the tape, conducting surveillance.

Sunday morning he, Lisa and Tom went to Mass. The two girls said they 'might go to evening Mass'; he left it to Lisa to push the matter if she wished. The girls, lately, had become irregular churchgoers, but did that make them mortal sinners? He couldn't chide them; he was a half-hearted Catholic. Or anyway, a half-hearted churchgoer. He had read recently that only twenty-nine per cent of Catholics now went to Mass regularly; he wondered how many of them felt like him, not sinners, just independent. He was forty-five years old and if he hadn't worked out his relationship with God by now there was something wrong with one of them. And, naturally, he didn't think it was himself.

Clements and Romy came to lunch with the new baby. After lunch he and Clements went out and sat by the pool, he with what was left of his lunch white wine, Clements with a large beer.

'The cleansing ale,' said Clements, raising his glass like a chalice though not in mockery. 'Nothing like it to revive you . . . So how's it going with Cyril?'

'Who? Cyril who?'

'The gay who's killing these bashers? We've got to call him something.'

'We're not getting very far. You want to take over from me?'

'No, thanks.' He looked at Malone over the top of his glass. 'Why? Are the poof – gays getting up your nose?'

He sipped his wine, pondered a moment or two. 'No-o. I'm getting used to them. But this bugger on the phone is. Right up it.'

'One of them has gotta slip up sooner or later –'

'That's it. I don't think there is a – a consortium. I'm beginning to think it could be the one bloke. Two of the killers have been left-handed. Two out of four? That's a pretty high percentage. He wore a wig in one of the murders – he'd have worn one, too, when he played the woman. The glasses I got back from Mr Needle – plain glass, fakes. Let's start thinking there's only one of him, not four.'

'Have you thought of putting out bait?' Malone looked at him curiously and Clements went on. 'Having someone play gay, go looking to be bashed up? Maybe our vigilante mate will then turn up and we grab him.'

'Are you volunteering?'

The beer splashed in the glass. 'Me? Christ, you're not serious?'

'Relax.' Malone grinned at the thought of Clements trying to look like an obvious homosexual; the farce would fool no one. 'Righto, let's say we set bait. But what if Cyril doesn't turn up and our feller gets bashed by some gang? How do we explain that when he fronts up for compo? I don't think the Compensation Board favours fellers who go out looking for trouble. Did you have anyone in mind?'

'John Kagal,' said Clements without hesitation.

Malone looked at him, wondering how much he knew. 'Why him?'

'I dunno. I just think he could play the part better'n the rest of us. He's got that – *smooth* look. If he ponced his walk a bit, he could pass for one.'

'Forget it, Russ,' he said, sliding Kagal out of the conversation as quickly as possible. 'We'll trap Cyril some other way.'

Clements was pensive, sipping his cleansing ale. 'Between you and me, I don't care how many of these bashers he shoots. Okay, not *kills*. But scares the shit outa them.'

'That's dangerous thinking.' But he had been guilty of the same thought.

'I know that. Which is why it's between you and me.'

The royal commission into police corruption was still going on, getting worse for the reputation of the Service day by day. The straight and narrow path for a cop had become narrower.

'But life would be easier, wouldn't it, if we could sometimes turn a blind eye to how law and order is enforced.'

'You're in favour of vigilantes? The gun lobby will be pleased to hear that. Keep your trap shut on that idea, Russ. We've got enough on our plate as it is, trying to please The Dutchman. Who'd have thought the old bastard would be trying to woo the gays? Any policy for a vote.'

Then Lisa and Romy came out and sat in chairs beside them. A thin layer of cloud took the glare off the sun and it was just pleasantly warm. Both women had the ease that affection, and not just social relationship, brought to their friendship. Each so different from her husband, foreigners both who had become Australians but not Australian, they had the same regard for each other as the two men shared. It was a four-cornered meeting of affection, even love, that was more rare than common.

'Where's the baby?' asked Clements.

'Call her by her name,' said Romy. 'She's not *the baby*.'

'Okay, where's Amanda?'

'Inside, in her carry-cot. Tom is singing her to sleep.'

'*Tom*?' said Malone. 'Singing to her?'

'Songs by the Grateful Dead,' said Lisa. 'He's just discovered them. He thinks they're battle-songs from the Punic wars.'

'Well, at least he's working backwards. Some day he'll discover Cole Porter or George Gershwin.'

'I wouldn't bet on it,' said Lisa.

Why can't every day in the week be like this? thought Malone. A wife I love, two people I also love, my son singing to their daughter. Then inside the house he heard the phone ring and then Tom came to the back door.

'Dad, it's for you. He wouldn't say who he was.'

'A nice boy, your son. Polite, just like his father.'

'Cut out the bullshit. How did you get my number? It's unlisted.'

There was a soft laugh. 'Oh, we have ways and means . . . Did you like the opera last night?'

So his apprehension last night had not been false, after all. 'Let's say I liked it better than I like Mardi Gras.'

'That's not saying much – I don't like it, either. Vulgar and so obvious. It's designed now to hit you straights right in the eye, don't you think? Kids' stuff, in your face.'

Why haven't I got a damned tape on this phone? 'Look, we have guests . . . What d'you want?'

'Just to pass the time of day, Mr Malone. We botched last night's service, but we made our point – scare the shit out of them. But we'll keep on until there is no more of this sort of persecution. You might call a press conference and make that statement on our behalf. For obvious reasons we can't call a conference.' Again there was the soft laugh. 'We're depending on you, Mr Malone. You and the police. You all hate these bash gangs as much as we do.'

Malone took a risk: 'I don't believe there is a *we*. There's only you.'

There was silence, broken by the sound of traffic in the background, then the soft laugh. 'I'll tell that to the others. I think they may be offended.'

Then the phone went dead.

Malone put it back in its cradle, stood a moment. When he turned round Tom was standing in the doorway. 'Who was it, Dad? Was it the gay who's been killing those bashers?'

Malone nodded. 'What did he say to you?'

'I dunno – nothing much.' Tom shrugged. 'He just asked was I your son. He said I had a good deep voice, like yours. I didn't tell him mine had just broken.' He grinned.

'That was all?'

'He asked where I went to school.'

'Did you tell him?'

'Yeah. Why, did I do the wrong thing? He sounded so nice and friendly. While he was talking to me he didn't sound like a – like a killer. I just thought he might be some guy from one of the papers or a TV reporter. Only when he wouldn't give his name, he said you'd know who he was, only then I sorta caught on. Well, sorta. I thought he might be one of your gigs, your informers. Then it clicked . . . That's the first time I've ever talked to a murderer.'

'Let's hope it's the last.' He put his arm round his son's shoulders; he was surprised how broad and muscular they were. 'This bugger's getting too close to home. Don't say anything to your mother or the girls, okay?'

'You think he's gunna come nosing around *here*?'

'No.' He tried to sound convincing; he was having too much practice at this sort of deception. 'But he might make a nuisance of himself on the phone. If he calls again and you answer it, hang up on him immediately. Would you recognize his voice again if you heard it?'

'I dunno – I might. But why would he wanna know what school I go to? It's creepy, I come outa school and think some murderer is keeping an eye on me.'

'I told you, that's not going to happen!' His grip on Tom's shoulder had tightened; but that was the giveaway. He relaxed his grip, turned it into a pat. 'If there's anyone in this family he's interested in, it's me.'

'But he could get at you through me. Or Mum and Claire and Maureen.'

He took his arm from round Tom's shoulder before he gave anything more away. 'Are you playing detective?'

'What d'you expect? Aren't you the role model around here?'

Role model: what did they teach kids at school these days? At Marcellin in his day the only role models, though they were not called that, mentioned by the Marist brothers and the lay teachers were Jesus Christ and an assortment of the more manly saints, preferably the ones who had died violent deaths. Women saints rarely got a nod, though the Mother of God, since the Marist order was named after her, got a chauvinist acknowledgement.

'Find some other role model. A surgeon or a writer.'

'A writer? You gotta be kidding. Okay, I won't play detective. But it's okay if I keep an eye out for him?'

'So long as you don't try fronting up to him. If you see someone you suspect, keep away from him. Maybe I should get you a mobile –'

'Great! There's one for nine hundred dollars, you can ring anyone anywhere in the world –' Tom's map of the world was a lay-out of price tags.

'You won't need to ring anyone anywhere in the world, you'll be ringing me right here in Sydney. I'll think about it . . .' He considered mobile phones one of the world's major pollutions; to have his teen-age son with one growing out of his ear would be the ultimate embarrassment. Yet . . . 'I'll think about it.'

He knew, though, even as he said it, that he wouldn't buy the mobile for Tom. Not because he objected to them in principle, but because it would be a surrender to The Voice.

5

Monday morning Malone got another phone call he didn't want.

'The Bristow kid's out of intensive care,' said Garry Peeples. 'I thought you might like to talk to him.'

'Why me?' But he knew why: you're the boss cocky, you take the crap, that's what you're paid for.

'Judge Bristow and I had a run-in about a year ago in his court. For once he wasn't on our side, hinted we'd done a verbal. He poured shit all over me while I was in the box –' One could almost smell Peeples' bitterness. 'I'd rather you took him on, Scobie.'

'Righto, Garry. But you'll owe me.'

He hung up, went back to looking at the computer's record of the weekend's homicides. Three of them, all horrific; he felt sorry for the uniformed cops and the medics who would have been first on the grisly scenes. He looked up as Clements came into his office. The big man had his new cheerful look, though Malone knew he would have read the print-outs before putting them on Malone's desk.

'Don't send Gail out on any of these.'

'I wasn't going to,' said Clements. 'So far the local Ds haven't sent for us. I talked to them on the phone – Campsie, Fairfield, Sutherland – they said there was blood everywhere. The killers went berserk, looks like.'

'Have they got them?'

Clements nodded. 'Picked up all three of them. All unrelated – just animals letting go. We won't be needed. What are you doing this morning?'

'Something more appealing. I'm going to have a run-in with Judge Bristow.'

'Over his son? Maybe he won't be at the hospital.'

'Not with my luck.'

Judge Bristow was indeed at St Sebastian's, sitting beside his son's bed with Mrs Bristow. They were not a handsome couple, but they had a certain dignity about them. Bristow was short and broad, with jug-handle ears, a blunt heavy-jawed face and a crop of neatly trimmed dark brown hair. His wife was as thin as he was broad, with a thin face that just escaped being pretty and greying hair that looked as if it had been too many times to the hairdressers. But they had a composure about them that dignified them; they would never create a scene here in the hospital. Still, Malone was glad their son was in a private room.

The son looked to be as broad as his father, but it was impossible to tell what his face was, or had been, like; his head was swathed in dressings. He raised a weak hand when his father introduced Malone.

'He's lucky to be alive,' said Bristow. 'Fortunately, there's no brain damage.'

Maybe he had that before he went out poofter-bashing. 'Who was with you when it happened, Clive?'

The boy's eyes looked round the curtain of the dressing at his father.

'Go on,' said his father. 'Tell the inspector.'

'Some guys from school.' The boy's voice was weak; or frightened. 'Six of us.'

His mother and father looked at each other; then Bristow said, 'We haven't questioned him on who was with him. From PBC?'

The boy nodded, then winced: it was impossible to tell whether from pain or fear.

'What made you pick on the two girls?' asked Malone.

'Do you have to ask questions like that?' said Mrs Bristow. 'Isn't the important question, when are you going to catch the man who did this to Clive?'

Malone looked at Bristow for support, but none showed in the judge's face. Then he looked back at young Clive, the lesbian-basher. 'Righto, we'll save it till you're in court on why you picked on the girls –'

'In court?' Bristow was stiff; with shock or indignation, it was difficult to tell which. 'The women are going to charge Clive and his friends?'

'Didn't you expect them to?'

'Well, no – after what's happened to Clive, I thought –'

'They'd think that was sufficient punishment? Maybe they will. But there are still the other five boys . . .' He turned again to the son. 'Clive, did you see the man who shot you?'

'Yeah, sort of. I saw him coming at us, but I didn't expect him to have a gun –'

'Why not? Haven't you read the papers lately? Kids who bash up gays being shot by this man?'

'Please –' But Mrs Bristow's plea was half-hearted.

She's still coming to terms with what her darling boy has done. 'I'm sorry to be so blunt, Mrs Bristow, but the judge will tell you we get nowhere in homicides if we pussyfoot with our questions. I'm just wondering why Clive was not more alert to what might happen . . .' The boy was silent, sullen. '*Clive* . . .'

Again there was the furtive eye round the curtain of the dressing, again at his father not his mother. Then, very reluctantly: 'It was one of the guys' idea – sort of Russian roulette, he called it. We'd been out before –'

'Doing what? Bashing gays and lesbians?'

The boy looked at both his parents this time, then back at Malone. He nodded.

'Jesus!' said the judge, got up and walked straight at the room's window as if he were going to plunge through it. He pulled up, thumped his fist on the sill, stood there.

Malone got up, joined him at the window. 'That's The Wall over there, Judge.' He nodded across the street at the high stone wall of what had once been a gaol. 'You've heard of it?'

'Of course! Dammit, man, I've sat in the court on the other side of the bloody wall.'

'That's where the bashers come to pick on the male prostitutes.

Sometimes there's a bashing a week, ones that are never reported to the police –'

Behind them there was a sound like a sob from Mrs Bristow. I'm pouring it on, thought Malone, but they need to know their son hasn't been out playing games in some game parlour. He's been in a more dangerous, shameful game than that.

Bristow turned back to his son. 'Jesus Christ, what got into you? You go out Saturday nights, you tell us you're going to a movie or a party . . . How long has this been going on?'

'This was the third time.' The boy's voice was just a mumble.

'The third bashing?'

The boy nodded.

The parents looked at each other. Malone tried to read the look: who was blaming whom? But they had enough dignity not to let the blame, if any, show. Then Bristow went back and sat down beside the bed again.

'Who was the ring-leader in this stupid bloody prank?'

'It wasn't a prank, Judge,' said Malone, still by the window. 'And if you don't mind, I'd like to get on with a few questions of my own. I'm more concerned with getting a description of the man with the gun than with what your son does with his Saturday nights.'

'Can you and I have a talk outside?' The judge's voice was cold, as if he were talking to a defendant in the dock.

'In a moment, sir.' Malone was a little more formal, took the rough edge off his tongue. He came back to the bed. 'Clive, what did the feller with the gun look like? Would you recognize him again if you saw him?'

'I think so. He was blond, had a pony-tail.' He paused. 'He looked familiar, I dunno why . . . When I saw the gun, I didn't believe it was happening – it was like I – I dunno, like I was in the middle of a movie –'

'What about your mates? They'd have got a better sight of him, after you went down. Did any of them chase him?'

'I dunno. After the gun went off, I lost consciousness. You better ask them.'

'You go to PBC, don't you?' Presbyterian Boys College. 'Name one of the fellers who were with you. The ring-leader will do, the

one who came up with the smart-arse idea of Russian roulette . . .
Sorry, Mrs Bristow.'

She looked as if she hadn't heard him.

Clive looked at his parents, then back at Malone. 'Sam Hindle.'

His mother blinked. '*Sam*? Sam Hindle?'

'Do you know the boy?' asked Malone.

'Of course we know him. We know his parents – his father's
Rupert Hindle. You must have heard of him, he's the leading heart
specialist in Sydney.'

'I've heard of him.' He stood up. 'You and I had better have our
talk, Judge.'

The corridor outside was deserted but for an old man in a dressing-
gown shuffling up and down at the far end with the look of someone
who had lost his way but didn't care; he looked to be at the end of
his life and all his ways were behind him. Malone glanced towards
him, hoped he would never reach that aimless stage of life.

Bristow ignored the old man, got straight to the point. 'Who are
the women, so that I can talk to them?'

'Do you think that would be wise?'

The judge looked at him quizzically; then he nodded, reluctantly.
He walked away from Malone, for the moment looking as aimless
as the old man further down the corridor and now coming towards
them. Then he turned back. 'I see your point. I go into court tomorrow
to sit on another murder trial.'

'Not one of mine.' *Thank God.*

'No, one from Northern Region. Skipps, the chap who beat to
death a man who made sexual advances to him. Ironic, eh?'

The old man passed them, took no notice of them, and continued
on. Malone said, 'It won't happen, of course, but what would you
do with a feller who shoots kids who bash up homos?'

Bristow walked to a window, looked out. Though Malone didn't
know it, from here the judge could see his home, safe amongst other
safe houses on a distant hill. But it was a shell, eaten away from the
inside. 'More importantly, what do I do with a boy of mine who
bashes up homosexuals? I hate violence – that's why I'm so tough
on offenders –' It was an admission he probably had made to no one
else but perhaps a fellow judge. He was talking to himself as much
as to Malone, still staring out the window: 'I'm in for some flak from

the media. Four of them have called so far and all I've commented is, no comment. But that won't satisfy them.'

'What's Dr Hindle like?'

Bristow faced Malone again. 'Flamboyant. Loud voice – he must wake his patients from their anaesthetic. Most of the time he wears double-breasted blazers with lots of brass buttons – has a showy handkerchief always dangling from the breast pocket.' The judge was as sober-suited as an undertaker; which in effect he was, with his sentencing. He was also a snob: 'Not my cup of tea at all.'

'His boy – Sam? What's he like?'

'Spoiled blind. He's still at school and he drives his own Saab convertible!'

Malone wondered if Clive Bristow was allowed to have a bicycle. 'And your boy? Is he spoiled?'

'Good God, no!' He sounded offended. Then he softened again, once more talking to himself: 'We have three boys and a girl – we're strict with all of them. Try to teach them all the *real* values. But sometimes – sometimes we shape our kids the wrong way? Do you think so?'

At least you're not a stepfather who sexually abuses his kid. 'We all have that problem. How's Clive going to get on at school?'

'I've talked to the headmaster about that. He's, as it were, out on bail.'

'I think I'll go out to the school now. Say goodbye to your wife and Clive for me.'

'Will you be back to see Clive?'

'I don't know, Judge. Candidly, I think he's more your problem than mine.'

He left before the judge could reply, walking down the corridor, passing the old man who looked at him with unseeing eyes; Malone felt a chill, as if he had passed a ghost. Sometimes he cursed his Celtic blood.

He drove out to Rose Bay, to the high hill above it where Presbyterian Boys College shared one of the world's great harbour views with the Catholic girls' school next door. It was a civic joke that, despite the persecution of the early Catholics in the colony of Sydney, Jesus Christ, Roman Catholic, had finished up as the better real estate agent over Jesus Christ, Protestant. Except here on what marathon runners called Heartbreak Hill: here the Presbyterians, with Scots canniness, had grabbed their share of the view.

It was not a large school, no more than eight hundred pupils, but it had solid Victorian buildings, a modern gymnasium and indoor pool and two large playing fields; it recognized that you could be too Calvinistic for the local hedonists. The fees were nine thousand dollars a year for day pupils and sixteen thousand for boarders. An immigrant road worker, mistakenly thinking that all education in Australia was free, had once brought his boy to the school and the playing fields had opened up in wide cracks as if from an earth tremor. The school's unofficial motto, coined by a cynical old boy who had made a fortune as a stockbroker, was *Élitism Beats All Else.*

The headmaster was neither a cynic nor an élitist; he greeted Malone with friendly politeness. 'We've had the Rose Bay police here, Inspector. But I wasn't expecting anyone from Homicide . . . That's a dread word, isn't it?'

'We get used to it, Mr O'Malley.' A Presbyterian headmaster with an Irish name? Or was he an Orangeman? Just as well Con Malone wasn't here. 'Are all the boys involved at school today?'

Stewart O'Malley was in early middle age and looked as if he might have been an athlete of some sort twenty years ago; he was lean-faced, with sandy hair brushed straight back and blue eyes in which the kindliness, if any, had worn thin. Malone wondered how many of today's teachers still had kindly eyes.

'Four of them, Year Eleven boys, have been expelled. We called their parents over the weekend and told them not to send their boys to school today. Between you and me, it wasn't easy – with the parents, I mean.'

'I can imagine. Four. What about Clive Bristow and Sam Hindle?'

They were in the headmaster's office, a large room in a modest Victorian house that stood aside from the main school buildings; Malone guessed it was also the headmaster's residence. Four separate windows in a large bay looked down on the playing fields, where a groundsman was preparing a cricket pitch on one of them. The larger of the two fields was surrounded by a fire of flame-trees, interspersed with the occasional jacaranda, like a blue gas flame. Any boy here would have had the best of everything, yet six of them, without thinking, had thrown it all away.

'Clive is in, shall we say, abeyance – I don't think we can pass judgment on him, not so soon after he almost died. You know they thought they had lost him while he was in intensive care?'

'No, I didn't know that.'

'As for Sam Hindle – well, we've put him on hold, too. He's in Year Twelve, he's doing his HSC right now. The boy is brilliant and he'll get top marks, breeze into university – he plans to be a doctor, like his father. I did a lot of soul-searching all day yesterday and decided he could sit for the exams, but in recess he's not to go near the other boys and as soon as he's finished the papers he's to go home. He's doing a science paper this morning, then I've asked his mother to call for him. I wouldn't let him bring his car to school. It's only a small punishment, but we have to make a start, let him and his parents know he's been brought up the wrong way.'

'I'm R.C. I always understood that Presbyterianism was much stricter than any of the other religions. Christian ones.'

O'Malley smiled, flicked the hem of his gown; Malone didn't think teachers wore gowns any more, but perhaps this was a badge of office. Or maybe it had been put on for his benefit. 'We are – in theory. But do you think Calvinism can flourish in our society today?' He shook his head. 'Fifty per cent of our parents send their boys here because they don't want the responsibility – the chore, if you like – of being strict with them. They leave that to us – then as soon as the boys go home, it's do-what-you-like. Don't quote me, but it's an uphill battle, Mr Malone. Teachers, both in private schools like this and in State schools, cop a lot of blame that is unjustified. I lay the blame for what has happened with Sam Hindle squarely on his parents. But again, don't quote me.' He looked at his watch, stood up behind his desk. 'Sam will be coming out of his exam now. I'll take you across to him.'

'I'd like to talk to him alone.'

'Of course. I'd just like to say a word in his favour, though. The boy is truly contrite about what happened. The attack on the women, I mean.'

'He should've been a Catholic. We're truly contrite every time we go into the confessional. Of course next day we're sinners again, but it keeps the priests on their toes.'

104

Outside Malone waited beside the curve of the long red gravel drive while O'Malley brought Sam Hindle across from one of the classrooms. He introduced the boy to Malone, then left, saying, 'Tell the truth, Sam. That will be easier for you in the long run.'

Malone said, 'Good advice, Sam. Do you take advice?'

The boy did not look like a leader, at least not physically. He was of medium height, slender, almost languid in his movements; nothing about his thin face was remarkable, except his eyes. They would never accept any façade, they would always look behind it.

'Not always,' he said. He brushed his almost-black hair back from his forehead and looked over his shoulder at the other boys who had come out of the classroom and now stood some distance away in watchful groups. He slung a schoolbag over his shoulder. 'Do you mind if we go down to the oval?'

'Sure, why not?'

They walked down the long green slope towards the main playing field, sat on a bench beneath the flame-trees. Out in the centre the groundsman was slowly driving a motor-roller up and down the cricket pitch.

'Do you play cricket?' said Malone.

'A little. Do you?'

So much for what I used to think was my fifteen minutes of fame. 'I used to. Are you any good?'

'Not really.'

'What makes you the leader of this gang of yours, Sam?'

He shrugged, unburdened by false modesty. 'Brains, I guess. None of the other guys are exactly intellectuals.'

'You didn't show much in the way of brains, going out bashing up gays and lesbians. Why'd you do it?'

The boy looked out across the oval. 'I've thought about that, since. Boredom. Weren't you ever bored at my age?'

'No.' Maybe he had been, but he wasn't going to admit it.

The boy sat with his arm along the back of the seat, relaxed, not at all as tense as Malone had expected he might be; yet he was not arrogant nor as antagonistic as that other gang leader, Les Coulson, had been. 'Sir, I'm not dumb. I appreciate how privileged I am –' He waved a hand at their surroundings, at the school up on the hill. 'I'm an only child, I'm spoilt like you wouldn't believe –'

105

This kid is likeable; what the hell possessed him? 'Sam, how will you look back on what you did Saturday night?'

'Ashamed.'

'You should be more than that. You almost got Clive Bristow killed, besides scaring the hell out of the women. What have you got against gays and lesbians?'

The boy took his time answering: 'Nothing, come to think of it. We just went out looking for targets . . . Stupid, I'll admit. Some of the other guys, Bristow in particular, they can't stand gays –'

'But you were the ring-leader.'

Sam nodded. 'I'm going to get it in the neck from the other guys' parents –'

'And from your own?'

'Yes.'

Malone sighed; the boy's problems were not his. He was just glad that this was not Tom he was talking to. 'Righto, let's get on to why I'm here. What can you tell me about the man with the gun?'

The boy thought a while. 'Not much. One of the guys and I chased him.'

'Were you being brave or stupid?'

'Stupid, I guess. I don't think I even thought about the gun, not till he suddenly pulled up, turned around and pointed it at us. That scared the hell out of both of us –' He smiled, an attractive smile. 'That was when I found out I'm not a hero.'

'Did he say anything?'

Sam nodded. 'He said, Fuck you, son, one more will be another public service.'

'And what did you or your mate say?'

'Nothing. We just waited for him to pull the trigger. I knew I was going to die –' A small shiver swept through him. 'Then he said, almost like talking to himself, No, not in cold blood. Then he took off again, but this time Chris and I were too scared to follow him, our legs had gone.'

'I've got a description of him from the two women you bashed –' The boy shook his head at that, but said nothing. 'He was blond, had a pony-tail and a goatee beard –'

'No. No beard – he'd either lost it or pulled it off.'

'So what did he look like to you?'

106

'I dunno exactly – I wasn't trying to remember him, all I was doing was looking at the gun. He was holding it like this –' He held out his hands clasped together in front of him. 'You know, the way they do it in the movies, the cops. But I do remember one thing now –' He stopped, concentrated. 'He looked *familiar*, as if I'd seen his face somewhere before.'

Malone felt a lift of excitement; but no one would have known it. 'An actor, maybe?'

'Could be. But it was just – subliminal? The way they flash images at you in a commercial, to influence you. Maybe that's where I've seen him, in a commercial.'

'If we picked him up, could you positively identify him?'

'Sure. You get him to stand the same way –' He put his clasped hands out in front of him again. 'Have you got a suspect?'

'Not yet. But there's always hope. It's a police dictum.'

Sam Hindle smiled again. 'That's my father's dictum, too. He says he's never lost a patient till the patient is dead.'

'The right sort of optimism.' *Morbid though it is.*

Then inside the boy's schoolbag there was the sound of a phone ringing. He took out a mobile, put it to his ear. 'Mum? . . . Okay, I'm ready.' He put the phone away. 'My mother's almost here.'

'Are you allowed to have mobiles here at school?'

'Actually, no. But you don't have a mobile, you're under privileged. Stupid, eh?'

'Sam, I'm sorry for you.'

The boy stood up, looked steadily at him. 'Do you have kids, sir?'

'A boy and two girls. They don't own a mobile between them.'

Sam looked away; in profile Malone saw him bite his lip. Then he looked up the hill towards the school. 'There's my mother now. Do you want to meet her?'

Not really. 'I think I'd better. You and I are going to have to keep in touch, Sam.'

They began to walk up the hill. The boy suddenly said with tears in his eyes, 'Christ, I've been really stupid, haven't I?'

Malone nodded, but said nothing because they were now approaching the silver Jaguar that had just arrived. A woman got out of the car, smiling brightly at them as if the world was full of only good news. Malone recognized her now. Claire and Maureen each Sunday had what they called their 'Sunday game': counting the number of teeth on display in the inane smiles on the society pages. Mrs Hindle was a regular there. She was on every invitation list; the Freeloaders Forum, as Maureen called it. The gamut of her living ran from Double Bay hairdressers to society *paparazzi*. Tap the bowl of her life and there would be a hollow ring.

Her son introduced Malone; the smile faded, bad news on the doorstep.

'Sam's not in *police* trouble, is he?'

'No, Mrs Hindle, not with Homicide. He will be in trouble if the women he —' He couldn't say the word *bashed*; he was beginning to have some respect for Sam Hindle. 'The women he upset on Saturday night, if they lay charges. I believe they're going to.'

'You didn't tell me that,' said Sam.

His mother looked at him, her bright pretty face clouded now. 'Darling, you're really in the poo, aren't you? What are we going to do?'

Stop spoiling him, for a start.

'Let's wait till it happens, Mum.' The boy sounded as if he had decided to be fatalistic.

Mrs Hindle looked back at Malone. 'Have you caught the man who tried to kill my son?'

'He didn't try to kill *me*, Mum —'

'Shut up,' said his mother without taking her eyes off Malone; she had decided to be firm with her son, at long last. 'Well, Inspector?'

'No, we haven't, Mrs Hindle. But we're hoping —' Malone saw the slight smile on Sam's face, but it was not a sneer. *The kid's actually on my side..*

'That's not good enough. He's killed — how many? Three, four? Almost killed Clive Bristow. How much longer is it going to go on?'

'We don't know. Maybe as long as gangs of kids go around bashing up gays and lesbians. Sorry, Sam.'

'No, you're right,' said the boy. 'Lay off, Mum. The police will get him eventually.'

He had gone round to the far side of the Jaguar, opened the passenger's door. Mrs Hindle looked from Malone to her son, then back at Malone. Then she said, all aggression gone, 'You can't blame me, Inspector.'

For what? But he kept his tongue in check, said only, 'No, Mrs Hindle. Just take care of Sam. He's all right.' He nodded at the boy across the roof of the car; the sun, shining on the silver of it, made Sam squint as if in pain. 'I'll be in touch, Sam, when we catch the feller with the gun.'

'Good luck, sir. And thanks.'

Malone watched the Jaguar drive away, the sun glinting on the silver of it as it might have on a trophy. Behind him O'Malley, appearing out of nowhere, said, 'Cars are the Hindle fetish. The father drives a Ferrari. It's a losing battle preaching the sins of materialism at this school. Don't quote me.'

Malone smiled. 'Do you go through life not being quoted?'

'I have since I became headmaster here. What's it like being a cop?'

'Hell, most of the time,' said Malone. 'You can quote me.'

Chapter Six

1

There were three quiet days, no homicides in Sydney. It was the sort of lull that soldiers sometimes experience in battle; it was welcome, but there was always the knowledge that the guns would start up again anytime. Thursday the guns did start again: a hold-up murder in a southern suburb, two domestics involving guns, one in the inner city, one in the western suburbs. That night there was also another gay bashing and the serial killer was on the scene.

Garry Peeples rang Malone Friday morning. 'They're at it again, Scobie. The woman this time. Some Tongans bashed up a drag queen last night and the woman appeared, just popped up like all the other times, and put a bullet right through the eye of one of the Tongans. Except for the mis-hit on the kid last Saturday night, this lot seem pretty accurate with their shots. One bullet, that's all they seem to need.'

'You got any of the Tongans in custody?'

'Paddington picked up two of them – the rest of 'em seem to have flown. Back to Tonga, I hope.' No police officer liked a case in which colour or race might become an issue.

'Righto, I'll talk to the feller who was bashed. Or is he – she a transexual?'

'Don't ask me. I wasn't game to look.'

Malone grinned and hung up just as Greg Random, the chief superintendent in charge of Major Crime Squad, Southern Region, came in, unhurried as usual, and sat down opposite Malone. He was a lean, weatherbeaten man who had grown up on a wheat farm in western New South Wales, joined the police at nineteen and served his first five years on a country beat. There was still a bush air to him, but he was no redneck hick. He was a shrewd politician, was a ballet fan and had, once or twice, surprised Malone by quoting poetry that had nothing to do with bush verse.

'I come, as they say, bearing tidings from our little mate, the Premier.' He had a flat dry voice that mocked his phrasing. 'Or more directly, from our other little mate, Assistant Commissioner Zanuch.'

Malone made a face. 'Don't tell me. They want results?'

'Got it in one. The Dutchman would like all gay-bashings stopped, the gay killer in custody, all before he announces the date of the Bligh by-election. I've just had a torrid time on the blower with Zanuch.'

Zanuch, the Assistant Commissioner, Crime, was not the most popular man in the service, but the betting was that he would be the next Commissioner. He and Malone were far apart in temperament, but each had respect for the other's ability. The difference was that one had ambition and the other didn't and the one with ambition had an ear, an eye and a finger always cocked for the way the wind was blowing in higher echelons.

Random was another who sometimes raised a finger to the wind; but always satirically. He wet his finger now and held it up: 'Things are going to get rough, Scobie. As my old man used to say when he'd stand out in the middle of a wheat paddock, "Storm's a-coming".'

'I've never heard a wheat cocky talk like that in all my life.'

Random grinned, took his empty pipe out of his pocket; it was a prop that Malone had never seen him light. 'I've been re-reading Thomas Hardy.'

'Never read him, but I saw a TV series about one of his books. Did he ever write about serial killers? Were there any gays in – where was it?'

'Wessex. Probably, but they wouldn't have gone around holding hands in public. I just wish some of our gays wouldn't be so bloody obvious – they're inviting a bashing.' Malone said nothing, just looked at him; after a moment Random nodded: 'Okay, I'm wrong, that's bigotry. One on one, some of them could give the basher some of his own. But Christ, a drag queen – what does he expect when he's flouncing down the street alone at night? It was nearly midnight –'

'The point is, who was the killer following? The drag queen or the gang who bashed him – her? What if the killer – or killers, if there *is* more than one – what if he lets the gays, or this drag queen, what if he lets them be the bait, doesn't tell them?'

'If that's the case, then he's more cold-blooded than we've thought so far.'

'I dunno, maybe yes, maybe no. When the kid Hindle and one of his mates chased the killer on Saturday night, he turned around and pointed the gun at them. Sam Hindle says he was sure he was going to be shot. Then the killer said no, he couldn't do it in cold blood and just started running again. The kids were too scared to chase him any further.'

'If he is using the gays as bait, then how are the gays going to feel about him? From your summaries I gather the gay community is sympathetic towards him. How sympathetic will they feel if they know they're just being set up?'

'It's a ploy we could try, it might flush him out, trick him into giving himself away.'

Random stood up, put his pipe away in his pocket. 'Not yet, too risky. Wait till Tilly the Profiler arrives.'

'Who?'

'I'm slipping. I've still got Zanuch blowing down my earhole.' He screwed his little finger into his ear. 'That's really what I came down to tell you. We're bringing in a woman from Canberra, Tilly Orbost.'

'Tilly? As in Tilly Devine?' A legendary brothel madam and sly grog seller from the nineteen thirties; Sydney no longer made women criminals like it used to.

'I gather her first name is Matilda. They used to call her Waltzing Matilda, but that was probably the male chauvinists.' He grinned as if he were not one. 'She's on secondment from Queensland, she's a detective-inspector. Your equal, son.'

'So why's she coming from Canberra?'

'She's seconded to the Bureau of Criminal Intelligence – she's with the Violent Crime Analysis Centre. She has a degree in psychology and she's done the FBI criminal profile course in Washington. Zanuch decided you could do with a little help and it looks as if you're getting the best. She's all yours, she'll be here this afternoon.'

Malone could feel his defences going up around him already; no cop ever liked outsiders coming on to his turf. He had read enough to appreciate the value of criminal profiling; the Americans had developed it to a high degree. He just wished he had been taken into the discussion before the woman, this Tilly, had been invited. He was still carrying the can in this case.

'Are you coming down when she arrives?'

'Not unless you need me. Somehow I think that till the Bligh by-election is over, I'm going to have an awful lot of paperwork that's going to take up all my available time. I'm beginning to think retirement can't come soon enough.'

Malone shook his head. 'You can't retire now, not while the royal commission's going on.'

'Bloody dreadful, isn't it? I always suspected some of those bastards were bent, but I never dreamed there were so many of them. No, if I took my superannuation now, it'd look suspicious.'

'When you do retire, you'll be lost – nothing to do, no paperwork. How will you fill in your time?'

Random wet his finger again, held it up. 'Listening to the wind. And reading some poetry. There's a Welsh poet, W. H. Davies. He once wrote:

'What is this life, if, full of care,
We have no time to stand and stare.'

'If that's all the Welsh have been doing, it's no wonder their rugby teams can't win a match.'

'My mother would tear you apart if she heard you say that. She's half-Welsh. Enjoy Tilly.'

When Random had gone Malone sent for Gail Lee. She came into his office and, as he had before, he wondered how she had managed to get into the service. She was almost delicate in her slimness and she wore outfits that accentuated her slimness. He wondered how much help she would be to her partner, whoever he was, in subduing a suspect. But he wouldn't judge her till there was some complaint. He would not be surprised if she proved to be an unarmed combat expert, a relative of Bruce Lee.

'Gail, I want you to chase up the actors' bible – I think it's called *Showcase, Showcast,* something like that. Check those FACE images against all the male actors under, say, thirty-five. Ten years younger than me.' He smiled.

113

She didn't return the smile. 'Sir, we've just had a call from Rock-dale. They want us in on that domestic homicide – I was going out there with Phil Truach –'

Russ Clements had briefed him on the case: *blood everywhere, like an abattoir.* 'Let Phil get someone else. This serial killer gets the priority.'

'Sir –' She looked composed, not at all rebellious: 'Am I being sent on this shopping errand because I'm a woman?'

He was as surprised as much as he resented her attitude. 'No, you're not! What makes you ask?'

She was still unruffled. 'Since I came to Homicide I've done nothing but paperwork or sat at the computer. I expected to go out on one of the cases at the weekend, but Sergeant Clements told me they were too gory. When I was transferred, I expected to be more than just a paperweight. That's all I've been so far, holding down paper.'

He did not want this hassle, yet he had brought it on himself. Unwittingly he had been trying to protect her, as he was Kate Arletti; he would have to stop playing father to the women on his staff, would have to forget gender. 'Righto, go with Phil. Had Russ okayed it?'

'Yes, sir.' She stood up. She wore a cream shirt buttoned to the neck and a neat pencil-line navy blue skirt; out on a hanger in the main office he knew there would be a neat navy blue jacket. 'Actually, I've ordered the copy of *Showcase* – I suggested it to Sergeant Clements two days ago. I've been reading the synopses, where it was suggested the killer might be an actor.'

He looked for smugness in the bland attractive face, but there was none. 'Tell Kate it's coming, she can attend to it.'

'Yes, sir.'

He had been put down; maybe it was his own fault. He was saved by the ringing of his phone. He picked it up, watched Gail Lee go out of his office as composed as when she had come in; then he said, 'Inspector Malone.'

'Good morning, how are you?'

He switched on the tape. 'I'm okay. What do I call you?'

'What would you suggest?'

Not Cyril. 'I could think of a dozen, none of them complimentary.'

'You're far too antagonistic, Inspector.'

'What do you expect me to be?' The tape still rolling . . .

'I wish you could bring yourself to see that we are on the same side.'

'That's asking too much. You give up killing people –'

'We're not killing *people* – we're killing scum. Scumbags, as our ex-Prime Minister would say. Ask those who have been bashed what they think –'

'We have.'

'Ah no, I don't think so, Inspector. None of them has come out and condemned us for what we are doing. They recognize a public service –'

'That line is becoming a bit tired –'

There was the soft laugh. 'You're trying to aggravate me. It won't work. We have faith in our cause, Inspector . . .' There was a pause, then he said, 'When the bashings stop, so shall we. Until then . . .'

The phone went dead and Malone turned off the tape. The call had come from a public phone, as had all the others; there were always traffic background noises. Tracing the calls would have been a futile exercise. He signalled through the glass wall and Clements came in from his desk. The big man still looked extra cheerful as if fatherhood was some sort of sainthood. He sat down in his usual place on the couch, nodded at the tape as Malone held it up.

'Cyril again? What's he got to say this time?'

Malone told him. 'I think we've got a bit more out of him this time. I want you to take it up to Professor Hamence, run it by him.'

'Now? I'm busy, mate –'

'We all are – *mate.*' *Why am I sounding as if I have shit on the liver?* 'Or would you rather go up to St Sebastian's and talk to a drag queen who's just had her crown dented?'

'No contest.' Clements stood up, took the tape.

'Oh, another thing. We're going to have a visitor attached to us for a few days. A woman from the Violent Crime Analysis Centre down in Canberra. Inspector Tilly Orbost.'

'A profiler?' Clements wrinkled his nose. There was still enough of the old-time cop in him to suspect theory. 'We'll see how she goes.'

'We co-operate, okay?' He would have to see that he was not

protective of her. 'Any help that brings in this bastard is welcome. Greg Random has just been down to tell me we're going to be tossed into the political shit again. The Dutchman's going to have his own Mardi Gras. I'll see you at lunchtime.'

He phoned Constable Beane at Surry Hills. 'I'll pick you up in ten minutes, Darren. We're going up to see last night's bash victim.'

Beane was waiting for him outside Police Centre. As he came towards the car Malone studied him. There was no suggestion that he might be homosexual, no tilt of the head, no delicacy of gesture. *Christ Almighty, why am I thinking like this?*

'Do you know this feller Billie Cork?' he asked as Beane got into the car.

'Not personally, no, sir. I've seen him perform at the Albury.'

'Is he a transexual?'

'I don't think so. I've seen him out of drag, he ponces about a bit, but that's all.'

Ponces about a bit: were there degrees of prejudice amongst gays? But Malone didn't ask. 'Righto, let's assume he's the same gender as us.'

Beane smiled, but said nothing.

As soon as they walked into the four-bed ward Malone knew he was going to be uncomfortable. Three of the beds were occupied by elderly men who had the stunned look of patients who had woken up in the maternity ward. The fourth patient wore a turban of bandages with a flower bobbing in it, two thick gold bracelets and a pink bed jacket that would not have been out of place on anyone from the actual maternity ward.

'From Homicide?' Billie Cork could have been anywhere between thirty and fifty; his skin was as soft and unlined as a young woman's. He held out a hand on which long fingernails glowed like neon beetles. Malone took it, pressed its limpness and handed it back to its owner. 'How thrilling! Do sit down. Darren, isn't it? I've seen you around, darling.'

The old men, though their heads were resting on their pillows, were as alert as old crows. Malone sat down with his back to two of them, and did his best not to look at the man in the bed next to Cork. 'Are you allowed out of bed?'

'I'm afraid not, darling –'

'Do you mind not calling me darling?'

'Oh, I am sorry.' The beetles rested on the breast of the bed jacket. Cork pointed to the sheet-covered cage over his right leg. 'The black bastards broke my ankle. I've always loved coloured men, too. When a coloured boy makes eyes at me, I'm like a parking space in a movie – always available.'

It was a line he had obviously used before; his big brown eyes looked from one to the other, waiting for appreciation. All he got was a cackle from the old man in the next bed.

'What'd he say?' asked one of the other old men.

The first man repeated the line and there was a burst of cackling like a corroboree of cockatoos. They all nodded appreciatively at Cork, who gave a little bow of his head. 'They're a wonderful audience,' he told Malone and Beane in a whisper. 'Much better than some I've had.'

'Much better than you got last night,' said Malone, trapped by discomfort into being cruel. 'Were you looking to be picked up?'

The indignation, like everything else about him, was over the top. 'How can you think such a thing! Good Christ, I'd never pick up anyone in the street! Rough trade's not my line.' He simmered down. 'I'm not that cheap, Inspector.'

Malone stood up, pulled the curtain around the bed and nodded to Beane to do the same on his side. Then he sat down, lowered his voice: 'Let's cut out the bullshit, Mr Cork. Constable Beane and I are not a paying audience, nor are we here as freebies. We're on duty, trying to solve a murder. Now why were you walking down a side street on your own, in drag? I've only seen drag queens in movies, like *Priscilla* –'

'You didn't see *To Wong Foo*?'

'No. With all due respect, once was enough. From what I saw in *Priscilla*, you tend to mince along, inviting someone to take the mickey out of you or, at worst, attack you like this gang did last night.'

Cork said nothing, lay with his elegant hands wrapped together on his stomach. Then he reached up and took the flower from his turban of bandages. The fluting had gone from his voice when he said, 'Okay, I should've been more careful. Maybe they'd followed me down from the Albury, I don't know. But when I'm on my own,

117

Inspector, I don't *mince*. Sometimes I walk barefooted, bloody high heels can *kill* you ... No, I was not looking to be picked up. I'm getting close to being over the hill –' He looked at Beane. 'You've heard none of this, Darren, okay?'

'Not a word, Billie.'

'Sweet.' He reached out and patted Beane's arm. Then: 'You can carry on your act just so long. Some queens can go on forever – Danny La Rue must have played before Queen Victoria – but most of us –' He shrugged, pulled the pink bed jacket closer around him. 'We're like over-the-hill chorus girls. If your act isn't good enough, false tits and good legs just aren't enough.'

Malone was glad he had closed the curtains: this was a confessional. 'So you think they followed you down from the Albury? What about the killer? Did you see him?'

'Him? It was a woman.'

'We think it's a man – or men – posing as a woman.'

'A man in drag coming to the rescue of a drag queen? Nice.'

Malone grinned and nodded; Beane, too, smiled. The atmosphere was easier, Malone no longer felt uncomfortable. 'Did you see her?'

'I think she came across from the other side of the street – it's a narrow street. Maybe because she was a woman, the thugs took no notice of her – they were just intent on bashing me, grabbing my handbag.' He closed his eyes. There were bruises on his face, but most of the damage had been done to his head. For a moment Malone thought he was going to weep, but then he shook his head, opened his eyes and went on, 'You know what it's like, Darren.'

Malone looked at Beane in surprise. 'Have you been bashed?'

'Not bashed, no, sir. Four guys tried to have a go at me – they'd followed me from the Albury, too – but I was carrying a gun –'

'You were on duty, in uniform, and they had a go at you?'

It was a long moment before Beane answered; he, too, seemed to be glad they were in the makeshift confessional. 'No, sir. I was off-duty.'

'And you were carrying a gun? You were in a hotel, having a drink with your mates and you were carrying a gun?' Beane said nothing and after a pause Malone said, 'Righto, we'll forget you broke the rules. What did you do -- draw your gun on the bashers?'

'Yes, sir.'

'Did you arrest any of them?'

Again the hesitation: 'No, sir.'

'Why not?'

'Well . . . Well, actually they hadn't done anything. And – and I was frightened by how I felt –'

'Go on,' said Malone.

'I wanted to kill the bastards. I'd seen what they had done to one of my friends – maybe not the same gang, but they had the same idea of beating us up . . .'

Garry Peeples had said, *He's not the sort of guy who'd go around avenging gay-bashings.* 'All right, leave your gun at home in future when you go socializing –'

Billie Cork had remained silent during this exchange, his eyes flicking from one to the other. Malone was aware of his attention and he wondered if there was any hierarchy amongst gays, if there was any discipline other than the mockery of bondage. But he would never feel comfortable enough to ask the question.

'Mr Cork, you're sure no single person followed you from the Albury? Just the bashers?'

'They wouldn't have been in the pub – they'd have been too obvious –'

Because they were coloured or because they were homophobes? That was another question he did not feel comfortable enough to ask.

'No, no one came out of the pub after me. I'm sure of that because I looked around to see if someone might – well, you *know*. You always hope someone you've had your eye on . . .'

'Anyone in particular last night?'

'Oh surc, but it wasn't *him* who followed me. I told you, it was a woman.' Suddenly he smiled again, but it was a wry smile. 'We girls stick together, don't we?'

'If the killer wasn't following you, then he must have been following the gang, waiting for them to hit someone. What happened after he – she – shot the Tongan?'

Cork shook his head, then winced. 'Ooh, I shouldn't have done that . . . The woman, guy, whatever, backed off holding the gun like this –' He held both hands out in front of him. 'You know, like cops do. Or cops in movies.'

'That's the way we do it – it steadies the recoil. Unfortunately, even first-time shooters have learned that's the way to do it.'

'He held the gun on them while I got to my feet – *staggered* to my feet. He told me to go back up to the Albury – he said, Go back and find a friend, Billie –'

'He called you by name?'

'That doesn't mean a thing. Everybody knows me, darling – oops, sorry, Inspector . . . I hobbled up the street – I dunno how. I fell over, I think I screamed with the pain of it . . . Then three guys came down the street and saw me . . .'

'What about the killer? And the gang?'

'I'd passed out by then – I just don't know –'

Malone looked at Beane. 'What does the report say?'

'Two of the gang stayed with the guy who was shot. Someone called an ambulance and the police. When the Paddington paddy-wagon got there, they took the two Tongans into custody – they'd hung around because, evidently, their mate didn't die instantly. They couldn't produce bail, so they were held to appear at Downing Centre this morning. They're probably out now, running around loose again.'

'I have Kate Arletti and John Kagal down there. The Hindle kid is being charged – Kate and John are there to keep an eye out, just in case the killer turns up to mark the Hindle kid and the others down for future disposal.' He stood up, pulled back the curtains. The three old men, who had been dozing, were suddenly wide awake. 'Get well, Mr Cork. You'll be asked to come to court when the two arrested men are brought to trial.'

'How shall I come? In drag?'

Malone grinned. 'Better not, Billie. Some magistrates are more old-fashioned than we cops.'

2

Dr Rupert Hindle was as slender as his son, but where the boy was dark, he was blond with a blond moustache and an unreal tan. He was a grabber, an embracer; he would have hugged a parking meter if it had shown unexpired time. He grabbed Kagal's hand, put the other hand on the detective's elbow.

'Splendid! You're here to give evidence?'

'No, sir.' Kagal had introduced himself to the doctor, but had not mentioned they were from Homicide. 'We're just here to observe.'

'Observe?' The mahogany brow furrowed; Kagal's arm and elbow were let go. 'Observe what?'

Kate Arletti touched Kagal's arm. 'John, it's time to go into court.'

Kagal excused himself and followed Kate. 'You almost cocked that up, mate,' she said. 'Were you going to tell him why we're here? That the killer might turn up to have another look at Dr Hindle's son and the other kids?'

Kagal was massaging his elbow. 'He was squeezing blood out of me. I said the first thing that came into my mind. Jesus, what a grip! He must tear the heart out of his patients with his bare hands!'

'Then we'd better see we get to the killer before he does.'

The courtroom was part of the government complex of departments that now occupied what had once been a leading department store. The family that had owned the store back in the Twenties and Thirties had had a policy of giving preference to Catholics in its employment; it was claimed, by Protestants, that the less numerate of the employees added up bills by counting on their rosary beads. On one dreadful occasion it was discovered that a Mason had been on the staff for two years; he was summarily dismissed and an exorcist was brought in to cleanse the store. At the same time preference in the Public Service had been given to non-Catholics, though lapsed Catholics were tolerated so long as they showed no Popish tendencies. Now religion never raised its head in the big building, though oaths were uttered and now and again profanity prevailed.

The courtroom was not drab nor forbidding; it was almost brand-new. Pastel walls, light oak timbering, overhead lighting: Justice, it seemed to say, had nothing to hide. Kagal and Kate Arletti, having explained to the sheriff why they were at court, had been placed in a box to one side where they could observe the whole room. The chairs at the back of the court were all occupied: by police officers, traffic wardens, relatives and friends of the accused, a small group of students. And the regulars: those who came because it was free theatre, because it offered a glimpse of others who, maybe only for the moment, were worse off than themselves.

The first few cases were the dreary litany of traffic offences. Three out of four pleaded 'guilty with an explanation': the roads, it seemed, were alive with drivers who, themselves, were never at fault. Then the two Tongans who had bashed up the drag queen were brought before the magistrate.

They were young, huge and looked bewildered, as if it had never occurred to them that they might finish up here and, eventually, in gaol. They had legal aid and their lawyer, a young man who sounded as if he knew he had an indefensible case, pleaded guilty on his clients' behalf.

'Good thinking,' said the magistrate, an elderly bald-headed man who was sufficiently well-dressed to suggest he might have been a floor-walker in the old department store. He obviously had no time for bash artists: 'Have your clients, with their high IQ, got anything they'd like to add?'

The lawyer conferred with the two young men, who shook their heads. 'No, sir, they have nothing to add to their plea, except to say they are extremely sorry for what they did to the – er – victim.'

'Naturally.' The magistrate was on the verge of retirement, his superannuation safe; discretion no longer worried him. And wasn't the government boasting that it was going to get tougher on crime? 'The probability of a gaol sentence brings on remorse in most of us. Bail is set at five thousand dollars each.'

The two Tongans paled visibly, shook their heads as if they had been rained on by falling coconuts. 'Your worship,' began their lawyer, 'they have no hope of raising such a sum –'

'Exactly,' said the magistrate. 'Next.'

The Tongans were led away, still looking like lost giants, and Sam Hindle and four other boys were brought forward. Kate noted that none of them was dressed in the school uniform; they all wore their Sunday best with plain ties. Presbyterian Boys College had disowned them.

The magistrate looked them over with the basilisk eye of a choleric headmaster; he, too, had been to a private school. 'Who represents this wayward lot?'

Four well-dressed men, all of them looking as if legal aid, in their understanding of the term, meant fees that kept them in the style to which they had become accustomed, identified themselves. Sam Hindle and two other boys were represented by individual lawyers; the remaining two boys shared the one lawyer. They were all middleaged men, fathers who would have sons as old as the boys they were defending. Maybe even sons at the same school, thought Kagal.

There was some preliminary discussion between the lawyers and the police prosecutor, a tall, crane-like man in an ill-fitting suit who, at this table, looked like the poor country cousin. Kagal and Kate Arletti turned away to scan the spectators. Kate focussed on four women sitting side by side in the second row, all young, all intent in their stares at the five youths standing at the front of the court. They're a bit old for the kids, she thought. Then it struck her: they were friends of the lesbian couple who had been attacked. Her gaze passed on, dismissed the middleaged and elderly: none of them looked spry enough to have killed someone and then out-paced pursuers.

'The guy in the horn-rimmed glasses,' whispered Kagal.

He was seated in the very back row of the court, a slim dark-haired young man. As Kate looked at him he moved behind a young Tongan who had arrived late to see how his mates had fared. The Tongan stood up, well over six feet tall and wide enough to fill a doorway; the man in the horn-rims might just as well have closed a door on himself. Kate and Kagal slid out of the box, gave a hurried bow of respect towards the Bench, and went quickly out through the back of the court. But by the time they got round to the big waiting lobby there was no sign of the young man.

Kagal approached a court attendant. 'Did you see a young guy come out of court, guy with horn-rimmed glasses?'

'Mate, people are going and coming all the time —' He was grey-haired and unconcerned, worn careless by years on the job. He waved a hand around the big space; there must have been two hundred people there. 'If I took notice of everybody who goes in and outa the courts . . .'

The two detectives thanked him for his non-help, went looking for the young man, but he was nowhere to be seen. 'Did you get a good look at him?' Kate asked.

Kagal shook his head. 'Just as I caught sight of him, he looked across at me. I think he smiled — I'm not sure — then as I spoke to you, he was gone.'

'He certainly knows how to disappear,' said Kate. 'Well, do we go back inside?'

As they turned to do so, the Hindle family, Dr and Mrs Hindle and Sam, accompanied by their lawyer, came out of the court. Kate remarked that Sam and the lawyer looked the most composed; the mother and father looked on the verge of going berserk.

'Jesus Christ, did you hear that magistrate? What gives him the fucking right to make such comments?'

'Watch your language, darling,' said his wife, though she was equally distraught. 'Couldn't you have protested, Derek?'

'Me?' The lawyer, a portly middleaged man, laid a spread hand on his stomach. 'Marcia, face the facts. What old Buggerlugs had to say couldn't be denied. Sam here is, if you'll forgive the language, in the shit.'

'Mum – Dad –' said Sam. 'Forget it.'

'Shut up,' said Mum and Dad.

Then behind Kate Arletti's shoulder a camera flash went off. Cameras were not allowed in the court's lobbies, but someone must have somehow sneaked one in past the security check. Dr Hindle blinked, got his vision back, saw Kagal and Kate and shouted, 'Get that bastard!'

The two detectives didn't move. 'It's a free country, Doctor,' said Kagal. 'You're free to chase him, if you like.'

But the culprit, whoever he was, had eluded the court attendant who had chased him, and disappeared behind the closing doors of a lift.

'Jesus Christ,' said Dr Hindle and looked at his wife. 'What's the fucking country coming to?'

'Watch your language,' said his wife automatically, as if it was a record she played over and over. 'God, it'll be in all the papers!'

'Consider ourselves lucky we won't be on TV,' said her son.

'How'd you get on, Sam?' asked Kate.

'Same bail as the black guys got. I was lucky – Dad could afford to pay.'

'Pretty stiff, I thought,' said his father. 'Five thousand!'

'The beak had to give you the same as he'd given the Tongans,' said the lawyer. 'He wanted to keep them in custody, they'd have skipped if he hadn't. The only way to do it was to slap them with bail they could never raise. So Sam and his mates had to cop the same. It's called equality of justice, I think.' He smiled at the two detectives as if he were in conspiracy with them. 'Sam and his friends are lucky that they, too, aren't going into detention somewhere, don't you think?'

'Yes,' said Kate and Kagal together.

On that they left the Hindles and went across to the lifts. Neither of them made any comment as they went down, but it was written on their faces: they had no time for the Hindle parents. They crossed the big ground-floor lobby and went out into the street. They stood on the sweep of steps that led down into Liverpool Street and looked at each other.

'Why should we bother?' said Kagal and Kate nodded.

Then Dr Hindle caught up with them. A photographer materialized like a one-eyed genie, flashed the magic eye and was gone.

'Bloody media!' said the doctor, as if he had spent his life dodging publicity. He put his hand on Kagal's arm, though his grip this time was tentative. 'You weren't here this morning to concern yourselves with my son's case, were you? Derek Armor – the lawyer – he told me you're from Homicide. So why were you here? The woman Sam and the others –' Uncharacteristically he was lost for a word.

'Bashed?' said Kate helpfully.

Hindle nodded, but still couldn't say the word. 'Has she – has she died?'

'No,' said Kagal. 'She's alive – she and her friend were the ones who asked us to lay charges against your son and his mates. They will appear when Sam goes to trial.'

Hindle winced, as if stitches had been removed from somewhere on his body. Kagal, who always dressed well, remarked how expensively the doctor was clad: the silk shirt, the Hermés tie, the dark blue suit that must have cost all of a by-pass fee. The mahogany tan seemed paler out here in the sunlight.

'So why were you here?'

'Our job is to find the killer who shot young Clive Bristow, the Tongan and three other bashers. We thought he might be here this morning looking over more targets.'

Hindle was acute: 'Meaning Sam and his friends?'

'And the Tongans,' said Kagal, easing the knife but not too much.

Detective Inspector Matilda Orbost was tall, six feet, and slim; she moved almost with a model's grace. She had curly black hair, cut short, regular features and big eyes that were almost black. She was dressed in a conservatively cut black slack suit and had an air of confidence that stopped just short of arrogance.

'Are we to be formal or do we start off on first name terms? I'm called Tilly.'

'Scobie. You're welcome here,' he lied. 'Experts always are.'

'So long as they don't show up the locals.' She had an attractive smile. 'I know how it is, Scobie, I've been twenty years a cop.'

'You don't look it.'

'I hope that's not idle flattery.'

'It isn't.'

'The scars are hidden,' she said. 'I had two strikes against me when I joined the force. A, I was a university graduate, B, I was a woman. When I was sent to Washington last year for the FBI course, there was still resentment. But you get used to it.'

'Not really.' He was beginning to like her.

'No, not really . . . I wish I'd been called in earlier to help you. In profiling we like to look at the crime scene, that's where we start.'

'The crime scene in every one of these cases has been the streets. He – or she –' He explained that sometimes the killer was a woman, but that they suspected there was actually only one person, a male, involved. 'He doesn't entice the victims into any secluded spot or break into their homes or cars – he just shoots them down in the streets as they attack the gays.'

'Any untoward violence?'

'No, that comes from the bashers. He just lets off one shot, usually at the head of the victim. He phones me –'

She leaned forward; he caught a whiff of perfume, something he never allowed Kate Arletti or Gail Lee to wear. Women detectives were not meant to use seductive aids. 'Phones you? You have tapes?'

Clements, as he so often did, made his entrance on cue. He stood in the doorway with the tape in his hand. 'Right here. I've just been to see our voice expert.'

Malone introduced him and the big man dropped into his usual place on the couch. 'Professor Hamence thinks this latest tape only confirms what he said before – the guy has a *trained* voice. He thinks he is either an actor or a singer.'

'What else has he read into the voice?' asked Tilly Orbost. 'Paranoia?'

Clements looked at Malone, who shook his head and said, 'We don't think so. Not in terms of being psycho.'

'They don't have to be psychotic to be paranoid. If they were, our parliaments would be full of madmen.'

The horrible prospect hung in the air for a moment; then Malone said, 'You can listen to the tapes, then go through the running sheets. I'm afraid the trail is going to be a bit cold and skimpy. Except –' He looked at both of them. 'Except he seems to be getting more daring. John and Kate –' He told Orbost who they were. 'They think he was at the magistrate's court this morning.'

'And they didn't get near him?' Clement's tone had the sound of an old hand's criticism.

'He was gone by the time they got out of the court.' He repeated the description Kagal and Kate had given him of the suspect. 'He could be a million men, except for the horn-rims. They could be his giveaway eventually.'

'If he's an actor, maybe he thinks he's Clark Kent,' said Clements.

'Or his daring could give him away,' said Tilly Orbost. 'Serial killing has a lot of causes, reasons. Revenge, a sense of persecution, of inadequacy, even ego. Perhaps this chap suffers from any one of those or all of them. In the end we find that in most cases it's ego, or carelessness born out of ego, that brings them in.'

'If he's an actor, that's on the cards,' said Clements. 'I've been on to the Actors Equity. There are thirty thousand actors on their books –'

'You're kidding,' said the other two.

'That's what they claim. Twice as many actors as there are cops in New South Wales. So where do we start looking?'

'You start looking here in Sydney,' said Tilly Orbost, then apologized: 'Sorry, that's stating the obvious. What I mean is, he's either out of work, which most of them are, or he's working in something here in Sydney.'

'I've sent for *Showcase*,' said Malone. 'The actors' meat market.'

'Good,' said Clements. 'There won't be thirty thousand photos in the book – Christ, I hope not! – but we'll narrow it down to guys who fit the description. Slim, dark – maybe –' He looked at Malone. 'He could be wearing a wig. Five-ten, say a hundred and seventy-five centimetres. Left-handed –'

'From what you said,' said Tilly Orbost, 'he's a pretty good shot.'

'Has only missed once, with the Bristow kid,' said Malone. 'Even that was close enough.'

She stood up, held out her hand for the tape. 'I'll listen to this and the other one, read through the running sheets. I'll check with you tomorrow, okay?'

He stood up, shook hands with her. 'Glad to have you, Tilly.'

When she had gone Clements said, 'Is she gunna fit in?'

Malone took his time, sizing up his partner. There was a certain honesty about Clements: he never attempted to hide his prejudices. 'Yes, I think she will, given a fair go. She may not come up with more than we've discovered ourselves, but the thing is – we have to *look* as if we're exploring every avenue. The Dutchman is stirring the possum again.'

'Who does he want us to nab? The killer or the bashers?'

4

'How did you go in History today?' asked Malone.

'Tough,' said Maureen, chewing on her steak as if today's exam papers had made her ravenous.

'History itself has always been tough. Not just the study of it.'

'The oracle has spoken,' said Claire and raised her glass of shiraz. 'They're a mine of information, cops.'

'I was reading today's report on the royal commission into cops –' Tom began.

'Don't,' said Lisa. 'You'll spoil his dinner.'

'I love youse all,' said Malone in his imitation of a well-known boxer. 'So how many more papers have you?'

'Just the one,' said Maureen, clearing her mouth of steak and taking a sip of wine. The girls were allowed a glass of wine with dinner, but Tom was still restricted to soft drink, a restriction that caused him no concern. He was already showing signs of being ultra-conservative in his habits, an attitude that caused no concern for his parents. His grandfather, the old socialist, on the contrary *was* worried: the boy might grow up to *vote* conservative. 'Geography. I'm good at that.'

'But she gets a D in modesty,' said Tom.

None of it was brilliant dinner-table chat, the sort Lisa kept reading about in the social pages but which she rarely, if ever, heard. She had heard it at dinner-tables in London, but that was long ago and she sometimes wondered if memory had given a gloss to the wit and wisdom of the time. But the chat round this table was part of the rope that, though it ravelled at times, kept them together. She always did her best to see that at least three or four times a week, unless Scobie was away on a case, they all sat down to dinner together. She did not lecture Tom and the two girls on the matter; she did not need to. She had come to realize that the family meant as much to the children as it did to her and Scobie. She knew good fortune, in these times, when it sat round the table with her. They were not the Brady Bunch nor Roseanne's family. They were somewhere in-between: average, she hoped, though she knew that might be delusion. Living with a cop, even one who did his best to leave his work at the office, did nothing to burnish one's illusions.

'Have you heard from that guy again, Dad?' said Tom. 'The gay killer.'

Then the phone rang. There were two phones in the house, one on Malone's side of the bed in the main bedroom, the other in the hallway just outside the kitchen door. Before Malone could stop him Tom, with a grin, was out of his chair. 'There he is now! I'll get it.'

Malone looked along the table at Lisa, who said, 'Has he called here? You didn't tell us.'

Then Tom came back to the table. 'It's not him. It's a Sergeant Peeples from Surry Hills.'

Malone got up and went out into the hallway; he knew it was bad news before he picked up the phone. 'Yes, Garry?'

'Sorry to disturb you, Scobie, but I thought you'd like to know. We got him, the gay killer. Picked him up twenty minutes ago.'

Chapter Seven

1

'Almost broad bloody daylight,' said Peeples. 'These four kids were walking down a back lane and he just steps out in front of them and plugs one of them. Right through the heart.'

Malone, selfishly, felt some disappointment; he would have liked to have been on hand during the arrest. He had come to look on The Voice as *his* pigeon. 'The kids weren't bashing anyone, rolling anyone?'

'As far as we know, no.' Peeples was doing his best to sound relaxed, but one could sense the excitement and satisfaction in him. 'Maybe he thought they were gunna do him, I dunno. He may have just got in early.'

'Who caught him?' He'd have been pleased if it had been one of his own detectives.

'He turned and ran straight into two of our guys on the beat – they were just crossing the end of the lane.'

'Did he try to shoot them?'

'No, he pulled up soon's he saw them, just stood there, then dropped the gun when they yelled at him to let it go.'

'Is he our bloke?'

'He says he is.'

'*Says* he is?'

'According to our guys' report, when they were bringing him in he said he wasn't sorry it was all over. Said he'd done enough.'

'Righto, I'll be in. Hold off questioning him till I get there, okay?'

He hung up, went back into the dining room. 'I have to go out. They've caught the serial killer.'

Tom jabbed a fist in the air, grunted *Yeah!* and the girls smiled.

Only Lisa remained unmoved; or seemingly so. 'Finish your steak.'

He went round the table, kissed the top of her head. 'Do you think I'd be able to taste it? What's for dessert?'

'Mango. The first of the season.'

His favourite fruit. 'Save me a double helping.'

He drove into Surry Hills through a beautiful evening. As he parked the car outside Police Centre he stopped for a moment, savouring the freshness of the air. Sometimes, for odd moments, a city can escape its pollution: a wind springs up, rain comes, the air is cleansed. It is not the freshness of bush air nor has it the sharpness of mountain air: it is itself, city atmosphere, tinged with stone and cement and asphalt. Perhaps not everyone smelled the difference, but Malone always did. Then an old bomb went past, trailing smoke from its exhaust, and he grinned and went into the Centre.

He found Garry Peeples with Neil Kovax, who also had left his dinner to come to the station. On the way over Malone had tried to sort out his reaction to the news. He was not unaccustomed to anti-climax; you expected that in police work, at least after the first year's experience. But somehow he felt let down that this case had ended the way it had. What had he been expecting? Another phone call – 'Meet me at Taylor Square, Inspector, and I'll surrender'? He and the killer had become the two main characters in the drama and the killer had let him down by surrendering to two cops on the beat. He felt a certain regret; no, irritation, almost anger. The bastard had no right to exit like this.

'I've had a look at him.' Kovax was in an electric-blue track suit and trainers. Out from behind his desk, out of uniform, he looked the most unathletic of men. He saw Malone looking at him and he grinned. 'I do bugger-all in this. I just wear it because it relaxes me. I sit in a chair and think about all the energy and sweat I'm saving by not doing anything. Do you want me to hang around while you question this bloke? No? Okay, put something on my desk, Garry, I'll look at it in the morning.'

He left and Garry Peeples said, 'He's taking his retirement, did he tell you?'

Malone's surprise showed. 'He's not had the finger pointed at him, has he? I'd never believe it –'

'Neil? Bent? Christ, no! The timing's unfortunate ... The poor

131

bugger has a bad aneurysm, they found out about it only yesterday. They're gunna operate soon's they can.'

Malone nodded sympathetically. 'It's a pity he's going to miss out on you nailing this killer. Most of it's happened on his turf.' Abruptly his own disappointment at not nailing the killer began to dissipate. Neil Kovax had borne the brunt of the frustration and criticism of the past six or seven months. 'Righto, let's have a look at this feller.'

As he followed Peeples down to the interrogation room he felt depressed. He had never been a friend of Kovax, just an acquaintance; their paths had criss-crossed over the years, that was often the pattern in the Service. Yet there was a sense of loss. Kovax had been a good cop, there had never been a hint that he had ever been bent, not even in his days in the Vice Squad. Now he was going, probably ten years before the proper time for retirement, and the Service, particularly at this time, could ill-afford to lose him.

'Poor bugger,' said Peeples as he opened the door to the interrogation room and Malone was not sure whether he was referring to Kovax or the young man sitting at the table in the middle of the room with his head in his hands.

'Okay, Terry, we'll take it from here,' said Peeples and the young uniformed officer who had been guarding the prisoner left the room, closing the door behind him.

Peeples and Malone sat down opposite the young man. 'We're gunna record this interview, Mr Conrad. Time is eight-forty. Detective-Inspector Malone and Senior-Sergeant Peeples present.' He set the video going. 'Okay, Mr Conrad, let's start. Your name is Travis Conrad and you live at –' He read an address from the notes he had brought in with him.

The young man was of medium height, slim: just as the witnesses had described him. He had dark hair, cut very short, and he wore a pearl earring, which none of the witnesses had mentioned. He had a thin, pinched face, large blue eyes that were heavily lashed and a girl's mouth. He was also very uncertain, despite the bravado attempt to appear laid-back.

'What's there to say? Your men caught me – I have to say they treated me okay. No rough stuff. Except –' He held out his thin wrists with a red mark on them. 'They did hurt me putting on the cuffs. But I suppose that always happens, right?'

'What's your occupation, Mr Conrad?' said Malone.

'Right now, I'm a waiter. But I act, too. Not much, but how many of us do?' The smile was an actor's, but not a good actor.

'Why did you shoot the boy? Were he and his mates attacking you?'

'They were going to, weren't they? It was obvious. They deserved what they got. You should be giving me a medal.'

'As we should for all the others you've shot?'

'Yes.'

'You were doing a public service?'

Conrad shrugged. 'If you like.'

'What are you – right-handed or left-handed?'

'Left.' He held out his hand, thin-fingered and bony, a large signet ring on the engagement finger.

'Which one of the consortium are you?'

For a moment he looked puzzled; then suddenly he was rat-cunning. 'I'm all of them.'

'What sort of gun were you carrying?'

'A Colt Forty-five.' He had a soft pleasant voice; but it was not The Voice.

'No silencer this time?'

'No.'

'So why did you swap guns?'

Conrad looked down at the table as he drew a circle with his forefinger. 'I thought you might trace me if I kept using the same gun.'

'We'd have done that – eventually,' said Malone. 'But you took a bigger risk changing to a gun with no silencer. Colts make a big bang.'

'I know that now.' With a rueful smile: he had slightly pointy teeth.

'So you are admitting to killing not only this boy – what's his name?'

'Kenneth Brodine.' Peeples had remained silent during the interrogation, watching Malone as much as he did Conrad.

'Him and Justin Langtry and –' Malone looked at his notebook, reeled off the other names. 'You admit to killing them?'

'Yes,' said Conrad, sitting up straight now, fitting the role of a

133

serial killer; there was almost a child-like innocence to him, someone striving to be bigger than he actually was. Malone wanted to laugh at him, but couldn't. In an odd way he felt sorry for the poor bugger. 'Like you said, it's been a public service. You p'lice should be thanking me.'

Malone nodded at the video and Peeples switched it off. Then Malone said, 'I think you're bullshitting us, Mr Conrad.' He glanced at the charge-sheet in front of Peeples. 'Travis. You killed this kid tonight, but you were nowhere near the other homicides.'

Beside him he was aware of Peeples suddenly still, but the big man said nothing. Travis Conrad just stared at Malone, then he said very slowly, as if weighing his words, 'I killed them all. I can give you time and place for every one.'

'The times and places are public record, Travis. They were in the newspapers and on TV.'

'I know all the kids I shot.'

'So do we, Travis. But we didn't shoot them.'

He stood up abruptly and went out of the room, Peeples following him. The young constable went in again to watch the prisoner. Malone leaned against the wall. 'He's not our man, Garry.'

'He could be one of the consortium, like they claim.' But Peeples didn't sound convinced.

'Which one?'

'The woman. He's slight enough.'

Malone could feel his own stubbornness in clinging to what he had believed all along. 'Garry, I've *listened* to this other bloke – you've heard the tapes. There isn't any consortium.'

Peeples shook his head doubtfully; the parcel had been all wrapped up an hour ago and now it was coming apart. 'I dunno. You may be right, but . . . If this is the only hit he's made, why's he claiming the others? Ego?'

'Could be. If he's going down for one, why not go down for the lot? Has he got a record?'

'Once, for prostitution. Darren Beane recognized him when he was brought in, said he'd seen him working The Wall occasionally. He's not a regular up there, does it, I guess, when he runs short of cash. Who'd be an actor?'

'Not all actors are poofs.' Now he was defending actors, which

134

was as bad as defending lawyers. 'You're holding him?'

'They'll keep him down in the charge cells next door.' Police Centre. 'He'll go before the magistrate tomorrow morning, probably down at Liverpool Street.'

There was a commotion at the front of the station. A drunken couple had been brought in, the woman swearing at the man, at the police, at men in general, in a high-pitched voice that sounded like the screech of a parrot. The man looked along the short corridor at Malone and Peeples, grinned drunkenly at them and waved a hand at the woman, implying she didn't belong to him and they could have her if they wanted her. Both officers shook their heads at the offer. The woman looked along the corridor and included them in her opinion of the male world. Then she and the man were led away, her screeching suddenly cut off, as if the man, or one of the officers, had suddenly decided to choke her.

'Aren't you glad you're not on patrol?' said Peeples. 'We get something like that practically every second night. Domestics are a cop's nightmare.'

'Back to Conrad – try and get him last on the list. I want a line-up. Get one of the witnesses from each of the murders and have them here tomorrow morning at nine o'clock – we'll run him by them. Bring in a couple of the bash victims if you can. Bob Anders is out of hospital, the feller who was done over two weeks ago – ask him to come in. Get Conrad a woman's wig, a dark one – we'll try him in a line-up of women. And a pair of horn-rimmed glasses.'

'What if someone fingers him? Or two or three?'

'I'm betting they won't.'

'Okay, you're the boss. But how'm I gunna get 'em all here tomorrow morning? Saturday?'

'Force and persuasion, Garry.' He grinned, though he had no amusement in him. 'I'll be next door tomorrow morning at nine for the line-up.'

He went home, disappointment riding with him like an unwelcome passenger. Yet there was also a certain relief: the real killer was still *his*. It was un-professional of him to think so, but it was a fact.

The night had suddenly changed in the past hour; this was a perverse summer. Last week's aluminium moon had turned to steel; an almost wintry wind came up out of the south in short, swift ambushes.

135

It was a night for dark moods and he arrived home in one.

'The mango is sour.'

'So are you,' said Lisa, sitting opposite him at the kitchen table. 'Why didn't you tell me that man had phoned here?'

'Who told you?'

'I got it out of Tom. How did he get our number?'

'I don't know.' He sprinkled sugar on the mango. 'If he calls again and you answer, hang up on him.'

'How will I know it's he? Does he announce he's the killer? I want our number changed.'

When she was adamant there was no point in arguing with her. It would mean notifying everyone at Homicide and half the senior officers at Headquarters, not to mention friends and in-laws. Some day she was going to ask for the Federal Constitution to be changed . . . 'Righto, I'll see it's done tomorrow, first thing.'

'Do that. First thing.'

He pushed the mango away from him; his appetite had gone. 'Darl, I'm sorry about this. He's a smart-arse, but we'll get him eventually.'

'I thought you'd got him? Tonight?'

He shook his head. 'No, he's what they call a copy-cat killer.'

She stood up, took the plate away from him, spread a sheet of Glad-Wrap over the plate of unfinished mango. Her Dutch thrift wouldn't allow her to throw out fruit at three dollars each. 'If there's a copy-cat, how will the original killer feel?'

'I haven't a clue.' He sipped the tea she had made for him. 'I'll have to ask Tilly Orbost about that one.'

'What's she like?' She was always interested in the women he worked with, though never in a jealous way.

'I still have to find that out. But she must be good – they wouldn't have sent her to Washington if she wasn't.'

'I didn't mean that,' she said, being wifely.

He grinned, put his arms round her hips as she came close to him, squeezed her buttocks. 'She's tall and dark and handsome.'

Then Maureen came into the kitchen, all lithe bustle; she never took her time going anywhere, as her mother and sister did. She wrenched open the refrigerator door as if only it lay between her and starvation.

'Okay, break it up. The kid's in the same room with you now.'

She grinned at them both, took some orange juice from the fridge and drank from the bottle. Then, wiping her mouth, she said, 'Monday's my last exam paper. I'd like to celebrate Monday night. There's a group of us going to a rave-in at a warehouse in Waterloo. Okay if I go?'

Malone looked at Lisa. 'It's up to you. The word from the Drug Squad is that at these rave parties you can buy anything you want.'

'Dad, you know I'll never touch drugs!' She obviously hadn't expected this reaction from him. 'God, give me credit for some intelligence! You can get drugs anywhere these days, if you want them, not just at rave parties. All the other girls and I want to do is let loose – we've spent a whole year studying – it's all over, we just want to celebrate –'

'It's up to you,' Malone said to Lisa.

'Will it worry you if she goes?'

It was not easy to say: 'Yes.'

Lisa looked at Maureen, but said nothing. She stared at her parents, her face a mix of emotion: of defiance, disappointment, incomprehension. Then she thrust the bottle of orange juice back into the fridge, slammed the door and went out of the kitchen, *Jesus!* floating behind her like the echo of a whiplash.

'You'd better iron it out with her,' said Malone.

Lisa, still gazing at the empty doorway, took his hand. 'Leave it to me.'

He lifted her hand, pressed it against his cheek. He felt he had betrayed her. He was the magnet who had brought the serial killer to the house, if only by phone: that had been bad enough. Now he was dodging the responsibility of trying to advise his daughter. He was losing the sense of certainty that had sustained him for so long.

2

'He's a copy-cat killer,' said Tilly Orbost Saturday morning.

She had come over with Malone from Strawberry Hills to Police Centre. Downstairs the holding cells were almost full, with Friday night's drunks and rowdies. She had been introduced to Garry Peeples, who looked at her approvingly.

'It happens,' said Malone. 'Not often, but occasionally. It seems to be more an American thing.'

'Is it ego with them?' The bruise on Peeples' cheek had begun to fade under ice-pack treatment.

'Sometimes,' said Tilly Orbost. 'Just as often it's a need to be noticed. Not out of ego, but as a resentment at being ignored.'

Peeples was obviously impressed by her both as a woman and a police officer. He even took her elbow as they went downstairs to the cells; when Peeples' attention was distracted by a junior officer, she looked back over her shoulder and winked at Malone. He grinned and winked back at her, but his mood was no better than it had been last night. Travis Conrad had thrown a spanner, or rather a gun, into a case where Malone thought he had worked out the parameters.

For all last night's reluctance and lack of time, Peeples had managed some recruits for the line-up. There were four men and three women, all slim, all medium height, all dark-haired. Malone recognized a policeman and two policewomen amongst them, but he had no idea, nor did he intend to ask, where Peeples had recruited the others. None of them looked like the usual mix in a line-up.

There were five witnesses: Bob Anders, Walter Needle, Les Coulson, Sam Hindle and Greta Bromley, all of them waiting out in the main charge-room. There were shouts and other noise from the cells, which were out of sight, but the witnesses seemed undisturbed by it. They did, however, look – well, *toey*, Malone thought: like runners who had at long last arrived at the starting line.

He addressed them: 'You will go into that room across the hall individually and just walk slowly by those in the line-up – each of them will be holding a number. Don't identify anyone out there, point your finger or anything – come back here, write the number of the person you suspect on the slip of paper and give it to Sergeant Peeples. Remember, take your time. And don't be afraid. This is important to us.'

'What if the killer's in there and he goes crazy?' said Les Coulson. 'If he recognizes one of us?'

He won't: he just stopped himself in time. 'You'll be perfectly safe.'

Walter Needle was the first to go into the room, followed by Malone, Peeples and a young constable. It was a windowless room, longer than it was wide: filing shelves against one wall, a table and chair, a raised platform along a wall, small numbered squares in front of the seven people in the line-up. Needle walked slowly up and down, ignoring the three women but studying the four men, all of whom wore horn-rimmed glasses.

'The women shouldn't be in this,' Malone whispered to Peeples.

'They've balled it up.' Peeples didn't say who *they* were. 'The witness Anders was supposed to come in first.'

Christ Almighty, what else can go wrong? In his ear, like a phantom phone call, he could hear The Voice laughing softly.

Walter Needle finished his inspection, going back down the line, then he walked straight out of the room without a glance at the police officers. Malone and Peeples followed him. He handed the sergeant the blank slip of paper.

'I thought Number Four at first, but no. No, none of them is the man who attacked us.'

Peeples grinned at Malone: Number Four was the police officer. 'Okay, thanks, Mr Needle. You may go, if you wish.'

'No, I'll wait. Just in case . . .'

Malone took Peeples aside. 'Get the women out of there, find another couple of men.'

'Where, for Crissakes?'

'I dunno. Shove a coupla more of your own men in there. Grab a couple from the cells. And you'll need at least two more women.' He could feel his temper fraying. 'Jesus, Garry, you're really making this a cock-up!'

'Hold on, Scobie.' They were talking in hoarse whispers. 'If you'd given me till midday today, I'd have got you a proper line-up. But you wanted it at fucking nine o'clock. What was I gunna do, go out and fucking shanghai people in here? It doesn't work like that, Scobie.'

Malone did his best to cool down; somewhere The Voice was still laughing softly. 'Righto, Garry, it's your show. Try and rustle up some other stand-ins. Give the witnesses a break, give 'em coffee. Sorry I got hot under the collar. You playing cricket this afternoon? You should be all fired up to bump a few at the batsmen.'

Peeples grinned. 'You should take up coaching.'

During the break Malone walked through into the cell area with

Tilly to get away from the witnesses. There were a few whistles from those behind the bars, but the two detectives ignored them.

'I had a peep into the line-up room,' said Tilly. 'Which one was Conrad?'

'Number Five.'

'He looked to me like he wanted to be identified.'

'That's what I'm afraid of.'

The whistling had increased and a grizzled sergeant came along the corridor to Malone and Tilly. 'If you wouldn't mind, sir, I think you're disturbing the animals.'

'Sure,' said Malone, then looked beyond the officer. 'Have you got cells boarded up down there?'

The sergeant nodded.'It's dynamite.'

'Dynamite? We're storing explosives down here?'

He gave a gap-toothed smile. 'It's all the evidence for the royal commission. We've got a twenty-four-hour guard on it. There's the death-knell for a lot of bent coppers down there.'

Malone looked at Tilly and she at him. 'There's a certain pleasure in being straight,' she said, 'that only straight cops know. I'm para-phrasing a poet named Dryden.'

'Know him well,' said Malone. 'Thanks, Sarge. We'll get out of here before the animals start tearing down the bars.'

They went back to the charge room where Peeples, miraculously, had rounded up some extras for the line-up. The examination started up again; Bob Anders and Sam Hindle went in individually, came out shaking their heads and with their slips of paper blank.

Then it was Greta Bromley's turn. She appeared composed, but underneath she felt fragile; the night of the bashing had suddenly come back like a nightmare. She walked slowly up and down the line-up of men; she paused twice, but only for a moment, then walked on. Malone, watching her closely, saw her hand opening and closing, as if she were trying to get a grip on something.

She walked out of the room, her slip of paper blank, and Malone and Peeples followed her. 'I'm not sure. It could be Number Five.'

Peeples looked at Malone and Tilly Orbost. 'Conrad.'

'He's practically pleading to be identified,' said Tilly, who had stood in the doorway again. 'What makes you think it's him, Miz Bromley?'

'I got the feeling he was trying to avoid looking at me.'

'He's play-acting,' said Malone. 'Righto, Garry, get the women's line-up ready. Do you want to stay, Miss Bromley?'

'I think so. This might be the end of it all, mightn't it? I mean if he's properly identified?'

'No, it'll just be the beginning. He'll still have to go to trial.'

She nodded. 'I suppose so. But you're wrong about the beginning. That was when those bastards bashed me.' She had her own starting-point.

The men in the line-up were replaced by women. Conrad came back in, wearing a dark wig and a black slack suit identical to those worn by the women.

'Where did you get all the gear?' Malone whispered to Peeples.

'I hired it from a dyke shop up in Oxford Street. I took their entire stock of Size Fourteens. Two of the women in the line-up are dykes from the shop.'

Malone could remember police line-ups from the old days: my, how the spectrum had widened. 'Righto, bring in the Coulson kid.'

Les Coulson had dressed for the occasion. Or at least he had changed out of the knee-length Keppers into jeans, wore a long-sleeved, dark blue shirt with no insignia, and no cap; he had, however, not forsaken his black Air-Max shoes. He was clean-shaven and his hair was brushed neatly back from his forehead. He had left his sneer at home and he looked almost handsome and certainly agreeable. He was here to help any way he could.

He walked up and down the line-up with slow, almost haughty deliberation, as if he were imitating a visiting dignitary inspecting a guard of honour. Malone grinned. 'Another play-actor.'

Coulson gave each of the women in the line-up a measured look; it struck Malone that Travis Conrad made such a convincing female that he did not stand out from the women. This time he made no attempt to look suspicious, just stared straight ahead. Malone wondered if he was suddenly afraid, if in Coulson he had recognized a vicious enemy of gays.

Coulson finished his inspection, went back out into the main room where he handed Peeples the slip of paper on which he had scrawled a number. 'It's Number Three.'

'You're absolutely certain?' said Peeples.

'Yeah. That's a guy, all the others are women. It's him, all right, the one who did Justin Langtry. The shit,' he said and the sneer was suddenly back in place.

Malone said nothing, let Peeples handle it. The sergeant took Coulson back into the line-up room and Malone and Tilly Orbost were left alone, apart from the witnesses.

'You don't believe him, do you?' Tilly said.

'No, I don't. He's recognized a gay and he doesn't care how he gets rid of him, whether by bashing or sending him to gaol.'

She was half-sitting on the edge of a desk, not awkwardly but with some grace. This morning she was wearing a beige suit and cream shirt and he could smell the perfume she had been wearing yesterday. He wondered how the men in the Queensland service, a once notoriously chauvinistic lot, responded to her. Whichever way they did, he was sure she could handle them. She would not mince words, even though most women liked to mince them, thereby making them harder to understand. The women, not the words.

'Homophobia is a real disease, I think we've been a bit slow to recognize it. All straight men suffer from it, to a greater or lesser degree. That boy Coulson is a chronic case, I'd say. I noticed you kept him and Bob Anders, his victim, apart.'

'I did that for Bob Anders' sake. He's still recovering from the bashing they gave him.' He looked across at Anders, who was about to go back into the line-up room to look at the women.

Tilly looked at Malone shrewdly. 'You're not comfortable with these cases, are you?'

'I'm learning. I guess I'm one of those who's homophobic to a lesser degree, but I'm learning. I never had the urge to bash one of them.'

'Would you have if he'd made advances, put his hands on you?'

'I'd probably have clocked him. But I wouldn't have *bashed* him. Have you ever been approached by a lesbian?'

'Once or twice. I think women handle that sort of thing better than men.'

'How would you handle a double-gaited lover, a man?' Thinking of Kate Arletti.

She smiled. 'Now you're getting personal . . . It would be interesting to know if that kid Coulson had ever been groped. I read the summary of the interview when he was brought in here originally and charged with the bashing. He's a real case.'

Then Peeples and Anders came back out of the line-up room. The sergeant came across to Malone and Tilly Orbost. 'No go, Mr Anders passed. So what do we do?'

'We just charge Conrad with the one homicide,' said Malone slowly. 'He can claim the others all he likes, but on our books he's done only the one killing.'

Peeples looked at Tilly. 'You agree?'

She nodded. 'His MO is too different from the other murders. A different gun, no silencer, attacking the kids who, as far as we know, were paying no attention to him or anyone else – there's nothing to identify him with the other killer. Or killers. I think Scobie is right. One murder, one charge.'

'He's on the record claiming he did all the others. What do we do – bury it?'

'For the time being, yes,' said Malone.

'And we just keep looking for the other killer? Or killers?' Peeples looked at Tilly. 'What have you come up with in your profiling?'

'Nothing much,' she admitted. 'He leaves so few clues, other than the sighting of him, either as a man or a woman – both times, I'd say, in disguise as the latter. All the offences are planned, but that's not unusual with a serial killer. The scene is always in gay territory, so that means he's familiar with it. The killings are random, to an extent, so that means the killer didn't know who his victim was going to be till the actual hit. There's no real signature to his crimes except that he has the compulsion to call Scobie and talk about it.'

'Could he really believe he's doing a public service?'

'Why not? It needn't necessarily be a fantasy with him – he could genuinely believe it. There is one distinguishing feature – there is always only a primary victim. He never hangs around to shoot any other member of the bash gang – it's as if one killing satisfies him for the occasion.'

'He told Sam Hindle he couldn't kill in cold blood.'

'Maybe that's it, if he has to take aim a second time he's killing in cold blood. I'm trying to profile him, but that doesn't mean I completely understand him.'

Malone had long ago given up trying to understand the extremes

143

of the criminal mind. Character was another of God's little puzzles. 'The trained voice – is that an actor's or a singer's or a public speaker's?'

She shrugged. 'Any of those three. To be any of those you need an ego – or anyway, the desire to step out of yourself. But I'd put my money on his being an actor, either professional or very good amateur – maybe that's his fantasy. There's an old rule we're taught to apply. It's called Occam's Razor –'

'A barber laying down rules for cops?'

She grinned. 'It was a fourteenth century philosophy –'

'They had criminal profilers *then*?' said Peeples.

'No, I don't think so – you'd better ask the man who wrote *The Name of the Rose* about that. William of Occam was a Franciscan monk who wrote philosophy about problems in general. It said, I quote, what can be done with fewer assumptions is done in vain with more. What that means to criminal profilers is that given a problem with several alternative solutions, the most obvious answer is usually the correct one. I think we go for the guess that this killer is a professional actor.'

'We're doing that,' said Malone. 'One of my detectives is going through the actors' bible right now. She'll narrow it down to male actors under thirty-five, dark-haired and, if they give their height, under one-eighty centimetres. Five-ten,' he added for his own benefit. He clung to the old standards like a sailor to wreckage: he was always near to drowning in the metric sea.

'There could be hundreds of them,' said Peeples.

'Due diligence,' said Malone. 'It's something lawyers and account-ants do all the time. Why shouldn't I be the same, so long as I have a junior to do it for me?'

The other two of senior rank nodded agreement.

Malone left them and went across to Bob Anders. The latter's face was still puffy and bruised and there was a line of stitches up the side of his left eye. He looked weak, almost frail, but he managed a smile that looked like a grimace on the ruin of his face.

'Scobie –' He had worked with Malone two years ago on a case that had involved the Securities Commission; he held no rank so he did not have to be deferential to it. 'That kid Conrad – is that what he's calling himself?'

Malone nodded. 'Travis Conrad. Has he got another name?'

'His real name's Joe Penda. I've known him since he was a kid. He's pathetic – and I don't mean that in a caustic way. He's always been the poor little bugger that is taken advantage of – he's been used all his life. Christ, has he been used! I can't believe he went out and killed that other kid, that *stranger*.'

'We think it was what we call copy-cat stuff. He wanted to be noticed.'

'That'd be him, then. At one time he wanted to be an actor – I never saw him, but someone who worked with him in a workshop production said he was bloody awful. Joe's been rejected all his life. Even his parents – a horrible bloody couple, real monsters. Yeah, I can understand him wanting to be noticed. But Christ, what a way to do it! He obviously hasn't thought through the consequences. Does he think he'll be a hero when he goes to gaol, a serial killer? No, he'll be just another little poof, they'll rape the arse off him.' He shook his head in pity. 'There's nothing that can be done for him?'

'The deed's done, Bob. He killed a kid, looks like without provocation.'

'This serial killer, whoever he is, has really started something, hasn't he? There's talk, you know, that the gay community is on his side. Some of them, anyway.'

'Have you heard anyone making any guesses who he might be?'

'Nobody. I honestly think nobody knows – he could be someone who's actually never come out of the closet. And if they did know . . .' Because of his damaged eye he had to turn sideways to look at Malone. 'If a cop was killing off crims, off his own bat, would you dob him in?'

Malone grinned wrily. 'Never ask that sort of question in a police station.'

Anders grinned in reply, another grimace. 'Sure, dumb question. But you see the parallel?'

'Up to a point.' He changed the subject though, to a more delicate one: 'How's your friend? John Kagal told me about him.'

'A matter of weeks.' He drew a deep breath, as if holding back sudden emotion.

'You're okay? No HIV?'

'So they tell me. They tested me while they were treating me for this.' He put a tender finger to his face. 'I wonder if they do it if you're not gay?'

'I'm glad to hear you're okay.' It was time to go; he didn't know what else to say but: 'Take care, Bob.'

'Oh, I shall. Now I've seen what it can do to one. And Scobie –' Malone paused. 'Yes?'

'Are you more understanding of us now?'

'Us?'

'You know who I mean.'

Malone took his time, then nodded. 'Yes, I guess so. But I'll always have reservations. Is that okay?'

'Sure.' Anders smiled, then winced as the wound beside his eye contracted. 'Even Jesus Christ had some reservations about some of the Apostles.'

'You mean some of them were gay?' Though he knew that was not what Anders meant. 'Just take care, Bob, that's all.'

Outside Police Centre Tilly Orbost was waiting for him with Garry Peeples. The sergeant opened the door of Malone's car for Tilly, handed her in, said goodbye to Malone and went along to his own station. Malone slid in behind the wheel.

'Is Garry doing a line with you?'

'He's trying.'

'You out-rank him.'

'Is that what you told your wife when you first met her?'

'She out-ranked me. She was private secretary to the High Commissioner in London. But it's worked – very well,' he said with grateful emphasis.

She was not looking at him, but straight ahead. 'I'll tell you about being out-ranked. My mother's mother was Fijian – that's where I got the hair and the eyes. *Her* parents, my great-grandparents, had been blackbirded – brought out as kanakas to work in the canefields up in north Queensland. My grandmother was the last of seven kids. She was taken away from her parents by the government and put on a mission station with Aboriginal kids and Thursday Islanders. The government out-ranked her parents. She was sixteen when she heard they'd both been burnt to death in a canefields fire. She ran away from the mission station, came south to Bundaberg and married a man who worked in the canefields around there. A white man, my

146

grandfather. But she was never accepted, she was out-ranked – she wasn't white. Same with my mother when she came along – she still had the tarbrush in her. My father's white, he was an Agriculture Department inspector, he met my mother on his rounds – she was a clerk in one of the country town offices. The tarbrush had lightened quite a bit by the time it got to me – just a smear here and there.' She touched her hair, rolled her big dark eyes. 'But there were still people who liked to remind me of it – who let me know they out-ranked me, especially when I joined the service. I'm okay now –' She buckled on her seat-belt, turned and looked at him with the almost black eyes. He was surprised at the vulnerability he saw there. 'But I've been out-ranked, Scobie. It's nice when someone respects me for what I am, a woman.'

It was not the first time he had had the thought: the world is full of strangers, even those one knows.

3

There was no call from The Voice. Malone sat at his desk waiting for the phone to ring: it did, often, but never with the caller he hoped for. The media had already run reports on the arrest of Travis Conrad and the police, for a change, were being congratulated on a job well done. The royal commission into police corruption had this past week produced yet two more bent coppers who had had their guts twisted by video evidence of their dealings with drug dealers and brothel keepers. Anything that put the police in a good light was being broadcast as a minor Second Coming by headquarters media relations. The arrest of Travis Conrad, the gay serial killer, was getting as much space as Australia's cricket test victory over the Pakistanis. No crim could hope for greater glory. For the time being the fact that Conrad had been charged with only one murder was being down-played. You never throw a whole beast to the vultures, said the head of the media unit, who had read natural history and saw himself as the David Attenborough of the service.

Malone stood up and went out into the main office. Being Saturday the office was deserted except for Kate Arletti and Gail Lee. He walked to the big windows that looked north towards the main part of the city. There had been a torrential downpour half an hour earlier and the last of the clouds were hurrying north, their rumps like a stampede of rhinos. Sunlight slanted in from the west, turning one side of the trees in the park across the road into a brilliant emerald green. A lone youth, hands in pockets, walked across the park, head down: even from this distance he looked worried, lost. Malone turned back into the room: he had his own problems.

'How's it going?'

Kate and Gail sat opposite each other at a desk, two big volumes open in front of them. 'Finished,' said Kate, leaning back in her chair. 'We have one-hundred-and-eighty-three actors who fit our description, who might be our guy.'

'That all?'

'We'll break it down further,' said Gail. 'A lot of these actors may not work out of Sydney. Most of them give only their agents' addresses.'

They were more at ease together than they had been. During the week she had come back unruffled from the Rockdale homicide. It had been gory, Truach had told Malone, a real abattoirs mess, but she had apparently suffered no ill-effects. It had proved an open-and-shut case; the wife-killer had his confession already written out, like a bill of lading; he was a long-distance truck driver. What lay behind the frankness, the openness of the confession was no concern of Homicide, as Truach had pointed out to Gail. That was work for the Director of Public Prosecutions, the judge and the jury. Never, Truach had warned her, take a step into other people's territory.

'Righto, when you've got the list down to what you think is the minimum, run off copies of the photos. Just the photos, leave out all the names and details – we'll show 'em to the bash victims. Have them on my desk in the morning.'

The two women looked at each other.

'You've got something else to do?' He could smell the shit on his liver. *What's the matter with me, for Christ's sake?*

'Tomorrow is Sunday,' said both women primly, like deaconesses.

He relented. 'Righto, I'm driving you, a bit *heavy* on the pressure. But the pressure's on me, too. Do the best you can. Monday morning, okay?'

The two women looked at each other again, then nodded.

He said nothing further, but went back to his office. Then Clements, whom he hadn't seen since yesterday, came into his office. He was still buoyant with fatherhood; Malone would knee-cap him if he started whistling. He dropped on the couch, all free-and-easy.

'What are you doing in here?'

'I phoned Lisa, she said you'd been out of the house since about eight-thirty. How'd it go?'

Malone gave him a rundown: 'We've got a killer, but not the serial one. How'd it go with you yesterday?'

'You've read the papers?' Malone nodded. 'Our mate Dwayne Harod got life. So did Alexandra Huxwood. The judge was in great form, he gave 'em both the rough end of the pineapple.'

The Huxwood case had caused Malone and Clements a lot of heartburn earlier in the year. They had been dealing with power: dynastic, political and police power; and they had come out on top by sticking to principles. Malone managed a smile. Any scrap of good news was welcome.

'Speaking of judges,' said Clements and nodded at the tape machine fitted to Malone's phone, 'we need to get the warrant renewed for *that*.'

'Forget Judge Bristow then. He's too involved now, with his kid one of the victims. Try Judge Casula, I was reading that gadgets are his hobby.' He looked at the phone almost longingly. 'Maybe the bugger won't call again.'

'He will. Like Tilly Orbost said, that's part of his fantasy.'

'You're coming to agree with her?'

'I never *dis*agreed with her. I just like experts to prove themselves, that's all.'

'Are you going to be like that with Amanda when she grows up?'

'I dunno. Maybe I'll come to you for lessons.'

'I'm no expert,' he said, thinking of Maureen. He wondered how many expert parents there were. Lisa, of course; but how many more? Parenting, other experts said, was dying.

Sunday morning, after taking the family home from Mass, Malone drove out to the gaol at Long Bay, where Travis Conrad was being held on remand. It was a fine sunny morning, a good day to be free; people were out mowing their lawns, washing their cars, the chores of freedom. In Malone's boyhood this southern suburb had been mostly scrubby sand-dunes; the gaol then had dominated the land-scape like a medieval fortress town. It had had high stone walls, guard towers at the corners, a suggestion of impregnable isolation. Three or four tall palms and half a dozen pine trees, foreign to the area, had given a bizarre hint of exotic location, a hint lost on the inmates and even the guards.

Over the years the complex had spread beyond its stone walls; outbuildings had been added and high wire fences were almost an invitation to look in at what was now called a correctional institution. Cops smiled cynically at the optimism of *correctional*.

Malone signed himself in and was shown into a sparsely furnished room to await Conrad. 'Is he in protective?' he asked.

'For the time being.' The prison officer was a young man, built like a weight-lifter, with thick black hair, wary eyes and a mouth that looked as if it might never smile. Neither would I, thought Malone: he could imagine few worse jobs than being a prison officer. 'Soon's a known homo comes in, everyone's looking at him. A homo serial killer, he's a rare one.'

'Yes,' said Malone and said no more.

Conrad was brought in. The green prison garb was a size too large for him and he looked boyish and vulnerable: jail bait, thought Malone.

'Sit down, Travis.' Malone sat down at the plain table and gestured to Conrad to sit opposite him. 'You can ask for a solicitor, if you wish, in which case I'll come back tomorrow.'

'No, it's okay.' Conrad sat down and looked around him, though there was nothing to see. Then he looked back at Malone: 'What's the use? It's all over, isn't it?'

'Not quite.' But it was, one way or another. 'Travis, we know you didn't commit the other murders, the bashers. No −' He held up a hand. 'No bullshit, Travis. We *know*.'

For a moment Conrad looked as if he might persist in his guilt; then he seemed to shrink within his clothing, as if it were now two or three times too large for him. He slumped in his chair. 'Okay, you *know*. But you haven't caught him, have you?'

'We're close.'

Conrad looked at him sharply, but Malone kept the lie behind his eyes and went on: 'You have some idea who he is, don't you?'

'Why would I know?' He sounded surprised.

'Because you tried to copy him. You don't go around copying the work of strangers, do you?' It happened too often, but Malone was banking on Conrad's not knowing much about serial killers.

'I haven't a clue who he is.'

'Then why did you copy him? You wanted to be a hero, that it? You're not, Travis, not even to other gays. What you did was stupid. You can alter the balance by telling me who the serial killer is. You've got some idea, haven't you? You're an actor, Travis. So is he.'

'If you know that, why haven't you arrested him?' Somewhere a door clanged, iron on iron; Conrad jumped, then hunched forward on the table. 'If I told you who I thought he was, do you think I'd be a hero? You know better than that, Inspector. Gays don't want him caught, he's doing a public service.'

The phrase caught in Malone's ear like a hook. 'Did he tell you that?'

'What?'

'That he was doing a public service.'

'That's what he's doing, isn't he? It's war, sort of, isn't it? Us and Them. Us and You,' he said, suddenly accusing.

'Not me, Travis. All I'm doing is my job – a public service. Tell me who you think he is.'

'I did, you think that is going to help me?' He shook his head. Iron clanged against iron again: a reminder. 'You're right, I was fucking stupid. But it's done now.' Abruptly he began to weep, his body shaking with sobs.

Malone wanted to reach across to comfort him; but held back. This pitiful kid was a murderer: he could not forget that.

Conrad heaved a huge sigh, wiped his eyes. 'No, I'm telling you nothing, Inspector. Whoever he is, I hope he goes on doing what he's doing.'

'You don't know who he is, do you?'

'You'll never know whether I do or not.' He tried for a smile, an actor's smile.

'Maybe not, Travis.' He was all at once angry and frustrated; he couldn't help his cruelty: 'But I know you're not a hero.'

Chapter Eight

1

Monday afternoon the new leader of the Opposition, Byron Lavenham, was on his feet in the Assembly, the green-upholstered Bear Pit of State politics. He threw no shadow across the government, nor did his policies. His guiding light was the last person he had spoken to; he had been known to have three visions, all contradictory, in the one day. But he was handsome and looked imposing on television, even if his sound-bites had no teeth in them; polls had shown that eighty-five per cent of the voters only half-heard what any politician said, anyway. He was fluent in cliché and platitude, the lyrics of politics.

'Now that we are long out of post-election mode, we look to the government to grab the bull by the horns and make good on their pre-election promise, In Time No Crime. But we look in vain –'

'A point of order, Mr Speaker,' said the Premier, rising from his seat like a turtle coming out of its shell.

'What point was that?' The Speaker, a Labor member, was known as Cut-on-the-Bias Cadwallader: he never let impartiality get in his way. He knew that if he did the Premier would have his balls for Christmas baubles.

'We are supposed to be debating finance –'

'I was coming to that, Mr Speaker –' said Lavenham, who had been a marathon runner in his youth and sometimes still thought he was out on the road.

Up in the public gallery sat a dark-haired young man who seemingly had eyes only for the Premier. He was goodlooking in an anonymous way; he had the sort of looks one saw at the back end of a group of male models, the one wearing the cheaper apparel. He sat very still, but there was no suggestion of tenseness; he had the air of a man who might be a good listener. On this Monday afternoon he was here to listen to the Premier, in hope that the politician, and Police Minister, would proclaim that certain crimes, so-called, were in fact a public service.

The Opposition leader waffled on, hand-fledged flummery floating around the chamber like transparent pigeons. At last he finished and The Dutchman, ignoring his own point of order, rose to speak on the government's war against crime. Cut-on-the-Bias, not wanting to spoil his own record, did not insist on procedure. The Opposition benches barked and howled, but no one, not even themselves, took it seriously. It was another game show for television.

'The honourable member, as usual, is talking with his hat on. We are stamping out crime day by day. Take the horrible murders by the so-called serial killer—'

The young man in the gallery could not believe what he was hearing. He had come here today with goodwill towards the Premier and his government; like all Labor governments they claimed to be more fair-minded than any other party, as if they had a monopoly on it. He came of a family that was ultra-conservative and he still voted, out of habit, for the Nationalist Party, the rural bloc. But he had believed Labor's rhetoric and now The Dutchman was once again proving that it was just words on the wind.

'The police have once again proved there are more good apples in the barrel than rotten oranges. They have caught the serial killer who has been wantonly murdering—'

No, no, no! He had never heard of Travis Conrad till he had read the newspaper reports. He had been surprised at his own anger; he had had no conceit about being the serial killer. But this man, whoever he was, had put a stain on the justifiable executions. They had been retribution for specific crimes, the random bashings; but Conrad's crime seemed to be a random killing. For him to claim that he had done all the other murders was an evil act in itself. What he had done was not a public service.

He would have to call his friend Inspector Malone.

'Bring them all in,' Malone had said. 'Including that kid Coulson. He's got to be made to see that Travis Conrad is not the feller who killed his mate Justin Langtry. I don't want any confusion when we bring in the real serial killer.'

So on this Monday afternoon everyone who had witnessed the killing of a basher was in the big office at Homicide. Kate Arletti and Gail Lee were acting as tea-ladies; or anyway, providing coffee and biscuits. Malone had waited for either or both of them to object to the role, but they had ignored him and joked between themselves about being the handmaidens of the service.

Clements was supervising the identification from the photos that had been reproduced from *Showcase*. It was a tedious business and the witnesses had to be kept in good temper. It was a lesson for some, if not all of them, that police work was not all riot control and flash work with weaponry.

'It's like you doing scale drawings of the architraves in a fifty-storey building,' Malone said to Walter Needle when the architect arrived.

'My dear man, architraves went out with Queen Victoria. But I see your point.'

Malone went into his office, shuffled back and forth through paper-work, and after some time Clements came in. This time he did not drop on to the couch, but sat down on the chair opposite Malone. He meant business: 'We've narrowed it down to sixteen guys, all of them based in Sydney.'

'What about the Coulson kid? Did he co-operate or is he still insisting Conrad is the serial killer?'

'A couple of the others leaned on him, Bob Anders and Greta Bromley.'

'How did he react to that, gays leaning on him?'

'Not very well at first, but then young Sam Hindle chipped in. At first we got the expected bit about young Hindle being an eastern suburbs silvertail — Coulson's got enough chips on his shoulder to make an epaulette of them. But he's not dumb, he started to see he was the odd man out.'

'Sixteen? You recognize any of them?'

'Oh sure, I've seen some of 'em on TV, but I didn't know their names. But the ones I recognized, I'd be surprised they were gay.'

'How would you know? A hundred-kilogram rugby league forward knocks blokes arse-over-head week after week, then he comes out of the closet – did you suspect he was gay? I've given up guessing who's in the closet or out of it.' *I'll bet you don't suspect John Kagal.*

He looked at the photos and not for the first time saw that good looks, especially amongst actors and models, often came out of a mould. At least two-thirds of the sixteen could have passed for cousins. But they all looked healthier than rock stars, even if, as rumour had it, there was no money in acting.

'Okay, so what do we do?' said Clements.

'We can't go out and bring in all sixteen of them, just on suspicion. The media'd make a meal of that, especially the trash magazines that gluttonize on that sort of thing. We'd be chewed up, if our mate isn't one of the sixteen. Send Kate and Gail and John out to see them, check what they were doing on the nights of the murders. When we've narrowed it down even further, say five or six, then we'll bring them and the witnesses in again.' Then he gestured at the phone and the tape machine. 'Did you get the new warrant?'

Then the phone rang and Malone reached for it. 'Inspector?'

Malone switched on the tape, nodding at Clements as he did so. 'Go ahead, Cyril –'

'Cyril?'

It had slipped out. 'Sorry. I was talking to one of my detectives.' Clements grinned, flipped a wrist. 'What's on your mind?'

'I've just been down to Macquarie Street, listening to that old fart Vanderberg. He's claiming you've arrested the serial killer. The *gay* serial killer.' There was a chuckle. 'The media love their little tags, don't they? I could be as straight as you, Inspector.'

'That's entirely possible. But what's your beef about the Premier?'

'It's not just him, it's that impostor you have in custody.'

'He's not an impostor – he actually murdered someone. Just like you did on several occasions.'

'Don't get nasty, Inspector – let's keep this civilized. This guy – Conrad? – what he did was not what I've been doing.' Malone noted there was no pretence now of a consortium. 'He did the public no

156

service – he wantonly killed an innocent kid. *That's* what I call murder, Inspector. I was hoping by now you'd know the difference.'

'Fred – do you mind if I call you Fred? I have to give you a name, just for my files.'

'Fred? I'd rather Nigel.' There was another chuckle. Malone cursed himself for beginning to like the man. 'Okay, Fred will do.'

'Thanks. Fred, is it getting under your skin that Travis Conrad is trying to steal your thunder?' The tape still rolling . . .

'Not *my* thunder, Inspector – do you mind if I call you Scobie? Since we are now on first-name terms?'

He was in two minds. Rank gave him a certain authority, some leverage. But here he was not dealing with a junior officer: 'Go ahead. What do you mean, not *your* thunder?'

Through the office window he saw that Tilly Orbost had come into the outer room. He signalled to her and she came into his own office. Clements gave her his chair and fell into his usual slouch on the couch. He mouthed the words, *the serial man.* She nodded.

'Scobie, I'm not in this business for self-glory. I really am dedicated to the public service of ridding Sydney of scumbag bashers. Once that is done –'

'Do you think it will be? Scumbags and bashers have been around since Sumerian times –' *John Kagal should hear me now.* Tilly Orbost and Clements both raised their eyebrows and nodded at each other, impressed by Professor Malone.

Fred was impressed, too. 'You're one up on me there, Scobie – I know nothing about the Sumerians. But even if I can only achieve temporary respite in the bashings, that will be something, won't it?'

'I guess so. Fred, why don't you come in and talk this over?'

Again the chuckle. 'Thanks for the invitation, but no. Just make sure the media knows the truth about that impostor. And try to get the word, somehow, to the Premier that I'm doing as much of a public service as the royal commission is doing on the police. Incidentally, I'm sure you're as straight as they come.'

'As opposed to gay or bent?'

This time there was a laugh. 'I love you, Scobie. I'll be in touch.'

The phone went dead and Malone switched off the tape. 'He's getting touchy. He thinks killing bashers is his domain. You want to hear the tape, Tilly?'

157

'I'd like to.'

'So would I,' said Clements and sounded as if he should have been asked first.

Malone left them and went out into the main office. The witnesses were grouped at one end of the big room, some of them looking impatient to be away. Though they were victims, to a greater or lesser degree, there seemed to be no camaraderie. Les Coulson sat apart, swinging his legs from a desk. The only three who appeared to have anything in common were Bob Anders and Greta Bromley and Liz Embury, though the latter looked as if she were here only under sufferance. The most relaxed of them was young Sam Hindle; he gave Malone a shy smile as the latter approached the group.

Malone thanked them all for their co-operation; then Walter Needle spoke up. Again he was immaculately dressed; he looked ambassa-dorial, sounded it too: 'Anything that brings this killer to justice, Inspector —'

'Speak for yourself,' said Liz Embury and everyone looked at her.

'Cool it, darling.' Greta Bromley laid a hand on her partner's arm, but the latter shook it off.

'Why should we? You think this — this killer is worse than those jerks there?' She nodded fiercely at Coulson and Sam Hindle. 'What do you think, Mr Stratton? Didn't this killer save you from being killed?'

Stratton was as elegantly dressed as Needle, but not for business; he had the two-thousand-dollar casual look. He was sitting beside Jim Gable, who by contrast looked as if he had wandered in from a Best & Less sale.

'I just hope we're not called to give evidence if ever he is caught —'

'You will be,' said Malone quietly. He was aware that the other detectives in the room, including those not on this case, were as still as pointer dogs. 'Just as Mr Coulson and Mr Hindle will be.'

'I can understand how you feel,' said Sam Hindle unexpectedly, addressing Liz Embury. 'What I and my mates did to you was stupid and unforgivable and I've apologized to you.'

'It's all right, honey,' said Greta Bromley. 'We all make mistakes. You're young enough to correct them.'

'What does that mean?' Liz Embury turned on her.

When women look to be on the verge of battle, men look the other way. Heterosexual men, that is: gay men are braver. 'Ladies,' said Bob Anders, 'don't let's start grinding axes till Inspector Malone has caught the killer.'

Malone was grateful for the intervention.

'Do you really think he's one of those actors?' Anders asked, while Liz Embury stood stone-faced and Greta Bromley all at once looked older, even sad.

'I think he could be,' said Malone and tried to sound convincing and convinced.

'What about the guy in the line-up Saturday morning?' Les Coulson still sat apart, self-contained. He had shown no reaction when Liz Embury had referred to him and Sam Hindle as jerks; he had barely glanced at her.

'He's a killer, yes, but he's not the man we're after. He'll go down, we'll see to that, but none of you here will be called to give evidence against him. You'll get your day in court when we catch the serial killer.'

'What if we refuse to give evidence against him?' Liz Embury was not retreating; nor was she looking at her partner.

'That will be up to the judge and the prosecutor.' He made a stab in the dark, an old ploy: 'You're an actress. Have you acted with any of the actors we've shown you?'

She was reluctant to answer. Today she looked most attractive; she had come straight from the shooting of a commercial. Her face was made-up, her clothes trim and conservative; in the commercial she was the nameless expert who told women how they could best avoid period pain. At the moment she looked as if she were experiencing some sort of pain herself.

'Miss Embury?'

'I've acted with a couple of them.'

'Which ones?'

Again she took her time, then she named two. 'The ones in Photos Two and Three. But I'd swear neither of them is the killer.'

'What about the others?'

'I haven't acted with them.'

'But you know them?'

'I've seen them around.'

159

'Are any of them gay?'

'What's that got to do with it?'

'A good deal, I should think.'

She abruptly was silent, sullenly so. She's holding something back, Malone thought. But this was not the place to grill her, not in front of the others. He turned to Anders: 'Bob? Do you know if any of them are gay?'

Anders, too, was cautious: 'You're supposing the killer is gay?'

'Wouldn't you? Why would a heterosexual —'

'My,' said Will Stratton, crossing a leg and showing a purple sock. 'Aren't we being a mite pedantic? Heterosexual?'

'Righto, a straight. Why would a straight go around avenging the bashing of just homosexuals —' He saw Greta Bromley smile and he smiled back at her. 'And lesbians? You don't want me to use the word *dyke*, do you?'

'No.' She had regained her good humour, a contrast to the mood of her partner. 'I much prefer the pedantic.'

Anders, too, smiled; he appeared to have no time at all for Stratton, though he had been affable towards Needle. He certainly got on well with Greta Bromley. 'The dykes of Lesbos — it doesn't have the right poetic ring to it, does it? . . . Okay, Scobie, let's say he's gay. Yes, one of the guys in the photos is gay — it's common knowledge. If you knew him, you wouldn't suspect him, no way. He's a motor-mouth, if he was doing the killings, someone would know about it.'

'Mr Needle?' Malone looked at the older man. 'You haven't offered an opinion.'

'I don't know any of them, if that's what you're asking. I may have seen them on TV or the stage, but I don't know them.' Whether he meant it or not, he had succeeded in sounding as if he and Will Stratton moved in a more exclusive circle.

'Mr Gable?'

Somehow Gable was the odd man out here, the gay from the suburbs, from the shopping mall and the hardware store, lost in the crowd on the hill at a football match. He looked so *ordinary*; but Malone knew that was some sort of prejudice even to think that. 'I guess my memory isn't as good as everyone else's. It might be better when I come face to face with those blokes. But right now . . .' He shook his head.

160

'Sam?'

The boy had a poise about him that gave him his own place in the group. How could he have been so stupid, Malone wondered, to have done what he did? Had he been bashing his parents as much as the two lesbians?

'I have my suspicions about one of them, sir. But I'm like Mr Gable – I'd like to see them face to face. I want to be absolutely certain I pick the right guy.'

'And you'll testify against him?' said Liz Embury: she was still on the attack.

'Yes,' said Sam Hindle, not defiantly, just matter-of-factly. 'Yes, I think we all should.'

'A moralist,' said Will Stratton and stood up. 'I'm going before the sermon starts.'

That broke up the group and Malone made no effort to stop them going. Except Greta Bromley and Liz Embury. He took the two women aside while Kate Arletti and Gail Lee showed the others out.

'Miss Embury, do you know something you don't want to tell us?'

'What makes you think that?'

'Intuition. It's something cops and women have in common.' He was trying to turn her bad humour to good, but he had clodhopped on that one.

'You wouldn't have a clue how some women, maybe most women, think. You've shown you don't know how *I* think.'

'You mean because you're lesbian? I'm trying, Miss Embury, even though it may not be too noticeable.'

He did not look at Greta Bromley, but guessed that for the moment she was neutral. She was standing to one side, not behind Liz Embury; on neutral territory. And looking unhappy about it, as if love were dying.

'I don't think you know how *I* think,' he went on. 'What I think is that you know more than you're telling us.'

She said nothing and Greta Bromley, after some hesitation, said, 'Go on, Liz. Tell him.'

No answer; and Malone said, 'Tell me what? That she knows who the killer is? That she's acted with him? Do *you* know who he is, Greta?'

161

'No, I don't. That's the truth, Scobie.' They were friends; or anyway more than just cop and witness.

'If you know who the killer is, Liz, you can be charged with withholding evidence.'

That did not seem to scare her. 'You can't charge me with withholding *suspicion* of evidence. And that's all I have at the moment.' It was an admission, she was weakening. Suddenly she turned on her partner. 'Jesus, why do you have to pressure me? Those shits could've killed you – the guy saved your life, for Crissake!'

'I know that,' said Greta Bromley quietly, and looked at Malone. 'Let it lay, Scobie. As Liz says, it's only a suspicion.'

'Even that would help.'

'And if I'm wrong?' Liz Embury was less belligerent now; she put out a hand and her partner took it. 'You drag the poor bastard in here, give him the works – I've read the royal commission reports, the going-over you cops give some of them –'

All at once Malone hated the bent cops, the stand-over merchants. 'We're not all like that –'

'Well, I'm not going to help. May we go now?'

Malone looked at Greta Bromley, who nodded and said something with her eyes: *maybe she'll change her mind?* 'Righto,' he said. 'We'll be in touch.'

He signalled to one of the detectives to escort them down to the security desk and out of the building. Then he went back into his own office where Clements and Tilly Orbost still sat.

'What went on with the two women?' Clements asked.

Malone told them. 'There's nothing we can do about Miss Embury for the moment. I just have the feeling the feller she suspects isn't in those six photos.'

'We're getting to him, whoever he is,' said Tilly, gesturing at the tape on Malone's desk. 'He's the star and now someone, this *bit* player Travis Conrad, is trying to take stardom away from him. If he's an actor, it'll be doubly hurting.'

'The media are still running Conrad as the serial killer,' said Clements. 'Do we tell them he's not?'

'Not yet,' said Tilly Orbost before Malone could reply. 'That will increase the pressure on him.'

Clements didn't look at her, kept his gaze deliberately on Malone,

162

the one he had been addressing: his boss. Malone was abruptly weary of undercurrents; they were rubbing against him like sand in a riptide. He looked at his watch, then reached for his hat. 'I'm going home. Start Kate and Gail looking for those six actors in the photos.'

Clements looked at his own watch. '*Now*?'

'Now. I'll see you in the morning, Tilly.' Occasionally he would invite home some officer from out-of-State, but he was in no mood to be hospitable this evening. Let Garry Peeples be hospitable.

As he was letting himself out of the security door Clements caught up with him, walked down the corridor towards the lifts. 'You've got shit on the liver again.'

'You noticed? What d'you expect? For Crissakes, Russ, the woman's only doing what she's expert at!'

'I'm being sidelined here. Put on the reserves bench.'

'Oh balls!' He pressed the Down button, waited for the lift. 'You and I are still running the show. When it comes time to arrest Fred, it'll be you and I fronting him, not her. She's okay, Russ, and she's only temporary. You've been in the game long enough, you know experts are always outsiders. Go home and bounce Amanda on your knee, tell her not to grow up to be an expert.'

'The wife's an expert.' Indeed, she was. When she put her mind to it, Romy could carve up men, dead or alive. 'One in the family is enough.'

The lift arrived and Malone stepped into it, managing a smile at Clements. They were both experts, they just didn't have degrees or diplomas to prove it. All they had was experience.

3

Bad news made good television. Malone watched the ABC seven o'clock news, wondering if being a ghoul was a necessary qualification for a TV cameraman. In Chechnya snipers were busy getting in their kicks before yet another projected cease-fire could get under way; desperate civilians raced across empty streets, the camera panning with them all the way: what price another death? There was a plane crash: many dead; a train wreck: many dead; a terrorist bomb explosion: many dead. One of the few cheerful items was yet another

Aboriginal dance ceremony somewhere up North; his mind had switched off as soon as the dancers appeared. He was not a racist, at least less so than the average voter, but he had grown tired of the ABC's obligatory Koori item each night; if it wasn't Aborigines, it was stranded bloody whales or more scruffy conservationists chaining themselves to trees. He was tired tonight and all the old prejudices had no difficulty in coming to the surface. He switched off the television before he turned into a fundamentalist, of whatever breed it didn't matter.

He went out to the dining room, where Lisa had just put dinner on the table. One night a week they had pasta: tonight it was fettucini with marinara sauce. He had two helpings, washed down with a Hunter Valley semillon. Dessert was lime pie, one of his favourites. By the time he was drinking his coffee his mood had improved. He might even have watched a Koori saving a stranded whale. Or a conservationist saving a stranded Koori.

'I think I'll watch *Sydney Beat* tonight, learn how easy it is to be a cop.'

'It's not on tonight,' said Tom, who kept watch on the family viewing. 'There's a day-night match on.'

'Oh God,' said Maureen. 'Bloody cricket. I think I'll go out.'

'Where to?' said her father.

'Not to a rave party.' They were on good terms again. Friction in the family was never a long-term thing. 'Over to Bondi Junction. There's a coffee lounge there, they play good music.'

'Such as?'

'Lots of Joe Cocker, stuff like that.'

'That's good music? I thought it was a gall-bladder attack with lyrics.'

She rolled her eyes. 'He's as old as you, maybe older, you know that?'

'Then he should be ashamed of himself. Stay home and I'll play you some Frank Sinatra.'

'Who?' She began to gather up the dishes. Her room was always untidy, but, like her mother, she liked a tidy kitchen. 'Can I borrow the car? You want to come, Claire?'

'No, thanks. I'll stay home with the oldies and cramp their scene. I might even watch the cricket. I love the way they're patting each other's butts this season, instead of kissing each other.'

'If someone had patted your bum, Dad,' said Tom, 'what would you have done?'

'Don't ask,' said Lisa.

The atmosphere was good, the family sort that pleased him, made him feel that this was what a home should be. 'Take the car, Mo.'

'Park it at least five metres away from anything else,' said Tom. 'You know what he'll be like if it gets a scratch on it. Or a dent in it.'

'I'll put a dent in you, mate,' said his father.

Later he gave the keys to Maureen and went out to the front of the house while she backed the car out of the garage. Both she and Claire were good drivers, though he did not make a habit of letting them borrow the car; sooner or later he and Lisa would have to scrape up the money to buy each of them a used car. So far he had held off because he hated borrowing money; the cars would be bought out of capital or not at all. It was a philosophy he was having trouble selling to his offspring, free spenders all.

He was happy, however, to lend Maureen the Fairlane: he was repairing the cracks in the cement that bound them.

'Thanks, Dad. I'll look after it. Did Mum tell you I've got a job at David Jones at Bondi Junction for Christmas?'

'Yes.' Both she and Claire had landed Christmas vacation jobs. For some odd reason Sam Hindle fell into his mind: would the Hindles let their boy take a vacation job? 'Take care.'

'Of me or the car?' She grinned. 'You take care, too. You're looking awfully tired lately.'

She drove away, slowly: twice she put the brake-lights on and he could almost hear her laughing to herself. Then she was gone round the corner and he stood in the garden looking up at the night sky. Close by him a gardenia bush threw up a fragrance, like a sweet-scented woman.

'What are you looking at?' said Lisa, his favourite scent, from the front door.

'The stars. Do astronomers have the same problems cops do?'

She was not without imagination, but she would comfort him better by being sensible: 'I shouldn't think so. Are you thinking of taking up astronomy? You can move out tomorrow.'

165

He put his arm round her waist. 'I was watching two women in love today. They have the same problems we do.'

'We have problems?' They had had them in their early days. Different worlds take time to meld; angry oceans of emotion had separated them at times. It was something they had kept from the children, but eventually she would offer it, along with other advice, to Claire and Maureen. She would leave Tom to him. 'The lesbians? How do you get on with them?'

'Better than I thought I would. The older one, anyway. The younger one –' He shook his head.

'What are they like? Butch? Attractive? What?'

'Attractive, both of them. But the younger one hates men, me included.'

She kissed his cheek. 'She doesn't know what she's missing. Do you want to watch the cricket? I'll sit and suffer it.'

'I think I'll read.'

Which he did: *Company Man*, which Jan Pretorius had sent over. The corporate jungle made the police service look like a comfortable club. *Downsizing the head-count* would have had a cop issuing a charge of obscene language; corporate raiding was murder without the blood, except for that of the odd suicide. He closed the book feeling that maybe a cop's life was not such a bad one after all.

Then the phone rang out in the hall. He looked at his watch: ten-fifty.

'I'll get it,' Tom called from the hallway on his way from the bathroom.

'No!' Malone just beat him to the phone. 'At this hour –'

'You mean it could be *him*?'

'Possibly.' He lifted the phone, gave just the number, which he always did.

'Dad?' It was Maureen, her voice faint and ragged. 'Could you get a cab and come and get me? I'm in Casualty at St Sebastian's.'

Chapter Nine

1

'It was horrible.' Maureen, bruised and cut, sat slumped in a wheel-chair, a blanket wrapped round her. Why do people in wheelchairs, even young people, always look so much older? Malone wondered. 'These hoons jumped me – I was walking back to the car park –' She closed her eyes and shivered, clutched the blanket a little tighter.

'Take your time.'

Malone had said that a hundred times, but never to one of his own. He and Lisa sat on either side of Maureen, each holding a hand. Monday night was evidently a slow night in Casualty; there were only three other patients waiting to be attended to. The pace was slow, the staff unhurried: this wasn't *ER* or *Chicago Hope* or all those other fictional hospitals where a crisis happened just before every commercial. A man sat crying quietly in the chair at the triage desk while a nurse patiently took down his details. A youth with a purple Mohawk crop sat with his leg, in temporary splints, propped out in front of him; he was reading a magazine, unconcerned, as if he were a regular visitor here. A thin middleaged woman, her face plum-coloured with bruises, sat with her eyes closed while her young daughter, no more than twelve or thirteen, sat holding her hand, looking the older and the wiser of the two.

Maureen was gathering herself together. Nothing had been broken; she was in the wheelchair because that was what had been closest after the duty doctor had examined her. She shook off the blanket and stood up; then she wavered and sat down again. She struggled to hold back tears.

'Not yet, darling.' Lisa was as pale and strained as her daughter; her bruises were in her gaze. 'Tell us what happened.'

'I was walking back to the car park – I'd parked the car well away

167

from anything else –' Her smile at her father was weak; he pressed her hand. 'Then these four guys jumped me – I didn't see them. They knocked me down – they were trying to drag me down under the by-pass – it's dark down there –'

'You were on your own?' Lisa said.

'I'd been with a couple of girls from school. They had their own car at the other end of the car park. These jerks came out of nowhere – and then –' She stopped, looked over Malone's shoulder.

He turned. Billy Logan, the ambulance medic who had brought Bob Anders here a couple of weeks ago, stood there. 'G'day, Scobie. I didn't realize she was your daughter – you okay, love?' Maureen nodded her thanks and Logan looked back at Malone. 'I see you a minute?'

Malone got up and walked out to the doors of Casualty. Another ambulance had arrived with two victims of what looked like a major car accident. A car pulled up and two youths got out and carried in an unconscious girl. Logan looked after them.

'Looks like another one who's OD'd. They'll never learn . . .' Then he looked back at Malone. 'Your daughter was bloody lucky, mate. If that bloke with the gun hadn't been on hand –'

'Hold on. She hasn't told us about anyone else being there. What bloke with a gun?'

'Oh. Sorry.' Logan worked his lips up and down his teeth. 'Maybe I better let her tell you, then.'

'No, go ahead. I don't want her right now having to give me all the gory details. She's been through enough –'

'Well.' Medics, like cops, are rarely bearers of good news. 'This bloke must of been following your daughter – the creeps who jumped her didn't see him. As soon as they grabbed her, he was on to them – he shot one of them –'

'Someone was shot? Dead?'

Logan nodded. 'A kid about sixteen, a skinhead, lives out at Bondi. He was gunna be first in – he had his dick out –' He shook his head at his gaffe. 'Sorry – there'm I going into details . . . We called the police – Paddington are handling it. I'm not playing detective, mate, but I wouldn't mind betting the bloke with the gun was the one who's been killing those bashers. That one you caught the other day, he's not the serial killer, is he?'

Malone looked at him curiously. 'How'd you know?'

'Mate, I've seen as many murders as you. I rang one of the guys at Surry Hills, he told me the MO was different.'

There would always be a leaking mouth ... 'This feller – he got away again, nobody chased him?'

'I think the dead kid's mates were too shocked –'

'How did my daughter get away from them?'

'I asked her that while I was treating her – I rode in with her in the back of the ambulance. She managed to get away from the hoons – she said she was screaming and a couple, a man and his girl, came running to help her. The bloke called us on his mobile and he and his girlfriend were with her when we arrived.'

'And the kids?'

'He'd also called the police – a patrol car got there before we did. The kids were still there, standing around their dead mate. They didn't seem to understand one of 'em might be shot, just because they were gunna rape a girl.' His obvious disgust excused his gaffe. 'Jesus, sometimes ...'

'Did you get the man's name?'

'Sure.' Logan glanced at his notebook, gave Malone a name and address. 'He did you a favour, Scobie.'

'Yeah, I'll find him and thank him.'

'No, I mean the bloke who shot the kid. I hate to think what would of happened to your daughter –'

He certainly did owe the serial killer, if indeed it was him. At the same time, as a man who always paid his debts, he was appalled at the idea. It was almost midnight: tomorrow mocked him.

'She'll be right, mate,' said Logan and Malone wasn't sure whether he meant Maureen or whether he was reciting the national anthem.

'Sure. Thanks, Billy, for looking after her.'

'Any time, mate. Well, no – not any time. Let's hope there isn't a next time.'

Then he was gone out into the night, heading for accidents, suicides and murders still undeclared. Another ambulance swung in before the entrance: casualties were piling up. Just like in a war.

Malone went back inside to Lisa and Maureen. 'Let's get you home, love. Mum'll take you by cab, I'll go and pick up the car.'

169

He called for two cabs and while they waited Lisa said, 'What did that ambulance man have to tell you?'

She would find out eventually, he would have to tell her; but not now. 'Just routine stuff.'

'Routine stuff? Ambulance men have to report to cops?'

'It was attempted rape —' He stopped when he saw Maureen flinch. Words were going to be as dangerous as other instruments, at least for a while.

Lisa put her arm round her daughter. 'All right, we'll talk about it later.'

Only when he had put her and Maureen into a cab did it strike him that Maureen had made no mention of anyone's being shot. Perhaps she didn't know one of the would-be rapists was dead, perhaps Billy Logan, riding with her on the way to St Sebastian's, had been wise enough not to tell her. Leaving it to him, the cop and father.

The second cab came and he rode out to Bondi Junction, sitting silently in the back, the driver, a grey-haired man, glancing continuously over his shoulder at him.

'Relax,' Malone at last told him, showing his badge. 'I'm a police officer.'

'You never know these days. Usually, I get a single fare, I make him ride in the front with me. I been done twice in the past year. We gunna have to do something about protecting us taxi drivers. We're a public service, the government forgets that. I been driving thirty years and the last coupla years, you wouldn't wanna read about it. Muggers, guys with knives, everyfuckingwhere. This where you wanna get out? Hullo, a crime scene? I recognize them tapes — I hope some day I don't look up and see 'em around me. What is it, a murder?'

'Yes. How much?'

'Seven-fifty.' Malone handed him eight dollars and waited for the change. 'Ain't you cops on a travel allowance?'

'Only during the daytime.'

He got out of the cab and stood for a few moments before approaching the two marked police cars and the unmarked Physical Evidence vehicle. Spotlights illuminated the area roped off by the Crime Scene tapes; there was no breeze and they hung as limp as last year's

Christmas decorations. The body had been taken away, the rough chalked outline the reminder of what had been there. The scene was all too familiar: except that the body might have been Maureen's.

One of the Paddington detectives came across to him. 'Hullo, Scobie.' He was George Noblett, a sergeant with a plain ugly face and a beautiful set of principles which, he said, he kept intact by never using them. He was cynical enough to have been adopted by a political party or a church, though the latter might have had hopes of redeeming him. 'You guys been called in already? I don't remember making any request.'

'I've come to pick up my car, George.' Then Malone explained the other reason why he was here. 'I'm on the case, anyway. I think the killer might be our serial killer, the feller who says he's avenging gay bashings. What've you got on how the dead kid was shot?'

'The kid's mates, three of them, have been taken down to the station. All I've got is that the guy must've used a silencer, nobody heard the shot. The bullet's still in the body, it's been taken to the morgue, so I dunno the calibre. Your daughter, she's okay?'

'She'll be okay.' He hoped he was right. 'I'll call you in the morning. Hang on to the kids till I get someone from Homicide to talk to them. What are you holding them for?'

'Now you've told me, attempted rape.'

He hesitated. Ropes were being woven here to truss up Maureen. 'I don't want my daughter testifying in a court, George, not on a rape case.'

George Noblett was the father of five. 'You want me to let them go?'

'If it's not too late, if the charges haven't been fed into the computer.'

'It'll all come out eventually, Scobie. The inquest on the dead kid –' He jerked at one of the tapes, as if trying to tear it apart. 'I've got three daughters . . . I'll do my best.'

Malone thanked him and went across to the Fairlane. He got in and sat looking at the complex of buildings across the street. David Jones was in there, the store where Maureen would start work in a week or two. If she was in a fit condition.

He punched at the steering wheel, missed and hit the horn. Across at the crime scene all work stopped. Then someone turned one of the spotlights on him.

2

He could not sleep. His mind was as cloudy as a rain-forest, but Maureen's bruised and cut face kept cruising through it. At three o'clock he got up and went out to the kitchen and made himself a cup of tea. Loose leaves: Brigid, his mother, would have disowned him if he had used tea-bags. He was sitting at the kitchen table, sipping the tea, when Lisa came out, poured herself a cup and sat down opposite him. Her eyes were red-rimmed, though if she had been weeping he had not heard her.

'She's going to be all right,' she said.

He shook his head.

'No, listen to me, darling.' She had, indeed, shed tears, but women have learned to cry more silently than men. They have had more practice. 'She wasn't *raped*. If she had been, things would be different.'

'She came that close –'

'I know. And she knows it.'

'She had that dead kid fall on top of her – Christ, isn't that traumatic enough?'

'Yes – and she won't forget that, not in a hurry.'

Then Claire, pulling on a shortie dressing-gown, came into the kitchen. She went to the fridge, poured herself a glass of milk and sat down beside her mother. 'A family conference?'

Lisa nodded. 'How's Maureen?'

'Sleeping soundly. I think she's going to be all right.'

'That's what I've been telling your father.' Lisa reached across and put her hand on Malone's. 'Darling, Claire and I talked to Maureen last night – she really is going to be all right. She's got guts, *real* guts. We don't want any counselling, understand? Claire and Tom and I can handle it. And Maureen herself.'

'Tom?'

'Yes. He was as angry as you are now when he first heard about it. But last night, before he went to bed, he'd calmed down. He saw

172

that it was better to be supportive of her than to be angry about what happened and not be able to do anything about it.'

'I can do something about it –'

'What?' said Claire. 'Whip the case up into a media event? Have reporters trying to get their foot in the door to interview Maureen?'

He said nothing for a moment; then: 'So I'm the odd one out?'

He saw that that remark had hurt Lisa; all he could do was turn over his hand and press hers.

Claire said, 'Dad, we were all angry to begin with. *I* was – bloody angry. Worse than that – four-letter angry. But where does it get us? Are you going to charge the creeps who tried to rape her?'

'No.'

'I'd never allow her to go into court,' said Lisa.

At least they agreed on that.

'Do you know who shot the jerk who was trying to rape her?' said Claire.

'We're just guessing.'

'Would it have been the guy who's been killing the gay bashers?'

He looked at her suspiciously. 'What made you ask that? Did Maureen see him?'

'Not as far as I know – she hasn't said anything. I just asked because you seem to be sitting on something, you're not telling us all you know. Or thinking.'

He had to smile, even though his face seemed to hurt. 'You'll make a good lawyer. Or cop . . . Yeah, it could be the same man.'

'So what are you going to do?'

Something in their steady gaze said his answer was important. He had often remarked that a woman's gaze, more than a man's, could be as straight and demanding as a gun barrel. Two barrels was one too many.

'Nothing,' he said. 'Unless I have to.'

That seemed to satisfy them; for the moment. 'Okay,' said Claire and stood up. 'But remember, we're all on Maureen's side.'

When they were alone, he looked at Lisa. 'You don't really think I'm not on her side?'

'Of course not.' She stood up, took their cups and saucers and washed and dried them. She was precise without being prissy; there would always be unwashed cups in anyone's life, including hers, but

173

she would always run the tap against the possibility. 'You're a cop. You think justice is important.'

'Don't you?'

'Not always. There are other considerations.'

They went back to bed. There is a certain comfort in flesh, even when not making love.

In the morning he was at breakfast when Maureen came to the table in her dressing-gown. The cut and bruises hadn't magically disappeared overnight; he felt immensely relieved when she smiled and he saw that none of her teeth were broken. 'I think I'll just take things easy today.'

'A good idea.' Tom had suddenly grown up, was no longer gauche. But he was a bit heavy-handed in his attempt to lighten the conversation: 'Any dents in the car, Dad?'

'None.' He reached for some toast. 'Are you seeing the doctor today?'

Maureen nodded. He noticed she was making no attempt to eat any breakfast but was just sipping slowly on her orange juice. 'Dr Stephens. I don't want to go back to the hospital – God, did you see some of those poor people there last night?' As if she hadn't been one of them. Then she said, looking down at her juice, 'That boy who fell on me – did he die?'

He felt the sudden stillness of Lisa, Claire and Tom; strangely, his hand seemed to lose its strength, he couldn't cut the toast on his plate. 'Yes.'

'What about the others?'

'Love, let's talk about it another time –'

'No, *now*.'

'No, they're okay. They were arrested, they'd have been charged at Paddington last night, then taken out to Waverley to be held.'

'Let them go, don't charge them. Not on my account.'

He looked at his three women: their expressions said the same thing. Even Tom seemed to be challenging him. He got strength back in his hand, cut his toast. 'Righto, I'll see what I can do.'

'Good enough,' said Maureen and reached for some cereal.

When he had finished breakfast he got up and went into the bedroom. He looked up the name and address he had been given last night; the man lived in Bronte, less than a kilometre from his own

174

home. He picked up the phone: 'Mr Kasper, this is Detective-Inspector Malone. You were kind enough to help my daughter last night –'

'Mr Malone, it was nothing –' He had a light, very young voice with a slight accent.

'I'd like to talk to you –'

'I'm sorry, I'm leaving for the airport almost immediately. I'm flying out to Europe – Vienna, actually – I don't know that I can help any more than I have –'

'Mr Kasper, did you see the man who shot the kid who was trying to – to rape my daughter?'

'Well, yes.' Malone detected the reluctance; Kasper did not want to be called as witness in a murder trial. 'He ran right by me – I didn't realize at first what he'd done –'

'What did he look like?'

'Damn, I don't know –' He was eager to get off the phone. He had been a Good Samaritan last night, but that was last night. 'He was young, I guess – but maybe he wasn't. He had a big bushy beard – you know, the sort that academics and hippies wear –'

Malone wondered what profession Mr Kasper had, but wasn't going to ask. 'Can you remember if he still had the gun in his hand?'

'Jesus, yes!' He sounded startled, as if he had had a delayed reaction.

'Which hand? Can you remember?'

A pause; then: 'His left hand. Look, Mr Malone, I'm sorry, I really have to go –'

'Sure, Mr Kasper. You've been a great help – in more ways than one. Thanks and enjoy Vienna.'

He hung up and sat on the side of the bed for a few moments. The bed was still unmade and he had the sudden crazy impulse to crawl back into it and pull the covers up over his head. Then sanity returned: *Jesus, what's the matter with me?*

'You all right?' Lisa said from the doorway.

'I'm okay,' he said, recovering. 'I've just been thanking the feller who helped Maureen last night.'

'Did you thank his girlfriend?'

He hadn't even thought about her. 'No, I forgot.'

'Typical. Leave the number and I'll ring her—'

'No,' he said. 'The feller said they didn't want to become involved. They don't want to go into court any more than we do.'

He kissed her, went out and kissed his two daughters, squeezed Tom's shoulder and left the house, somehow with a feeling of escape. He said goodbye each morning in the same way, but this morning each kiss, each gesture, was a shade prolonged.

He did not drive to Strawberry Hills, but cut across town to the morgue out on Parramatta Road opposite Sydney University. As he went into the Institute of Forensic Medicine building he met Romy Clements.

'Hello, I thought Russ was joking when he said you were coming back to work so soon.'

'I come in just one morning a week, just to look at the paperwork.' He had always thought she had her own particular beauty but today there was a bloom to her. Motherhood, it seemed, became her. 'I have an ex-nurse looking after Amanda.'

'How is she?'

'Amanda? Looking more like me than her father, thank God.' She smiled; she had no vanity. 'Why are you here?'

He told her what had happened last night. She was visibly upset at what might have happened to Maureen; but: 'So why are you here?'

'To see the kid who was shot. He was the one with his dick out, he was going to be the first to rape her.'

'Jesus!' He knew she could be angry, but usually coldly so; he had never seen her like this. 'Come into my office. Sit down. *Sit down*, hear me? God Almighty, Scobie, what's the matter with you? This kid, whoever he is, he's dead. *Dead*. What the hell's the point of looking at him?'

'We're not going to lay charges against the other hoons, but I just want to see this one—'

'And I'm not going to let you!' She had not sat down but was leaning forward over her desk, temper flaring out of her. 'You are officially banned, you understand? And don't you dare mention to Lisa or Maureen that you came here, you hear?' Then she said something in German, the language harsh to his stranger's ear.

'What did you say?'

176

'I said, you've acted like a bloody idiot! But that's between you and me.' Her English sounded even harsher.

He tried to make a joke; 'Do they use the word *bloody* in German?'

'No,' she snapped, still on her feet. 'I used a good old Anglo-Saxon word that I never use when I'm speaking English. Don't be more idiotic by trying to joke.'

He was silent for a long moment, totally squashed; then he slowly stood up. It is one thing to be called an idiot; it is another to realize the truth of it. 'You're right. Okay, this is just between you and me?'

'Of course.' She softened just a little. 'I think Russ might have acted the same way if —' She came round her desk, paused and looked hard at him. He expected another blast, but then she kissed him on the cheek. 'I'll call Lisa now, but I shan't say you've been here.'

When he had gone she checked the Completed Bodies list, then went out to the body storage room. She found trolley number nine and the tag E51801 on the green plastic bag. She unzipped the bag and looked in at the thin bony youth who had tried to rape Maureen Malone. His head was completely shaven but for a long fringe hanging down over his forehead; he looked ridiculous, she thought, but he had been dangerous. He was the sort of animal that lay in the jungle years ahead of Amanda.

She zipped up the bag with a movement as savage as a knife slash.

3

Outside in his car Malone phoned Paddington police station.

'No, sir,' said the duty sergeant. 'They weren't held. Sergeant Noblett said just to take their names and addresses and let 'em go.' His tone implied he would have held them.

'Put the names and addresses on the fax and put them through to Homicide. I'll have a couple of my detectives go and talk to them.'

'Will do, sir. How's your daughter?' So George Noblett had let it be known why no charges were to be laid. Malone wondered if the duty sergeant was married, had children.

'She'll be okay, thanks.'

He put down the phone and sat for a while. He had been saved a second time from being a bloody idiot; had the three would-be rapists

177

been held he would have gone out to see them. They would have been charged at Paddington, then taken out to Waverley police station where they would have been held overnight. He would have gone out there and, before he could talk to them, would have had to face the patrol commander, a superintendent. He was newly promoted, had come from Murwillumbah in the north of the State, and Malone did not know him. There would have been the danger of another lecture, this time in more basic English than Romy had used.

He was aware of someone standing by the car's open window. 'Have you lost someone, sir?'

He was an old man, brown and gullied, bushy eyebrows sticking out like wire-grass above faded blue eyes. He was curious, even inquisitive, but it was curiosity born out of sympathy.

'I live just down there.' He nodded down the street. 'Every day I see people come here. Must be terrible for you, identifying your loved one. I say a prayer for each of you.'

Malone felt too weary of himself to identify himself. 'Thanks, dad. Say a couple for me.'

'You're very welcome.' He had an old-world politeness. 'I don't know if The Lord listens, but one always hopes. Do you believe?'

Malone waited for the tract or pamphlet to be produced, but there was none. He was no theologian and a philosopher only because of police experience, but by short-cuts down the back lanes of intelligence that are called commonsense he had arrived at the same reasoning as St Augustine, that doubt is an aspect of faith. A drunken priest whom he had once arrested had told him that.

'Now and again, dad. Take care.'

'You too, son. Always remember, the dead are the only ones with no regrets.'

He had heard that one before: death, it seemed, always produced more philosophy than birth. He hated the thought that the dead kid inside the morgue was better off than Maureen. He drove away, leaving the old man to his watch on the bereaved. He wondered why he had been mistaken for one of the bereaved.

Back at Strawberry Hills he sent for Kate Arletti. 'Kate, three names and addresses are on the fax —'

'I'm sorry to hear about what happened to Maureen. She okay?'

'Bruised and shaken up, but I think she'll be all right. These three kids, I want you and John to go out and talk to them, get their line on who the killer was —'

'Sir —' She was very formal, very neat in her dress this morning, all buttoned up. As if being interviewed for the first time. 'I'd rather not work with John Kagal.'

'Why not?'

'It's just personal.'

He sat back. Problems were falling on his desk like bird droppings on his car; he was used to them, but he didn't like them. Particularly this one, which he had been expecting. 'Care to talk about it?'

'I'd rather not.'

He had to protest, if only to disguise what he was guessing at: 'Kate, I can't run this office according to your personal problems. We have to work together.'

'I know that.' But she was stubborn. Hands in her lap, knees together, just as the nuns had taught her to do when dealing with men who did not understand.

Then, the relief in all cheap drama, the phone rang. He reached for it as for a lifebelt. 'Malone.'

'Scobie?'

'I've been expecting you.' He switched on the tape.

There was a moment's silence; then, with what could have been the chuckle again: 'Then you guessed?'

'Not a guess, Fred. We're familiar now with your MO.'

'Method of operation? You're smart, Scobie — I've never under-estimated you. But I did you a service, you know that, don't you?'

'You're wearing that line a bit thin. If you were an actor, you'd know.' It was a dangerous throw, but he risked it.

'Scobie —' He didn't take the bait; instead, he sounded aggrieved. 'Come off it, man. What would have happened to your daughter if I hadn't come along?'

'Why were you following her? How long have you been doing that?' He could feel the anger boiling up in him. 'Have you been following others in my family?'

'Don't get shitty with me.' There was no chuckling any more. 'No, last night was the first time. Fortuitous, wasn't it? I don't want to sound cruel, Scobie, but just think what would have happened if I hadn't been there.'

Malone had thought about it. 'You still haven't told me why you were following her.'

Opposite him Kate was frowning, as if she had forgotten about her own problems. She was motherly, perhaps it was the Italian in her. Thank Christ, thought Malone, she's decided not to mother John Kagal. Then he repeated his question to the killer, who, apparently, was looking for an answer.

'*Why* were you following her?'

'She's a pretty girl, Scobie.' He laughed. 'But don't misunderstand – I had no designs on her. Not like those other jerks. I should've shot them all. Have you arrested them?'

'They'll be charged.' He made the lie sound convincing.

'Then your daughter will have to go into court.' This time there was a clucking noise. 'That won't be a happy experience, Scobie. For you or her.'

'We know that.' He saw that the tape was running out. 'It won't be enjoyable, either, when she has to give evidence at the inquest on the kid you shot. You still haven't said why you were following her.'

'Oh, for Crissakes, I did you a service! Why can't you accept that? Why do you have to look for fucking reasons?'

The tape had almost run out. Malone said quietly, 'Fred, leave my family out of your public service.'

'Are you threatening me?' The angry, almost hysterical note had gone from his voice: he was as quiet as Malone. 'Don't do that, Scobie. You and I are on the same side.'

Then he hung up and Malone reached across and turned off the tape. Kate said, 'Why was he following Maureen?'

'I don't know.'

'He's getting scary now. I mean for you.'

'Yeah.' He was silent with his thoughts, which were scrambled. He put them aside, gave his attention to Kate again: one problem at a time. 'I'll talk about you and John some other time. For now, get Andy Graham and go out and trace those three kids, get what you can out of them. How do you get on with Andy?'

'It's like going out with an Airedale, I feel I should have him on a lead.' She sounded less uptight now. 'But he's okay. I can handle him.'

180

But she hadn't been able to handle John Kagal. 'Where's John now?'

'He's doing the rounds of the gay baths with Darren Beane.' She had got to her feet, abruptly sounding prim again.

'Better him than you and me.' It was the wrong thing to say: he could have bitten his tongue.

'Yes,' she said and went out of his office.

It was Idiots' Day. He thumped his desk, hurting his hand, and looked up to see Clements and Tilly Orbost in the doorway.

'He gets like this quite a lot.' Clements waited till Tilly had sat down opposite Malone, then he dropped on to the couch. He seemed more at ease, more accepting of her. Impending departure, like absence, can make the heart grow fonder. 'It's the Irish in him.'

'I've been recalled to Canberra,' she told Malone. 'I think I've done all I can to help here.'

Without comment he set the tape going, sat back while she and Clements listened to it. Out in the main room John Kagal had returned, was sitting at his desk and seemingly ignoring Kate three desks away. The tape finished and Clements switched it off.

'So it was him who saved Maureen?'

Malone gave him a hard stare and Clements waved an apologetic hand.

'Sorry. I didn't mean that the way . . .' He trailed off, looked at Tilly Orbost. 'What d'you reckon?'

'He's starting to fray at the edges,' she said. 'You're getting to him, Scobie.'

'I don't know that I want to get *to* him —'

'He's going to slip up — soon rather than later, I'd say. But he didn't react when you slipped in that bit about him being an actor. I thought that might've got a reaction . . . The thing is, you've become important to him.'

'A father figure?' said Clements.

'If you like. He wants approval and he's chosen Scobie.'

'I'm glad you're going back to Canberra,' said Malone. 'You'll have me adopting him next.'

Tilly smiled. 'That might not be a bad idea. Suggest it next time he calls.' She reached into her briefcase, handed him a folder. 'There's my report. I've sent a copy to Superintendent Random. Let me know how things turn out.'

'If I don't adopt him, what'll he do?'

She stood up. 'He might turn the gun on you.'

Clements, too, had stood up. 'She's a real comfort, isn't she?'

She looked at both of them. 'You wouldn't want it any other way, would you?'

Both knew the truth of that. Clements bit his lip, then nodded. 'I'll get a car for you,' he said and went out of the room.

Malone stood up. 'Thanks for all your help, Tilly.'

'I know how it must have been when I first arrived. But I felt you were on my side. Was I right?'

He nodded. 'Yes, but you were on trial. It'd be the same if I came to Canberra, down there in the Hub of the Universe ... Maybe I shouldn't ask – how did it go with Garry Peeples?'

She smiled. 'Do you mean was I on trial there?'

'Of course not!' Or had his tongue slipped again?

'He's a nice man, but that's all – *nice*. It was what do they call it? An interlude. That sounds better than what you men would call it.'

His tongue showed some sense: it didn't ask if there was a man in Canberra: some lonely politician far from home and family. Or a senior Federal Police officer with enough silver braid to dazzle a girl. 'Good luck, Tilly. Don't ever be out-ranked.'

She looked at him with amusement for a moment, then she came round his desk and kissed him. Out in the main room Kate Arletti and Gail Lee clapped. 'Good luck, Scobie. But, as I've heard you say – take care.'

Then she left, waving to everyone in the main room as she headed towards the security door. Malone, though he was a republican, thought she looked queenly. His mood lightened. Till he scanned the room and saw John Kagal looking at him. He raised a beckoning finger.

As Kagal got up from his desk, Kate Arletti and Andy Graham went out of the security door after Tilly Orbost. Kagal and Kate did not look at each other; each might have been only a vacant space in the room. Kagal hesitated, then came into Malone's office.

'How'd it go around the baths?'

182

'Nothing.' Kagal sat down, a little stiffly; there was none of his usual quietly arrogant ease. 'If anyone knows anything, or guesses anything, they're not telling.'

'What about Darren Beane?'

'What about him?'

Don't be difficult, son; we haven't reached the difficult part yet. 'He's sympathetic to the killer.'

'He hasn't said anything to me.'

He sounded like the sort of cop the royal commission was investigating: hear no evil, see no evil, speak no good. But Malone, though he was no fisherman and hated to cook, had another fish to fry: 'Kate tells me she doesn't want to work with you.'

Kagal shifted stiffly in his chair. He was wearing a double-breasted suit and he hadn't unbuttoned it as he usually did; he looked encased. 'She hasn't said anything to me.'

Malone kept his temper. 'Well, she has to me. What happened between you two?'

'With respect, I don't think that is any of your business.'

'Oh, you're wrong there, John.' He was surprised at how he was holding in his temper. 'If it disrupts this office, makes Russ change the manning, then it is very much my business. Has she found out you're double-gaited?'

After some hesitation: 'Yes.'

'Who told her? You or someone else?'

'I did.'

'Well, I'm glad you were honest with her.' Though he wondered how any man could divulge something like that to a woman. He was learning the many layers of sophistication, if that was what one could call it.

'She didn't appreciate it.'

'I'm not surprised. You thought she'd be more understanding?' Kagal nodded and Malone wondered at the younger man's sophistication in understanding women. He went on, 'Are you in love with her?'

'Oh, for Crissake! What is this, a confessional?' He undid his buttons, burst out of his stiffness.

'Don't lose your temper with me.' Surprised that his own temper was still under control; and proud, too. Or anyway, Lisa would have been proud. 'If it's as deep as that, then you can't work together and you can't stay in this office together. One of you will have to transfer.'

'You mean it'd be okay if I'd said no, it was just an office affair?'

'No, I'm not saying that. I don't know how Kate feels about you.'

Kagal had cooled down. He was not normally given to nervous habits, but now he folded his hands together and twiddled his thumbs, looking at them as if puzzled by the meaninglessness of the gesture.

'Unfortunately,' he said at last, 'she is serious.'

Malone looked for smugness, which he expected; but there was none. Whatever else he was, Kagal was not a bastard. 'Righto, then I'll have to have another talk with her. I don't want to lose either of you, if it can be avoided.'

'She's a good detective.' He had stopped twiddling his thumbs.

'So are you. Righto, leave it with me.'

'Am I still on this case, then?'

'Do you want to see it through, bring this feller in?'

'Yes. I think I'm like you – to me, he's a killer, that's all. Not an avenger or anything else.'

'Not a public servant?'

'No.'

'You're still on the case.' He couldn't see himself doing the rounds of the gay baths with Darren Beane. But what was he afraid of? Too much sophistication?

When Kagal had gone back to his desk Malone sat on staring out of the window at nothing, trying to think of nothing. The threat that the killer might turn his gun on him was a worry: not for himself but for what it might mean to Lisa and the children. He was no braver than the next man and he certainly had never suffered from bravado; but he was a fatalist and somehow the odds always seemed to favour them. Then the phone rang.

It was Greg Random: 'What are you doing for lunch?'

He looked in his desk drawer: 'Two salad sandwiches, two peaches and a glass of non-fat milk to come.'

'I can do you better than that. Machiavelli in Clarence Street. One o'clock.'

'Why here?' said Malone.

'Because if two commissioned police officers were seen having lunch in some out-of-the-way place, like a motel restaurant in the outer suburbs, there'd be instant suspicion. The commission is turning us into honest cops by default.'

'Who's paying for lunch?'

'It's off expenses. I'll put it down to interviewing a reliable source of information.'

'Is that what I am?'

The Machiavelli restaurant was in a large basement in the heart of the business district. Back in the early days of the colony the military barracks were in the next street; here in Clarence Street the wives of the soldiers had lived in huts on one side of the dirt road and the whores, not yet called hookers, had worked the other side. The whores, like the soldiers and their wives, had long gone, but whoredom, under other names, still flourished in the neighbourhood.

If the author of *The Prince* had been amongst the waiters he would have picked up enough footnotes to have produced another volume. Politicians, political minders, political columnists: they all came here. Intrigue, or what passed for it, was as thick as the minestrone. The Florentine had proposed his set of rules almost five centuries ago and politicians, supplanting princes, had embellished the rules, if they had not refined them. Someone had once said that the end of the line was Tammany Hall in New York, but their view had been too narrow and short-sighted. They should have looked to the other end of the world. Anyone in this restaurant would have been pleased to add an addendum. Including the two police officers at the corner table.

While they studied the menu, with an impatient waiter hovering by like a magpie in the nesting season, Random said, 'How's your daughter?'

'She'll be okay.' Malone gave his order to the waiter, waited till Random had done the same, then said, 'Is that why I'm on a free lunch?'

'Ease off, Scobie. I haven't brought my rank to the table.'

'Sorry. Russ tells me I've had shit on the liver for the past week or so.'

'The gay case getting you down?'

The restaurant was noisy, ideal for drowning secrets. Random, who was in mufti rather than his silver braid, knew that he and Malone had been recognized as soon as they had sat down. The royal commission had made police an endangered species; the hunters were out in force. Eye-strain and ear-strain were endemic here; but the big room was awash with secrets, gossip, false information, and, unless there were lip-readers amongst the diners or waiters, Random knew that whatever he and Malone discussed would be safe.

Malone nodded. 'It's not as cut and dried as I like a case to be.'

'That sort come along now and again. Is the killer still calling you? What's he saying now?'

Malone hesitated; but Random was a friend as well as his superior officer. 'You know he thinks he's doing a public service?'

'I've read the summary of the tapes.'

'He called again this morning. He said that last night he did *me* a service.'

Random broke a bread roll, chewed on a piece of it. '*That's* why we're here. I'm taking you off the case, Scobie.'

Malone also chewed, but on his cud; then he shook his head. 'No, Greg, I know this bloke better than anyone else. Have you read Tilly Orbost's report?'

'Yes.'

Malone waited till the waiter had put their first course down in front of them and then quick-stepped away. 'There should have been a P.S. on it. She listened to this morning's tape, then told me I've become a father figure to him.'

'You think that should impress me?'

'I don't care whether it does or not, Greg. I don't think he's going to talk to Russ or anyone else the way he talks to me.'

'Scobie, it's become too *personal* for you. He saved your daughter from rape, maybe saved her life. You're in his debt. Like he said, he's done you a service.'

The antipasto, through no fault of the chef, had lost its taste. 'I admit all that. But it doesn't mean I'm giving up on bringing him in. He's a killer, Greg, that's all he is in my book.'

'I'd like to believe that —' Random picked at his fettucini.

'Give me credit, Greg —'

'I'm doing that. Giving you credit as a father as well as a cop. And that's my problem. And yours, too.'

The food was good, but Malone was beginning to wish that Random had called on him out at Strawberry Hills. He could have argued more forcibly there; but perhaps that was why Random had chosen here. Yet Random was not Machiavellian, he was just a decent cop who was also a father.

Then Grace Ditcham, snatching a chair from a neighbouring table, was sitting with them. 'You don't have to buy me lunch, gentlemen. I've eaten.'

'Whom?' said Malone.

She was the best crime reporter in the State, the sort that one paper poached from another; she had more sources than a mountain stream. She was blonde, short and attractive, though too many days on the beach had begun to shrivel her edges; fifteen years of crime reporting had also shrivelled her emotions. But she still had a pleasant smile for those she liked and Malone was one of them.

'I've been watching you two — you don't look happy. Are we talking royal commission and more cops about to roll over?'

'We're talking Christmas greetings,' said Random.

'This early? Come on, Greg. Off the record . . .' She put on her expectant look, though it was fake.

'Grace,' said Random, 'the last time I told a reporter something off the record, it was a headline the next day.'

'Not me. I shan't tell a soul —'

'Grace, I don't think you know anyone who has a soul —'

'Watch out,' said Malone. 'Her husband is a part-time wrestler. We've got nothing for you, Grace, that's the truth.'

'What about this serial killer you're working on? Did he do last night's murder at Bondi Junction?'

Malone hesitated, then nodded. 'He might have.'

'Was it another gay bashing?'

So she didn't know Maureen had been involved. 'We think so. Whoever it was got up and ran.' Which was part of the truth.

'Are you any closer to nabbing this guy?'

'Quote, the police are hopeful of an early arrest, unquote.'

She gave him a tired smile and looked back at Random. 'You guys sound like trained seals at times. I dunno why I love you all so much.' She stood up and instantly had her chair snatched from under her by a waiter. 'I'm covering the commission. I sit there some days and weep for the honest cops.'

Random softened. 'Grace, I promise you – when the breakthrough comes on the serial killer, you'll be the first Scobie will call.' He looked at Malone. 'Right?'

Malone nodded. Sometimes the media, especially the television reporters, could be a pain in the arse; but Grace Ditcham had always played fair and sometimes been a help.

She leaned forward, grinned, then straightened up. 'I was about to kiss you, Greg. Think of what Judge Wood would make of that.' Justice Wood was the royal commissioner. 'Ring me any time, Scobie. Even if I'm home in bed with the part-time wrestler.'

When she had gone, a hundred pairs of eyes following her as if digitally produced, Malone said, 'So I'm still on the case?'

'You have another week, that's all. By that time it's sure to have leaked that your daughter was the one who got up and ran away last night.'

The main course, miraculously, was suddenly full of taste. 'Thanks, Greg. I just hope a week is enough. I'll do my best.'

'A prince should also show himself a lover of excellence by giving preference to gifted men.'

'Let me guess. Another Welsh poet?'

Chapter Ten

1

Les Coulson, all laired up for Saturday night, was unhappy. He had had a haircut, told the barber to go easy on the sideburns; he had noticed they were coming back into fashion. He had put on a button-down shirt instead of the usual T-shirt; new chinos; and had kicked off the Air-Maxes to put on leather-soled loafers. He looked almost – what was that old-fashioned description – Ivy League?

He wasn't sure whom he was out to impress; certainly not Stefanopolous and the others. He had met them and the night had immediately started to turn to shit. He had drunk two stiff vodkas, which he didn't like but which he could not refuse: he had to match everyone, including the one-bottle screamers. A leader, the politicians were always saying, had to prove himself. Vision, they said, that was what was needed. It was bullshit, of course, but that was the way of the world nowadays. He occasionally paid enough attention in the lectures at university to know that history itself was bullshit, always the victors' version of things; he had never bothered to look up who had said that but he knew it was true. He could never see himself as a victor, not the way his life was going. What was he? Leader of a gang of semi-morons? He hated them, he hated the world and, worst of all, he was beginning to hate himself. Not for what he had been or done, but for what he wasn't going to be and wasn't going to do. Under his arrogance and apparent self-confidence he had found someone he had long suspected: a no-hoper, lazy, unambitious, getting by because he had more brains than those who surrounded him.

The vodka had made him sick and he had left the guys on a pretext that he had a date, gone to a back lane and vomited. Then he had gone to the dance along King Street, taking on the old swagger, John Travolta in *Saturday Night Fever*, the video of which he had run at least half a dozen times. He was light on his feet, he had rhythm and, if he had to say it himself, he wasn't bad-looking. But it wasn't his night: Saturday Night fever was no more than a bad cold.

He tried his luck with a goodlooking blonde who had invitation written all over her. She turned out to be a bikie's girlfriend and the bikie and two of his mates had loomed up like a trio of strays from *Mad Max*. He had escaped just in time from having a chain wrapped round his skull. He had come out of the dance hall and wandered along the busy narrow street. Once upon a time, long before his time, Newtown had been a typical Australian working-class inner suburb. British and Irish descendants who worked in the railway sheds at nearby Eveleigh, as gangers and fettlers on the railways, as labourers for the Water Board; there had been white-collars amongst the blue-collars, but most of them had worked as clerks in the Public Service. The only wogs had been Italians running fruit-and-vegetable shops; the only Chink had run a café that served reputable Aussie dishes such as steak-and-eggs and, for the occasional gourmet or drunk, dim sums. Now, you couldn't move for bloody ethnics: the line ran from China right across the Middle East and down to South America. A racist like himself, and proud of it, was a stranger in his own country. He had idly thought, once or twice, of shaving his head and joining the National Action Group, who had a shop-front office about half a k down this street. The Nazi salute was a real macho gesture, not like the poofter salute the Army demanded.

He passed a coffee lounge, run, of course, by a wog. He stopped, looked in and saw Jillian Langtry sitting by herself in a booth. Without thinking, lured by the smell of the coffee, he went in and sat down opposite her in the booth.

'Hi.' He had always felt uneasy with her, as if she knew that behind that plain face of hers she had as many brains as he did. He had felt more uneasy with her since Justin had been shot by that fucking maniac.

She took her time acknowledging him. She ate a small piece of Danish pastry, sipped her cappuccino. Then she said, looking around her, 'What are you doing in here? Gunna cause more trouble?'

He frowned, wondering what she meant; the last thing he wanted tonight was trouble. Then he looked around and saw where he was. He picked up the menu, looked at the name at the top and shook his head at his stupidity. The Isle of Lesbos was not a coffee lounge where Bruce Willis would be a pin-up nor Henry VIII a favourite even amongst monarchist dykes.

He leaned forward, whispering, 'What are *you* doing here? Are you a dyke?'

A small smile played round the edges of her mouth. She leaned forward and whispered, 'What if I am? You gunna bash me?'

Two girls stopped by the booth and he looked up. One of them was a real butch dyke, the other not a bad sort at all. The butch one gave him a look that would have cut his balls off if they hadn't been hidden beneath the booth table; he knew at once that she had recognized him, the leader of a gang that bashed up gays. Then she said to Jillian, 'He giving you any trouble, Jill?'

'Nah. He's reformed, he's just been telling me.' Jillian was sitting back, amused. 'He's gunna take me to hear Melissa Etheridge, ain't you, Les?'

He was in enemy territory, even if they were only dykes. 'Yeah, sure. Melissa Whatever-her-name-is, k.d. lang, Snow White and the fucking Dwarfs.'

The three girls smiled at each other and the butch one said, 'I didn't know Snow White was one of us. Watch out for him, Jill. If he doesn't like Melissa, kick him in the balls. It never misses changing a guy's mind.'

They went on out of the coffee lounge, but their stopping by the booth had caused interest. The place was almost full: all women except for two guys, slightly older than himself, and they looked gay. He suddenly wished for the bikies to burst in, even if they came looking for him. When they recognized where they were, they might go to work on the poofters and the dykes first. He was angry but, to his surprise, helpless.

The proprietor's wife, middleaged and stout with dark poached eyes that had seen everything, appeared beside the booth. 'You wanna order?'

She could have been double-gaited: right now she sounded like the leader of the pack in a dykes' football team. He thought he had better order: 'A cappuccino and a lamington.'

'A lamington?' She was from Salerno; she didn't even understand why some pastries were called Danish. 'Wassat?'

191

What the hell had made him order the Australian national cake in a wog dyke café? He was nervous, that's what: maybe he should have ordered a lady's finger? 'Okay, I'll have one of those she's got. A Danish.'

'Apple, peach or raisin?'

She's standing over me. Around the broad edges of her he could see the women in the other booths grinning like monkeys. He looked for the proprietor, but he was hidden behind the counter, only the top of his head showing: was she married to a midget? Opposite him Jillian was still smiling, still mocking him. When he had sat down here he had felt years older than her; abruptly the situation had been reversed and he didn't know how it had happened. He tried a smile on the big woman standing over him, but he might just as well tried smiling at Godzilla's mother.

'Apple.'

The woman went away and he looked back at Jillian. '*Are* you a dyke?'

'No. But I like their company. It's a bloody sight better than you and your crappy mates.'

He wasn't going to answer that; he had no answer, not here. 'How's your mum?'

'How d'you think she'd be? She's fucking near outa her mind.' They were still low-voiced, only just above a whisper, but she was hoarse with sudden anger. 'Jesus, Les, when are you gunna grow up? You're the one with brains – Justin was always telling me how bright you were . . .' She gulped at her cappuccino, wiped the froth from her mouth with the back of her hand, smearing her lipstick. 'I dunno why I'm sitting here talking to you –'

'I dunno why I'm here, either.' It was a confession, not a jab at her.

She seemed to sense that he was not all antagonism. Taking her time to change gears, she took out a small compact and repaired her lipstick. He watched her, thinking: Is she ever going to make it, have a guy really interested in her? Is she here in this dykes' retreat on a Saturday night because she has nowhere else to go? He was surprised at the pity he suddenly felt for her. He had felt pity, an unfamiliar emotion, when he had looked down at the dead Justin, but that had been different.

She was not aware of his pity, did not need it. She closed the compact and it was impossible to tell whether she was satisfied or sad at what the mirror had shown her. 'What're you studying at uni?'

That also surprised him, that she should ask such a question. 'Arts. History is my main subject.'

She looked at him: with pity? 'What the fuck's the good of that? You think kids are interested in history today? You oughta be studying, I dunno, economics, computers, stuff like that. Jesus, if I had your brains, that's what I'd be doing. You're a dead loss, Les, you know that?'

'I know it.' More confession.

The proprietor's wife brought him his coffee and pastry. 'No apple. You like raisin?'

He'd better. 'Sure, it's okay. Thanks.' Then he gave his attention to Jillian again. 'Maybe in the new year I'll change.'

She watched him while he ate the pastry and drank his coffee. Out in the street a small horde of bikies rode past, the thrum-thrum of their Harleys like a war-cry. The women in the lounge turned their heads, then looked back at each other and sneered. Macho men: who needed them? Some of the women looked across at him, but he kept his eyes on Jillian. It sourly amused him that she had become his protection in here.

'I hope so, Les, for your sake. But I dunno – I don't think you ever will.'

'And you?' For a moment his natural nastiness re-surfaced. 'What're you gunna be?'

'I dunno. A fucked-up suicide, maybe.'

He frowned, paused with the cup halfway to his mouth. 'Jesus, don't talk like that!'

She smiled again, a very old smile. 'That's all it is, Les – talk. I'd never lay that on my mother, not while she's got – You know about my sister?'

'Yeah, Justin told me once. I'm sorry – for your mum, I mean.'

'Yeah . . .' She sat a while, then abruptly gathered up her handbag. 'I'm going home.'

The words were out of his mouth before he had thought about them: 'You want me to see you home?'

She had looked old for the past few moments; now surprise made

193

her look young again. 'Yeah. Yeah, that'd be nice. Mum's always scared for me these days—'

He paid both their bills, even leaving a tip to impress the dykes. He walked out of the Isle of Lesbos after Jillian. He could feel the stares in his back: he was a dartboard. Outside on the crowded pavement he said, 'I'm lucky to get outa there alive.'

'Lesbians ain't man-eaters. It's the nymphos you gotta watch out for.'

He grinned. 'Don't tell me you're one of those?'

She was incapable of flirting; she was too down-to-earth, knee-deep in matters of fact. 'No. Bad luck.'

Now they were out in the street, away from the menace of the dykes, he regretted he had volunteered to see her home. But, he guessed, he owed it to Justin: he had been the least moronic of the semi-morons. She was nothing to look at, but at least she wasn't a semi-moron.

They hardly spoke as they turned out of King Street and walked down Erskineville Road. He was awkward with her, a condition that usually didn't affect him when he was with girls. He was no Lothario, whoever he was, but girls responded to him. He had been screwing girls since he was fourteen and he guessed he was lucky he hadn't picked up fucking HIV; he was lucky, too, he hadn't picked up love. Not that he ever thought about it and he wondered if Jillian ever did. But he wasn't going to ask her.

'You don't like me, do you?' It was out of character for him to ask a leading question like that, but he couldn't get into step with her.

She stopped dead under a street-light and looked at him. 'Les, do you really care what I think of you? Honest?'

He was honest: 'Well, no, I guess I don't care what anyone thinks of me. It's what you think of yourself that counts.'

She was still not moving. 'Then why do you care what I think of you?'

'I dunno. Maybe because of what happened to Justin.'

'I'm glad you're starting to feel guilty about that.'

He wasn't feeling *guilty*; but he had the sense to say nothing.

She began to walk on. 'What do your parents think of you? I dunno nothing about them. What does your dad do?'

194

'He manages a service station. All he cares about is the up-and-down price of petrol. His idea of Hell is the boardroom of Shell. He thinks they meet every week just to persecute him.'

They had turned off Erskineville Road, reached the front door of Number twelve Billyard Street. She stood on the narrow front porch, the spiked gate between them, and looked at him with eyes far older than his. Behind her lay her own Hell, one she could never leave, not while her mother and Jasmine were still alive.

'It's a pity,' she said, 'that you're such a fucking idiot.'

Then she had turned and gone inside before he could whip up a reply. Jesus, he thought, where does she get off with an opinion like that? He stepped back into the roadway, looked up at the dilapidated house, dark and blank-faced. He wanted to shout at her – but what was there to say?

Then a quiet voice behind him said, 'It's in cold blood this time.'

He turned. A young guy stood there, dark-haired, wearing horn-rimmed glasses. He raised his left hand; in it was a gun with a silencer. Les Coulson tried to say something, but all he could manage was a gurgling in his throat, like a death rattle.

The killer steadied his left hand with his right, then he fired the gun.

2

The Malones had been to Mass as a family. Nothing was said, but it was understood that it was in joint thanks for Maureen's escape last Monday night. Whether God listened was neither here nor there, as far as Malone was concerned: Maureen was safe and that was all that mattered. He did not have much confidence in God's all-encompassing ear. The air was loud with prayers from other parts of the world: Bosnia, Rwanda, Chechnya.

As they approached the Fairlane his pager beeped. Instantly there was a moan of disgust from the family. He opened the car door, picked up the phone and dialled Russ Clements at home.

'This had better be good – Lisa and the kids have their knives out –'

'We had another one last night,' said Clements. 'The kid Les Coulson.'

'Coulson?' He frowned. Parishioners streamed by him, shining, if dully, with piety; sin was on the back-burner. 'Was he bashing another gay?'

'No. He'd just taken home the sister of the Langtry kid who was shot. It happened right outside her house.'

'Did she see it?'

'Not as far as I know. I'll meet you there – I've told Kate Arletti to be there. You still coming to our place for lunch?'

Malone took the family home. 'I'll be back to pick you up, noon at the latest. You coming to the lunch, Claire?'

'Sure. I'm bringing Jason.'

Jason Rockne's mother was doing life for the murder of Jason's father. Jesus, thought Malone, I'm surrounded by murder. But Claire and the Rockne boy had been teenage sweethearts and, though they had drifted apart over the past year, if they were together again, no matter how temporarily, he would have to accept it. He always dodged the issue of his daughters' friends, leaving it to Lisa. He hoped he would not be so cowardly if and when he had to pass judgement on some friend of Tom's.

'You bringing anyone, Mo?'

She had recovered from last Monday night; or at least on the surface. What trauma lay behind her smile he had no way of guessing. 'I'm bringing a really nice guy, Luther.'

Whatever had happened to Mick and Clarrie and Ned, names that had slipped off the tongue so easily? 'Does he nail proclamations to church doors?'

'I don't know. You can ask him.'

'Tom?'

'I rang Pamela Anderson, but she's having her boobs polished.'

'You're too gross,' his sisters told him.

Malone looked at Lisa and she said, 'I'll settle for you. But you'd better be on time or –' She ran a finger across her throat.

He left them and drove across town to Erskineville. He drove unhurriedly but without that intention; he was halfway to Billyard Street before he realized his reluctance. When he reached the short narrow street it was blocked off by police cars. Crime Scene tapes stretched across the road in front of Number twelve, but the Physical Evidence team had come and gone. Kate Arletti was there and so was Irving Rubens, a detective-sergeant from the Newtown station.

'G'day, Irv. What've you got?'

Irv Rubens was one of the few Jews in the Service, an overweight goodlooking man with a Jewish sense of irony and a total lack of interest in things Semitic. Not out of a sense of protection against anti-Semites, of which there were a number in the Service and many more in the criminal classes, but because he had decided long ago that religion and race meant little to him. The other side of the coin, which he remarked with wry amusement, was that as soon as he mentioned his name other ethnics were instantly wary of him.

'It happened about eleven-thirty last night.' He had a deep voice with gravel in it: ideal for questioning reluctant suspects. 'One bullet, right through the heart – the bullet's still in him. No one heard the shot, so we presume the killer used a silencer. You know who the deceased is? Was?'

Malone nodded. 'Russ Clements told me.'

At both ends of the street a small crowd had gathered: Sunday spectators. Rubens looked around, then beckoned to a youth in the front row of the crowd at the north end of the street. He came forward hesitantly: it was Steve Stefanopolous.

'Mr Stefanopolous was a mate –'

'Hello, Steve,' said Malone. 'Did you expect this? What happened to Les?'

'Shit, no!' He looked ready to run. 'He was with us last night for a while, then he went off on his own . . .' He frowned, his thin face pinched into lines. 'You think the same guy done it, the one killed Justin?'

'I'd think so, wouldn't you? I think you'd better make yourself scarce for a while, Steve. You and your other mates, the ones who bashed up the gay. Go bush, go fruit-picking or something. Go up to Queensland, to Cape York – the further the better. I'd start now, Steve, or you might be next.'

He kicked at the chalked outline where Les Coulson's body had lain. He was being theatrical, he knew that, but anyone connected with Les Coulson angered him. They had no right to be in this street, outside the Langtry house.

Stefanopolous looked down at the chalk marks, then abruptly he

197

scurried away, already in his mind halfway to the bush, to Cape York, to anywhere.

'I was waiting for you to kick him up the arse,' said Rubens.

'I would have, but there are too many spectators.'

Then Clements arrived, casual in a green polo shirt, off-white moleskins and Reeboks. 'Who found him?'

Kate Arletti had been standing in the background. She, too, was casual: pale blue slacks, dark blue shirt and blue-and-white boat shoes. Her blonde hair was pulled back and tied with a blue bow. Malone, though he was in slacks and an open-necked shirt, felt over-dressed in his blazer. Irv Rubens, in a grey suit, looked to be the only one on duty.

Kate said, 'Jillian Langtry found him.' She nodded at the upper storey of Number twelve. 'He brought her home, they'd met in some coffee lounge up in King Street. They said goodnight, she went upstairs to bed – she sleeps in the sleep-out on that balcony there. She said she was about to get undressed, when she looked out and he was lying in the middle of the road.' She gestured at the chalked outline.

'She see the killer?'

'No. At first she thought Coulson was putting on some sort of act – she said she'd called him a –' she cleared her throat '– a fucking idiot before she closed the door in his face. Then she saw he wasn't moving . . . She came downstairs, came out, had a look and saw he was dead. Then she ran next door – her mum doesn't have a phone – and they called the police.'

'A patrol car got here about five minutes after the call,' said Rubens. 'I didn't come on the job till eight this morning.'

'You interviewed the girl?'

'Not yet. I left it to Constable Arletti, for the time being. I gather she's pretty upset.'

Malone looked at the house, as close to demolition as the lives inside it. Paint hung down like staghorns from its front; the front door was a running sore. The one window on the ground floor, half-boarded up, had had graffiti scrawled on the boards since he had last been here: nothing legible, just a scrawl that could have been a hex.

'Righto,' he said and felt as if he were trying to lift a heavy weight, 'we'd better go in and talk to her. You and me, Kate.'

She looked reluctant but said, 'Yes.'

Jillian opened the door to their knock. She looked washed-out, pain painted on her plain face. 'Shit,' she said, 'can't you leave us alone? My mum is going outa her mind –'

'We shan't come in,' said Malone, glad of the excuse; he was ashamed of why he wanted to retreat from misery. 'We'll stay out here, just one or two questions, Jill.'

'What else've I got to tell? I seen him lying there –' She nodded towards the middle of the road. Then she said, frowning a little, 'When're they gunna rub out that chalk-mark? Kelly come out here this morning, stood here asking what it was for. Am I supposed to tell him, a little kid?'

'I'll get them to wash it out before we go,' said Malone. 'I understand you came home with Les Coulson. Was there anyone following you?'

'I didn't see no one. If there was and I seen him, you think I'd identify him? Forget it.' She had the cynicism of despair. 'He'd come back and do me.'

'I don't think he's that sort of killer.'

The bright intelligence of her eyes sometimes took the plainness from her face. 'Are you sticking up for him?'

Even Kate had looked startled at what he had said. He did not look at her as he said, 'No, I'm not. But –' Then he ran out of reasons why the killer would not come back and kill again. It suddenly hit him that this latest murder had been done in cold blood. All at once he wished Tilly Orbost was around to offer advice: the profile, like a sketch under water, had changed. 'I'll tell the police not to trouble you and your mother any more, Jill. Just be careful, right?'

'You gunna gimme protection, just in case?' She sounded ironic.

'If you want it –'

She shook her head. 'Nah, don't bother. Just go away and leave us alone. I know you're trying to be helpful, Mr Malone, you're just doing your job . . .' She stopped. Somewhere in the back of the house there was a whimpering sound, of someone in pain. Without turning her head she called back into the dark hallway: 'I'm coming, Jasmine . . . Leave us alone. Mum and my sister don't want any reminders, okay?'

Then she stepped back and closed the door in their faces.

Malone turned away, not looking at Kate. She moved away from him, put her hand to her eyes. Clements and Rubens stood in the middle of the roadway, one on either side of the chalked outline of Les Coulson, like pallbearers ready to lift a ghost. In the background the uniformed police were holding back the silent, curious neighbours. The quietness was palpable, as if everyone had heard Jillian's plea to be left alone.

Malone walked towards Clements and Rubens. 'Get that chalk washed off at once, Irv. Take down the tapes, keep your men, a couple of them, here for an hour or so, see that nobody goes knocking on that door. Have you talked to the dead kid's parents?'

Rubens nodded. 'I saw them an hour ago. The mother's hysterical – she won't even believe that her loving son actually beat up gays. The father – I dunno. It's almost like he's been expecting it. I gather he didn't have much time for the loving son.'

'We are the ones who should of been expecting it,' said Clements.

There was no denying that and Malone wondered why he had ignored the possibility. He had become too close to The Voice, he had fallen into the trap of trusting it. It happens to police as well as to soldiers. The enemy becomes a relative.

'He could start on the others,' said Clements, belabouring the point without realizing it; he's telling me how to do my job, thought Malone. And he's right. 'We better start warning them. The Bristow kid – he might come back to finish the job there. The Hindle kid. What about the Tongans?'

'Tongans?' said Rubens. 'How many have you got mixed up in these cases?'

'Too many,' said Clements. 'We seem to be breeding a new class. One time they used to bash up drunks and women, now they put the boot into gays. You look at the charge-list, it runs right across the spectrum – you can't leave poofter-bashing out of multiculturism. The only ones missing are the Asians. They're too busy running drugs.' One mustn't forget one's prejudices.

Malone had forgotten the Tongans, the ones who had bashed up Billie Cork, the drag queen. The cast of a murder, in this case several murders, didn't always have speaking parts. The Tongans had been almost no more than walk-on characters; they had walked on and off and he had never even seen them. 'Are they still on remand out at the Bay?'

'Could be.' Clements had his own lot to remember; the file room back at Homicide was jam-packed with names and evidence. Since he had become Supervisor he had discovered how thick was the undergrowth of paper; if he had had his way, he would have invited the Greens in for an orgy of re-cycling. 'I'll check. If they're still out at the Bay, they're safe.'

'Who's safe at the Bay?' said Rubens. 'Pack rape is part of the afternoon sports.'

'Would you rape a couple of six-foot-three, sixteen-stone Tongans?'

'No,' said Rubens. 'But I'm celibate.'

'Well, the killer's not gunna get into the Bay to take a shot at them. It's the others we gotta worry about.'

'I'll call Judge Bristow now,' said Malone. 'You want to come with me?'

'I've gotta go home,' said Clements. 'We've got a lunch party on, remember?'

'A lunch party?' said Rubens.

'My wife's German. She wouldn't have a bar of a barbecue.'

'Geez, you're a social lot in Homicide, aren't you? Us working Ds don't get to lunch parties.'

'What about bar mitzvahs?'

'I didn't even go to my own. Okay, I'll clean up here. Enjoy your lunch party.' Then he looked at Malone. 'Enjoy Judge Bristow.'

'You know him?'

'I was a bit sloppy one time with evidence. He circumcized me in open court. Very painful.'

'He's not going to enjoy what I'm going to suggest to him.'

Malone walked back to his car, called Kate over to him. She had recovered, had even surreptitiously applied some make-up; if she had wept as she had turned away from the Langtry house, there was no sign of it now. She had pulled herself together, even had all her buttons done up.

'Judge Bristow and Dr Hindle – have you got their home phone numbers?'

He was not surprised when she read them out of her notebook;

201

like Clements, she was a grab-bag of miscellany. She was too good to lose: he would have to find some way of keeping her in Homicide. 'How'd you get out here?'

'In the Goggomobile – I came straight here from home, soon's I got the call.' She pointed up towards the end of the street, where the tiny car glistened in the sun like a giant soap bubble, where half a dozen kids clustered around it, poking at it with their fingers as if trying to burst it. 'You want me to come with you?'

'No, this won't take long.' He hoped not. He wanted his message to be to the point and the point taken. 'Go home. Let Irv Rubens handle it today. We'll take it up tomorrow. And Kate –'

She had been about to walk away, but turned back.

'Kate, never be afraid to weep in front of me.'

She stared at him, then she nodded. 'Thanks.'

He got into his car, called the Bristow home out at Bellevue Hill. 'Judge, I think I'd better come and see you ... No, *now* ... I'll be there in fifteen, twenty minutes. What's the address?'

He hung up, dialled the Hindle number. A girl answered: 'No, I'm the maid. Dr and Mrs Hindle are down on their boat ... Rushcutters Bay, at the Cruising Yacht Club. Do you want their mobile number?'

Malone rang the Hindles' mobile number, got the doctor himself. 'I'll be there in half an hour at the outside, Dr Hindle –'

'I'm sorry, Inspector, but my wife and I are taking people out for a picnic –'

'I'm sorry about that, Doctor, but if you don't listen to me, you may find yourself in for another sort of picnic altogether. Judge Bristow will be coming to meet me there. If you have any guests on board your boat I suggest you get rid of them for half an hour ... This is police business, Dr Hindle, not a courtesy call. It might be an idea if you asked your wife to join your guests in the clubhouse or wherever.'

He hung up, cutting off Hindle's reply, then called Judge Bristow again. 'Judge, would you mind getting down to the Cruising Yacht Club at Rushcutters Bay? I'll see you on Dr Hindle's boat.'

'Hindle? Why on his boat? I can't stand the man.'

'Judge, what I have to say to you I'd rather not say in front of your wife. Twenty minutes, down at Rushcutters.'

He hung up, sat back: it had been an exercise in logistics. Ahead

202

of him lay what might be an exercise in diplomacy: getting Hindle
and Bristow to agree to what he was going to suggest. If they didn't
. . . There was a burst of cheering and he looked up the street to see
the Goggomobile drawing away from the kerb to a loud send-off
from the kids who had been admiring it. A Ferrari or an Aston-Martin
could not have been farewelled more warmly. In the little bubble car
sat another problem: Kate.

He sat for a minute or two wondering whether he should drive the
couple of blocks to call in on his mother and father. But no: it would
be only for a minute or two and what would be the point? More to
the point was that he did not want to drop murder on their doorstep.
Brigid Malone spent most of her time spraying prayers on the weeds
of misfortune. They would read about the murder of Les Coulson;
his father, if not his mother, would know that he was involved. Better
to stay away, call another day when the air was clear of murder. His
mother's rosary beads would do nothing for Les Coulson: it was too
late for them.

He drove over to Rushcutters Bay, a tiny inlet on the southern
shore of the harbour. The wealth of the eastern suburbs began here,
climbing the ridge of Darling Point like runaway ivy. The inlet was
crowded with boats, like a huge nesting of gulls: millions of dollars
floating on water. The message was clear: you're in rich territory,
son: it was a gigantic leap from Number twelve Billyard Street and
Malone wondered if Jillian Langtry had ever travelled the five kilometres to look at it. There would be problems here, as everywhere:
domestic strife, ill-health, worry about the job; but there would always
be the cushion of wealth to support the despairing head. Con Malone,
the old socialist and trade union man, would have stood on the shore
and bombed the fleet with invective.

Malone squeezed his car into a No Parking zone and a security
guard appeared immediately. They are like parking police, they will
be there on Judgement Day, guarding the No Parking zones. 'You'll
have to move your vehicle, sir. That is just for an emergency – '

'That's what this is,' said Malone and showed his badge.

'Oh. Can I help?' The guard girded himself for action.

'No, it's nothing like that. Where's the office?'

In the office they told him where Dr Hindle's yacht could be found.
He walked out along the long dock and almost at the very end

he found *Hippocrates*, a fifteen-metre ocean-going yacht. Malone wondered what the bankers and lawyers and stockbrokers called their boats. He was in a sour mood, the red blood of Con Malone pumping in him at a great rate.

Rupert Hindle and Richard Bristow were waiting for him on the deck of the yacht, the judge looking as if he wished he could pass sentence on the indifferent doctor.

'I must say this is a bloody nuisance,' said Hindle, getting off on the wrong foot but unaware of it. He was in white shorts and a blue-striped white shirt and the mahogany tan looked as if it had been given another coating. 'I've got eight friends expecting to be out on the water now. My wife is blowing her top —'

'This won't take long, if you'll just listen to me.' Malone stepped over on to the deck, his leather soles slipping slightly on the deck boards. It was Bristow, not the yacht's owner, who gave him a steadying hand. 'It's more important than a day out on the harbour.'

Hindle could take a rebuff, though not gladly. He looked at Bristow, then back at Malone. 'This concerns our sons? Mine and the judge's?'

'We think their lives may be in danger.' He then told the two men what had happened to Les Coulson. They were both abruptly grave. 'It looks as if the killer has decided to widen his target. There have been no gay bashings for the past week or ten days, so maybe he's decided he's won his point there. Now he's coming back to get rid of the bashers he let go the first time around.'

'Do you have to keep referring to our sons as bashers?' said Hindle.

'What else were they?'

Hindle shut up, took a pair of dark glasses that had been hooked into the neck of his shirt and put them on. Malone, who rarely wore dark glasses, hated dealing with people who did. The glasses had become the greatest evasion tactic since lying had become a habit.

Bristow had said nothing. He was in shorts and a polo shirt; but, unlike the doctor's, his legs and arms were pale. He wore a broad-brimmed straw hat, the sort of hat a wife buys for her husband; it sat squarely on his head. He was obviously no waterman; boats were not his territory. Criminals whom he had jailed would have laughed at his unease as he tried to steady himself on the gently rocking boat.

People were coming and going along the dock, carrying lunch

baskets, liquor coolers, bags full of sun lotion; scraps of conversation that had nothing to do with murder or impending danger floated like the gulls above the boats. Sunlight bounced back from the white yachts and the water and Malone wished now that he had worn a hat. He could almost feel the sun cancers coming out of his skin like termites.

'What are you suggesting then?' said Bristow at last.

'That you get your boy and Sam –' He glanced at Hindle. 'Get them out of Sydney, hide them somewhere till we catch this feller.'

'And when's that going to be?' said Hindle.

Christ, thought Malone, do you carve up your patients as aggressively as this? 'I don't know, Doctor. But before you find a cure for blocked arteries.'

Abruptly and surprisingly Hindle laughed. 'You're a tough bastard, Inspector. Okay, so you don't know when you'll catch him. But tell us – are you getting close?'

Malone looked at the judge, who knew the odds in police work. 'We're closer than we were at the beginning, that's about all I can say.'

'You've narrowed the field?' said Bristow. When Malone nodded, the judge looked at Hindle. 'That'll have to do us, Rupert. We're in the inspector's hands.'

Thanks, Judge. Passing the buck, it seemed, was no more difficult than passing a sentence; though in this case they might be the same thing. 'The safety of your sons, Judge, isn't police responsibility –'

'I shall have a word with the Premier about that.' Bristow had been appointed to the Bench in one of The Dutchman's earlier terms. He was not a Labor voter, but the Premier didn't know that nor had he ever asked. He handed out tough sentences and that was all that Vanderberg, who at heart was a feudalist, required of a judge.

'Yes,' said Hindle, but dubiously: he and Hans Vanderberg would not have exchanged a word if they had been marooned together on an ice-floe.

'You can probably get police supervision, but I doubt if you can get round-the-clock protection from them.'

'You give protection to criminals who have grassed.'

Malone smiled, though it was no laughing matter. 'Judge, are you putting Clive and Sam in the criminal class?'

Bristow gave him a ten years' hard labour look. Watch your tongue, Malone told himself. He went on, 'I'm sorry, but you'll have to provide your own security guards –'

'Jesus.' Hindle all at once seemed to realize the enormity of the situation. He sat down, looked up at the other two. 'This fucking thing is getting out of hand!'

'Don't be obvious,' said Bristow as if speaking to a junior counsel. 'It's been ready to get out of hand since our boys committed their stupidity. Their fucking stupidity,' he said bitterly and turned away for the moment.

'The safest thing,' said Malone before *this* situation got out of hand, 'will be to get the boys out of Sydney. You'll have to warn the parents of the other boys who were in the bashing –'

'Stop saying that!'

This time it was Bristow who objected; but Malone ignored him. 'Do either of you have any suggestions? Anywhere the boys can go, somewhere a bit isolated, preferably?'

The two fathers looked at each other, then Hindle said, 'I have a half-share in a vineyard up outside Pokolbin, in the Hunter. There's a fair-sized house, four bedrooms . . . There's a manager lives on the property and his wife looks after the house for us.'

'That suit you, Judge? Or have you got a place?'

'No-o.' Bristow sounded reluctant to accept the offer; it obviously disturbed him to have any sort of relationship with Hindle. 'How long would the boys have to be there? Who'd keep an eye on them?'

'The security guards. And we'll ask the Cessnock police to keep a check. You'll have to impress on Clive and Sam and the other boys what danger they'll be in, if the killer finds out where they are. There'll be no leaving the place to go into town, they'll be – well, prisoners there. How long it'll be, I dunno. A week at the most, I hope.' *Or I'm off the case and you'll be dealing with someone else.*

'He killed someone last Monday night,' said Bristow. 'What about the bashers in that case? Will he be after them? Are they going to be herded in with our boys?'

It sounded like class distinction; but the judge wouldn't have known who Monday night's gang were. 'No, they'll be looked after,' he said, but wondered whose responsibility they would be. His, for whom the killer had done a service?

'Was it another gay-bashing?' Hindle, this time, seemed to have no trouble with the words.

'No,' said Malone and left it at that. Yet he wondered what the doctor and the judge would have said if he had told them his daughter had been in danger and had been saved by the killer.

Then Mrs Hindle, all aglow in pink cotton and indignation, came along the dock. 'Rupert, for God's sake, how much longer –?'

'The picnic's off,' said her husband and explained the reason for Malone's visit.

She looked at Malone as she might have at a paparazzo who had snapped her in a bad light. She was a little slow at taking in what her husband had said; then her face went blank: 'You mean someone's going to try and kill Sam?'

Three couples, passing along the dock behind her, stopped dead. None of the three men on *Hippocrates* said anything. It was Bristow, not Hindle, who stared at the three couples, challenging them to move on and mind their own business. Which they did, congealing into a stumbling group, snarled by their whispers.

'That's it,' said Hindle and clambered up on to the dock and put his arm round his wife.

She was frowning now, lines appearing as if her make-up was cracking. She looked down at Malone and said accusingly, 'Can't you stop him?'

She was distraught, unwilling to listen to reason: one could not blame her. Malone merely said, 'I've explained to your husband, Mrs Hindle. We'll do our best.'

A big motor cruiser eased past the stern of *Hippocrates*; the yacht rocked gently in the swell and Bristow grabbed at a stay. He had been standing stockstill, but the boat's movement made him suddenly active. He jumped up on to the dock, and said, 'We'd better get started. Can you recommend a security firm, Inspector?'

Malone named one. 'It's run by ex-police officers. They'll understand the problem.' He climbed up on to the dock. 'The sooner you get the boys up to Pokolbin the better. Give me the address and phone number, Doctor.'

Hindle, still with his arm round his wife, did so. All his arrogant bluster had gone: he was stripped to being just a worried father. 'Will you come up there with us today?'

'I don't think there's any point.' *I'm going to a lunch party with my family.* Self-interest won out over duty. Bugger 'em, he thought. 'Call me at home this evening, after they've settled in.'

'You sound so – so bloody calm about it all.' Mrs Hindle was still accusing him, as if he were to blame. Her husband pressed her shoulder warningly, but she ignored him. 'It's unbelievable –'

Malone had no answer. He had tried before to explain the unbelievable to the incredulous. It was Bristow who rescued the moment: 'We'll call you this evening, Inspector.' Malone gave him the number, but reluctantly; he should have asked them to call him tomorrow at Homicide. They were intruding on him. 'And thanks – I mean for warning us so promptly.'

'Yes,' said Hindle. 'Will you let the police up in Cessnock know?'

'I'll call them now. You phone them as soon as you're in the house at Pokolbin. And remember, the boys aren't to leave the property.' He looked at Bristow. 'Impress that on the security guards. They are the boys' jailers.'

'I don't believe all this –'

You had better, Mrs Hindle: the fun life is over. But he clamped his tongue on those words, just said goodbye and left. Going along the dock he passed the fleet of yachts and cruisers, their owners pottering about on them, preparing to move out for a careless day on the water. All at once, for no sane reason, he felt utterly bolshie. Con Malone, a bolshevik from another time, would have been proud of him.

3

'What do you do, Luther?' Sometimes, he thought, I sound like a Victorian father. He should be standing with his hands behind his back, in front of an ornate fireplace; instead of which, he was standing here in the Clements' back garden, a glass of chardonnay in his hand and Courtney Love singing softly (silently would have been better) somewhere in the background.

'Nothing,' said Luther. 'I'm on the dole.'

He was a cheerful-looking boy with sun-and-salt-streaked hair drawn back in a pony-tail, a gold ring in his left ear-lobe, a black Mambo T-shirt, baggy black shorts, black socks and black Air-Max shoes: he would not have been out of place in Les Coulson's gang. Just the sort of no-hoper you wanted hanging around your daughter.

'What would you *like* to do?'

'Get into computers. But there's a million guys trying to do the same. Or get into movies. You know, films.'

Yes, I know movies are films. Of course, I haven't got past Laurel and Hardy yet. Courtney Love expired in the background.

'He plays in a rock group,' said Maureen in a voice that said, *Lay off, Dad.* 'A record company is listening to them.'

'What d'you play, Luther?' Lute, maybe? The sun and the chardonnay were getting to him.

'Drums.' Luther did a riff on empty air.

'Gene Krupa-style or Chick Webb?'

'Da-ad,' said Maureen ominously, 'stop showing off . . . He thinks all music stopped when Benny Goodman died.'

'My dad's the same. Worse even. He listens to Perry Como. *Perry Como!*' The ring wobbled in his ear. Thank God, thought Malone, he doesn't wear one in his nose.

He grinned at the two of them, left them and went through the house and joined Lisa on the front verandah. This solid Victorian house with its large garden and view across the waters of Iron Cove might have raised queries about Clements' probity if he, as a detective-senior-sergeant, had been the Clements' sole source of income. But his and Romy's combined annual income was one hundred and fifty thousand dollars plus and so far no royal commission investigators had come sniffing at the front door. It was the sort of house that Romy, in particular, had wanted: anchored to the earth with certainty, a bulwark against storms. And, God knew, she had experienced enough of those: losing her mother only a year after they had arrived in Australia from Germany, losing her father to his murderous spree.

'Did you have an easy time this morning?' It was the first time he and Lisa had been alone since they had arrived at the Clements'.

'No, I've had a bugger of a morning. I tried to explain to a silly woman what the facts of her life might be from now on, and I couldn't.'

209

'Did you feel sorry for her?' She knew he had to be guided amongst the shoals of women's minds.

'Ye-es. Yes, I did,' he said, realizing it belatedly. 'Let's talk about something else. Is Maureen serious about this Luther?'

'Are you kidding? He's this week's toy boy. She's starting a collection.'

'You don't seem worried.'

She sipped her wine, stared out across the water. On the ridge rising up from the opposite bank of the cove there had stood a mental asylum; she could imagine the pain and despair that had been endemic there. 'I'm not worried about the boys, no. I told her to choose one or two boys she could trust not to — well, put their hands on her. She has to get over last Monday night, but she mustn't start distrusting men, hating them for what might have happened to her.'

'You're tough,' he said, but admiringly.

'Dad was in the Dutch air force in the war. He said that when a pilot crashed, they put him back in the air again as soon as possible — they thought it was the best way of fighting the trauma. I think they were probably right. Dad was shot down, but he said he went back up again the next day. The treatment worked, he said.'

'There's a difference between being shot down and being raped.'

'Of course there is. And if Mo *had* been raped, Claire and I would be protecting her — sheltering her till she got over it. I've had two long talks with her — she's not over Monday night, but she's trying. I don't want her distrusting men. You're not all bastards —' She reached across and put her hand on his.

He was silent a while, then he said, 'I didn't tell you. The killer phoned me Tuesday morning. He said he'd done me a service, saving Maureen.'

She was still holding his hand, but she was looking out across the water again. A rowing eight went slowly by on the far side, looking like figures on a frieze. 'I suppose he did. But I hate the thought that we owe him something.'

'So do I.'

She took her hand off his, changed the subject; or almost. 'Jason is back in favour with Claire. Very much in favour.'

'He's a nice kid.' *Forget his mother, the murderer.* He tried to remember what the Bible said about the sins of the fathers; did the

210

sins of the mothers ever get a mention? Had Salome ever had kids? 'Do they talk about his mother?'

'How would I know? I don't ask, she doesn't tell me.'

Then Clements and Romy came out on to the verandah. The four of them sat in wicker chairs and enjoyed the Sunday peace. Well, what passed for peace. A 747 flew overhead, then another a few minutes later. The flight path into Kingsford Smith airport had recently been changed with the opening of a new runway. Once peaceful areas were learning the price of progress. Armies of protestors had been recruited; placards were as numerous as banners and standards at medieval tournaments; everyone was loud and had a good time, no matter how futile. So far the authorities had been stone-deaf, a common affliction in governments and bureaucracies. Hearing would only be restored when an election was announced.

'A nice lot of kids,' said Clements. 'Even the one with the earring. He asked me what are the prospects for being a cop, now all the bent ones are rolling over.'

'He was into computers and films five minutes ago,' said Malone.

'Another fifteen or sixteen years, I guess we'll be throwing parties for Amanda and her friends. I'm looking forward to it.' He sounded smug, which is affordable when you are fifteen years from your child's adolescence.

'Don't let's rush her,' said Romy. 'God knows what the world will be like in fifteen years' time . . . Do we talk shop or not?'

'No,' said Lisa. 'We don't talk shop.'

Thank you, said Malone silently. He had had more than enough shop for today. Out on Iron Cove a lone sculler slid along the water, drawing a fading line behind him. Another jet roared overhead and Clements raised an imaginary gun to his shoulder.

'What would they charge me with if I shot it down?'

'A public service,' said Malone and this time his tongue bit him.

Chapter Eleven

1

All day Monday Malone waited for *the* phone call, but it didn't come. The Voice had either retreated in petulant anger or was playing a waiting game. Either way, Malone wished he would call: time was running out. Up till now he had not realized how much he wanted to be in on the end of this case, to meet The Voice face to face, preferably alive rather than dead.

Sunday night Rupert Hindle had called Malone at home. He had been agreeable and quiet-voiced this time, hardly related to the man of Sunday morning. 'The boys are here at Pokolbin. Just Sam and Clive Bristow. The other boys' fathers decided they would do their own thing.'

'I know.' Kate had told him she had contacted the other parents. 'It makes it difficult for us, the police, but there's nothing we can do about it. The Witness Protection scheme is still voluntary.'

'The Witness Protection – Christ, it sounds like the boys are running away from the Mafia.' For a moment he sounded like the Sunday morning Hindle.

Malone wasn't going to get into comparisons. 'Keep 'em under wraps, Doctor. I'll call you each evening to see how things are making out. Are you staying up there, you and the judge?'

'We can't – I wish I could. But I have two ops tomorrow that can't be put off. And the judge is in court. But my wife will come up tomorrow morning –'

'No,' said Malone flatly. 'With all due respect, Doctor, your wife is the last person who should be there.'

'Christ Almighty, she's Sam's mother –' Then his voice cut off. There was silence while Malone waited patiently; he wondered if Mrs Hindle was already up there at Pokolbin. Then Hindle came back on the line, subdued once again: 'I see your point. But it will be tough on her – how do I explain it to her?'

He had lost patience with Dr and Mrs Hindle; he showed his own toughness: 'As you would to a patient who has only a fifty-fifty chance of surviving.'

Then he had hung up and gone in a sudden black mood back into the living room where Lisa was watching the Sunday Night Movie. 'I don't want to know,' she said, recognizing the look on his face. 'Save it for the office.'

Television was out of the ratings season; sometimes the high points were the commercials. Tonight's movie was another Hollywood true-life story of a woman who, for love, murdered her children. All these crimes seemed to take place in quiet rural towns and Malone wondered if mothers killed their kids in cities like New York and Los Angeles. Or weren't those murders worth two hours of film? He fell asleep halfway through the accused woman's trial.

Now, Monday, he sat at his desk, an ear to the call of the phone, an eye on the weekend summaries. There had been two murders in South Region, both domestics; the local detectives were handling them and had not called in Homicide. John Kagal and Andy Graham were out at Newtown with Irv Rubens, tidying up what few clues there were on the Coulson murder. Actually, as Malone knew, there were no clues but the MO and the identity of the victim.

Then Kate Arletti came into the office. 'Got a minute, boss?'

'Sit down.' He could tell from the note in her voice that she was going to say something he didn't want to hear. 'What's on your mind, Kate?'

She was all neatness this morning, as buttoned-up as one of the more conservative bishops. 'I'm applying for a transfer. To the Fraud squad.'

'Are you asking me to approve it?'

'Yes.'

'Kate –' He was not a counsellor; he was stumbling here. 'I know the situation between you and John –'

She looked even more buttoned-up; 'You know? He *told* you?' Malone nodded. 'Jesus God! He talked with you about *us*?'

Malone got up, went round his desk and closed his office door. Out in the main room Gail Lee and some of the other detectives glanced curiously at him but he turned his back on them and went back to his desk. He was treading water, but felt he was sinking fast.

'It wasn't like that, Kate. We got into a discussion when we were first called in on the gay-bashings. He told me then he was – bi-sexual.' Double-gaited, in the circumstances, sounded flippant, insulting. He was paddling furiously, trying to stay afloat; there was no help at hand. 'He didn't mention you till I brought it up – I asked him if you knew how he was. He said no. He's told you since, I understand.'

Suddenly she was unbuttoned; she actually fiddled with a button and it came loose in her fingers. 'Is it office gossip?'

'Oh, come *on*! Do you think I'd spread something like that?' Indignation is always a resort for the cowardly. 'Or that John would?'

'He told *you*.'

'I've told you –' Now he had adopted exaggerated patience: another resort. 'I *asked* him if you knew.'

'Do any of the others know? I mean, about him?'

'I don't think so. Maybe one or two suspect, but they've never said anything.' He wanted to keep the situation here in his office, if he could.

'Are you going to let him stay on?'

He was losing patience; but he had been doing a lot of that lately. 'Kate, right now we're working on cases where I'm trying not to pass judgement on other people's sexual preferences. John's a good detective – he says the same about you. I'm not going to transfer him because occasionally he gets out of the other side of the bed.' He was desperate for euphemisms.

She smiled wryly at that; maybe, he thought, her sense of humour is going to save both of us. But he didn't place much hope in it. 'Boss, you don't seem to appreciate – I'm in love with the guy. D'you expect me to come in here every day, just pass the time of day with him and let it go at that? Not feel anything?'

'Have you tried –' He was almost under water now. 'I mean, can't you work out something between you?'

She looked at him pityingly. 'Jesus, you men are dumb!' She turned away, looked out the window. Fraud was there in the opposite wing; was fraudulence in love ever investigated there? Then she

214

turned back. 'Some women can forgive a man playing around with other women – some can, but I couldn't. I'm not built that way. But playing around with other *men* –' She closed her eyes and shook her head. 'No, I could never stomach that.'

'Have you got anything against homosexuals?' It was almost an irrelevant question, but he couldn't think of anything else to say. He wondered what she thought of lesbians, but that was a can best left unopened.

'You know better than that,' she said sniffily. 'I've proved it on this case. But there's a difference between tolerating what men do with each other and having your – your own man do it with them.'

He could think of nothing to say and they sat in silence for a while. Out in the main office, for no reason, one of the smoke detectors started to ping-ping-ping. Phil Truach got up, reached up with a broom handle and pressed the warning button. Then he looked in at Malone and lifted his hands defensively: *I wasn't smoking.*

Then Kate stood up, adjusting her blouse, trying to look buttoned-up again. 'Will you approve my transfer? I've been across to Chief Inspector Cronje and he says there's a vacancy. I can have it if you say okay.'

He stood up, put his hand out to her. 'I'll be sorry to lose you, Kate. Counselling wouldn't help?'

'Are you kidding? I'm sorry I called you dumb, but you are, you know. Most men are, when it comes to women. Even the ones who think they're New Age Guys.' Then she shook his hand. 'I'll be sorry to go. There's always a certain excitement here in Homicide, even if you hate what's caused it.'

Then she opened the office door and went out into the big room and everyone there bent their heads to their desks as if the solutions to all homicides were engraved there. Some of them suspect what's happened, Malone thought.

Kagal and Andy Graham came back to the office just before Malone left for home. Kagal came into Malone's office, looking as fresh and dapper as if he were just beginning his day. He had stopped by Kate's desk and said something to her, but it seemed perfunctory and could have been nothing more than a comment on the day's work.

'Nothing new,' he told Malone. 'I got on to Physical Evidence, the bullet had been taken out of the Coulson kid. Same calibre, I'm sure Ballistics will confirm it's out of the same gun. Who does he hit next?'

'No one, I hope. Close the door and sit down, John. Kate has been in to see me.'

The main room was almost empty; only Kate and Andy Graham remained. Kate appeared to be cleaning out her desk: a little prematurely or was she filling time till Kagal emerged from the smaller office after *his* talk with the boss?

'She's applied for a transfer, to Fraud. They've said they'll take her.'

'She'll be wasted there.' Kagal sounded suddenly angry. 'Why the hell has she got to sacrifice herself? We can get on together, work together — I've told her that —'

'I don't think so, John. Are you in love with her?' You never found situations like this in the police manual. Maybe there should be a royal commission into love in the Service.

Kagal did not seem disturbed by the question. He's a Sensitive New Age Guy, Malone thought: a bloody sight more sensitive than me. Kagal considered a moment, then said, 'I don't think so. And therein lies the problem, right?'

'Therein,' said Malone, wondering if he had ever used the word before. 'I've said I won't stand in the way of her transfer, but I don't want to lose her. Or you, either,' he said, trying not to sound hurried.

'I don't want a transfer, if that's what you're thinking. I like the work, it's more interesting than any other division. And —' He stopped.

It's where you can be noticed, where it might lead to promotion elsewhere. 'How ambitious are you, John?'

Kagal was not put out. He had the assurance of someone who knew his own credits and those of everyone else. Malone began to wonder if that self-assurance ever bothered Kate. Or did women dismiss it, look underneath it? He would have to ask Lisa.

'Very ambitious,' said Kagal. 'You're not surprised, are you?'

'No.' Malone was candid. You could always be candid with those whose self-assurance was iron-clad. It was the impostors who always looked hurt. 'But knowing the police culture, double-gaited as you are, do you think you'll ever make Assistant Commissioner?' Let alone Commissioner.

216

'You mean that might be a problem?'

'Therein.' Malone grinned and was pleased when Kagal smiled.

'It's never interfered with my work, has it?'

'Not so many years ago you rarely got anywhere in the Public Service if you were a Catholic. Your religion didn't interfere with your work, it was just the wrong colour. One thing about being a Catholic, it's pretty hard to be blackmailed about it – unless you're a priest who interferes with altar boys. But there are still a lot of cross-eyed cops who'd blackmail you if they knew about you, especially if you were going for promotion over them.'

'So what are you suggesting? I give up my friends like Bob Anders?' His voice was getting an edge to it now.

'No. I like Bob. I like one or two of the other gays I've met on this case. I'm less homophobic. If I ever was,' he added defensively.

'Oh, you were, you were.' But Kagal smiled as he said it. 'Would you go to bat for me if I was up for promotion and someone brought up that I'm bisexual?'

Malone sighed. 'I should've seen this coming . . . Yes, I would. But in the meantime, I'd suggest you try finding more appeal in women.'

'Oh, I find that easy, as much as you or any of the straights here in Homicide. Trouble is, I find the other just as easy.'

Malone stood up, reached for his hat; the pork-pie dated him as if he were stamped. 'I'm going home. I was never cut out to be a counsellor. Do me a favour, though. If you and Kate have a row, tearing out each other's hair, don't do it in the office. Or you'll both be on the transfer list.'

Then he left, nodding to Kate but saying nothing as he passed her. He fumbled at the security door like an intruder, then he was through it and heading for the lifts and home, where all the problems were straightforward. Or so he hoped.

2

'We're watching *Sydney Beat* tonight,' said Lisa.

'There she goes again,' said Claire. 'Getting her kicks out of that cop's muscles.'

'So what's wrong with that?' said Maureen. 'It means she's got a healthy mind.'

'What is unhealthy,' said Tom, 'is that she watches such a lousy show.'

'She, as you call her, watches it because everything else on at that hour is even lousier. I can't wait for *Four Corners* to come back.' Lisa gestured at the table. 'Now you can all clear the dishes and wash up, since you're all so damned superior about what's on television.'

Ten minutes later, when he and Lisa were side by side in front of the television set, Malone said, 'Why *do* you watch it?'

'Because I thought you liked it?'

He shook his head. 'I'd never miss it if they took it off tomorrow.'

'They are taking it off – tonight's the last episode. You still haven't said why you watch it.'

'To pick fault with it.'

But that wasn't entirely it. The series was more than the junk food that was served up in the non-rating season. An episode rarely held him till its end, but it usually had some bite in its opening sequences and he was interested in how the script writers handled material that he and Homicide took for granted. *Sydney Beat* was not about Homicide, but the detectives in it occasionally dealt with murder. A script writer and a director had once come to Homicide looking for background, but he had let John Kagal deal with them.

Tonight's episode didn't hold him. It was about murder, but the detectives appeared to have to do no donkey-work: clues, connections, coincidences fell out of the woodwork. The lead actor, in no situation where he could be shirtless, seemed to be walking through his part; only his sidekick, the detective-constable, made any impression. He underplayed the part, yet there was a suggestion of strength in him; or perhaps it was repressed violence. He played against the way the role was written and the director gave him his head. He's not the hero's sidekick, Malone thought, he's his enemy. Were they setting up a new situation for next season's series?

He had been dozing off as the film seemed to lose its plot; then he heard someone say, 'It's a public service –'

He was instantly awake, saw who had spoken, then closed his eyes and strained his ears. 'It's him!'

'Who?' said Lisa, and the children, who had now all come into the

218

living room and were sprawled in chairs, looked at him in puzzlement.

'What's his name? The actor, the one playing what's-his-name?' He rarely knew an actor's name, never knew a character's name unless the actor was playing a title role. 'The feller with the moustache.'

'Lloyd Chase,' said Maureen.

Claire, the lawyer in training, suddenly had her shrewd look. 'It's him, you said. You mean he's the guy you're after, the serial killer?'

'Shut up.' He leaned forward, watching the actor closely, almost as if lip-reading him. Lloyd Chase was slim, dark-haired, medium height; the only feature that didn't fit was the moustache, the thick brush adornment popular with some gays. But his voice was The Voice: no doubt of it.

'It can't be him,' said Maureen softly, leaning forward in her chair, studying the actor as closely as her father was. 'I'd have recognized him —'

'You said you didn't see him,' Malone reminded her without looking at her.

The story was coming to its climax: the storming of a suburban house where the murderer was holed up. The State Protection Group was on the scene, fit-looking men in their flak jackets and dark caps, their Remington twelve-gauge shotguns adding menace to their look. But the star and his sidekick were not going to be denied their roles.

'Now!' shouted the star and he and Lloyd Chase followed the Protection Group men into the house. Lloyd Chase was holding his gun in his left hand and steadying it with his right.

Malone snapped off the remote control. 'What channel is that?'

'Fifteen,' said Tom in the voice of someone to whom television channels were better known than the Ten Commandments.

They were all sitting forward, even Lisa. The atmosphere was almost crackling; only later would he realize that he had dragged them into something he had always tried to avoid. He sat still, trying to quieten the chaos of excitement that had gripped him. It was no comfort to know that he had been watching the serial killer only two weeks ago here in his own living room.

Then he said, 'I'm going out there, get that tape. Darl, call Russ and tell him to meet me at the office as soon as possible —'

'I'll call him,' said Tom and was on his feet, halfway to the hallway phone.

Malone went to call him back, but Lisa pressed his knee. 'Let him. We're all in it now, whether you wanted it or not.'

'Yes,' said Maureen, and beside her Claire nodded.

He looked at them all, then nodded at Tom. 'Go ahead. Tell him what I've just come up with. But get it right. Tell him to get Professor Hamence – got that? Hamence – get him and Liz Embury to the office. I want them there when I get back from Eastwood – No, wait a minute, I'd better do it.'

'Dad!' Tom was indignant. 'I'm not a bloody idiot! You want Russ to get Professor Hamence and Liz Embury to your office – right? Geez!' He went through into the hallway, taking his disgust with him.

Malone grinned, trying to take some of the excitement out of himself. He stood up, kicking off his slippers. 'Where are my shoes? Don't wait up for me. I dunno how long this is going to take.'

'I'll be awake. Get his shoes, Mo.' Lisa stood up, trying to remain calm. She felt little excitement, just trepidation. She knew the inherent danger in his job and had experienced fear before; but now, in her own living room, she had been given a preview of what might confront him. 'Are you going after him tonight?'

'That depends if we can find out where he is. That film would have been shot weeks, even months ago. I'll get my shoes, Mo.'

He didn't want her in the bedroom while he not only put on his shoes but also slipped on his shoulder-holster. He was in the bedroom, putting the Smith & Wesson into the holster, when he saw Claire, holding an open phone-book, standing in the doorway.

'Is there going to be shooting? Don't let Mum see that.'

'I'm going to do my best to see there's nothing like that.' She looked dubious and he went on, 'Claire, he and I have an understanding. He's killed other people, but I don't think he's going to try and kill me.'

'I'll try and tell that to Mum.' Then she held up the phone-book. 'I've gone right through the Chases – there's no Lloyd Chase. There are five L. Chases –' She tore out the page, gave it to him.

He grinned again, though he had little humour in him. 'You training to be a cop?'

'Yes.' She was going to be a cop with a law degree. 'Good luck and keep your head down.'

At the front door Lisa, who had followed him, kissed him. 'As you tell everyone – take care. Ring me from the office –' She kissed him again and he could feel the grip of her hand on his arm. 'Good luck. Bring him in, stop the killing.'

Behind her he could see the two girls and Tom in the hallway. It struck him that there had never been this scene before. Lloyd Chase had come like an alien being into the house and set the small opera.

'I'll be okay,' he told them and went out to the Fairlane, feeling slightly ridiculous as the image came into his head of a soldier going off to the wars.

Channel Fifteen was out on the Epping Road, a main artery running north-west into middle-class suburbs. The night gateman was surprised when Malone showed his badge, but asked no questions and directed him to the main entrance. There was no one behind the reception desk, but a young girl came through the lobby as Malone came in through the front doors.

'Oh, you'll want Production Control. But I dunno you can go through there without a security pass. They're very strict on that –'

Malone produced his badge again. 'Which way, miss?'

She blinked, then capitulated and gave him directions. 'Ask for Ricky –'

Ricky turned out to be a twenty-two-year-old, long-haired and long-nosed king for the night: 'Look, mate, I dunno I can give you the tape –'

'We'll ring the managing director then, or whoever.'

'You tell me, mate, what you want it for –'

Malone had met his type before, when he had worked some years ago for a couple of weeks as technical adviser on another police series, also called *Sydney Beat*, which had sunk without trace. Ricky was in television, mate, than which there was no higher firmament. Malone had never been on a film set, but he imagined the snobbery there would be much the same. But he had news for Ricky:

'I don't have to tell you anything, Ricky – I'm a cop doing his job. Now direct me to a phone, give me your boss's name and number and we'll stop fartarsing around.'

He knew he was being overbearing, but it couldn't be helped; he wasn't going to waste time bandying words with Ricky. The kid was doing his job, but his attitude got up Malone's nose. He got the name of the production control manager, rang him at home.

'I can't tell you why we need that tape, Mr Indelli. Not now, anyway – you'll learn why in due course. But I need the tape *now* – immediately. It'll be returned to you undamaged tomorrow. Okay?'

He hung up, held out his hand for the tape. 'Thanks, Ricky. I'll tell your boss how well you held the fort –'

'No worries, mate,' said Ricky, unworried.

Malone drove back to Homicide, resisting the temptation to put the flashing light on the roof and use the siren; but he drove fast and was fortunate enough not to be stopped and delayed by a patrol car. Clements was waiting for him with Kate Arletti and John Kagal. With them were Professor Hamence and Liz Embury and Greta Bromley.

'I felt Liz needed some support,' the last explained to Malone. 'I hope you don't mind?'

'Glad to have you ... Thanks for coming in at such short notice, Professor. I'll run the voice tapes again for you, to refresh your memory, while John here puts this TV tape into our VCR ... Fast-forward it, John, to the last segment. I'd like you to hear the voice tapes, too, Miss Embury.'

She was here under protest; but so far the protest was unspoken. She just nodded and followed Malone, Clements and Hamence into Malone's office.

Malone ran the last two tapes of The Voice: then Hamence nodded. 'That's enough.' He appeared to have caught some of the suppressed excitement that the detectives felt. 'I take it you've recognized that voice on the TV tape? An actor?'

'Yes, an actor named Lloyd Chase.' Malone looked at Liz Embury. 'You know him, Liz?'

She and Greta Bromley looked as if they had been caught on their way to bed. Neither of them wore make-up; their clothes looked as if they had been pulled on hurriedly.

Liz Embury said nothing and Malone repeated his question. 'Do you know him?'

At last she nodded. Malone gave her a hard stare, then he led them out into the main office where Kagal was ready with the TV tape on

222

the VCR. 'I've fast-forwarded it, Inspector. This is the last segment.'

The tape began to roll. Malone stood to one side watching Hamence and particularly Liz Embury; at the same time he was aware that Greta Bromley was watching him. The professor nodded to himself several times, but Liz Embury remained expressionless. Then the credits were rolling. Kagal switched off the set.

'That's him,' said Hamence. 'No doubt in my mind.'

Malone looked at Liz Embury. 'Well?'

She was sitting on the edge of a desk beside her partner. The latter took her hand and Malone was pleased to see that the younger woman did not snatch it away.

'He's wearing a moustache,' he said. 'That was never mentioned in any of the descriptions of him. Certainly not when he was disguised as a woman,' he added, trying to lighten the moment.

Liz Embury was not yet ready to smile. Whether she was acting or not, Malone could not tell. The world is full of actors better at hiding their true feelings than displaying their affected ones. At last she said, 'The moustache was a prop. He used to put it on each day before shooting started.'

Malone didn't ask why an actor would not *grow* a moustache for a continuing role in a series. He had met few actors and didn't pretend to understand them. 'Is Lloyd Chase the man you recognized as our serial killer? The one who possibly – probably –' *lay it on thick, Malone* 'saved your lives. Is he the man?'

For a moment it looked as if she was going to refuse to answer; her partner squeezed her hand. Then she nodded. 'Yes.'

There was a concerted sigh, of relief, of suppressed excitement. 'You could have saved us a lot of trouble, Liz, maybe saved some other lives, if you had told us that earlier.'

'I – I wasn't sure. Anyhow –' She stopped.

'Anyhow what?'

'If he'd saved your life, wouldn't you feel you owed him something?'

None of the detectives in the room turned their heads; but Malone could feel the stares of Clements, Kagal and Kate as if they had faced him with fingers pointed. He wondered how much longer Maureen's name could be kept out of the case. Would Lloyd Chase, when brought to trial, shout that challenge across open court at him?

223

'There's one point,' said Greta Bromley, still holding her partner's hand. 'What if he finds out Liz has identified him and he comes looking for her?'

Malone skirted the question by asking Hamence, 'Are you afraid he'll come after you, professor?'

'He will only know what I've done after you catch him and I testify in court — that's if you want me to. I've testified in other cases.' It was a statement of fact, not one of bravado.

'There you are,' said Malone to the two women. 'You're safe till you testify in court. And you'll be safe after it.'

Clements came in: 'When he came to your rescue he knew who you were. He didn't pick two lesbians at random — he picked you. He hasn't been near you since, has he?'

'No,' said Liz Embury, sliding off the desk, ready to leave. 'I haven't said I'll testify against him if he's caught.'

'Oh, we'll catch him, all right,' said Malone; but he was in no mood for further argument tonight. 'Thanks for coming in. None of this will be released to the media — we don't want Mr Chase reading about it. You'll continue to be safe.'

'From bashers too?' said Greta Bromley.

All Malone could do was wave a helpless hand. 'I hope so, Greta.'

The two women and Hamence left, escorted out of the building by Kagal. Malone, suddenly tired, sat down at Kagal's desk, looked up at Clements and Kate Arletti.

'Why wasn't the bugger in *Showcase*? It was sheer bloody luck I caught him tonight in that film.' He looked at his watch. 'It's late, but I'm trying Channel Fifteen's production control manager again. We have to find out who produced that series —'

'I've got that,' said Kate and produced her notebook. 'I took it down off the opening credits. Coolabah Productions.'

'What would we do without her?' Malone said to Clements, but didn't look at Kate. He had noticed that she and Kagal had shown no sign of their differences; they had worked as partners. 'I wonder if she has their address and phone number?'

'Naturally,' she said and gave a phone number and an address in Ultimo.

He did look at her then. 'You'll never have this sort of excitement in Fraud. The adrenalin never runs over there.'

'Maybe not,' she said. 'But there are other things that run in a woman's blood besides adrenalin.'

'Such —?' Then Clements saw Malone's warning glance and did not finish the question.

'I'm sure there are, Kate. Be here at nine in the morning and we'll go down and talk to Coolabah Productions.'

She said goodnight to both of them and left. Clements heaved himself to his feet. 'Do you think we're gunna lose her?'

'It's either her or John.'

'Are you gunna tell me why? I *am* the supervisor.'

Why do I feel as if I'm treading on eggshells here? But he explained carefully and flatly the problem between Kate Arletti and John Kagal. Clements listened carefully, only biting his lip, as was his habit.

'I'm not surprised – what you've told me about John. I don't see why Kate should be the one to go and he stays. *His* problem is our main problem.'

'I was afraid you'd say that.'

'Well, isn't it? What are you afraid of – being accused of homophobia? Frankly, mate, I'm tired of being politically correct. If he's the one with the problem, then he's the one who goes.'

Malone and Clements had argued before; but never on a subject as delicate as this. They had argued on politics: Clements was conservative, Malone still brushed by his father's socialist beliefs. They had argued about degrees of guilt in murder cases. But this was different: somehow it touched on their maleness.

'The real problem is that she's in love with him. If it was just an affair, they could iron it out between them . . . She's the one who's asked for the transfer. I didn't suggest it. Ask yourself – who's the better detective, who's got more to offer us?'

Clements took his time: 'Okay, it's John. But —'

'But?'

'It's not gunna be the same, working with him from now on.'

'So long as he doesn't put the hard word on you, what's to go wrong?'

Clements grinned at the thought of any man putting the hard word on him. 'How has he worked with you on this case?'

'Absolutely straight – whichever way you want to read *straight*. When it comes to nailing Lloyd Chase, he's not going to back off.

225

You'll just have to learn to live with him, Russ – the world is changing, whether we like it or not. It's just a pity we're going to lose Kate, but it's her decision.'

He got to his feet; he was ready to fall into bed. Clements, unusually sullen, buttoned up his jacket, which was usually undone. He had never worn kid gloves, never practised diplomacy: he was honest and prejudiced and would always be politically incorrect. He would survive, if he did, on his honesty.

'I'm not gunna like it.'

'Neither am I, Russ. But right now I'm more concerned with nailing Lloyd Chase. He's my main problem.' *And more than you know, mate.*

3

Tuesday morning Malone and Kate went down to talk to Coolabah Productions. They were housed in part of a converted wool store in Ultimo, an inner-city area. The huge warehouses had once been the banks for the primary wealth of the nation, back when Australia had, as the saying went, ridden on the sheep's back. Wool had flowed in here from the Monaro, from the Riverina and the Black Soil plains, from sheep runs with liquid-sounding names like Illilliwa and Mulberrygong and Terrinallum. But that was long ago and wool was barely a cash crop these days; millions of bales were stored elsewhere while woolgrowers waited without much hope for prices to rise. The huge old stores had been converted into apartments and studios and offices and all that remained of the past was the occasional floorboard glistening with wool-grease and the faint echo of an auctioneer's shout.

'Coolabah,' said Walter Claven, the executive director. 'We wanted an Aussie name and there's nothing more Aussie than the coolabah tree, is there?'

Malone was not well-versed in things arboreal. 'No, I guess not. But we're not here, Mr Claven, to talk about Coolabah. We'd like to know about an actor you employed in *Sydney Beat*, named Lloyd Chase.'

Claven was bald, lean and energetic, tanned as if he spent all his working days on location. He wore a diamond stud in one ear, a red neckerchief knotted round his throat and a gold bracelet: another one, thought Malone, letting his prejudice out for an airing. Yet behind Claven, on a shelf, was a photo of a pleasant-looking woman and three children. Malone decided it was time he gave up classifying men.

'Lloyd? A good actor, he'd go a long way if he had more ambition. But he just cruises – you know, does a good job but never exerts himself. As if he's got other things on his mind. He doesn't need the money, I guess.'

'He makes a living at something else?' said Kate.

'Not as far as I know. He's always been a bit of a mystery man – keeps his mouth shut, doesn't tell you anything more than you want to ask him. Never was interested in promotion – not like some of these kids who'd lie down in front of a bus to get their name in the magazines. But we liked Lloyd and we've used him a coupla times.'

'When did you finish *Sydney Beat*?'

'Oh, almost six months ago. I haven't seen Lloyd since . . . Why do you want to see him? He been up to something?'

'No,' said Malone. 'It's just routine.'

Claven smiled. 'We use that line of dialogue a lot in our cop series. Lets us segue into the next scene. What's your next scene?'

'A talk with him, we hope. Where can we find him?'

'I haven't a clue – is that what you cops ever say?'

'Never.'

'You'd have to see his agent. Josie Everett, she's just along the street from here, in this same building.'

'You don't have the whole building?'

'Christ, no! We have these two offices and two small sound stages. We're not Rupert Murdoch, you know. If I come across Lloyd, will I tell him you're looking for him?'

'Why, does he occasionally drop in here?'

'Well, no.' He was bursting with curiosity. 'But you never know.'

'Yes, tell him. He's talked to me once or twice on police procedure.'

'Really? Well, you'd never know – he never seemed that interested in background stuff.'

'Maybe he wants to be a director?' said Kate.

'Don't they all?' said Claven wearily.

Out in the street, with traffic roaring past, Kate shouted, 'A mystery man? I always thought actors were an open book?'

'Let's go and see if his agent can open him up a bit.'

Josie Everett was a large lady with tiny gestures. Malone had never seen anyone so economical with her hands; they rested on her bosom like decorations. She wore a loose dress of multi-coloured diamonds; she was a one-woman chorus of jesters. Except that she didn't jest; she was a very serious lady.

'I don't give out information about my clients, not even to producers. Their private business is their own.'

'Mr Chase's private business happens to be ours,' said Malone.

'Why? What has he done?'

'*That* is our business. I don't want to play the heavy cop, Miss Everett —' He had recently seen *Heat*, in which Al Pacino had played the heavy cop, chewing up the scenery like Luke di Lammermoor. He hoped neither he nor any of his staff would act like that. 'But could we cut out —' He almost said *fartarsing around*. But Miss Everett, for all that she was theatrical in her dress, sounded as if she preferred to be treated as a lady.

'The fartarsing around?' said the lady. 'Well, if you're going to mean business, issue me with warrants and all that bullshit, I suppose —' The hands came down off the bosom, moved to other diamonds on the dress as if on a checkerboard. 'I haven't seen Lloyd in, oh, I guess three or four months.'

'We looked for him in *Showcase*,' said Kate, 'but he wasn't there.'

'You were searching through *Showcase*? This is serious, isn't it? It's not just a courtesy call.'

'Yes, it's serious,' Malone admitted. 'Why wasn't he in the book?'

'He was in last year's edition. But this year he said no, he was going to take six months, maybe a year off. Said he was going to do some community work.'

'Has he ever done that before? Community work?'

'I don't know. He never talked much about his life outside what work I got for him. He's a sweet guy — polite, no ego . . . I hope he's not in serious trouble? Really serious?'

Malone dodged that one. 'Do you have an address for him?'

'Yes, but he's gone from there — we had some mail returned that we sent him. The letters had come addressed to him here — probably fan mail. Girls liked him, especially the kids.'

'Would you have those letters?' asked Kate.

'Oh God, I dunno. Trix!' She had a shout that went with her size. A thin blonde girl came in on the back wash of it. 'Trix, do we keep any fan mail that our clients get? What we don't send out to them?'

'It's in a bag somewhere,' said Trix, as if fan mail was trash. 'I can look for it. Who do you want?'

While they waited and small talk filled the waiting, Malone looked around the office. It was large and open, a single partition splitting the big space that was the agency's office. The original beams of the wool store supported the ceiling; the walls were open brick. Attached to the bricks were wallboards and attached to them was a gallery of Everett clients. Malone got up and looked closely at a young good-looking man who gazed at the camera with eyes that dared it to expose him.

'That's Lloyd,' said Josie Everett. 'About three years ago. When he first came to me I thought I could make him, promote him. Another Sam Neill — you know, everything held in. But that would come later, I told myself — first, I had to get him started. They were making a late-night soap, you know, a local *Melrose Place*, and the producers wanted him. But he said no, he didn't need the work that badly. An actor in this country saying he didn't need the work that badly! Jesus, there are —'

'We know,' said Kate. 'Thirty thousand actors in this country.'

Josie Everett was impressed. 'You've done your homework.'

'We always do,' said Kate.

'So what's Lloyd done that you've been so thorough?'

'It's not what he's done,' Malone lied, 'it's what we hope he can do to help us. These the letters?'

Trix, the secretary, had come back with a dozen or more letters, addressed to Lloyd Chase in a variety of handwriting, some of it childish-looking. One letter stood out with the name and address in a neat copperplate hand.

'We'll take these,' said Malone, 'and return them to you.'

'Are you going to open them?' Josie Everett was ready to throw her weight around for her client. 'You can't do that —'

Malone tried to look patient. 'We can come back with a warrant and all that bullshit, as you call it — you want us to go to all that trouble? We'll present you with the warrant and then just to prove what utter bastards we are, we'll ask you to come along with us to Homicide and take up a lot of your time —'

'Homicide?'

That had been a slip. 'Oh, didn't I say where we were from? Didn't you mention it, Constable Arletti?'

'I forgot,' said Kate. 'I'll mention it now, if you like.'

Josie Everett smiled for the first time, big cheeks ballooning. 'Who writes your dialogue? You've been to see *Get Shorty*.'

'We're not fooling, Miss Everett,' said Malone, gathering the letters and standing up. 'You'll have these back tomorrow, hand-delivered. Thanks for your help.'

'I won't say anytime,' said Josie Everett, hands once more at rest on her bosom. 'Cops frighten me.'

Malone grinned at her reassuringly and led Kate out on to the street. They crossed the road to their car, dodging the traffic that appeared to use this one-way street as a speedway. Standing by their unmarked car, just finishing the details on the parking ticket, was the usual ubiquitous parking policeman. Kate showed her badge and the grey bomber shook his head in disgust and scrawled something in his book.

'You could cause a pile-up, parking along here.' He watched the traffic speeding by. A semi-trailer, like a terrace of houses on wheels, roared past, sending back a gale of disturbed air. 'I wish I was a motorcycle cop, I'd have a ball. I'd be writing tickets like a bookie's clerk.'

'I think you all have a streak of malice in you,' said Malone.

'That's the first thing they ask you when they interview you for the job. Have a nice day.'

Kate drove them back to Homicide. Once upstairs she came into Malone's office and they began to open the letters. 'Should we steam them open?' she asked.

'No, just slit 'em.' He picked up the letter addressed in the copper-plate hand. 'This isn't a fan letter, unless Mr Chase also appeals to the old biddies. My mother has a hand like this.'

The letter was indeed from an old biddy, possibly his biggest fan:

his mother. It was dated three weeks earlier and she had not heard from him for a month before that ... *Write, darling. You know how much I worry about you. Why don't you come home for a break? Love, Mum.*

'What's the address?' said Kate.

Malone felt a chill as he read it out: 'Manhattan Winery, Broke Road, Pokolbin.'

'Pokolbin? Where the kids are?'

He nodded. 'Manhattan — that's one of the old Hunter wineries. He's not a —' Then he shook his head at the farcical thought: 'Chase Manhattan? He's gotta be kidding!'

'Chase Manhattan? That's a bank, isn't it?' Kate didn't deal in high finance, never looked at the business pages in a newspaper. Her dealings were with the St George Bank, a one-time building society that catered for people like herself, the low-flyers. She had never heard of Barings till Nick Leeson had made news with his withdrawals. She would have a lot to learn when she moved across to Fraud.

'Lloyd Chase — it's obviously his stage name. Lloyd Manhattan sounds a mouthful.' He looked at his watch. 'What's it up to the Hunter? Two hours? Two-and-a-quarter?'

'Just over two hours,' said John Kagal from the doorway. 'Less if we use the siren. I go up there every year for the wine festival. What's on?'

Kate hadn't turned to look at him. Malone explained developments: 'I'm going up there to talk to his mother. You two had better come with me.'

Kagal nodded, but Kate just sat very still.

Malone's patience was wearing thin. 'Righto, forget your private war. You two have been on this case right from the jump — you're staying on till the finish. We're going to be civilized cops and you'll both do your jobs as well as you've done them up till now. I'm not going to start at this late stage having to brief someone else on all the detail. We leave in ten minutes. You'll drive, Kate.'

Kate nodded, got up without a word and went out past Kagal. The latter raised his eyebrows at Malone, shrugged and went back to his desk.

Malone picked up his phone, rang Lisa at home. 'I may be late this evening, darl. I have to go up to the Hunter.'

'Wine-tasting?' Then she said, 'Sorry – I shouldn't be flippant. You've got a lead on Lloyd Chase?'

'You remembered his name?'

'I'm a cop's wife. He also saved our daughter from rape, remember? Good luck. And don't be brave . . .'

'I never am. I love you.'

'Of course you do.'

He hung up, sat for a moment deeply in love; then he sent for Clements, gave him a quick rundown. 'Get on to Cessnock, tell them we're on our way. Just a protocol call, don't ask for any help.' You never did that unless absolutely necessary. 'Call Greg Random and tell him what's on.'

'Will you need the Protection Support Unit from Newcastle?'

'I hope not. I don't even know if he's gone home to Mum for a break. Crumbs, if he's up there – he can't be more than a mile or two from the Hindle winery . . . On second thoughts, ask Cessnock to have the Support Unit stand by, just in case.'

Clements nodded out into the office. 'You're taking both of them?'

'Yes. They'll be okay – they'd better be.'

'I wish I were coming with you. Stuck at that bloody desk –'

'I wish you were, too – like old times. We were never in love, but we held hands a lot.'

Clements grinned. 'Don't ever let anyone know. Good luck. And if Fred *is* up there, don't be a hero. Be careful.'

Neither of them would have called it love, but they knew it was more than mateship.

Chapter Twelve

1

The Hunter Valley lies about two hundred kilometres north of Sydney. At the mouth of the Hunter River is Newcastle, the State's second biggest city, its fortunes originally built on its steelworks and its coal docks. Behind it, running west, then north-west, lies the wide shallow valley, one of the two principal wine-growing areas of the nation. Grapes have been grown there since the eighteen twenties, encouraged by the early colony's authorities. In those wild early days rum, most of it from illicit stills, had been a major currency; soldiers, free men and convicts alike indulged themselves in the democracy of drink. Then the authorities, with that talent for knowing what is best for everyone but themselves, trumpeted the benefits of wine. Free men, aspiring to be like their betters, besides seeing a profit, took to the grape. The convicts, uninterested in their betters and unconversant with profit, stuck to the grog. It took almost a hundred and fifty years before the descendants of the convicts began to take wine with their meals and wine snobbery grew like *phylloxa*.

'There are over a hundred and fifty wineries in the Hunter,' said Kagal from the back of the car.

'Don't you find that interesting, Kate?' said Malone, beside her in the front seat.

'Very,' said Kate, as if she had just been told that Tuesday followed Monday.

Malone gave up. Conversation had been desultory all the way up from Sydney; Kagal had spent most of the time reading a paperback of *The Shipping News*. Kate had used the siren and the flashing light most of the way on the freeway, keeping the car at a steady hundred and forty ks an hour. Then they had left the freeway, come through timbered country and were approaching Cessnock, once a major coal-mining town, now the starting point for the Hunter. Tiny vineyards, some no more than two or three acres, created a broken pattern on either side of the narrow road; but the valley proper had not yet begun, the ribbed acres and acres lay ahead. Malone hoped that no crime scene lay up there amidst the vines.

All three had lapsed into silence by the time they pulled up in front of Cessnock police station. It was a nondescript brick building built in the nineteen thirties when architects, particularly government ones, had been intent on not spoiling the mood of the Depression. The courthouse beside it had more imagination to it, as if Justice had decided to lift her skirts and show a bit of leg.

Malone left Kate and Kagal alone in the car, hoping they would not be at each other's throat while he was gone, and went in to pay his courtesy call on the patrol commander. Chief Inspector Des Flagg was a tall grey-haired man with a broken nose and a laugh that sometimes rang a little hollow, as if he had heard all the jokes about life and found most of them unfunny.

'I've had a couple of my men check out the Hindle place a coupla times a day. You really think this serial killer will come up here and try to do them?'

'I don't know, but I had to get them out of Sydney. I think we've identified him – a TV actor named Lloyd Chase, he's been appearing in the police series *Sydney Beat*.'

'We never watch anything up here that has to do with Sydney.' It was difficult to tell whether Flagg was joking or not. 'Playing a cop? That's going to look good in the papers.'

'It's going to look even better when they learn his real identity. We think he's one of the Manhattan family.'

Flagg made a noise halfway between a laugh and a cough; then he flattened his nose with a broad finger, as if that helped him think. Then he said, 'Do you know about the Manhattans? No? I've lived in the Hunter all my life – I was hearing about them when I was in nappies. My old man worked for them all his life, out at the winery. They've been in the valley since God knows when – they came up here not long after the Lindemans, some time in the late eighteen forties. They've got this mansion out along the Broke road – it was built, I think, in the late eighteen eighties. They're – well, I guess you'd call them valley aristocrats. Their name wasn't always Manhattan – it was

234

some German name that they changed, the beginning of World War One. They've got neighbouring vineyards besides the main one – they're run by one of the sons. There's a daughter somewhere, but I dunno where. I seem to remember there was a second son –'

'That's him, then. Who's on the main vineyard?'

'Mrs Manhattan – Vera. A lady, every inch of her. She's not from the valley, she's from Melbourne, but no one holds that against her.' He smiled at last, showing big teeth. 'She's looked upon as the First Lady of the valley. And you're going out there to tell her her son's a serial killer? Better you than me.'

'I was hoping you'd come with me.' He hadn't hoped that at all, but now it seemed wiser in the circumstances.

'Okay, I'll come. Do you think the son's up here?'

'I don't know. If he is, we might need back-up.'

'Yeah, you might.' Flagg picked up his phone, called Newcastle and asked for the Support Unit. He outlined the situation, then hung up. He stood up; he was at least two to three inches taller than Malone. 'They're on their way. They'll stop by here at the station till we call them out. We don't want to frighten the horses. Or the tourists,' he added. 'The Chamber of Commerce would be down on me like a ton of bricks if that happened.'

'Righto, let's see if our luck is in and we don't need the Support fellers.'

Kagal and Kate Arletti appeared to have arrived at a truce; at least they were affable when Flagg got into the car with Malone. The chief inspector gave Kate directions and she drove out of the town and soon the vineyards stretched away on either side in an almost too-neat design. Everything appeared so ordered, a blue-print, or green-print, for harmony. Yet everything was still at the mercy of the weather. As the Manhattan family, it seemed, had been at the mercy of the weather of human nature.

'There it is,' said Flagg and pointed to a large two-storied house on a hill to their right. They turned in through the ornamental gates, past the big ornamental sign, *Manhattan Estate*, and drove up between the vines, past the sheds of the winery and in through another set of gates to the house. Trees formed a barrier round the perimeter of a large lawn and garden: this was a private house, not open to tourists or wine-buyers.

235

'Vistors are coming here all the time, all year round,' said Flagg. 'Coachloads of them. But they're never welcome up here at the house. I've only been here once, myself.'

Malone didn't ask whether he had been here in his official capacity or as a guest. He looked up at the house. White stone, verandahs running round three sides of it, black lace ironwork, slate roof. It had the dignity that old colonial houses have achieved, as if it had come with the ageing of the people who had lived in it. It was, Malone guessed, a Down Under chateau. Or would the Manhattans, originally German, have thought of it as their *schloss*?

'Go down and talk to the workers,' he told Kate and Kagal. 'Ask 'em if our actor friend has been up here lately.'

If the big house ran to full-time servants, none of them was evident. Mrs Manhattan herself answered the front door, ready to tell the strangers that they were trespassing. Then she recognized the chief inspector and she frowned. 'Inspector – Flags?'

'Flagg. This is Detective-Inspector Malone, from Sydney. Could we have a word with you?'

'Of course. But why –?' It was hard to guess her age: she could have been either fifty or sixty. Natural beauty, a lively mind and perhaps a glass or two of the grape had held back the years. Her dark hair was only slightly touched with grey; there was still shape to her cheekbones and jaw. She had blue eyes with a touch of purple in them; Malone could imagine them growing dark with anger. If Mrs Manhattan allowed her anger to show.

She led them off a wide, high-ceilinged hall into a drawing room about three times the size of the Malone living room in Randwick. It was beautifully, almost elegantly furnished, and Malone wondered who was entertained here. The other aristocrats, if any, of the valley? Or no one at all?

'Inspector Malone will explain why we're here,' said Flagg, throwing the ball at Malone with all the practised ease of a man who knew how to sidestep a delicate situation.

Malone began cautiously. 'Do you have a son who is an actor, plays under the name of Lloyd Chase?'

She was suspicious at once; it showed in the eyes, though they didn't appear to tighten. 'Yes. His name's Carl, with a C. The Chase bit was always a family joke and when he decided to become an

actor, he chose it. Lloyd is his middle name. But why –' Her long
fingers moved nervously amongst each other, but only for a moment.
'What has he done? Why do you want to see him?'

It was not easy telling her; it never was. '. . . We have reason to
believe he is the killer.'

'You have reason to believe? You actually do use phrases like
that?'

She's playing for time. 'Sometimes it softens the blow.'

She thought about that for a moment, then nodded. 'Perhaps. Words
have their uses . . . Did you know about this, Mr Flagg?'

'No, ma'am. You don't seem surprised at what Inspector Malone
has told you.'

'You don't know how I feel,' she told him with some asperity.

'Has Lloyd – Carl been in touch with you?' said Malone.

She hesitated; then nodded. 'Yes, I've spoken to him.'

'When?'

'Last night. I hadn't spoken to him for almost two months.'

'Where was he then? Is he *now*?'

A wind had sprung up. Through the large French doors Malone
saw the trees dancing, sunlight bouncing on their tops. There was
silence in the big room, accentuated by the sudden creaking in the
rest of the house, as if it were moving in the wind. Had been loosened
on its foundations by the news the police had brought into it.

At last Mrs Manhattan said, 'I don't think I shall answer that.'

'It would be better if you did,' said Malone. 'It's not going to do
your son or you any good not telling us where he is. We'll find him.
He and I have talked on the phone – we're almost friends. Almost.
We want to bring him in before he gets hurt. Or kills someone else.'

She ignored the last sentence. 'Won't he be hurt when you do
bring him in? Won't he go to prison?'

'Probably. Unless –' He stopped: the question was too difficult to
put to a mother.

'Unless what?'

'Is Carl – is he mentally unbalanced?'

'Insane, you mean?' She shut her eyes at that, as if he had struck
her. When she opened them they were dark, with pain. 'No, he's not
insane, not in the least.'

The two men waited. Flagg put his hand in his jacket pocket, as if searching for something; then changed his mind and withdrew his hand. A window-pane rattled.

'Has he told you he is a homosexual?' Mrs Manhattan said.

'I've guessed it, but he's never actually said he is. Is he?'

She nodded, her fingers weaving constantly now.

'How long have you known?'

She sighed. 'I think I suspected it when he was about – I suppose sixteen. He ran away from home twice, but came back each time after a month or so.'

'Why did he run away?'

She looked down at her hands; then at Flagg. 'You knew my husband, didn't you?'

'Yes, ma'am. I first met him when he was young, before – before he married you. I used to come here occasionally, not to the house but down at the winery. My father worked here.'

'I remember your father now. But did you know my husband after we married?'

'I'd see him now and again – he was president of our rugby league club. He was a fine man, highly regarded.'

'You didn't know him at all,' she said bitterly, but she was talking to herself.

Both men waited for her to go on, both acutely uncomfortable, although Malone was sure that Flagg, like himself, had been through this sort of thing before. The wind came and went in gusts, the house protested and somewhere a door banged.

At last she said, still apparently talking to herself; certainly not looking at them, but out at the swaying trees: 'Jacob Mannhaussen came up here in 1849 – he was from a small village on the north bank of the Mosel in Germany. He was a hard man, so the family history goes – he should have been a stone-cutter, not a wine-grower. It was his grandson who changed the family name in 1914 – there was a great deal of anti-German feeling in those days. We're not the tolerant people we claim to be, are we? Blacks, foreigners, homosexuals –'

Each man kept his intolerance secret; neither looked at the other.

'That Manhattan actually joined the AIF and went to fight in France – he was a hard man, too, I'm told –' Then she looked at them. 'Why am I telling you all this?'

'Because you're looking for excuses for Carl,' said Malone gently.

She studied him carefully, as if seeing him for the first time. 'Perhaps you're right.'

'What about Carl's father, your husband? Is he still alive?'

'No, he died two years ago . . .' She looked out at the trees, frantic now under strong gusts. 'He came to Melbourne in 1956 for the Olympic Games – he was a discus thrower. My father was a doctor, an honorary with the Australian team. He was a wine lover – when Australians generally were drinking only beer – and he invited my husband home to South Yarra. Jake was big and strong and handsome and I was young and impressionable. You make choices when you are young . . .' She looked at them again. 'The marriage was happy for a while. You can't imagine what it was like for a young girl to be mistress of a house like this –' She waved a hand about her, but, oddly, didn't *look* about her. Does she hate the place now? Malone wondered.

'I had three children . . . Jake was like his grandfather and his great-great-grandfather. A hard man. That was the thing with all the Manhattan men. They were *men*. Do you understand what I'm saying?'

'Your other son, too.' Flagg said it as a statement.

She nodded. 'Not quite as bad as his father – but yes. My daughter left because of the male atmosphere – she lives in London, she is our agent there. But Carl –' She was silent again; then she said, 'He and his father never got on. Right from the time he was a little boy, Jake called him a sissy. He would hit him, call him worse than sissy –' She stopped again, the fingers locked tightly together now. 'No, I'm not going to tell you any more. I've told you too much already.'

'Not quite,' said Malone quietly. 'You haven't told us where Carl is.'

'I don't think I wish to do that,' she said and sounded prim.

Malone looked at Flagg, who raised his eyebrows: what do we do now? Then Malone looked back at Mrs Manhattan. 'We want to look through the house. We can go and get a warrant, if you insist, but Mr Flagg and I –'

Flagg nodded. 'We don't want fuss, ma'am. I'll sit here with you while Mr Malone goes through the house –'

And thank *you*, thought Malone.

Flagg must have read his thought, because he grinned. 'I don't think Carl is going to be dangerous, is he, ma'am? Not with you in the house.'

'He is not here.'

Malone stood up. 'I'm sorry I can't take your word for it, Mrs Manhattan. I shan't be long—'

He went out of the room into the big hall, went through all the rooms on the ground floor, counting them as he went: Lisa would want a description of the house. The furniture was grand and old, old enough to shine with its age; the long table in the dining room, long enough to seat twenty-six, was polished till it looked like dark glass. There was a library, two of its walls stacked with books to the twelve-foot-high ceiling; the books, too, looked old, as if no one had been in here since World War Two: A. J. Cronin sat beside Churchill, Maugham beside Mauriac. The kitchen was almost big enough for a restaurant, furnished, except for the electric range and the huge refrigerator, in a style that suggested turn-of-the-century. The cook was the only furnishing in the kitchen under thirty.

She was plump and tanned and might usually have been cheery; today she was quiet and suspicious. 'No, I haven't seen Mr Carl.'

'Have you always called him Mr Carl? Is it always that formal around here?'

'I hardly know him. He's only been back here a coupla times since I came to work here.'

'You're sure you haven't seen him this time?'

'Quite sure.' She was slicing celery into dices, chopping neatly and quickly, as if the knife was a natural part of her hand.

She's lying. 'I'm going upstairs. Maybe you'd like to show me the way?'

'I'm the cook, not the upstairs maid.'

'Well, let's have a look above stairs – is that how you say it? I live in a house all on the one floor.'

'Poor you.' She put the celery dice in a strainer, held it under a tap and ran water through it. Then she emptied the dice on to a sheet of paper on a bench, wiped her hands on her apron and said, 'You're making a mistake, coming here.'

240

'We often do,' said Malone. 'But you'd be surprised the number of times we're right.'

She led him out of the kitchen, along the hall and up the carpeted stairs, with the polished sideboards, to the upper storey. 'How many rooms in the house?'

'Thirty,' she said.

'Who uses them?'

'Nobody, these days. But in the old days, so my mother told me . . .' She was still unfriendly, she was not going to be trapped into small talk.

'Your mother worked here?'

'Yes, she was the cook before me.'

'So you would have known Carl when he was a boy?'

She said nothing, paused as they came to the landing at the top of the stairs. He stepped round her, took out his gun, said softly, 'You'd better stay here.'

'There's no need for that.' She nodded at the gun, did not seem in the least surprised or upset to see it; as if she had been around guns all her life. Or had become inured by seeing too many violent movies. 'He's not here.'

He went through all the rooms on the upper floor, approaching them carefully, gun at the ready, feeling slightly ridiculous as he came out each time into her view to see her still standing at the head of the stairs, a slight smile on her broad pretty face.

The rooms were all as well furnished as those on the ground floor, but all the furniture was old; the house was a museum. He came back along the landing to her.

'Why would anyone want to run away from all this?'

'I wouldn't. But Carl was different –'

'He's been here, hasn't he? What's your name?'

'Sharon. I told you, he's not here.'

'That wasn't what I asked you. He *was* here, wasn't he?' She was stubbornly silent and in exasperation he raised his voice: 'For Crissake, Sharon, I'm trying to help him! I want to get to him before they come hunting him –'

'Who?' she said calmly.

'The cops with guns –' Then, wondering why he hadn't asked the question before: 'Do you know what Carl's done? Why we're here?'

She hesitated, for a moment looked unsure of herself. 'I heard you telling Mrs Manhattan. I don't believe any of it.'

'Unfortunately, it's true, Sharon.'

'He's the nicest guy—' Then she shut up, shook her head: he was going to get no more out of her.

He went ahead of her down the stairs, left her and went into the drawing room. 'I should've taken your word, Mrs Manhattan. But I still think Carl has been here.'

'You may think what you wish, Inspector.' She stood up. 'If I hear from Carl, I'll tell him you called. He might be pleased to hear from someone who was almost a friend. Almost.'

He had to admire her; but he had to say: 'Don't be sarcastic, ma'am. I am seriously trying to help him. Thank you for your time.'

Outside, with the wind whirling up red dust from the driveway, Flagg said, 'You were a bit rough on her, that last bit. But she asked for it.'

'What d'you think? Has he been here?'

'He's been here, all right. Let's go down and talk to someone in the winery.'

2

They walked down the hill, leaning against the wind. Out on the wide slopes the vineyards looked like a rippled canted lake. Clouds were massing on the Brokenback range, but they were not dark enough to suggest rain.

Two coachloads of tourists had just been decanted into the winery. The bouquet, as the wine writers would describe it, of crushed grapes was enough to tip an alcoholic over the edge. Several of the men getting out of the coaches raised their noses and sniffed appreciatively as if at the gates of some drunks' heaven.

John Kagal and Kate Arletti were talking to a small round man who would not have been out of place amongst the barrels in the big shed behind him. 'Lachie Langer,' Flagg told Malone. 'The estate manager, been here all his life.'

'Any luck?' Malone asked Kagal, who shook his head.

'Mr Langer, Chief Inspector Flagg tells me you've worked here all your life? So you'd know Carl Manhattan pretty well?'

'Sure.' He had a deep smooth voice. A real wine-taster's voice? 'A nice kid.'

'Nice enough for you to protect him if you knew he was in trouble?'

Langer frowned at that. He had a round face in which the years of wine, either tasting it or just enjoying it, had come to the surface. But the bright blue eyes were not a drinker's eyes: they were clear and shrewd. 'Are you accusing me of something?'

'I'm just asking, Mr Langer. We know Carl has been here in the past day or two. We're looking for him before he gets into further trouble. You've told Mr Langer why we want Carl?' he asked Kagal and Kate.

'Yes,' said Kate. 'We thought it best to be frank with him.'

'So you be frank with us, Mr Langer. Has Carl been here?'

Langer sucked in his breath, looked at Flagg. 'It's that bad, is it, Des?'

'It's bad, Lachie, and it's true. He's killed – how many, Scobie?'

'Six and nearly killed a seventh.'

Langer ran a hand over his thick black hair. 'Jesus, I can't believe it! He was a nice guy – a little, well, *soft*? When he worked here, some of us guessed he might be a poof – you know, a closet one –'

Malone didn't look at Kagal or Kate.

'– but it didn't worry us. We get a lot of gays up here buying wine – they like all the good things in life.' *Who doesn't?* Almost unconsciously his hand rubbed his ample stomach. 'But we *liked* him, we never made fun of him. Not the way his old man did . . .' His voice trailed off for a moment. The wind had suddenly stopped. The tourists were still milling around behind him. Jokes, flat as stale wine, filled the air. Bottles clinked as they made their purchases: a good time was going to be had by all. Langer looked over his shoulder at them as if he had never seen so many buyers; then he looked back at the police. 'Yeah, I saw him yesterday afternoon, late. He drove by here and up to the house.'

'He's not there now,' said Malone. 'Where else would he go around here? To his brother's place?'

'Maybe. But I was working back last night – I saw him leave.' Langer was doling out information drip by drip. 'He was heading up there, I'd say.' He nodded towards the ranges shouldering a white burden of cloud. 'Maybe he's gone up there – the Manhattan kids

243

used to go up there when they were young. We tried to start a small vineyard, but it never worked, the ground's too rocky. There's a cottage – the wife and kids and I go up occasionally for a picnic.'

Malone looked at Flagg. 'I think you'd better get the Support fellers up here.' He nodded towards the ranges. 'How far would that be? Three, four ks?'

'About six up to the cottage,' said Langer. 'The road winds up the mountain.'

'Righto, Des. Get them up here and we'll close off the road. Is there a phone at the cottage, Mr Langer?'

'Yes. It's been kept up.' He gave the number. 'Vera's grandkids go up there with mine – they call it camping out. With all mod cons.'

'I'll call the Support Unit on your car phone,' said Flagg, and Kate led him across to the police car.

'He's really killed all those people?' said Langer. 'Why, for Crissakes?'

'Who knows?' said Malone. 'What was he like when you knew him? When he worked here?'

'Okay. He worked hard – but maybe that was because his old man drove him. Jake was a great winegrower, one of the best we've ever had. But – well, just between us, he was a real bastard. I dunno how I've stuck it out as long as I have. Except to belong to the Manhattan wines – well, it's a cachet. Top vintage, if you like. But Carl – no, he was okay. Everyone liked him, especially the girls. But he wasn't interested . . . Well, now we know why, don't we?'

Kagal had stood silent, almost as if he were an uninterested bystander, someone come just for the wine. Now he said, 'Did he have a male friend up here, someone special?'

Langer shook his head. 'I can't remember anyone. Maybe he had someone down in Newcastle or Sydney.'

'As far as we can gather, he had no affairs down in Sydney,' Kagal said. 'Maybe he's a virgin gay.'

'Are there any?' said Langer and Malone was glad his own tongue had been slow.

'Occasionally,' said Kagal with a tiny smile. 'Gays are a mixed lot, aren't they, Inspector? We've learned that on this case.'

Then Kate and Flagg came back before Kagal could tease out the conversation any further. 'The Support Unit's on its way. We'd better

244

see about getting the mountain road blocked off. I think we should get the brother and his wife in here to look after Mrs Manhattan, just in case . . .'

'Just in case what?' said Langer. 'Christ, you're not gunna shoot him, are you?'

'No,' said Malone. 'Where does the brother live?'

'Out along the same road.'

'Righto, I'm going out there now. You stay with Inspector Flagg, Kate. You come with me, John. You, too, Mr Langer. I think you'd better close the gates down on the main road, tell the visitors the winery's closed for the day. Get rid of this lot –' He waved at the tourists still in the winery. 'But don't tell them why. Tell 'em there's been an outbreak of mad grape disease or something.'

Langer looked dubious. 'I dunno I can do that without Vera's say-so –'

'You're doing it on my say-so. Just in case Carl takes it into his head to come back this way before the Support Unit arrives.'

'Jesus!' Langer shook his head abruptly, unable to believe the situation that had swamped the Manhattan family.

'I'll get some of my own men out here,' said Flagg.

Malone turned to Kate. 'Mrs Manhattan is your responsibility. She's going to need all the support you can give her. Whichever way this thing ends, she's going to lose her son. Go up there and introduce yourself, but don't mention the Support fellers. We don't have to frighten her that much – it may not be necessary. I hope not.'

'If he's up at the cottage,' said Kate, 'and there's a phone . . .'

Malone nodded. 'I've thought of that. He'll know we're on our way. I just hope he doesn't come running home to mother. I'd rather he stayed up there on the mountain.'

Two minutes later he, Kagal and Langer were heading out of the estate. It had been an exercise in logistics; it was time-consuming but necessary. There were no jump-cuts from one sequence to another as there was in *Sydney Beat*: real life was step-by-step. He had thought of phoning the Hindle property, but decided against it; the boys there had their own security. Unless, of course, Carl Manhattan was not up at the cottage on the mountain but was already scouting the Hindle vineyard . . . He put the thought out of his mind.

The road dog-legged between the vineyards; all, it seemed, that

245

strayed from the straight and narrow. The paved road ran out, turned to dust. The ranges loomed before them, rising steeply like a wave about to break, the clouds the foam on top.

'That's where Richard, the other brother, lives,' said Langer, breaking the silence that had ridden in the car since turning out of the Manhattan gates.

The house, single-storied but large, built in colonial style but obviously fairly new, stood on a hill, a windbreak of trees to the west of them. 'We'd better see them,' said Malone. 'I'll bet Mrs Manhattan has already been on to them.'

They turned in through the gates and drove up the long curve to the level stretch in front of the house. A man and a woman stood at the front steps as if expecting the visitors – which they were: 'My mother said you were on your way out here.'

Richard Manhattan was taller and thicker set than his brother Carl, but he had the same dark good looks, except that there was a sternness, a hardness that was not in the photo Malone had seen on Josie Everett's agency wall. He wore moleskins, a faded blue shirt and heavy boots, ideal for tramping the hillsides amongst the vines. There was a strength to him that, one suspected, he would not hesitate to use.

'Why are you after Carl?' Emma Manhattan had a suggestion of strength about her, too; maybe, Malone thought, she needed it to handle her husband. She was tall and slim, with sun-streaked blonde hair and a long angular face that only escaped plainness because of her heavy-lidded eyes and sensual mouth. She was dressed exactly the same as her husband except for the heavy boots. There was no mistaking that she was a working wife, wealthy though the Manhattans might be. 'What's he done?'

'Mrs Manhattan didn't tell you?' said Malone; then explained why Carl was wanted. There was disbelief on Emma's face, but Richard showed no emotion at all.

Malone nodded up towards the mountain, carved into angles now by the lowering sun. 'He's up there, isn't he? Did he call in on you last night when he came by here?'

Husband and wife looked at each other, then Manhattan said, 'Yes. He didn't say anything, except he'd come up here to do some thinking. I thought he meant he might come back to work here.'

'Would he have been welcome?' It was a blunt question. There was another question Malone asked himself: why am I on Carl's side?

Again husband and wife exchanged glances, then he shook his head. 'No.'

Malone was aware of Langer shifting uncomfortably beside him. He wondered how often the grapes went sour around here.

'Then he's up there at the cottage?'

Manhattan said and showed nothing, but after a moment his wife, still apparently unbelieving of what her brother-in-law had done, nodded.

'Did you phone him after his mother phoned you?'

Again Manhattan was silent, but this time his wife said, 'I tried, but the phone was engaged. Or off the hook.'

'Would he listen to you, if you could get through to him? Either of you?'

This time it was Manhattan who answered: 'Probably not. I have to be blunt – Carl and I never got on, never. But I also have to tell you – I don't believe he's done what you told us. He wouldn't be capable of it.'

'Why?' said Kagal, who had been standing in the background. 'Because he's always been a sissy? A poof?'

Hold on, John. Malone glanced at him; even Langer gave him a hard look. But Kagal took no notice of them; he continued to face Manhattan, who frowned, put his head on one side and looked at the young detective as if he had not been aware of him up till now.

Then he said coldly, 'Is that any business of yours?'

'No.' Malone got in before Kagal could answer. 'We know what he's done, Mr Manhattan, and that's all that matters. I understand you have children – are they here at the house?'

'No,' said Emma. 'They'll be on their way home from school now.'

'They'll be stopped down the road – we've closed it off. You'd better go back there and meet them – are they on a school bus? I think you'd better go, too, Mr Manhattan, if you're not going to help us with your brother.'

'I'll stay,' said Manhattan flatly, but said no more.

A few minutes later Emma Manhattan, visibly upset now, drove

247

down the curving driveway in a Land Rover, turned right and headed back towards the main vineyard. The four men watched her go, then Malone said, 'In a little while, Mr Manhattan, we'll have the Support Unit up here – there may be some shooting, but I'm hoping not. Constable Kagal and I are going further up the road. I'll try and get Carl on my car-phone. I think you and Mr Langer had better stay here.'

'No.' Manhattan had changed his mind; but there was no softening. 'I'll come with you. Carl won't listen to me, but just in case –'

'I'll come, too,' said Langer, but looked as if he would rather be miles away from the situation. 'He might talk to me – just might –'

'That's our only hope,' said Malone. 'That he'll talk to someone.'

The wind had dropped, the air suddenly still. The sun, too, dropped and shadows crept over the hillsides, darkening all the grapes. The four men, in the police car, drove up the winding road till the cottage came in sight, about four hundred metres further up the road.

Kagal pulled the car into the side of the narrow road. As they got out, Malone looked back down the valley. In the distance he could see flashing blue-and-red lights, like cheap jewels catching the sun: the Cessnock police had blocked off the roads. He wondered how much longer the Support Unit would take to arrive.

He got back into the car, picked up the phone and dialled the number Langer had given him. It was answered immediately. 'I can see you, Scobie. I have the glasses on you.'

'Just so long as you don't have a gun on me. We have to talk, Carl.'

'Carl? Not Fred?'

'No, nor Lloyd Chase. We're down to basics now.'

In the distance the flashing lights had multiplied; the Support Unit had arrived. Soon their vans would be coming up the road, the men would be spilling out, running crouched over like dark four-legged animals, dropping behind cover, their shotguns aimed at the cottage . . . 'Carl, things are serious now. Come on down.'

'No, Scobie. As you say, things are serious now.' There was silence on the line, then he said, 'Will you come up and talk to me? There are some things I want to explain.'

The flashing lights in the distance had been reduced; the vans were on their way, lights turned off. The sunlight in the valley was turning to pale gold, the green of the vines showing their yellow tinge. As far as one could see there were acres and acres of pale green corduroy. The whole scene was so peaceful; if one strained one's ears, one could just hear the faint hum of the approaching vans. In a minute or two Malone would no longer be in control of the contact with Carl Manhattan; if he ever had been.

'Carl, I'll only come up if you promise you're not thinking of me as a hostage. I'm not going to be in that.'

'Trust me, Scobie.' It sounded more like a plea than a commitment. 'You can even bring your gun.'

Malone hung up the phone, got out of the car. 'I'm going up,' he told Kagal. 'You sit by the phone. When Flagg arrives with the Support Unit, tell 'em there's to be no shooting till I come back.'

'I'll come with you,' said Richard Manhattan unexpectedly.

So you're not a total bastard, after all. 'No, I think it's better that you don't. I'll be okay. Remember, John – no shooting while I'm up there. I hope I can bring him back down with me before anything like that happens.'

'Take care, Scobie,' said Kagal, as if there was no difference in rank.

'I don't think he'll harm you,' said Langer. 'Not in cold blood.'

'That's the way I want it,' said Malone. 'Cold. Or anyway, cool.'

He started up the road, which was now in shade; the sun cut slantwise across the steep mountainside. Something hurtled at him out of a tree; he ducked under the attack of a magpie defending its territory. It came at him again and, because his nerves were stretched, he wanted to laugh hysterically. He was going to be pecked to death by a bloody bird! He picked up a large stick and as the bird came at him a third time he hurled the stick. His aim was good: the stick struck the magpie a glancing blow and it whirled away in a flutter of wings. Then he was beyond the trees, past the nest and coming up to the cottage.

It was a neat weatherboard house, though the paint had long ago peeled off and the timbers had paled to a silver-grey. The corrugated iron roof was a faded red, the water tank beside the house the same grey as the timbers. Carl Manhattan was waiting for him on the verandah that stretched across the front of the cottage.

'I didn't think we'd ever meet like this,' he said.

'No.' Malone turned and looked out on the valley again, keeping the moment as calm as possible. 'It's a long way from the Cross and Oxford Street.' Then he turned back. 'Pleased to meet you, Fred.'

'Likewise.'

Carl Manhattan grinned, though it seemed to be an effort. He looked exactly as he did in the agency photo; but the good looks were strained now, even a little gaunt. Then he twisted his head to one side, listening; then he raised the binoculars he held and looked down the road. When he lowered them he was no longer smiling.

'Jesus, what are you doing to me? Those guys down there — with guns!'

'Carl, what did you expect?'

Manhattan continued to stare down the road, then abruptly he turned and went back into the cottage. Malone hesitated. He had hoped to keep Manhattan out here in the open, perhaps to sit and talk on the verandah, where everything that went on between him and Manhattan could be seen down the road, where, he hoped, they would recognize there was no danger and so would not use their firepower.

But Carl Manhattan showed no sign of coming out again. Malone reluctantly went up the steps and into the cottage. It was strictly functional, a workman's cottage, as great a contrast as possible from the big house further down the valley. There was a medium-sized room that served as living and dining room; if anyone who had lived here had ever 'dined'. Two bedrooms opened directly into the larger room; through an open doorway he could see a tiny kitchen. If there were a bathroom and toilet, they were somewhere out the back.

Manhattan was sitting in a chair, a pistol, a Browning Thirty-two, held negligently in his lap. Malone took his time sitting down opposite him. He looked around the room, then back at the younger man. 'There's no need for the gun, Carl. Unless —'

'Unless what? Unless I'm going to hold you hostage?' He shook his head. 'No, you're my friend — I wouldn't do that to you.'

'Then give me the gun.' Malone held out his hand.

'No, Scobie. I haven't decided yet what I'm going to do.' He was sitting so that, at an angle, he could look out through the open front door and down towards the road. 'I never thought it would come to this, you know.'

'How did you think it would finish? We were always going to catch up with you eventually. That is, if you went on killing –'

'That's why I came up here – I wasn't sure I wanted to go on. I didn't kill for the thrill, you know that, don't you?'

Malone nodded. *Let him talk.*

'It was a public service –'

Malone said nothing.

'You never believed that, did you? But that was how I honestly felt.'

'Didn't you feel any guilt?'

'Not while I was doing the actual shooting, no. Afterwards –' He shrugged. 'Yes, I guess there was some guilt. Sometimes.'

'What started you? Did you have a friend who was bashed?'

'Yes.'

'Someone who was reported as being bashed? Someone we know?'

'I don't think it was ever reported that he was bashed.' He considered for a moment, then said, 'Darren Beane.'

Malone felt a flash of anger, but held it in before it could show. So his early suspicion of Beane had been right. 'He wasn't on our list of those who'd been bashed.'

'It happened last January when he was on leave. He didn't report it. Think of the headlines – Gay Cop Bashed. *You* don't like headlines – you've kept your daughter's name out of the papers.'

Don't keep implicating me in this. But he saw the truth and the sense in what Manhattan had said. 'Okay. But did Darren know you were the killer?'

He winced at that. 'Don't use that word, please.'

'Righto, what word do I use?'

'Public servant?' It was weak, as was the smile; but Malone saw that he was trying hard to keep friction out of the relationship. It was obvious that he thought of them as related.

'Were you and Darren – lovers?'

'For a while, back last year. We kept it – discreet? I was never a gay who wanted to strut my stuff – being in love with Darren was

251

my business, not anyone else's. Darren kept it quiet – after all, he's a cop. It was only after he joined the police liaison unit that he owned up to what he is. Are you anti-gay?'

'I don't know, Carl. Sometimes I am, sometimes I'm not. I haven't any time for the exhibitionists. I like sex – with a woman – as well as the next man, but I don't go around hanging out my dick like some kid who's just discovered what it's for. Tell me more about Darren.'

'I still loved him when we broke up – he was the one who wanted to move on. You do stupid, juvenile things when you're in love. Didn't you when you were young?'

'I guess so. Such as?'

Behind Manhattan, through the open window that looked out up the mountainside, he caught a glimpse of movement.

'I started following Darren, to see who he was going out with. Jealousy is a curse – that's original, isn't it?' He gestured as if in embarrassment, the gun an extension of his hand. 'He was with someone when he was bashed. That was when I got the idea –'

'Did Darren know?'

'No. I met him once in the street, but he didn't want to talk to me. By then I was committed –' He nodded out through the open door, down towards the valley and the big house that he had fled. 'I was teaching my father something –'

'Your father was dead before all this started.'

'Sure. But you can still kill ghosts, didn't you know that? I'm not nuts, Scobie. Obsessed, if you like. But that's no crime, not in today's society.'

The movement beyond the window had stopped.

Manhattan went on, 'I think I wanted you to catch me. It struck me after a couple of the phone calls that you were understanding, that if I was going to be caught I wanted it to be you. Did you tape the calls?'

'Yes.'

'Did Darren ever listen to them? He'd have recognized my voice.'

He had made a mistake, one of several, in not having Beane listen to the tapes. But why would he have asked the young cop to listen to them? 'No. But do you think that he might've guessed you were – were doing a public service?'

'Why would he?'

'Was it widely known that you are homosexual?'

'You mean did I go around the baths? Did I strut my stuff at Mardi Gras? No. In a way perhaps I'm ashamed of being gay – my father did that to me. If I could turn myself inside out, I could show you bruises.'

Up on the mountainside there was more movement: a dark figure slipped behind a bush.

'Let's go outside, Carl.' Malone stood up.

'No, Scobie, I haven't finished explaining. Sit down –' He raised the gun, not threateningly but pointing it at Malone to emphasize he should sit down.

'Don't do that!'

But Malone was too late. Carl Manhattan died with a bullet in the back of his neck at the same moment as Malone heard the shot from up the mountainside.

4

'I'm sorry, sir,' said the Support Unit sergeant. 'He raised the gun and I thought he was gunna shoot you –'

'It was a cock-up, a bloody cock-up. He wasn't going to kill me.' Malone sounded bitterly sad, as if he were a relative.

They were on the road down from the cottage: Malone, Kagal, Flagg and the sergeant. Other police, including the Support men, were congregated around the cottage; tapes were already being strung across the front of it. Richard Manhattan and Lachie Langer were inside with the body of the dead man.

'Is that what we say in our report?' said Flagg. 'Come on, Scobie. Don was doing what he was brought up here for. Once you went in there you were at risk.'

Malone nodded, reluctantly. 'I know, Des. Righto, that's the way we report it – necessary action. But how much did his brother see?'

'No more than I did,' said Kagal. 'We were down there –' He nodded down the road. 'We couldn't see into the house. There was only the one shot – there wasn't any fusillade.'

'We don't go in for *fusillades*,' said the sergeant, whose name was

253

Cadogan, and made the word sound as if he had never used it before.

'Righto, Sergeant,' said Malone. 'We're not meaning to criticize you. You did what you thought was right, from where you stood. I was inside –' Inside the dead man's mind? he wondered. Had he become too sympathetic towards Carl Manhattan? 'We've settled on the story. You took necessary action.'

'Thanks, sir,' said the sergeant and called to his men and went off down the road towards their vans. That was a feature of support groups, Malone thought, bitter again for the moment: they never had to hang around for the emotional clean-up.

Then Richard Manhattan and Lachie Langer came out of the cottage and down into the road. Both looked dazed; all the hardness had drained out of Manhattan's face. 'What do we do with the body?' he asked.

'It'll go into the morgue, Richard,' said Flagg. 'Then you'll be called in to officially identify it.'

'Christ, I've just been staring at him for five minutes. Isn't that enough to identify him?'

'It's the system,' said Malone sympathetically.

'Was he going to shoot you? I saw his gun –'

'Yes,' said Malone, not looking at Flagg or Kagal, feeling treacherous towards the dead Carl. 'We had an argument – he threatened me. I – I don't think you need to mention that bit to your mother.'

'No, maybe not.' Manhattan looked back down the valley, towards the big house on the hill that couldn't be seen from here. 'But how am I going to explain it to her?'

'I'll come with you,' said Flagg. 'I'll explain our men acted out of necessity and let's hope she doesn't ask for details.'

'*Was* it necessary?' Manhattan asked Malone.

'I think so, Richard. The alternative might've been worse for him.'

'What alternative?'

Why do you keep asking questions that are so bloody hard to answer? 'He'd have gone to prison for life. He'd have been a known homosexual –'

Manhattan understood the implication; he nodded. 'I suppose so. But I can't tell that to my mother, can I?'

'Let's go, mate,' said Langer, who had said nothing up till now,

254

and took his boss's arm. He looked at Malone. 'We'll work it out, somehow.'

He, Manhattan and Flagg moved off down the road; Kagal and Malone were left alone. The younger man said, 'You don't want to hang around, do you?'

Malone shook his head. 'We'd better pick up Kate – no.' He had thought of two other players: 'We'll go and see the Hindle and Bristow kids. They can go home now. Then we can pick up Kate.'

They had reached their car. They stood on either side of it for a moment looking at the wide valley. The sun was low now, the shadows long. On a distant road dust was a golden snake behind a moving car. Crows flew home on harsh mournful cries; in the trees by the roadside the magpie carolled a warning to anyone who came too close. The vineyards stretched away forever, a static inland sea.

'You can hear the peace,' said Kagal. 'Why would anyone ever want to leave here?'

'Depends whom you had to live with,' said Malone and got into the car.

Chapter Thirteen

1

Summer was over: not a vintage season for the winegrowers: too much rain, too many cool spells. Lachie Langer sent Malone a case of 1995 shiraz: 'A great season. Much better than the one just past, in more ways than one . . .'

Overseas the world went its own way: Australian news was only worth a filler. Bosnia settled for what it hoped would be peace but which looked like a fake; stock exchanges fluctuated with serial fevers; a misfit massacred sixteen small children in Scotland and the world wept. Time, the one constant, passed, oblivious of it all.

Then another misfit on a peaceful Sunday afternoon massacred thirty-five people in Tasmania and Australia was suddenly news. Foreigners learned for the first time where Tasmania was and that it was part of Australia; though Tasmanians themselves, neglected for so long by mainlanders, sometimes wondered about their nationality. But the massacre united the nation in a call for gun control and Malone wished that he were not a cop so that he could add his voice to the protests.

In other events at home, in order of national importance, there had been a Federal election and a new government installed; there had been an attempted take-over of rugby league, an event just below Pearl Harbor on the treason scale; and the Bligh by-election had been won by the Premier's candidate, a lady with a short haircut, a deep voice and four children, two of them gay. Vanderberg himself had been invited to ride on the lead float in the Gay and Lesbian Mardi Gras parade, a sight that would have doubled the crowd of six hundred and fifty thousand who turned out to watch the parade. Lechery mixed with disbelief at their own stirrings as wharf labourers and construction workers and coalminers found themselves flirting with naked poofters; mothers of five and childless nymphomaniacs gasped in admiration at buttocks and codpieces not meant for them; and countless brats trembled with a mixture of fear and curiosity at what might entice or assault them in a few years' time. Voluptuous fancy reared its flamboyant head while conservative zealots dropped to their knees and prayed for The Lord to piss on the parade.

The Premier, had had a sudden attack of political shyness, a hitherto unknown disease, and had sent his regrets. Or rather Ladbroke, his minder, sent the regrets. The Dutchman himself had been so apoplectic on receiving the invitation to float with the fairies that his mangling of the language was even more unintelligible than usual.

The morning after Malone returned from Cessnock, Chief Superintendent Random sent for him. 'I've read the report, Scobie. What happened?'

Malone told him, frankly.

Random shifted in his chair, as if he were uncomfortable. 'So you don't agree it was necessary action?'

Malone shifted in his chair. 'No.'

Random looked out the window of his office, as if hoping there might be some message written on the clear blue sky. 'Scobie, you got too close to this man.'

'It happens, Greg. You know that.'

Random nodded. 'But it doesn't alter the fact that cops and crims are on opposite sides of the fence. If you'd brought him down alive, you think you'd have been doing him a favour?'

'I guess not.'

'The gay press have been defending him on the grounds of retribution for the gay-bashings. There's a fine line between retribution and murder, but it's not a line we cops are allowed to draw. I respect your feelings, but keep 'em to yourself. The report was right – it was necessary action.'

Malone could do nothing but agree, but doubt would always gnaw at him.

Constable Darren Beane was questioned and denied that he had even suspected that Lloyd Chase, as he knew him, was the serial killer. However, he asked for a transfer from Surry Hills and was posted to a suburban station on the North Shore, where homosexuality was discreet and bashers did not prowl the leafy streets.

Travis Conrad was sentenced to life imprisonment but three months into his term was raped and murdered by another inmate already serving two terms for murder.

Garry Peeples was promoted inspector and succeeded Neil Kovax as acting patrol commander at Surry Hills – 'But you know the system, Scobie. There have already been five objections from other guys.'

Tilly Orbost left the Bureau of Criminal Intelligence and went back to Queensland, where she was promoted to the rank of chief inspector and received twenty-two objections from other police officers, all men.

The royal commission was still in session, bent coppers doing their best to straighten themselves out with mass confessions that had the judge rolling his eyes like a cardinal under the onslaught of heretics rushing to convert.

Dr Hindle, free of charge, performed a heart transplant on a wino, who, hand on his new heart, swore off the drink till next Tuesday. Mrs Hindle attended six charity luncheons in five days, breaking her own record. Sam Hindle came second in the State in the Higher School Certificate and went to university, opting not for medicine but for the humanities.

Judge Bristow, coming back after the summer recess, refreshed and relieved that his son was no longer in danger, sentenced a rapist to nine years, then looked at the cases on his calendar, all of which promised long sentences. Clive Bristow failed his HSC and took a job at McDonalds, where he is being trained as a hamburger *sous-chef*.

Jim Gable, told that he now had AIDS, committed suicide. His body was discovered when the police were called in by the old biddy across the road who objected to the loud music she hadn't heard for three days. On the tape-deck, where the volume had been turned up to the maximum, had been Saint-Saëns' *Organ Symphony*, the tape broken.

Jasmine Langtry died two weeks after Christmas. Though saddened by their loss, Mrs Langtry, Jillian and Kelly were a little better off. But not much.

Greta Bromley and Liz Embury split up. Greta went back to Ohio, where she was temporarily reconciled with her parents, but was estranged again when she started campaigning against Pat Buchanan.

Liz moved west to Perth, got a job in radio and found a new lover. Greta sent Malone a Christmas card, but he heard nothing from Liz Embury.

Walter Needle and Will Stratton remained together. Needle retired from business and the two of them left on a world cruise. Stratton had brief affairs with an officer on the cruise ship, and with pick-ups in San Francisco, Panama, New York and Tangier; but he always came home to Poppa. Needle hated being called Poppa, but it was a small price to pay for love.

Billie Cork, tiring of self-mockery, abdicated as a drag queen. He bought a coffee lounge in Oxford Street and installed himself at the cash register, just as he had seen bar madams do in French films.

Bob Anders' partner died of AIDS. When told of this by John Kagal, Malone phoned Anders and offered his sympathy.

'Thanks, Scobie. I just have to see now that I stay clear of it.'

'I hope so, Bob. Take care.'

Now the mornings and evenings were tinged with autumn. Malone came out of the building late one afternoon as Kate Arletti followed him out of the front doors. 'How's it going?' he asked.

'In Fraud? Boring, after Homicide. But no, I like it. They are nice guys and there's no blood.'

There had been a spate of murders in the past week, most of them brutal and bloody. 'Yeah, it's been grim.'

Then John Kagal came out of the doors behind them. 'You ready?'

'Yes,' said Kate and they walked off holding hands. She looked back over her shoulder and shrugged and Kagal, without looking back, raised a hand in salute.

Well, Malone thought, we all solve our problems in our own way.

Then Clements said behind him, 'I hope she knows what she's doing.'

'Sometimes you have to make the best of what cannot be helped,' said Malone.

Kirribilli
September 1995–March 1996